# The Second Coming

## Book 3: The City of Nis Trilogy

P.J. Fenton

PJ Fenton

# Acknowledgements

The author would like to acknowledge the works of Dante Alighieri, particularly his masterpiece, *The Divine Comedy*, for the inspiration that it played in the writing of this story.

Thanks also to Roberta J. Buland, Editor, Right Words Unlimited, for her professional editorial guidance.

# Dedication

This book is dedicated to my nephews: Seth and Packy, and my niece, Madison.

# Table of Contents

Part 4: The Final Moments before the War

Part 5: War Comes to the City of Nis

Part 6: Paths Converge Within an Ocean of Chaos

# The Second Coming

# Part 1: The Past Returns to Hunt the Present

# Chapter 1

*From the size of this crowd, just about every member of the Hammers of the Orange Light must be here,* Virgil guessed, as Hammers continued to flow out of the buildings in the camp and toward the terranaut ship, the Antaeus. All of them were wearing suits similar to the ones he and Dan-te—Virgil's friend and member of the underground civilization, the Remnant of the Tribe—were wearing.

Surrounded by so many Hammers of the Orange Light, Virgil could not help feeling afraid. The memory of their first encounter, the attack on the Alien Astronaut Movement's camp, and the slaughter of all its members except him, replayed in his mind. But even more frightening was the unseen danger below them.

*If Tanas manages to ignite the supervolcano, it's going to erupt right beneath our feet.* Virgil eyed the ground nervously as the thought danced in his mind. *We have no way to tell how close Tanas is to triggering the eruption. If it happens now, we might only have seconds until we're incinerated by the magma, with the rest of Prism—on the surface and beneath it—soon following.*

Virgil had reviewed his friend Ann's supervolcano theories enough times to know that once it started, very few things could be done to stop it. That was why he decided to bring Dan-te to the Tri-Dominion Caverns. He hoped they could find a way back to Nis, home of the Tribe of Shadows—the other underground civilization, so they could try to stop the Third Great Attempt.

1

*If nothing else, at least it has been a* revealing *trip,* Virgil mused, trying to distract himself from the fear of being surrounded by so many Hammers of the Orange Light.

Virgil Virt Indigo-Castitas, a.k.a. Virgil Wood, Woody, and Worm, never guessed that when Dan-te, an emissary from the Remnant of the Tribe, first appeared in his room in Spectral Academy he would face his own nightmare again. Nor did he think he would find so many of them, and so well-equipped, in one place.

*When Dan-te and I first met, she was scared, confused, and starving,* Virgil remembered, thinking back to their first encounter. *After she learned that we Hy-muns had our own story about Tanas, realizing that the "Light Bringer" who led "The Coming," and the "Lord Tanas" who rules the city of Nis, were the same person, she broke down in tears over the revelation; one I had yet to comprehend. That was when we started comparing notes.*

Virgil could not forget *that* conversation even if he wanted to. It opened him up to a far greater world, and a newer understanding of his own, than he ever thought possible.

*When we first started comparing our histories, I learned how long before Hy-muns ever walked on this planet. Dan-te's ancestors, the Ancient Tribe, lived on the surface. Back then, the land was untouched by sunlight and radiated a bio-luminescent light called the Glow until "The Coming."*

Regardless of how frightening it was to be surrounded by the Hammers of the Orange Light again, or how terrifying it was the first time it happened, Virgil did not doubt that it could be compared to the fear of seeing legions of Beings of Light attack in "The Coming."

*Watching the Beings of Light pierce the sky, letting* deadly *sunlight shine onto the planet for the first time, burning it to ash, while they* joyfully *slaughtered the Ancient Tribe, would have made the Alien Astronaut Movement (AAM) raid seem timid by comparison,* Virgil guessed. Even after seeing two of the Tribe of Shadows' Tempters burn to death in sunlight, one in Tri-Dominion City Hospital and the second outside of the Hammers' tent. He did not want to try to imagine the same sight on the planetary scale Dan-te described.

*Members of the Ancient Tribe, plants, animals, all burned to death from the sunlight or exterminated by the Beings of Light, the Hy-muns' Nag-el. The Ancient Tribe ran and did everything they could to try and hide from both the Beings of Light and the sunlight until the few survivors found shelter deep underground, literally right beneath our feet. That's where Hy-mun mythology takes over and when the Nag-el shift from being destroyers to the creators of the "new world" and the Hy-muns, until Light Bringer and his legions betrayed Ash Addiel and was banished underground. Reappearing before the Greater Tribe,* the portion of the Ancient Tribe that wished to devote themselves to vengeance, as "Lord Tanas" and eventually lead them.

Virgil could still see Dan-te's face in his mind when he showed Dan-te the Tome of the Ouroboros. Explaining how its passages, translated differently, could easily fit with Dan-te's description of "The Coming." He could see her confusion, shock, anger over her peoples' omission, and resignation when she finally understood him. Yet no matter how shocked she was, it could not compare to Virgil's shock over the realization of what the Third Great Attempt meant for them all. Nor that he would face his own personal nightmare, the Hammers of the Orange Light, as they surrounded him; forcing his mind to relive the raid years earlier.

*I can still hear my friends' screams from when the Hammers first showed up in the camp. They attacked us without mercy. They shouted that they were doing Ash Addiel's good work as they set fire to everything, destroyed our rocket and equipment, and killed everyone but me. A few members of our project even tried reasoning with them by telling them to stop, citing the Tome of the Ouroboros as the reason for our efforts and explaining how the Hammers' actions went against it. The Hammers took extreme delight in killing them. If they found the two of us now...*

Along with the memories of the AAM raid, the possibility of what would happen if not only he was discovered, but also Dan-te, continuously danced in his mind.

*If we're caught now, my death will make what happened to my friends seem like a joke. Plus, the embarrassment that is sure to reach the Indigo Dominion might destroy it, especially considering the support the Hammers must have. As for Dan-te, her Veil will be stripped off her, and she will be burned alive in the sunlight as a glorious spectacle for everyone to see. Thankfully, no one is questioning us. As far as everyone here is concerned, we're just two more Hammers boarding the ship. Dan-te, we have sure come a long way, haven't we?*

Since their first meeting at Spectral Academy, Virgil had revealed to Dan-te not only Hy-mun history and beliefs but his own also. He confided in her that he was the only survivor of the heretical AAM that was slaughtered by the Hammers of the Orange Light. He showed her different aspects of his own world. He revealed to her his true identity as the son of Hesiod Virt Indigo-Castitas, the Virt Prince of the Indigo Dominion. It was a position that, under normal circumstances, would make him the subject of awe for the Hy-mun majority and unable to move around as freely as he wanted to. But it was Dan-te's own way of experiencing the surface world. The process the Remnant of the Tribe and the Tribe of Shadows used, called *Knowing*, that utilized all five senses plus intuition and study to experience the world, brought about the most significant revelations.

*Since we first walked out of my room together, she revealed Spectral Academy, a place of learning, to be a stressful place that lacked belief,* Virgil remembered, thinking back on their journey. *Wanton City, a city of entertainment and commerce, was a swirling storm of lust. The Hotel Avery mud bath turned into a filthy wallow for the gluttonous, followed by a gym that became a den of greed. Then we walked through the sports arena, and that was the place that knocked Dan-te out. When we walked through that arena, Dan-te* Knew *it as being no different from the Grand Coliseum in Nis, exploding with wrath from the spectators and athletes alike. Worse, she found Tempters from the Tribe of Shadows enjoying the spectacle alongside the Hy-muns they were supposed to be tempting, a scene that shouldn't have been possible by the Tribe of Shadows' own beliefs. Yet despite being knocked unconscious by the sights in the arena, the worst experiences happened after we arrived in Tri-Dominion City.*

Virgil trembled in his suit as he remembered some of the things they witnessed while they made their way from the Stone Gate of Tri-Dominion City to here. Several things invoked a particular fear in both of them.

*After we arrived in Tri-Dominion City, we were detained by the Furies. We saw their Medusa Machine reveal and capture a Tempter in the shadow of another Hy-mun. If Mr. Geryon didn't show up when we did, then you would have been the next one to be revealed, captured, and sent to Purification.*

Just the thought of Purification back at Tri-Dominion City Hospital was enough to make Virgil sick.

*When we first entered the hospital, I thought the worst thing we would be dealing with would be the delay from taking the tour and the way Dan-te* Knew *the place. First was the hot water baths that Dan-te* Knew *as pools of boiling blood for the patients who were suffering from physical injuries caused by own actions. Then there were the people on life support,* Knowing *them made Dan-te vomit. Dan-te described them as being "rooted to their beds and the very floor itself," that their energies, "turned a dark charcoal color as it continued to be corrupted by the machines," that the patients* wanted *to die. They had given up hope, and were growing envy for the healthy because of their mobility. I thought that was the worst Dan-te could have reacted in the hospital. I was wrong.*

Virgil could still see that second doctor running up to them to ask Dr. Ness to join them in Purification to administer a sedative to Bruno Lat. What Virgil and Dan-te witnessed in that room changed everything.

*We watched doctors. Hy-muns who were supposed to be dedicated to* saving *and* preserving *lives, killing a Tempter from the Tribe of Shadows. They neutralized his Veil of Shadows with a device they called a Lightning Lamp and then executed him from the head down by exposing him to sunlight. Those Lamps, plus a couple of other tools I didn't recognize, are now all around us.*

# The Second Coming

Virgil cautiously peered upward. Besides the Lightning Lamps, several spheres radiating light, almost like miniature suns, floated in the air. Virgil did not know what they did, but he guessed they must work with the Lamps.

*Those spheres must be another way the Hammers of the Orange Light are looking for Tempters from the city of Nis. I just hope these suits are protecting us. Dan-te is probably more frightened than I am.*

Virgil was right. Dan-te was more scared than she ever thought she could be. Mentally she forced herself to not only keep walking forward but to also avoid gripping Virgil's hand so tightly that she ended up crushing it. Ever since they approached the massive tent concealing the Hammers' camp and a Lightning Lamp neutralized the Veil of Shadows, Dan-te had been in a heightened state of alertness. She realized all someone had to do now was pull off the Veil, and she would die, especially after seeing a Tempter killed right outside the tent.

*Thank the First Ones they can't* Know *like me,* Dan-te thought to herself, trying to will her mind into relaxation as she walked through the crowd with Virgil. The entire mob was dressed in the same suits that the two of them were wearing, complete with the opaque masks that blocked anyone from seeing their faces. Only the energy emanating from both herself and Virgil made them appear different. Everywhere else Dan-te looked, the Hammers were a sea of orange-yellow hypocrisy, appealing on the outside, but truthfully not believing or caring about what they supposedly stood for. Dan-te remembered the few Hammers she encountered before with Virgil at the Sand Spa Hotel. She realized now they were just the beginning.

*The Hammers in the Sand Bath were laughing as they boasted about how they would "soon be striking the Lord and Master's Divine Light through Tanas's darkness." They couldn't "wait to get underground and shine the light of our hammers into the face of Tanas and his monsters." All of them laughed like they were on some kind of good and noble mission when, in truth, they only wanted to kill something that they considered "unlike" themselves.* Dan-te *Knew* the Hammers surrounding her now were not only no different from the ones in the Sand Bath, but they were also worse.

Virgil, however, was a storm of blue, violet, white, and pink energies of loyalty, protection, mental, and fear that stood out like a beacon among the orange-yellow energy of the Hammers. Even without the ability to *Know*, Dan-te knew Virgil was scared. From the energy swirling around him, Dan-te *Knew* Virgil did not want to let go of her. He feared something would happen to her, or to himself, making it impossible for him to help her. He was also scared that if he did let go of her, he would not be able to find her in the crowd again.

*As soon as I get the chance, I'm letting you know I will always be able to find you.* Dan-te thought, wishing she could do something to help remove some of his fear.

*Regardless, I'm still incredibly grateful to you for protecting me. guiding me across the surface, coming with me as far as you did, and being the hand I can hold onto. At least now you can actually* see *me whenever you want,* Dan-te mused. The Veil's disabled invisibility did give her that one satisfying comfort. Unfortunately, she did not have much time to think about it. The crowd soon stopped at the camp's central plaza where a stage had been set up in front of the Antaeus's launch platform.

The Antaeus was bigger than any other terranaut ship Virgil had seen or the digging machines that Dan-te had seen the Tribe of Shadows take into the Great Tunnel. It was oriented vertically—held in place by a launch platform. At the base of the ship, glittering in the yellow-orange light, was a massive spiral drill that looked like it was made of the same metal and gemstones as the Platinum Throne. The drill was pressed against the ground, ready to bore its way down to the city of Nis. Above the drill, several cylindrical compartments were stacked on top of each other. Some contained open doors; others had conical ports attached to hoses oozing stinking gas. The name "Antaeus" was visibly written across the entire ship from back to front.

"Wow," Dan-te whispered in awe. She knew the Hammers were not the allies she was hoping to bring back with her. Still, Dan-te could not help being amazed over the sheer number of them and the size and scope of their operation. Even their terraship, the Antaeus, was an impressive sight. "They really did all this and still managed to keep it a secret from the public."

Dan-te suddenly felt her hand squeezed by Virgil. Looking at him, she *Knew* he had heard her whispering and had become even more alarmed and scared than before. Virgil's pink fear energy was becoming more erratic. His focus continually shifted from one Hammer to the next as he tried to tell if one was moving toward them offensively. The suits might have provided them with excellent disguises, but it still did not change the fact that they were surrounded, by Hy-muns who would kill them both if they knew who they were.

*Remember where you are,* Dan-te chastised herself. *All it could take is one whisper overheard, or the right person getting suspicious, and they'll know we're not Hammers. You might be able to* Know *if someone is threatening you beforehand, but Virgil doesn't. Still, this entire scene is incredible and a little eerie. All of these Hammers surround just me and Virgil, and not one of them realizes who we are. If the Hammers were broken down to a few units after the Great Rainbow War, how did they grow to such massive numbers? I* Know *Virgil is wondering the same thing. The fact that his mental energy is still pulsing, trying to process all of these Hammers, is proof of that.*

Dan-te did not have time to figure out an answer to her question as a siren pealed throughout the compound. Every Hammer looked up as the image of an extremely old and withered Hy-mun appeared in front of the terraship.

*A 3-D projection*, Virgil thought, slightly amazed again by the technology the Hammers had access to.

"My brother Hammers of the Orange Light," the image shouted to the deafening roar of the assembled crowd. "I, Grand Hammer Kai Aphas, give thanks to the Great Master Ash Addiel. He has given me enough life and health to be with you today. Today we bring our Light, the Orange Light of Ash Addiel, to the city of Nis, the city of Tanas, the root of all evil, darkness, and shadow upon our world and destroy it. Finally, we will fulfill our mission and return our world back to its former glory, a world without darkness or shadows, one fit for the Great Master's return."

*He's the biggest hypocrite out of them all*, Dan-te thought among the deafening roar rising from the other Hammers. *This Grand Hammer, Kai Aphas, is radiating far more of the orange-yellow energy of hypocrisy than all of the Hammers combined. I can see his energy flaring up from where he's standing by the Antaeus from here. Not only that, but his voice is soaked in hypocrisy. Every word coming out of his mouth is double-sided. He praises Ash Addiel. He claims Nis is the root of all evil, darkness, and shadow, that they are trying to return the world to its former glory, without darkness or shadows, a world Ash Addiel can return to. But he's lying, to himself most of all, and he knows it. He knows Ash Addiel wouldn't want praise, that they use* extreme *violence, that evil doesn't come from Nis, and even if they were to succeed, Ash Addiel still wouldn't return.*

"I still remember what happened like it was yesterday," Kai Aphas continued. "The Great Rainbow War was in its closing stages. I was examining underground caverns with my betrothed, Hope, and stepbrother, Able, to seek out new locations for technology bunkers. But while spelunking, we ran into a patrol from Tanas's Tribe of Shadows and was taken to his city, Nis."

*He's telling the truth about that*, Dan-te realized, listening to Kai Aphas's story and seeing his mental energy flare in the retelling. *Now we know who convinced these Hammers and others on the surface that Nis and the Tribe of Shadows were real in the first place.*

"We were later joined by another captured Hy-mun, Noah Heart. The four of us were forced into battle as gladiators for the amusement of Tanas and his demonic people. It was there I learned the horrible truth of their constant meddling in the lives of Hy-muns everywhere, including the instigation of the Great Rainbow War that was decimating Prism. I watched as the arenas, the

7

constant contact with Tanas's Tribe of Shadows, twisted my stepbrother, betrothed, and Noah Heart. So, when our chance at escape finally came, they did not take it. Instead, they trusted one of the demonic Tribe of Shadows to help them find a way to end the very war *they started*—if you can believe it. I tried to convince them otherwise, to leave Nis, escape, and gather the strength of the Dominions to smash Tanas and his vile Tribe of Shadows forever. Instead, they believed the demon's lies and let it lead them into the city, myself following reluctantly. It was on that journey where my betrothed was lost to me forever." Screams and boos echoed through the crowd as Kai Aphas told his story, but Dan-te already *Knew* there was more to his story than just what he was telling them.

He's trying to make it sound like the Tribe of Shadows are entirely irredeemable, and beyond any act of goodness, Dan-te thought, hearing how Kai Aphas was intentionally making the Tribe of Shadows into demons who corrupt anything and anyone they touch, except himself who resisted their influence. Then there's Noah Heart, that's the name of Professor Heart's father. I'll bet my horn that they are the same people. Now, what else isn't he telling us?

# **Chapter 2**

"I eventually did manage to escape from Nis, Tanas's city of demons," Kai Aphas continued. "But not without suffering my own personal losses. My betrothed Hope, stepbrother Able, and Noah Heart were seduced by Tanas's lies, delivered by that demonic warrior from the Tribe of Shadows my stepbrother and betrothed chose to trust. I still remember his name and spit it with disgust, Cacci-guida."

*Now I know he's lying.* Dan-te twitched, listening to Kai Aphas's story and very familiar with both the former gladiator Cacci-guida and his story. *Cacci-guida's daughter is the current Seat of Hope. His story is about how he was once one of the greatest gladiators in Nis until he learned* the truth *about Tanas, breaking free of him with the aid of a group of Hy-muns. He abandoned Nis for the Remnant, and he took a large number of its women who were captured and turned into breeders with him. The story is almost legendary. Actually, in that story, while Cacci-guida never named anyone, he did say that the Hy-muns who aided him also helped him learn* the truth *about Tanas. But one of the Hy-muns later betrayed them so he could save his own life. That betrayal almost got the rest of them killed. Cacci-guida himself considered it pure luck that they all managed to make it out of Nis after that event. I think I just found the betrayer.*

"I never saw my betrothed Hope again after she was lost to me in Nis," Kai Aphas said, the sorrow in his voice almost sounding genuine. "Noah also managed to escape, but Nis's corruption turned him into a recluse, caring more about machines than people. As for my stepbrother, Tanas personally turned him into a weapon that he would have used to kill the Virt Princes of the Dominions under the guise of an emissary of peace."

The assembly began shouting in rage over the idea of Tanas directly using a Hy-mun to do his bidding. Dan-te, however, heard something different over the crowd, the venom of lies and hypocrisy dripping off each of Kai Aphas's words as the orange-yellow energy of hypocrisy flared even brighter.

"Tanas gave my stepbrother the documents that would later end the Great Rainbow War, the bait to lure the Virt Princes close to him. Once they had gathered around him, my stepbrother was programmed to take *this dagger* and kill them all." The image of Kai Aphas produced an old dagger from his clothes, brandishing it before the Hammers.

*That's an old dagger from Nis*, Dan-te thought, recognizing its design. *It's similar to the one I picked up in the Grand Coliseum just before I came to the surface when I captured the Veil but it is much older. I lost it when I put on the Veil, but I haven't forgotten what it looked like. The blade is short but zigzagged to the point, and the hilt looked like two griffon talons.*

"Thankfully, I was there to put my stepbrother out of his misery and finally free him from Tanas's influence forever. For the stability of the Seven Dominions, my stepbrother's fall was kept a secret from the world. Today, he is remembered as a hero. But since that day, I have been working tirelessly with most of the Virt Princes. I've been saving and recreating the Hammers of the Orange Light, all for this day. Today is the day our brothers here at the Antaeus, as well as our other five ships: the Og, Nimrod, Typhon, Alops, and Tityos, will travel down to Tanas's city, eradicating his shadows once and for all."

The crowds of Hammers began cheering and hollering over Kai Aphas's proclamation. Dan-te, however, was trembling. After listening to Kai Aphas's story, she *Knew* there was one grim fact behind it that he was refusing to tell anyone.

*It a lie,* Dan-te thought, listening to the fake words tumble out of Kai Aphas's mouth, burning her ears. *He's lying to his people and himself. He knows what he's saying isn't true. That his stepbrother didn't become Tanas's puppet, and his betrothed vanished. But he is desperately creating and clinging to his own personal fantasy to give himself and his followers' justification. And that only makes him and the Hammers all the more dangerous.*

Dan-te and all the members of the Remnant of the Tribe *Knew* just how dangerous someone could be if they were desperately clinging to an illusion or something to believe in. They had seen the Tribe of Shadows do that for generations. The cheering and energy echoing from the Hammers left Dan-te with a frightening vision of being back in the Grand Coliseum. The sounds the Hammers were making, and the horrible red energy they were releasing, were the same as the Tribe of Shadows and the gladiators' energy just before they fought them.

*I knew the Hammers would be dangerous, but not* this *dangerous,* Dan-te realized, taking in the noise and energy around her and really believing for the first time what she was seeing. *These Hammers really are the Hy-mun version of the Tribe of Shadows' warriors. We can't let them run rampant underground because it would mean everyone's destruction.*

Dan-te squeezed Virgil's hand and looked over to him. During Kai Aphas's story, she never noticed how Virgil was reacting to it. But looking at him now, she *Knew* the story was affecting him personally. Virgil was generating the same painful red energy from when he first told her about how his friends in the AAM were slaughtered by the Hammers of the Orange Light. Only now the energy was fresh, a new injury had been added to the ones he had already sustained. He was using everything he had to keep himself from breaking down.

"Virgil," Dan-te asked, pulling him closer to her so no one could hear her, "what's wrong?"

"I'll tell you later," Virgil said, and Dan-te *Knew* Virgil was struggling to be able to say those words, the pain and worry in his voice as fresh as the energy. "I need to process a few things in my head."

Dan-te nodded to Virgil, letting him know she understood, but still not letting go of him.

"Tell me when you are ready," Dan-te whispered, *Knowing* full well that Virgil was hurting inside but also trying to figure something out. Virgil's white mental energy was adamantly sparking despite all the internal pain he was feeling. But before Dan-te could give much more thought about it, the image of Kai Aphas spoke again.

"Now, my brothers, I want you to turn your attention to the main podium. I want to introduce a special member of our Brotherhood, the one responsible for making our first strike against Tanas with our new Sun Spheres and whose trackers have led the way to our insertion point, above the center of Nis itself, my grandson Sol Aphas!"

"Sol! Sol! Sol!" the mob of Hammers chanted. Dan-te, however, noticed an immediate shift in Virgil the moment the name was spoken, as a young Hy-mun walked onto the stage before the assembly.

"You know him," Dan-te whispered again, seeing Virgil's white mental energy flash in recognition the moment Sol walked on to the stage.

"Thank you, Grandfather," Sol said before turning his gaze to the assembly. "My brothers, I can't tell you how good it feels to be back among you. The days at Spectral Academy, studying undercover under my mother's family name of Sol Sword until I could take our miniature Sun Sphere underground, was nothing short of mediocre. The classes were filled with nothing but idiotic students who had no idea what the world was really like or of the threats that existed throughout it and beneath their very feet. The worst students were the silly ones who had their own delusional and warped ideas about the world. One of the worst that I met was a girl from the Orange Dominion. She seemed to think I had a romantic interest in a girl from the Violet Dominion. As if something like that could ever happen."

Laughter, *honest* laughter, began echoing from the assembled Hammers over Sol's comment.

"No self-respecting member of the Yellow Dominion would have anything to do with the Violet Dominion," one Hammer said.

"The Violet Dominion's citizens are as inclusive as it gets, to marry outside of the Dominion means banishment," another shouted.

*This Sol seems to have made some sort of joke,* Dan-te thought, listening to some of the comments from the other Hammers. *I'm guessing none of the Hammers, would ever consider a relationship with someone from another Dominion. They're bigots as well as hypocrites.*

Yet at the mention of a girl from the Orange and Violet Dominions, Dan-te felt Virgil's grip tighten. Dan-te looked back to Virgil and saw more of his white mental energy of recognition flaring around him, as well as the red energy of anger. He knew *precisely* who Sol was talking about.

"Virgil—"

"Reye and Stella," Virgil murmured before Dan-te could even finish asking the question.

"Oh," Dan-te whispered in complete understanding. While Dan-te may not have known her for a long time, she knew just who Reye was from their time trapped together in Wrath Eras. As for Stella, Dan-te may never have met her personally, but Virgil had met her. And Dan-te remembered Reye screaming Stella's name during that first week she was unconscious in her cell. Dan-te *Knew* Stella and Reye were good friends.

"But in the end, those fools were best ignored," Sol continued. "Any energy I needed to deal with them I could better use for my work, in preparing for my underground dive where I would make our first strike against Tanas and his city."

More howling cheers echoed from the assembled Hammers, but Sol ignored them and continued retelling his story.

# The Second Coming

"I arrived at the decent site at the Demp Caverns, a site our allies in the Deep Earth Mining Corporation and the Red Dominion believed would have a high probability of contact with Tanas's Tribe of Shadows. Upon arrival, I gave each one of those arrogant fools a pin, a deep earth tracker. I developed them so that if anyone were taken to Nis, we would finally know its exact location. Once we were underground, I waited by the One-Man Return Rocket, and as we hoped, the Tribe of Shadows attacked. They cut the lights so no one could see them. Those fools squealed and cried like lambs to the slaughter, but I was able to keep my cool. I saw the Tribe of Shadows through the night vision glasses I brought with me and launched our miniature Sun Sphere just as directed. The Sun Sphere worked like it was made by Ash Addiel himself, it burned the monster's bodies black just like when they are exposed to sunlight."

*I was wrong about the Hammers,* Dan-te realized, listening to the cheering, and feeling the energy radiating off them. *They're* worse *than the Tribe of Shadows' warriors. They sound more like the Beings of Light in "The Coming." They don't just massacre their "enemies," but also their own people, joyfully, like they're on some kind of noble crusade and think nothing of it or the Hy-muns they sacrifice. It sounds precisely like something the Beings of Light would do. Even the Tribe of Shadows, who values martyrdom and remembering every life lost or given to their Plan, hasn't sunk that low.* Glancing toward Virgil, Dan-te could tell through his tightening grip and the energy swirling around him that he was struggling to maintain his composure. She *Knew* that Virgil had known Sol, Reye, and Stella before their journey began, and to hear Sol talk the way he was now was infuriating.

"Once I saw that the Sun Sphere test was a success," Sol continued, "I used the One-Man Return Rocket to go back to the surface. Our contacts in the Deep Earth Mining Corporation, the Red Dominion, and the media were more than helpful to make sure our cover story remained intact. The lives of the fools we chose beforehand to sacrifice for the greater good of defeating Tanas and his Tribe of Shadows now at least have some merit. The pins I gave them have led us to this spot right above the city of Nis. It is time to destroy Tanas!"

"Death to Tanas! Death to Tanas!" the Hammers chanted.

"I share your enthusiasm, my fellow Hammers. I still remember my first mission: erasing the heretical Alien Astronaut Movement who sought to violate the Great Lord and Master Ash Addiel's sacred space. Dozens of heretics were destroyed for the glory of the Great Master Ash Addiel, our fellow Hy-muns, and the Hammers of the Orange Light."

At the mention of the AAM, Dan-te quickly turned to Virgil. He was flaring with not only his natural blue energy but also with white mental and the same horrible red energy she had seen Reye generate. She *Knew* what was on his mind.

*Sol was a part of the raid that wiped out Virgil's friends,* Dan-te fretted as Sol continued speaking.

"I still carry the scar from that fight," Sol boasted, opening his shirt and revealing a scar running from the bottom right side of his waist up to his left shoulder. At the sight of the mark, Virgil's energy grew brighter. "Nor have I forgotten the masked heretic who gave me this scar and the strange transparent sword he carried. Both were reminders to not let myself become overconfident again. But now that we have enough Sun Spheres, we can launch them throughout Nis and blanket the city in both their light and the radiance of our Lightning Lamps. Once that is done, neither the Tribe of Shadows nor Tanas will be able to hide from us. They will find themselves at the tips of our weapons and never threaten the Hy-muns or the Seven Dominions again. The order is to begin boarding now!"

All at once, the gathering of Hammers began moving toward the Antaeus. Yet Dan-te could not help worrying about Virgil, who was now gripping his chest—right where his sword was hidden—along with her hand.

*Virgil gave Sol that scar,* Dan-te realized. She remembered Virgil telling her that his sword could identify him far more than his face could. But finding a Hammer that could identify it, one responsible for so much of Virgil's pain, literally *right next to him*, almost seemed like another cruel joke. Dan-te wanted to talk to Virgil. But the most she could do among the bumping and pushing from the other Hammers was keep a tight grip on Virgil's hand, realizing Virgil felt the same way. His own grip tightened and his own energy was a chaotic mix of colors and sharp feelings. Simply being among the Hammers who were responsible for the destruction of the AAM, and hearing Kai Aphas's story, were painful enough. Now finding out that Sol, a fellow student from Spectral Academy, was a Hammer and hearing him talk disrespectfully about Reye and Stella. Calling the other students who died in the mining project, a "sacrifice for the greater good," was all increasingly disturbing, and worse since he and the Hammers were anticipating it. Finally, learning that Sol was part of the attack on the AAM, bearing a scar that Virgil gave him, was rattling Virgil to his core.

*I'm going to have to talk with him the first chance I get,* Dan-te decided. But with the way the crowd was moving, she did not know when that would be.

# Chapter 3

The Antaeus's launch platform bustled with noise and activity. Hammers of all shapes and sizes, dressed in the same colored outfits, crowded every platform waiting to get a seat for the event of their lives. While Dan-te did not want a single one of the Hammers of the Orange Light to enter the underworld, she was grateful for the noise they were making. It made it extremely easy to talk in whispers to Virgil again since no one seemed to notice one conversation over another.

"Virgil, you and Sol, did you know?" Dan-te asked.

"I didn't know," Virgil mumbled. "Right next to me was one of the murderers who slaughtered all my friends. I *remember* giving him that scar, and I never knew it was him, nor did he know it was me."

Dan-te decided to change topics. She could tell from Virgil's chaotic energy that Sol was *not* someone she should talk about. And after what happened with Reye in Wrath Eras, she knew better.

"I know something about the characters from Kai Aphas's story," Dan-te continued. "Cacci-guida is well-known among my people, and he is *not* how Kai Aphas described. You've also mentioned Noah Heart before, he was Professor Bridget's Heart's father. But the other two, Kai Aphas's stepbrother Able and betrothed Hope, I *Know* you have some connection to them. The moment Kai Aphas mentioned Hope, your white mental energy, along with painful red energy, reacted like some new injury was just handed to you. What was it?"

15

"My maternal grandmother was named Hope," Virgil replied.

Alarm flashed in Dan-te's mind. She did not need to guess if it was a different Hope. From that one sentence, she *Knew* Virgil had meant the same Hope who was Kai Aphas's betrothed.

"Then, does that mean you are also Kai Aphas's grandson?" Dan-te muttered, wondering if *that* was the cause of his suffering. If it were true, she would not be surprised. The Hammers have done more than enough harm to not only him personally, but also to his friends. Finding out now that their leader was also his grandfather would just add massive insult and shame to those injuries.

"Kai Aphas is *not* my grandfather, and Sol and I are *not* related," Virgil snapped. His own voice revealed alarm and insult at even being considered a direct relative to the leader of the Hammers of the Orange Light.

"My maternal grandmother, Hope, may she rest in peace, never talked about where she came from, or who my maternal grandfather was. She just showed up one day in the Indigo Dominion, pregnant, and asking for sanctuary in what would later be the house where my mother was born and raised. My mother told me she hardly left her house, doing everything—including growing her own food and schooling my mother—from her home. When I was nine, I met her for the first time, and when she saw me, she dropped to her knees and started crying."

"Your grandmother started crying when she saw you," Dan-te said. "Why would she do that?"

"I asked her the same thing myself, as did my mother, who had never seen her act that way before. My grandmother said it was because I was the spitting image of my grandfather, only younger. She said she was happy to see my grandfather's face again."

"I imagine you and your mother must have been surprised," Dan-te said, catching a tone of bewilderment in Virgil's voice as she noticed the colors of energy shifting around him as the red energy began to diminish and be replaced by a hazy white mental energy. She *Knew* he remembered the encounter.

"We were. Both my mother and I looked at each other like we had grown new faces, the first time I met my grandmother and the first thing she said to me was that I looked exactly like my grandfather. It was also the first time my mother had ever heard anything about her father."

"Did she say anything else?" Dan-te asked.

"Not much, but it was still more about her past than she had ever revealed before. She did say, on that very day, that she was once betrothed to a man from another Dominion. At the time, she thought he was the kindest and most loyal Hy-mun alive, filled with life and the desire to help others. Yet something happened to him. She never said what it was, but it challenged him in

16

ways that nothing could have prepared him for beforehand, and the experience revealed his true colors. She saw that the man she thought she loved was actually cold, cruel, and cowardly. Every kind act he had made before was done with full knowledge of his own safety. Once his safety was compromised, he showed he only cared for himself, eventually leaving her alone to die, breaking her heart in the process."

"Clearly, she survived," Dan-te whispered, but her own hands were beginning to tighten in rage. Dan-te might have been a member of the Remnant, but she was still a woman like Virgil's grandmother. She understood what it meant to know someone who was extremely kind, tenderhearted, and loyal; someone who she could say would drop everything he was doing, leave the comforts of his home, and help her on a suicidal journey. She could imagine how much it would have hurt Virgil's grandmother when her betrothed abandoned her so he could save himself. "So, what happened?"

"My grandfather happened," Virgil said, his face radiating the teal energy of pride. "And I think I now know *who* he was. My grandmother said he was the stepbrother of her betrothed and was also abandoned when her betrothed ran away to save his own life. My grandfather, however, managed to save my grandmother from the danger, a danger she never described. With the help of two other friends she wouldn't name, she then made it safely to the Indigo Dominion."

"Pregnant with your mother," Dan-te added. A slight smirk crossed her face as she imagined Virgil's grandparents traveling together and, in the process, falling in love with each other.

"My grandmother never gave any details about what they faced that caused her betrothed to abandon them and later split up. She did say she knew my grandfather died shortly after sending her to the Indigo Dominion. After that, all she cared about was living as inconspicuously as possible, and raising my mother, until she saw me. Then she said she had to tell us that much at least so we would know about him."

"Did she tell you anything else?" Dan-te asked.

"No," Virgil hung his head slightly. "My grandmother died on that trip shortly after she told us the story. I never fully understood it, but I do now."

"So do I," Dan-te whispered, but privately adding, *in more ways than you realize.*

*Every member of the Remnant knows the story about how Cacci-guida walked into Rem with dozens of the Remnant's captured women who were being used in Lust Atrophied,* Dan-te remembered, thinking about Cacci-guida's part of the story. *Cacci-guida talked about four Hy-muns that were caught and used as gladiators. One of them he called the strongest being he ever faced, not because of his fighting ability, but because of his spirit. He made him question Lord Tanas's motives and learn more about It than he ever realized, so much that he left Lord Tanas and decided to join the Remnant of the Tribe. When Tanas almost killed him, Cacci-guida was stunned to see the same Hy-mun not only stand and defend him but also actually* strike *Lord Tanas. That story was also one of the reasons why we thought Reye would be able to kill Tanas. If It could be hit by a Hy-mun, It could be killed by one. Cacci-guida later took that Hy-mun, along with the other Hy-muns and the Remnant women he rescued out of Nis, to safety. It was a plan that almost failed when one of the Hy-muns, one he called the Traitor, betrayed them, almost getting them all killed so he could escape to safety.*

*Now I understand how their stories connect,* Dan-te mused as she reassembled Virgil's, Cacci-guida's, and Kai Aphas's stories into a complete picture. *Kai Aphas's stepbrother was Able, and also Virgil's grandfather. He, along with Kai Aphas, Hope, and Noah Heart, were snatched together, just like Reye, and brought to Nis. They're all shocked beyond belief when they learn the truth about Lord Tanas, the Tribe of Shadows, the Remnant, and the shared histories of our peoples. Kai Aphas can't believe it. Instead, he writes off everyone in Nis as servants of Tanas. But Able, if he was anything like Virgil, tried to learn and find out as much as he can. Able gets the attention of Cacci-guida, and the two develop a friendship.*

*Cacci-guida begins questioning Tanas, eventually taking Able to Decca-Ju Tower, where they learn the truth about Tanas and his motives. Tanas discovers them and tries to kill them, but Able somehow manages to fight It, and the two of them escape. Cacci-guida leads Able, Hope, Kai Aphas, and Noah Heart out of Nis, freeing dozens of women from the Remnant in the process. Kai Aphas, however, refusing to accept the truth, betrays them—breaking Hope's heart in the process—and escapes on his own. The others thankfully still manage to escape. Cacci-guida goes to the Remnant, and Able and Hope—having fallen in love—along with Noah Heart, returned to the surface before going their separate ways.*

*Noah Heart returns to the Red Dominion. Able sends the now pregnant Hope to the Indigo Dominion while he heads off to stop the Great Rainbow War, where he is killed in the process of doing so by Kai Aphas. Kai Aphas, knowing in his heart that what he did was wrong, starts to lie to himself to make himself believe he was right. He casts his stepbrother as a pawn for Lord Tanas and recreates the Hammers with the mission to destroy Lord Tanas and Nis to justify himself. Meanwhile, Hope and Noah Heart decide to live a reclusive lifestyle to keep from attracting attention to either of themselves.*

# The Second Coming

"Your grandparents were very brave," Dan-te finally said, quickly gaining Virgil's attention.

"Thank you," Virgil said, his face glowing with the energy of understanding. Dan-te *Knew* Virgil had reached the same conclusion she did.

"If we live through this and you ever get the chance to visit Rem, there's someone I think you might want to meet. She might be able to tell you more about your grandparents if you are interested." Dan-te chastised herself as soon as the words left her mouth. She *Knew* that Virgil had already given up his safety, security, and potentially his life, helping her. She also *Knew* Virgil would not abandon or betray her, it was not a part of his being. But asking Virgil to join her in Rem—even for a little while—was a wish she dared not put into words.

*Virgil's still from the surface,* Dan-te scolded herself. *I can't ask him to stay with me underground.*

Virgil, however, just squeezed Dan-te's hand back and whispered to her. "Let's just live through this first. Our group is going to be boarding soon."

Dan-te peered over Virgil's head to the front of the line and noticed he was right. With all the noise from the other Hammers and the loading equipment, it was easy to lose track of how close they were to the elevator they were using to board the Antaeus. Throughout the commotion, Dan-te was thankful she managed to keep a hold onto Virgil's hand for the entire time they had been moving through the mob of Hammers. She knew she could have easily picked Virgil out by his energy, but Dan-te didn't want to try to force her way through the crowd. especially when her suit was the only thing keeping the other Hammers from realizing she wasn't a Hy-mun. It was not long afterward that Virgil and Dan-te were raised up on an elevator platform and herded into the Antaeus. There they were seated in a cramped capsule marked "Pod 33-ES" with a dozen other Hammers. Each one laughed and joked about how many lives they would take once the fighting started.

*I wonder how they plan to attack Nis like this,* Dan-te asked herself before a voice started speaking throughout the capsule.

"Attention all capsule occupants," the voice said. "Please remain strapped into your seats at all times. Once the Antaeus reaches Nis, your capsule will be launched into the city. If the capsule fails to launch, it will automatically open. You are to then disembark through the ship. You will then proceed to your designated positions, terminating any monsters you encounter along the way. You will find weapons under your seats; the ship will depart as soon as boarding is complete. Good luck and all praise to our Lord and Master."

"All praise!" Dan-te heard the other Hammers shout in unison and was thankful none of them noticed that neither she nor Virgil joined in the cheer.

*I guess this is it,* Dan-te thought, swallowing a breath as she prepared herself for when the Antaeus would take her back to Nis. *I always thought I would go back through the tunnels with an army of Hy-muns who were ready to fight with us to save our world from Lord Tanas and the Third Great Attempt. Instead, I get the Hy-mun equivalent of the Beings of Light, Hy-muns already planning to attack Nis and filled with the desire to kill anything that moves beneath the surface—Tribe of Shadows or Remnant. This is going to be a bloody catastrophe. The worst thing is they might still be our best chance to either kill Lord Tanas, or provide the distraction we need to try and prevent—or mitigate— the effects of the Third Great Attempt.*

"Very soon now, it's all going to end," Dan-te mumbled as a clock appeared in the capsule displaying how much more time remained until the Antaeus departed.

# **Chapter 4**

"You're the last one, rest well."

The Tribesman's work in the ruins of the Hy-mun camp was complete. He finally finished burying every corpse left behind by the Tribe of Shadows after they invaded it over a week ago.

*You were all once alive and full of hope,* the Tribesman mourned, walking among the graves. *All of that changed in the Tribe of Shadows' attack. It ended your lives and set Reye on the path to becoming the Hy-mun Horror. But it was my old self's apathy and weakness, something that developed long before the attack, that fixed Reye's path and caused the death of my former self, eventually leading me here.*

The Tribesman, formally known as Ice, had suffered the Death of the Self. It was when his "self" changed so much that he became unrecognizable to anyone, a point where his old "self" died, and a new "self" took its place. When the Tribesman—than known as Ice—first saw the Hy-mun girl Reye, she was suffering from the loss of her friends, Ann and Stella, and her brother, Raymond. They were lost after an attack by the Tribe of Shadows on the very spot he now occupied. Reye burned with a horrible red energy and a desire for revenge, wanting to make the Tribe of Shadows feel just what she was feeling.

*Ice had no problem pointing her toward Yam-Preen, letting her create death and chaos across the Circles of Nis in an attempt to kill its leader, Lord Tanas, while he stayed relatively protected, safeguarding her back.* the Tribesman remembered, thinking back to his time as Ice. *Reye broke out of the*

21

*Grand Coliseum, melted an E-gle Building in Greed U-Sez, destroyed the Great Staircase in Sloth Cur-Nos, and cut a volcanic chasm straight through Circle Emporium before assaulting Lord Tanas itself at Decca-Ju Tower. That was where Ice's "plan" fell apart.*

The attempt on Lord Tanas proved unsuccessful. Reye showed herself to be even *more* susceptible to Lord Tanas's influence than the members of the Remnant.

*So much for Cacci-guida's story about a Hy-mun being able to strike Lord Tanas*, The Tribesman lamented. He remembered how he—when he was Ice—thought a crazed Hy-mun would be able to kill Lord Tanas partially because of the story passed down by Cacci-Guida, one in which a Hy-mun struck Lord Tanas. *But what happened to Reye wasn't her fault, it was* my *fault. And after we were captured and I learned my old self died from the Seat of Kindness, the other members of the Remnant, and my reflection, I* Knew *it.*

After the failed attempt, the Tribesman was sent to work at the entrance to the Great Tunnel, the tunnel connecting Nis with the magma vein that was crucial for the execution of the Third Great Attempt. Thankfully, luck was on his side.

"It's been a long walk getting from the entrance of the Tunnel to this point," the Tribesman murmured, thinking about how an explosion let him escape down the Tunnel. "And it's given me a lot of time to think and reflect over all of the things I've done, and more importantly, over the things I didn't do."

Walking, reflecting, and escaping from Tunnel Diggers was all the Tribesman could do as he slowly made his way down the Great Tunnel, making his way to the Keyblast Point where the Third Great Attempt would be triggered. While walking, he disguised himself in a Hy-mun suit and snuck past one team of Diggers in a smoke-filled section of the Tunnel. He was then captured by another group that tried to crush him under a drilling machine—only to survive through pure luck. Most recently, he ducked down a side tunnel that led him to the remains of the Hy-mun camp littered with rotting corpses. Every step and encounter gave him one more thing to think about.

"I've been a prideful, envious, apathetic, and selfish Tribesman," the Tribesman mumbled as he looked out over the camp. The mossy green, decaying brown, and sickly yellow energy from the corpses that once filled the camp now barely emanated from beneath the ground. "I've done nothing but hurt instead of heal since I was 'born.' I'm a pathetic example of my people."

During the Tribesman's first imprisonment at the entrance of the Tunnel, he came to the realization of how he let his pride get the better of him. After finding the Hy-mun suits and painkillers, he began to realize just how envious he actually was of the Hy-muns and their abilities. The realization of that envy later turned to the discovery of how much his bad decisions and poor leadership only stoked the fires of Reye's wrath instead of quelling them. It was a revelation that came from an unlikely source.

"Good leadership is key, right, Lom-ardo."

The Tribesman remembered the words from the Tribe of Shadows' taskmaster, the words sticking in his head, mainly because they reminded him how it was the good leadership of the Council of Rem that preserved it. His own bad leadership had only led to Reye taking all the real risks while she rampaged through Nis. Reye's anger and wrath erupted from her with every step. Meanwhile, he stayed in the safety of her back, basking in how she could do things he would not even dare to try. When he first saw the massive drilling machine that the diggers later attempted to crush him under, his first impulse was to wonder how Reye could use it. A part of him was still envious of her, something he *Knew* he could not be anymore.

"At least the digging machines are gone now," the Tribesman said to himself, no longer hearing the sound of the machines rumbling back to Nis, echoing through the camp. "It's time to get going, there's not much time left until…

But the Tribesman's words were abruptly cut off as the cavern began shaking.

# Chapter 5

"It can't be," the Tribesman screamed. "The Third Great Attempt can't be starting *now*!"

The Tribesman could not feel any energy approaching him from the direction of the Great Tunnel: no heat, fearful energy, or anything else from the Land. Instead, something else was approaching. Putting his hand on the cavern's floor, the Tribesman searched through touch for where the unknown object was approaching.

"It's coming from the far end of the cavern, away from the passage leading to the Great Tunnel."

The wall of the cavern crumbled immediately afterward as the largest drill the Tribesman had ever seen bore through it. Ducking for cover behind some rocks, he watched as a colossal metal vehicle forced its way into the ruined campsite.

*At least it's not over the graves*, the Tribesman realized, looking at the vehicle and not knowing what to make of it. *It looks like one of the digging machines used by the Tribe of Shadows only much bigger. The word "Arc" was also written in Hy-mun letters across the front of it. What is going on?*

The Tribesman's thoughts paused as a part of the machine near the drill opened up, and the strangest figure the Tribesman had ever seen walked out.

*Is that some kind of Hy-mun?* the Tribesman wondered as the figure slowly walked out of the vehicle. The Tribesman *Knew* it was a Hy-mun, and a woman like Reye from the energy she emitted, but much older. Her energy felt more stable and weathered, giving him the same sensation he received whenever he met one of the Council members. The Tribesman *Knew* she had lived a long life. But aside from her energy, he could not tell anything else about her. She contained herself in a white suit filled with a liquid that erased all of her scents. Inside the helmet, a mask covered her eyes, nose, and mouth, giving her an extremely bizarre appearance. The strange Hy-mun appeared to be looking around the cavern, examining it.

"So, the story *was* faked," the strange Hy-mun proclaimed, more to herself than anyone. From her voice, the Tribesman *Knew* she was not using her real voice but a projected one, similar to the announcer's voice in the coliseum. The Hy-mun was also generating the golden energy of shock and awe, but not as much as her voice would lead others to believe. She was shocked not because she was surprised, but because she learned she was right. "No lava, no eruption, the whole thing faked, what else are you trying to hide, Sol, and for who?"

The Tribesman did not understand what the strange Hy-mun was talking about, but he *Knew* she was angry. As soon as she overcame her shock, she started generating a red energy similar to Reye's energy, but not as horrible. The Hy-mun then noticed the graves of the other Hy-muns who were killed in the attack. Realizing the graves were fresh, she looked around the cavern and projected her energy and suit's lights in every direction.

"Who else is in this cavern?" she screamed. "Are you a Hy-mun, a member of the Tribe of Shadows, or the Remnant of the Tribe?"

*What?* The Tribesman did not know what to think, the appearance of the strange vehicle and its Hy-mun occupant were already enough to stretch his mind past the "incredible" point. But for the Hy-mun to ask if he was a member of the Remnant or the Tribe of Shadows, meaning she already knew of their existence, was entirely beyond expectations.

*Well, I might as well try talking,* the Tribesman decided. *I can't just look at myself and say, "I let myself be almost crushed by a digging machine," and think that's risk enough. I need to do more.* Raising his hands in a gesture of surrendering, the Tribesman stepped out from his hiding place and into view of the strange Hy-mun. The moment she saw him, the Tribesman *Knew* she instantly relaxed, her energy quickly calming.

"You're a member of the Remnant," the Hy-mun woman beamed, "I thought I had something to worry about."

"And what makes you think you don't?" The Tribesman asked, unsure how this Hy-mun woman knew he was a member of the Remnant. "How do you know I'm a member of the Remnant?"

"Members of the Remnant of the Tribe have chalk-white skin and hair, silver eyes, pointed ears, and silver and gold horns. The horns wrap around their heads and form a single horn on their forehead, just like yours," the Hy-mun explained.

*So, this must be what Reye felt when I first told her how we could* Know *things about her.* The Tribesman mentally grumbled, understanding now how Reye must have felt when they first met.

"Whereas the Tribe of Shadows have no horn, blue skin, red eyes, and would have tried to kill me instead of talking to me first."

"Okay, I am a member of the Remnant," the Tribesman said, realizing the Hy-mun *did* know more about who he was than what she was telling him. "But who are you, and how do you know about the Remnant and the Tribe of Shadows?"

"My name is Professor Bridget Heart," the Hy-mun said as she settled herself into a seated position. "As for how I know about the Remnant and the Tribe of Shadows, I only learned about them recently through my father, Dr. Noah Heart. During the Great Rainbow War, the Second Great Attempt, my father was captured by the Tribe of Shadows and forced to become a gladiator alongside three other Hy-mun: Able Kane, his stepbrother Kai Aphas, and Kai Aphas's betrothed, Hope Crys. In Nis, the four of them learned about the Tribe of Shadows, their Plan, and Lord Tanas from a gladiator Able managed to gain the respect and then friendship of, a gladiator named Cacci-guida."

*Cacci-guida,* the Tribesman thought, instantly recognizing the name. *He was one of the greatest gladiators in Nis until he abandoned Nis, taking a number of the women who were stolen from the Remnant with him, and joined us. His daughter, a child of one of those women, is the current Seat of Hope. The Seat of Hope often spoke about her father and his friends who helped him* Know *the truth, but never gave their names. Those must have been them, and this Professor Bridget Heart is Dr. Noah Heart's daughter.*

"Able and my father told Cacci-guida that the Great Attempts would not allow the Tribe of Shadows to return to the surface," Professor Heart continued. "Instead, they would destroy it and the Tribe of Shadows in the process. To prove this to him, Able convinced Cacci-guida to take the three of them deeper into Nis to find proof of their claims. Those plans, however, were complicated by Kai Aphas, who betrayed them. He sold out his betrothed Hope in the process so he could create the disturbance needed for him to escape Nis and return to the surface alone. Thankfully, by then, they had already found the proof they needed and more, a means of stopping the Great Rainbow War and making their own escape to the surface.

"After escaping, Cacci-guida left them and defected to the Remnant while Able, Hope, and my father returned to the surface. Once on the surface, Able sent Hope to his mother's home in the Indigo Dominion, where he believed she would be safe. Meanwhile, he delivered the documents that ended the war, getting himself killed in the process. My father then spent the rest of his life and resources building this ship, the Arc, preparing for the Third Great Attempt."

"Wait one moment," the Tribesman said. "If your father knew about Nis and the Third Great Attempt, why didn't he try to alert the rest of the Hy-mun population about it after he escaped. Shouldn't he have tried to stop Lord Tanas in the past instead of waiting until now? And why do you seem so shocked about it? From the moment you started telling me your story, you've been generating golden energy of shock and awe alongside white mental energy. I *Know* you are shocked to find out this is real, meaning you've only just learned about it and had trouble believing it. So, why *did* you believe his story?"

"Fair questions," Professor Heart conceded, thinking back to the last time she saw her father a few days ago on his deathbed.

# Chapter 6

"You can't expect me to believe this," Professor Heart had shouted after hearing her father's story. "A city, two cities actually, populated by a native race of beings that predate everything we have been taught to believe in. And in this city, Nis, you were held prisoner by the Tribe of Shadows, the descendants of the original native inhabitants of Prism and the banished Legions of Light Bringer from the Tome of the Ouroboros. Not only that, but Light Bringer himself is still alive, only he's called Lord Tanas now, and rules that city. And this ship you've spent the last forty years building is meant to stop a supervolcano Tanas is attempting to ignite. And also to save the people of Rem, the second city populated by the Remnant of the Tribe."

"I know it's a lot to take in, Bridget," Dr. Noah Heart coughed weakly from his cot. "But it's the truth."

Professor Heart honestly did not know what to call "truth" anymore. Shortly after the Demp Cavern Mining Project Disaster, she left Spectral Academy and returned home to the Red Dominion. Everything about the disaster seemed wrong to her, so she decided to talk with her father, Dr. Noah Heart, the greatest expert on volcanoes on Prism. The two of them had a strained relationship. After disappearing underground, her father miraculously reappeared later but changed. He buried himself in his research, secluded himself in darkness, took very few guests, and eventually drove away both his wife—

Professor Heart's mother—and herself. Still, despite their relationship, Professor Heart knew that her father was the best in the world when it came to volcanoes. If anyone could answer her questions, it would be him. What she did not expect was to find him lying on a cot almost dead from getting the Arc prepped from launch, struggling to continue, and retelling a strange story in the process.

"You're telling me that there are a race of beings living deep beneath the surface that secretly helped incite the Great Rainbow War and further its progression," Professor Heart said, repeating parts of her father's story, "until you, along with the martyr, Able the Peacemaker, his stepbrother Kai Aphas, and his betrothed Hope escaped from Nis with the help of one of Nis's gladiators, Cacci-guida. Who provided Able with the documents that ended the war. And that during the escape, Kai Aphas betrayed you to escape on his own and later become the security gunman who killed Able the Peacemaker when he presented the documents that ended the war. Since then, the Tribe of Shadows has been stealing Hy-mun technology from underground bunkers across Prism so they can further their final plan by digging a tunnel that would connect them to the volcanos in the Red Dominion so they can set off a supervolcano to darken the skies—since sunlight is lethal to them—and allow them to return to the surface to take it back. As for the Arc, which you publicly called 'a testament to what Hy-muns could still do despite the technological losses of the Great Rainbow War.' It's actually meant to stop Tanas's supervolcano and save the lives of the people living underground. Father, I think it's time I call a doctor."

"No doctors," Noah Heart exclaimed. "No one on the outside can know what I've just told you."

"Because the Tribe of Shadows can watch us from our shadows, the general public might not be able to handle the truth about the underworld. And our own government will do anything it can to keep the truth buried," Professor Heart said sarcastically, remembering what else her father told her about Kai Aphas. That after killing Able, he secretly revived the Hammers of the Orange Light following the Great Rainbow War and was still running it. "If you can prove any of this is more than just a delusion brought on by your age, then maybe I'll believe you."

Dr. Heart reached into his clothes and pulled out a small device with a switch on it. Flipping it, the Arc's launch bay and workshop became lit in yellow-orange light. Professor Heart needed a second for her eyes to get used to it, having only ever seen her father work by candlelight and flashlight. But once her eyes adjusted, she found herself unable to breathe at the sight before her.

"What is this?" Professor Heart gasped as several forms, some obviously weaker than the others, bulged from her father's shadow. Turning around to check her own shadow, she found that there were not any similar forms protruding from it.

"Tempters from the Tribe of Shadow," Dr. Heart explained. "They've been caught in my shadow over the years because of the Lightning Lamps throughout the lab, a 'gift' from Kai Aphas when he and several members of the Hammers of the Orange Light approached me years ago. That was when I learned about his work, how deep it ran, and what he was up to. He wanted the Arc but settled for a copy of its plans provided I keep out of his way. Otherwise, there would be *consequences.*"

By "gift," Professor Heart knew her father meant "payoff." And from the way he was trembling when he mentioned consequences, she guessed that if he did anything afterward, then they might not be having this conversation right now.

"If you still doubt me, read this," Noah Heart reached under his covers and pulled a book out from underneath. "It's my own private journal detailing what happened after I was captured and my own calculations concerning Tanas's supervolcano plan."

Professor Heart took the journal from her father and began reading through it. Inside was the same story she had been told, only more detailed, along with sketches of what members of both the Tribe of Shadows and the Remnant of the Tribe looked like. She did not doubt his story anymore, but it still seemed too incredible to believe. The journal was also filled with diagrams and calculations predicting the size and scope the supervolcanic eruption needed to completely darken the skies over Prism and what effects that darkening would have on the planet.

*He's still decades ahead of me or anyone else who has ever worked on volcanoes*, Professor Heart thought in admiration, awed by the genius work her father had laid out on paper. *Ann and I worked on supervolcano theory before the Demp Cavern Mining Project, but Father took it far beyond theory and put it into* practice.

Professor Heart continued to read, examining the notes, maps, charts, and equations her father sketched throughout the book. She realized her father already discovered that none of the volcanoes in Red Dominion could provide a suitable ignition point for a supervolcano. The *real* site of the eruption would have to be the city of Nis itself and that the Great Tunnel connecting Nis and the Red Dominion were meant to feed magma from a volcano to Nis so an explosion there would trigger the eruption.

"All this information about a supervolcanic eruption seems correct," Professor Heart admitted, marveling at her father's work. "But it still depends on the Tribe of Shadows' activity. Also, if they are such a big threat, why did you hole yourself up in here instead of working with Kai Aphas. Regardless of what happened between you in the past, if he is trying to stop this from happening, should you not have done more to help him then give him a copy of the Arc's plans? I can't believe you were really that scared of him and a few guys he brought along."

"Keep reading," Noah Heart replied.

Professor Heart continued to read; following her father's supervolcano work was a series of news clipping, photographs, and charts. The articles were about the destruction of hospitals, factories, and projects working to bring Hymun society back to Pre-Rainbow War status and beyond.

*I know some of these stories,* Professor Heart thought to herself, looking at each article. *The hospital in the Violet Dominion that was experimenting on new medicines until a fire destroyed all inside. The failed submarine voyage to the bottom of the Great Lagoon, the sub launched from the Blue Dominion, malfunctioned, and all hands were lost. The explosion at the site revealed to have been operated by the heretical AAM, they tried to launch a rocket, but it exploded and killed everyone. The Demp Cavern Mining Project disaster right here in the Red Dominion is present too, and more. All of them go back to just after the end of the Great Rainbow War. But why are all these pictures here?*

Professor Heart soon found her answer as her blood ran cold from looking at the pictures, each one about one of the previous articles.

"What did you have to do to get these? And where did you get them?" Professor Heart mumbled, shocked at what she was seeing.

The pictures showed security camera footage of men in orange robes carrying hammers—the garb of the Hammers of the Orange Light—attacking the hospital, killing doctors and patients alike, and destroying whatever they found. They showed the submarine from the Blue Dominion being sabotaged by similarly garbed men. There was also a picture of the shooting of Able the Peacemaker, the shooter's face circled and labeled "Kai Aphas." Other photos included the current Virt Princes of the Red, Orange, Yellow, and Violet Dominions, and in each one, listed as someone different—but still as a personal advisor, was the unmistakable face of Kai Aphas. The last pictures showed the aftermath of the Demp Cavern Mining Project and Sol's interview, and in each one, Kai Aphas, again using a different name, was present and alongside Sol at each move.

"All right," Professor Heart admitted, realizing not only that the Hammers of the Orange Light were real, but also that Kai Aphas and the Hammers were dangerous. "Anyone who can get as close to the Virt Princes as Kai Aphas can, using false names each time, and never be noticed by anyone for as long as he has is definitely someone to avoid. You're right to be scared of him, he's *extremely* dangerous. So, what do we do now?"

"We?" Noah Heart asked.

"Yes, we," Professor Heart answered. "I'll do whatever I can to help you. I'm in."

Dr. Noah Heart smiled and reached back under his sheets, this time pulling out a key which he handed to his daughter.

"Take the Arc and finish what I started," Noah Heart said with a cough to his daughter's stunned expression. "The so-called 'disaster' surrounding the Demp Cavern Mining Project must have been the work of the Tribe of Shadows. It must mean they've reached the Red Dominion like I estimated. Take the Arc, my journal, the plans inside it, and see for yourself. I know you've always wanted a reason to go back underground again, here is your chance. I've equipped it with everything you need. Go, save as many as you can, I know you can do it."

Noah Heart looked into his daughter's eyes one last time before closing his own and giving up his last breath. Professor Heart stood stunned, looking at both her father's body and the Arc's key for what felt like an eternity before cremating her father's body, hoping that if his death did not free the Tempters trapped in his shadow, destroying his body would. After that, she boarded the Arc, suited up, and launched it, heading to the Demp Cavern disaster site to see how much of it *was* a disaster.

***

"Kai Aphas," the Tribesman whispered. "He's the Hy-mun who betrayed Cacci-guida, your father, his stepbrother, and betrothed when they all escaped from Nis, correct?"

"Right," Professor Heart agreed. "According to my father's journal—he left me more details on his experience in Nis inside it—Kai Aphas did not handle the discovery of Nis, the Tribe of Shadows, or their history very well, especially 'The Coming.' My father initially described him as being 'deeply religious but far more open-minded than most of the other Hy-muns from the Yellow Dominion.' But once he confronted life other than what he believed was created by Ash Addiel below the surface, the story of 'The Coming,' learning that the Nag-el caused it, and how Lord Tanas, or Light Bringer, was still alive in Nis, he became closed-minded and violent."

"Wait, Light Bringer?" The Tribesman interrupted. "Lord Tanas is *Light Bringer*?"

"Yes, he is," Professor Heart confirmed. "My father's journal mentioned the members of the Tribe of Shadows and the Remnant of the Tribe didn't know that. A good part of the reason for Cacci-guida's defection was his own discovery of that fact. Sorry for dropping it on you just now."

"Dropping it" was an understatement. Yet the Tribesman could not feel anything about this new revelation beyond the initial shock. After everything that had happened from Nis onwards, the revelation barely registered with him. He could not devote the strength to produce a reaction.

"When Kai Aphas betrayed my father and the rest of their group," Professor Heart continued, "he claimed they had been 'charmed by Tanas's lies' and that 'you are all dead to me,' breaking Hope's heart in the process. When he ran off, the last words my father heard him say were that he 'would find allies to crush all these Tanas-born creatures.' The next time my father saw him, he was on a broadcast where he was the one who killed his stepbrother Able as he delivered the documents that ended the Great Rainbow War."

"He killed his own brother," the Tribesman gasped.

"Without any hesitation or remorse," Professor Heart replied. "As far as he was concerned, Able wasn't his brother anymore. After the war, Kai Aphas, when he was known as simply 'the Shooter,' was supposedly executed for killing Able. Obviously, that didn't happen. My father later heard rumors and talk of a Hy-mun matching his description leading a reformed group of government endorsed religious vigilantes, discovering the pictures afterward. That's why my father decided to be so secretive about how he operated, not telling anyone what he was really trying to do; he didn't want Kai Aphas to notice him."

"Your father was scared of Kai Aphas," the Tribesman stated matter-of-factly, "And of what he could do."

"Very scared," Professor Heart agreed, her voice ringing with truth while a new pulse of pink fear energy pulsed from her. "Anyone who can fake his own death, make allies of over half the Virt Princes and the media, assume multiple identities, lead an army of religious vigilantes, and never get caught once is *definitely* someone to be afraid of. My father was terrified of his work being discovered by the wrong people."

The Tribesman *Knew* just who Professor Heart meant when she said, "the wrong people." If the Tribe of Shadows were not enough to watch out for, anyone who could willingly betray and take the life a family member and not show any remorse over it, must be seriously wrong in the head. And if there are more Hy-muns like that, then perhaps it would be better for their two worlds to stay separate for as long as possible. Unfortunately, the Tribesman *Knew* they did not have that luxury.

"Professor Heart, there is something I need to show you," the Tribesman said, pulling out a dirty timetable from his suit and handing it to her.

# Chapter 7

"The Third Great Attempt is starting when?"

The Tribesman had shown Professor Heart the timetable he carried outlining the final stages of the Third Great Attempt. Unfortunately, Professor Heart's reaction was far from what he had hoped.

"The Third Great Attempt can't be starting that soon," Professor Heart panicked. "I checked and rechecked my father's work a dozen times. He predicted it wouldn't be for another month. Before he died, my father said that the attack on the mining project meant that they reached the Red Dominion. That they were getting close, but not *that* close."

"But you can still use the equipment on the Arc to stop it, right?" the Tribesman asked.

Professor Heart did not answer with words, but with the energy she started to emit. White mental energy and fearful pink energy rapidly exploded from her head, giving him more than a good idea of what their chances were of stopping the Third Great Attempt with the Arc.

"I don't know," Professor Heart squeaked, shocked over the revelation. "For the Arc to do its job, and assure maximum safety and effectiveness, it needs another week to create vents between the Red Dominion and Nis, and that's not even counting how long it will take to evacuate anyone underground. With the timetable you presented me, and if I work really fast, I *might* have enough time to create the exit points along the Yellow and Green Dominions' border and then go straight to Nis and Rem to begin evacuations. And I do mean *might*."

# The Second Coming

"You need to keep going to Nis," the Tribesman encouraged, shoving the timetable further into her hands. "There are more Hy-muns there that need to be rescued. Afterward, continue on to Rem. Do whatever you can along the way. I always planned to try and stop the initial detonation, and I'm going to do that. If I succeed or at least delay it, you'll at least have more time to reach Nis and Rem."

Professor Heart looked at the Tribesman solemnly, knowing that if he continued on alone, he would die. But if he did not go, they would all die anyway, and that he had already decided to use his remaining time to do something instead of waiting around for something to happen.

"Wait here," Professor Heart instructed, returning to the Arc before coming back atop a small self-propelled cart on four wheels, carrying another suit similar to the one she was wearing.

"Change into this," she said, giving him the suit. "It's a heat repellant suit. As you get closer to the magma vein, it will get hot—really hot—you might even feel like you are walking through fire. This suit will protect you. Also, take this electric cart. It's designed for working in high heat environments, it will help you get to the vein faster."

The Tribesman put on the suit and took the cart while Professor Heart gave him a brief explanation on how to operate it. The Tribesman *Knew* Professor Heart was right about it being resistant to high temperatures as soon as he felt it. It was tough and repellant, especially to heat.

"Thank you, Professor Heart," the Tribesman said, clasping her gloved hands in gratitude before riding off in the cart. "And good luck, if you get to Rem, tell the Seat of Hope you're the daughter of one of Cacci-guida friends. That will clear away any doubts anyone might have about you."

"Good luck to you, err, I'm sorry you never told me your name."

"I don't have a name anymore," the Tribesman said in a remorseful tone. "I did have a name once, but that name and person is gone now. Call me, Tribesman."

Professor Heart looked at him inquisitively, the Tribesman *Knew* she did not understand what he had just told her and would have liked to find out more— her white mental energy was buzzing intensely. Unfortunately, she knew she did not have the time to find out every little detail of the Remnant's society and ways of life.

"Good luck then, Tribesman." Professor Heart replied. Her voice was painted with curiosity, fear, remorse, understanding, respect, and courage.

"And good luck to you as well, Professor Heart. If you tunnel in that direction," the Tribesman pointed toward the far end of the cavern where he originally came from, "you'll eventually reach the Great Tunnel, which leads back to Nis. If you take the Arc down it, you might save some time."

"I will. Thank you again," Professor Heart shouted as the Tribesman rode away while Professor Heart returned to the Arc. The ship powered up soon afterward and almost made the Tribesman jump out of his suit.

*Relax, it's just the Arc,* the Tribesman said to himself as the Arc came to life and began moving toward the far end of the cavern. Watching it go by, the Tribesman realized just how long and big it really was.

*It could take up the entire size of the Great Tunnel and not leave any room for anything else to get by,* the Tribesman marveled. *And if its length and width are any indications about how many people it could hold, then almost all of Rem should be able to fit inside of it.*

The Arc slowly lumbered past the Tribesman but quickly gained speed and was soon out of sight, yet the Tribesman could still hear it moving down the Great Tunnel toward Nis.

*Well, I better get going myself,* the Tribesman decided, driving the cart into the Great Tunnel and back toward the Keyblast Point.

*This will help me make up some time,* the Tribesman realized, a small bubble of hope welling up inside of him. *But will it be enough?*

# Part 2: The Festivities Begin

# Chapter 8

"Two hours since we were last inspected," Ann reported. She had taken a position near the front of their cell and was counting seconds between cell inspections. "We now have two hours where we are completely unguarded. Yesterday it was one. You see, Reye, all that chaos you caused was helpful to us."

"*Helpful* to us," Reye mourned, sitting in the corner of the cell she kept for herself. "In no way was it helpful to anyone."

Reye was keeping to a distant corner of the cell, surrounded by members of the Remnant, while she played the role of the simpering Former Horror thrown into the mass cell a few days ago in Maestri.

Maestri, the First Circle of the city of Nis and its primary defense and incarceration facility, was changing its guards again. Ever since Reye, then known as the Hy-mun Horror, ripped through the city, destroying pieces of it wherever she went, guards transferred in and out of Maestri regularly to work throughout Nis. They were providing social services to replace the ones Reye destroyed. Reye Jasper, the Hy-mun Horror, had been a crazed Hy-mun girl who escaped the Grand Coliseum along with a single member of the Remnant of the Tribe. With his help, she had left her mark on the city. She caused more chaos and devastation through Nis than anyone ever thought possible until she was subdued and captured by Lord Tanas, reducing her to nothing more than a whimpering little Hy-mun girl not even worth killing. The Former Horror, her new nickname, was then thrown into a cell with a large group from the Remnant that had been captured a little over a week before the Horror's rampage when they arrived in Nis to protest the completion of the Third Great Attempt. Along with the members of the Remnant was another Hy-mun, Ann Branley, another survivor of the same raid that resulted in Reye being brought to Nis.

Ann had convinced Reye to undergo a Remnant Reconciliation Ritual to come to terms with her past actions as the Hy-mun Horror. Saying the ritual was psychologically intense was an understatement. Reye spent the entire encounter in a dreamlike state being slammed by the phantom of her dead twin brother, Raymond. He accused her of taking pleasure in the slaughter of the Tribe of Shadows, destroying Nis, and willingly abandoning any chance to escape or find her best friend Stella just to pursue revenge. He claimed that maybe she should join the Tribe of Shadows because of how much she had in common with them. The experience also included a vision of Tanas, when he was still a Nag-el, tempting her to slaughter a group from the underworld that was intermingling with her family. Instead, Reye struck down the phantom of Tanas before realizing what she was actually witnessing was a happy gathering of her family with the members of the Remnant at the Evening Supper Meal, complete with her brother—now looking like a member of the Remnant, before finally waking up from the ritual.

Since completing it, Reye slowly regained the spirit she once possessed. She knew she would not be the same person she was before being brought to Nis and did not want to be. The ritual not only made her face her past but also her personal flaws, flaws she knew she ignored before and would have kept ignoring if she was not captured, and would now have to correct if she lived long enough. But first, there was the matter of escaping.

"But do you think that is enough time for us to make it to the city's main entrance," Reye whispered, dropping her moping persona.

"If we are going to move before anyone returns, we'll need one and a half hours to reach the main gate," the Seat of Kindness, one of the Remnant's Council members, interjected. "It's enough."

"So, what are we waiting for?" Reye asked, eager to be moving again and start correcting her past mistakes, especially since she knew right where she wanted to start. "We have the keys. Let's move."

"I *Know* you are eager to get moving again," the Seat of Kindness pointed out. "But you must be patient. We don't know yet if all the digging equipment has been brought back from the Great Tunnel. It makes no sense to break out only to be captured again by returning diggers."

"Yes, Seat of Kindness," Reye replied, hanging her head low. She did not like waiting, it let her mind drift back to all the mistakes she made before ending up in this cell. Even the way the Seat of Kindness said "*Know*," indicating the special way the members of the Remnant and the Tribe of Shadows could perceive one another, served as another reminder of when she did not look at them as "people" but as "creatures."

"You will get the chance to look for her," the Seat of Kindness encouraged, placing his hand on Reye's shoulder and causing her to look into his silver eyes. "Just don't lose hope that she is still alive, just like we still hope that there are more of our own people back home waiting for us to return."

Since waking up from the Ritual and learning more about the details of both the Tribe of Shadows' plans and the Remnant's plans from Ann and the other members of the Remnant imprisoned in Maestri, Reye had decided on what she would do once they escaped.

*I'm not making the same mistake again,* Reye mused, thinking about the upcoming jailbreak. *Just stay alive for a bit longer, I'm coming for you, Stella.*

While the main group—a group that Ann was joining—would attempt to commandeer some of the digging machines used to dig the Great Tunnel so they could create vents to diffuse the supervolcano, a smaller group would head to Lust Atrophied. That group would find and rescue any members of the Remnant still being used there as breeders. Reye was eagerly waiting for the moment she could set out with that group.

"*So, you abandoned any hope that your best friend could have been alive all because you wanted to kill someone. Is that how you value friendship?*" Reye's stomach turned at the memory of her phantom brother's question during the Reconciliation Ritual, and at *how* she already answered it beforehand.

*I am going to save you. No matter what, I'm not leaving Nis until I go to Lust Atrophied, find you, and get you out of here.* Reye's thoughts were interrupted as an immense roaring sound began echoing through Maestri.

"What is that?" Reye shouted.

"I think the diggers are starting to return," Ca-to said. Ca-to, the member of the Remnant who led Reye's Reconciliation Ritual, was also in charge of the team going to Lust Atrophied to look for more members of the Remnant.

"I agree with Ca-to," the Seat of Kindness said, jumping to his feet. "Do you hear the cheers echoing through Maestri? It is honest, welcoming, and excited. The scents are the same too. The air of adrenaline is making its way through Maestri."

"Does this mean it's time to move?" Reye asked, excitement building in her for the first time since facing Lord Tanas.

"Not yet, but *very* soon now," the Seat of Kindness answered.

# Chapter 9

"Finally," Tanas said, looking through a secret camera installed at the city's main gate and watching as the diggers arrived in Nis. "Thousands upon thousands of years among these savages is finally going to pay off!"

In preparation for his departure, Tanas had secretly left Decca-Ju Tower and was now in his escape ship on the bottom of the Great Lagoon. Hidden away from anyone who could overhear him, he had no problems speaking his mind as he continued to watch the proceedings from various cameras spread across Nis while he continued to go over both his plans and contingency plans.

"The Third Great Attempt Plan," Tanas squealed, reveling in its coming fruition. "Objective, artificially creating a supervolcano that will remove sunlight from the surface, shutting down the Ziggurat Security System, which needs sunlight to operate, and allowing me to leave the planet. To do that, I convinced these savages to create a vast chamber to serve as the magma chamber for the supervolcano and a pipeline that will funnel magma from a ready source into it. I have also convinced them to create the conditions which will cause the magma to flow upward once the chamber is filled to capacity. The city is laced with Magnesium Mining Charges that will trigger the eruption once the magma arrives, forcing the magma up in one supervolcanic explosion. It couldn't be more perfect." Tanas smiled proudly and arrogantly as if he did all the work himself without the aid of either the Tribe of Shadows or the technology he had them steal from the Hy-muns.

# The Second Coming

"Final preparations," Tanas continued, walking over to a monitor and keyboard. "Welcome message, Invitation Message, Purging Message, and Initiation Message, all set and ready for activation."

Tanas had pre-programmed messages to play across Nis. Once the first message was activated, a three-dimensional image of himself would be projected over the city using Nag-el projectors, illustrating him delivering it. Tanas had rehearsed each one to make sure every word and gesture would make the most impact on its listeners. He calculated how much time would be needed between messages, given the capacities of the listeners, so that each of them could be played one after another with anyone realizing it wasn't actually "him" reciting them.

"Contingency plans." Tanas created his contingency plans in case something or someone tried to stop the Third Great Attempt. "'Failure at Keyblast Ignition,' I'm ready for that. 'Tunnel Sabotage,' the digging machines have all been appropriately outfitted. 'Invasion by Savage Rodents.'"

Tanas scoffed at that one. The Remnant of the Tribe was a minor annoyance at best. Every time the Tribes of Shadows came close to confronting them, they would run away. Tanas's contingency plan for the Remnant was nothing but letting the Tribe of Shadows have their way with them.

"Invasion from the surface." Now that possibility was one Tanas was slightly worried about, ever since that particular Hy-mun broke into Decca-Ju Tower near the end of the Second Great Attempt and struck him. That Hy-mun proved it was still possible to be born without the genetic programming that would make Hy-muns submit at the sight of him.

"That Hybrid Mutant might have been killed later on the surface, but his companions weren't. If he or any of them were able to convince others about me—"

Tanas worried about what could have happened.

"After the Mutant escaped, I began running simulations to try and find out what percentage of the Hybrid Mutant population could have been born without the programming. At best, only a tiny portion of the population should be 'anomalous.' So, even if a large force of Hybrid Mutants assaulted Nis's main gates armed with either martial weapons or the best weapons their science could produce, the odds are that the bulk of them *will* have the genetic programming and submit to the sight of me. Of course, they would have to get to me first."

Tanas knew that his main contingency plan against a Hy-mun Invasion counted on both the genetic programming within the Hy-muns and warriors of the Tribe of Shadows.

"Both that Mutant during the Second Great Attempt and the Hy-mun Horror were flukes, no one is *ever* going to get that close to me again unless I want them to."

The Methuselah Drug might have kept Tanas alive, but it did not make him immortal. Tanas was fully aware of his own mortality and the boundaries he could not cross if he wanted to stay alive. But once the Third Great Attempt succeeded, those boundaries would be gone for good.

"Now that I'm safe and far away from the city, I'll be able to sit back and watch the fun from here." Tanas laughed as he programmed his final instructions and recordings for the Tribe of Shadows to be played in the event of a surface invasion. "I'm just happy. I'm *finally* leaving all this behind me for good and forever."

Tanas entered a few final commands into the keyboard. Watching eagerly as the diggers approached Nis, it was time to begin the festivities. Tanas excitedly pushed the first button.

***

"My proud Tribe of Shadows!" Tanas's voice boomed and echoed across Nis as a colossal image of him appeared above the city, gaining the attention of everyone.

"For generations, the Tribe of Shadows labored and struggled while the Beings of Light, and then the Hy-muns after them, have enjoyed the comforts of the surface world. A world that originally belonged to you and your ancestors until it was unjustly stolen and desecrated by invaders who slaughtered entire families without mercy. They shattered your culture and way of life and destroyed a world that might never be restored. But now, the Great Tunnel the Tribe of Shadows has labored on is completed. Soon the vengeance that your ancestors have long called for will finally be answered. Rejoice!"

All throughout Nis cheers and hollering from every member of the Tribe of Shadows echoed in the circles. While in Maestri, Ann, Reye and the members of the Remnant were having their own thoughts on the proceedings.

"You were right," Ann said, moving to join Reye and the Seat of Kindness. "Lord Tanas *does* like to put on a show. Tell me, how is it that anyone here in Nis even believes what It is saying?" The Seat of Kindness did not answer. Instead, he looked past her to where Reye had suddenly collapsed onto the ground.

*Submit, Submit, Submit...*

The words coldly echoed through Reye's head as the same primal fear that froze her in place the first time she faced Lord Tanas surged through her again.

# The Second Coming

*No,* Reye whimpered. *I can't, I won't, it's not Lord Tanas. It's just an image. I don't have to submit to an image.*

But the word "submit" only echoed itself louder in Reye's head while Ann and the Seat of Kindness tried to shake her from her stupor. With each second, Reye felt herself falling back into the submissive form that resulted from her first encounter with Lord Tanas until Ann wrapped a blindfold across her eyes.

"Ha…" Reye coughed. The effect was instantaneous. Once Reye's eyes were covered, she instantly felt herself turning back to normal. "Ann, what did you do?"

"Don't take off the blindfold," Ann warned. "I think just seeing Lord Tanas will trigger the reaction."

"But why didn't anything happen to you?"

"I don't know," Ann answered. Looking back up at the projected image of Lord Tanas, and listening to the delightful cheers throughout the city, she could feel nothing but the desire to smash him in the face. "I wonder how many members of the Tribe of Shadows would still follow It if they knew It was also Light Bringer who first led the Beings of Light to their world?"

"We've already seen what happens," the Seat of Kindness replied. "As far as the Tribe of Shadows is concerned, any attempts to paint Tanas as Light Bringer is considered Hy-mun propaganda, just a Hy-mun trick to make members of the Tribe of Shadows lose faith in Tanas, their deity, savior, and benefactor."

"Still, with all that slop coming out of Tanas's mouth, can't you or the Tribe of Shadows tell it's all a lie."

"But it's not a lie." Reye interrupted, quickly gaining Ann's attention. "Lord Tanas is a deceiver who tells no lies. The trick is how It gets others to interpret them."

"Exactly, Reye," the Seat of Kindness agreed. "Notice, Lord Tanas is talking about what the Tribe of Shadows has gone through, which is true. It also referred to the Beings of Light, including itself, as 'invaders' without mentioning itself. Its use of words is one of Its most dangerous weapons." Gazing back at the image, the form of Lord Tanas soon started to speak again.

"Now that the Great Tunnel is complete, the Tribe of Shadows is connected to the magma vein in the Red Dominion. From there, we will trigger the eruption that will darken the skies over the entire continent, removing the accursed Light from the surface world and making it safe for us to return. Once we return, it will be the Hy-muns who know what it is like to see their families destroyed, their culture smashed, and their only refuge to hide in the very same caves that we have been forced to hide in since 'The Coming.' Cheer for the Third Great Attempt!"

The image of Tanas paused again as more cheering resounded throughout Nis. Chants of vengeance for "The Coming" and the blood of the Ancient Tribe echoed throughout the streets. However, in the Remnant's cell, orders were given as the members of the Remnant began putting their own plans into action.

"This is the moment we've been waiting for," the Seat of Kindness said as the other members of the Remnant, as well as Ann and Reye, gathered around and prepared themselves for action. "Once Tanas finishes Its speech, It's sure to call the Tribe of Shadows together in one place away from the digging equipment. Partially for the sake of performance, but mostly to keep anyone from trying to alter the tunnel. That is when Team A comes with me to get the digging machines. Ann, you're with me, you are the expert on supervolcanoes, so I want you to stay close."

"Yes, Seat of Kindness," Ann replied with a nod.

"Ca-to, you are going to take Team B to Lust Atrophied and find the women from Rem. Reye, let Ca-to lead you. As long as that image is up, you can't take off that blindfold, so let Ca-to be your eyes. You wanted to act, now is the time."

"I'm ready," Reye eagerly replied, and the Seat of Kindness *Knew* she was ready to get going. The second he started rousing the members of the Remnant into action, he saw Reye's energy come to life in a vibrant explosion of silver and blue. Now that Reye was going to have something to do, she felt more alive than ever before. Especially since she was resolved to doing the right thing, finding her friend and her getting out of the city instead of letting her anger consume her and pursuing her own vengeance.

"Seat of Kindness, what about the Tribe of Shadows' women, should we try and bring them with us as well?" Ca-to asked.

"You can try, but sadly I don't know if they'll even want to go," the Seat of Kindness responded. His head drooping as sad taffy-colored energy slightly radiated out from him. "The Tribe of Shadows' women were raised from birth to believe that their only purpose is providing future generations in Lust Atrophied. They may not want to leave, but if any do, bring as many as you can."

"We will," Ca-to replied as Reye stood next to him, ready and willing to charge back into the city, but this time to search for Stella, not to kill every member of the Tribe of Shadows she came across. Above them, the booming voice of Tanas resumed its proclamations with the next part of his speech.

# Chapter 10

"The Tribe of Shadows has endured countless hardships over the generations." Tanas's image continued as it broadcasted its message over the entire city, captivating the members of the Tribe of Shadows. Met-on was no exception. The broadcast began just as he was making his way to Lust Atrophied to see Stella again. But now, all that mattered was the image above him.

*This is the first time I have ever* seen *Lord Tanas.* Met-on whiffed, unwilling to say the words out loud in fear of interrupting Lord Tanas's proclamation. *I wonder what else he is going to say.*

"Unlike the Hy-muns, living in comfort on the surface, with their weak wills that allow them to be easily tempted to turn on each other, the Tribe of Shadows is a strong-willed people who won't be tempted from their goals. The Tribe of Shadows know the true meaning of sacrifice. While the Hy-muns on the surface have clung to foolish notions like hope, you have abandoned hope and devoted yourselves toward the success of The Plan, which is now only a step away from completion, sacrificing what you didn't need in the process. You sacrificed the weaker half of your people by cutting the Rodents of the Remnant out of your company, sacrificed the weakest members among you so that only the best and strongest would survive, and you will continue to do what is necessary until The Plan is complete. The countless names of martyrs inscribed on the walls throughout Nis, who are remembered for the lives they gave for The Plan, are remembered in every action you take here and on the surface. Now, I ask for the city of Nis to make another sacrifice before the Third Great Attempt begins. I,

Lord Tanas, order every man in Nis, along with every being who carries the blood of the Rodents, to go to the Grand Coliseum of Wrath Eras's main arena. It is finally time that they, too, are acknowledged and allowed to make a sacrifice worthy of the Tribe of Shadows. I will watch and not speak again until everyone has gathered in the Grand Coliseum."

"The Grand Coliseum," Met-on whispered. He could not believe it. "Lord Tanas just called me, and every other member of the Tribe of Shadows with Rodent-blood, into the Grand Coliseum." Since his last visit to Stella, Met-on had been torn and holding himself up in his small back-alley nook in Envy Opal-lo. He had been lying on his mat, trying to figure out why Stella had made the request of him that she did, and come up with a solution.

When Met-on last saw Stella, it was just after Warden Cha-Les told him that there would soon be a gathering in the Grand Coliseum of all members of the Tribe of Shadows who were like him and to listen for an announcement as to when it would be. At the time, Met-on was overjoyed. He had never heard of any member of the Tribe of Shadows with Rodent-blood ever being allowed into the Grand Coliseum. Not only that, there would be the added bonus of seeing every member of the Tribe of Shadows like himself in one place. Yet when Met-on told Stella about it, her reaction was not what he expected.

*"I don't want you to go to the Grand Coliseum,"* Met-on remembered Stella blurting. *"I don't want you to go to the Grand Coliseum. Instead, I want you to take me outside the city."*

That was not the end of Stella's reactions.

*"If you go to the Grand Coliseum, you'll die. Please, you need to trust me. Don't go. Instead, take me outside the city. I'll do anything for you if you can do that, I'll even tell you that I'm in love with you."*

*When Stella first told me that, I was overjoyed,* Met-on remembered. *Warden Cha-Les gave me the mission of making her fall in love with me, say that she was in love with me, or get her pregnant, for me to receive my first branding. Throughout our relationship, Stella had been submissive, curious, welcoming, and I definitely enjoyed being with her more than I did the company of other members of the Tribe of Shadows. But I hadn't heard her say that she loved me, or seen the energy of love around her, not that I've ever seen the energy of love before or could recognize it. But the last time we met, she showed me a new side, she was defensive of me and was worried about my life. At first, I didn't know what to do until I realized she must be falling in love and testing me.*

*"More than a test,"* Stella admitted. *"This a challenge from me to you. The purpose of a challenge is that it has to be passed for you to claim the reward. Instead of going to the Grand Coliseum, come here instead and take me outside the city. Do that, and I'll tell you exactly what you want to hear."*

# The Second Coming

*That was when my real mental torment began.* Met-on remembered, thinking back to how his mind kept trying to decide how he could pass Stella's challenge and still go to the gathering. *I kept trying to figure out ways to get rid of the guards so I could take her out of Lust Atrophied, send her on her way, or even chance the Jac-ob Way to get to the city's main gate and back as quickly as possible. None of them worked. But now, it doesn't matter any more. Lord Tanas himself has appeared over the city and personally ordered me to go to the Grand Coliseum, along with every other member of the Tribe of Shadows with Rodent-blood. I am going!*

Met-on began running toward Wrath Eras and the Grand Coliseum. The thrill of following Lord Tanas's command and the possibility of meeting more members of the Tribe of Shadows like him fueled his every step.

*I assumed the announcement would have been made regularly,* Met-on thought to himself as he darted toward Wrath Eras. *To think Lord Tanas would make it, and before the entire Tribe of Shadows, it's incredible!*

Meanwhile, in Lust Atrophied, Stella was having an entirely different reaction to Tanas's message.

***

Stella frantically searched her room, looking for a loose stone, a way to break apart the bed, anything she could use as a weapon. She knew *exactly* what Tanas's proclamation meant for both her and the baby she carried.

*Well, this is it for us.* Stella thought anxiously as her arm rubbed her womb where her child was slowly growing. *I was hoping that when Met-on was ordered to go to the Grand Coliseum, he would have found a way to get us out of here first. The desire to complete his mission and get his first branding winning out over going to the Grand Coliseum, but not anymore. There is no way Met-on would* ever *refuse a direct order from Tanas.*

Stella knew that the only reason she was still alive was that she had not told Met-on that she loved him and had managed to keep her pregnancy hidden. If her pregnancy was discovered, or if she said that she loved him—which she knew was not going to happen—the guards outside her door would kill her immediately. She also discovered, thanks to listening in on the guards when she attempted to escape, that at the gathering of members of the Tribe of Shadows with "Rodent-blood" that the Tribe of Shadows was going to kill them all, Met-on included, and then afterward she would be next.

*I didn't tell Met-on what I overheard because I knew he wouldn't believe me, and I didn't want him to know I was trying to escape.* Stella spoke internally to the child inside her. *I'm still a prisoner here, and he's still a member of the Tribe of Shadows, loyal to Tanas above all else for the services he gave them after he, ironically, tried to wipe them out of existence when they lived on the surface. Now it's only a matter of time, Met-on will be killed in the purge along with every other member of the Tribe of Shadows with mixed ancestry under the eyes of every pure-blooded man from the Tribe of Shadows—wait, every man?*

Sudden realization sparked into Stella as she hurried to the door of her room.

*If every man in the Tribe of Shadows is going to the Grand Coliseum, then the guards should be gone.*

Stella had not tried the door since her first escape attempt when she learned about the guards, Met-on's "mission," and the plans being made against both of them. But now, gripping the handle, she took a deep breath as she prepared to try it again.

*Well, here goes.* Stella tried the door.

It did not budge.

*The guards must have locked it before they left,* Stella thought to herself as she turned around and leaned back against the door, looking around her room.

"The guards won't come back until after the purge is over," Stella said to herself, no longer worried about being overheard by anyone. "So, now what do we do?"

Stella looked around her room, her mind now working calmly, taking inventory of everything in it.

"I've got a bed that's bolted down. I know how to work the gas. I got the slip I'm wearing, and the bedsheets. Okay, let's see what I can do with that."

Stella opened the panel above the door and saw the rope that controlled the gas. It looped under a slit in the wall above it. When Stella watched Met-on slow the gas, he pulled one side of the rope, and by tugging it the other way, the gas increased.

"This rope must connect to a valve that increases or decreases the gas," Stella figured as she pulled the rope so the gas would be completely shut off. "If I'm going to do something, I'll need my mind as sharp as it can be."

When the rope would not move anymore, Stella grabbed both ends of it and began pulling at it until it ripped out of the wall. Once it was free, Stella took the rope and her bedsheets and started tying them into a series of knots.

"Thank the Great Master for my talent at knots," Stella laughed at how her own talent was now hopefully going to get her out of trouble. When she was done, she had formed a cord almost as tall as she was.

"Well, I doubt I'll be stopping any swords with this," Stella figured, feeling the soft bundled material she had bound together. "Knotted together like this, it will be stronger, but it's still old rope and sheets. One good sword swing will probably cut clean through it. But at least I can bind, choke, or control a guard for a second. It might give me a chance to escape. A small chance, but it's still better than waiting to be killed. Now, where should we wait?"

Stella knew it was the most obvious hiding place in the room, but still she could not think of anywhere better, she stood on the opposite side from where the door would open. That way, when the guards entered the room, there would be a moment when the door would be between her and them, and she could jump them from behind.

*This is a crazy place to hide,* Stella puffed. *So crazy, it just might work.*

Stella waited with her back against the wall. All she could do was wait until someone opened the door and came to kill her.

*When that door opens, I'm either going to follow Raymond's last piece of advice and run, fight, and live, or do what he did when the Tribe of Shadows attacked the mining project, and die.*

# Chapter 11

"Wow…"

Met-on almost forgot to breathe. He'd never been allowed in the Great Coliseum before, he had only seen the outside of it from the streets of Wrath Eras. From there, he thought he had a rough idea about how big it actually was. He was wrong. The Grand Coliseum was more massive than anything he could imagine, and he was walking right into the middle of it.

"I always knew that the Grand Coliseum took up the entire width of Wrath Eras," Met-on whispered in awe. "But still, to see it all at once."

Met-on was not the only one to be stunned as more members of the Tribe of Shadows like himself slowly entered the Grand Coliseum. Each one was equally stunned by the sheer volume of empty space that had hosted some of the finest gladiators and martyrs Nis had ever produced. Each entry, like Met-on, showed signs that they carried the blood of the Remnant of the Tribe in their veins. Everyone who entered the Grand Coliseum had the same ash-grey skin and two jet-black horns that formed a coronet around their heads until they met on their foreheads, spiraling together into a small horn. Some were about the same age as Met-on, a few younger, but the bulk of them were older, in some cases many times older. Met-on noticed that some of the older ones bore a branding that they proudly showed off like a badge of honor.

*I wonder how long it took them to get those brandings,* Met-on thought to himself, his own unbranded body feeling more exposed than the ones with the brands on them. His mind flashed back to Stella in Lust Atrophied and her challenge.

*Stella asked me to go to her and take her outside of the city instead of coming here,* Met-on remembered. *She told me if I did, she would tell me exactly what I wanted to hear, that she was in love with me and that I could get my first branding. But if I did that, I'd be disobeying Lord Tanas's orders, and I couldn't do that, could I?*

Met-on knew that by choosing to follow Lord Tanas's orders without question, just like any other member of the Tribe of Shadows, he was giving up a chance—in essence, failing his mission—for a branding, something that everyone would defiantly criticize him for harshly. But he was following an order from Lord Tanas. He had to do it. How could he even *think* of disobeying it?

*I'm overthinking this,* Met-on decided, shaking his head a few times to clear his thoughts. *I should be celebrating, I'm in the* Grand Coliseum*! And I'm being surrounded by members of the Tribe of Shadows who are Rodent-blooded like me. I'm actually amazed there are so many of us throughout Nis. All of them must have been scattered throughout each of the different circles between Maestri and Sloth Cur-Nos, living in holes, back alleys, under staircases, or wherever else they could, just like me, for all this time. Ah, I wish...*

Met-on stopped his own thought, shaking his head out again when he realized he was about to wish for Stella to be here to see him in the arena as well.

*Why can't I get Stella out of my mind?* Met-on fumed, as the image of Stella's face, either pleading with him or challenging him not to go to the Grand Coliseum, remained stuck in his head. *What is happening to me?*

Met-on stopped questioning himself when he noticed a familiar face in the growing crowd. He was old, far older than any member of the Tribe of Shadows he had ever seen; Rodent-blood or not. If he were a pure-blooded member of the Tribe of Shadows, he would probably have a complete set of brandings by now and be allowed to retire to Circle Emporium with full honors. Yet he had only two brandings on his chest. As Met-on approached him, the old member knelt down, tears filling his eyes as he looked out upon the Grand Coliseum.

"Teacher," Met-on gasped, recognizing the ancient member of the Tribe of Shadows who served as his teacher in Envy Opal-lo. He was so old, he could not remember his own name.

"Young One," Met-on's teacher, coughed. "I finally made it here. No one said I would stand here, but I am finally here."

Met-on *Knew* his teacher was both reliving a past memory and proud to be here. He was generating waves of teal prideful energy, like most of the other members of the Tribe of Shadows present. Hazy white mental energy that Met-on had seen him produce whenever he remembered how he managed to earn his two brandings also pulsed from him.

"Now I can get my third branding, Young One," Met-on's teacher sobbed. "They said if I ever managed to be invited onto the Grand Coliseum, I could get my third branding. I'm finally here!"

"Congratulations, Teacher," Met-on exclaimed, his own problems temporarily forgotten in the face of his teacher's joy. For any member of the Tribe of Shadows with Rodent-blood, receiving a branding—bringing them one step closer to full citizenship into the Tribe of Shadows—was something to be praised.

"You'll now have three brandings! You're now closer to full citizenship in the Tribe of Shadows than any Rodent-blooded member of the Tribe of Shadows that I have ever heard of."

"What about you, Young One?" Met-on's teacher inquired. "Have you been given a mission by any of the Wardens to earn your first branding yet? How is that going?"

"Well, about that," Met-on stuttered, but was cut off as the image of Lord Tanas began speaking again.

"Tribe of Shadows," the image boomed above and throughout the entire city. "The *entire* Tribe of Shadows, now that you have all gathered in the Grand Coliseum, let us begin."

# Part 3: Across the Underworld, Forces Begin to Move

# Chapter 12

"Just the words we were waiting to hear."

The Seat of Kindness took one of the keys the members of the Remnant managed to acquire and unlocked the cell's door. Soon all the members of the Remnant, along with Ann and a blind-folded Reye, were standing free in Maestri listening to Tanas's image preach over the Grand Coliseum.

"Nis was nothing more than a refugee village in its beginning," the image boasted. "But the Tribe of Shadows grew stronger. Building from that village, now the heart of our city, Yam-Preen, until it reached Maestri. It is in Maestri where some of the greatest dangers to the Tribe of Shadows are imprisoned, including Rodents from the Remnant of the Tribe and, most recently, the Former Hy-mun Horror that assaulted our city until she was destroyed by my own hand."

Reye winced at the cheering she could hear echoing to Maestri from the Grand Coliseum in Wrath Eras.

*Not too long ago, I basked in those very same voices,* Reye remembered, trembling as she listened to the echoes. *Voices cheering for the lives I had taken, for more lives I could take, and for the warrior who would take my life. And I was enjoying every second of it.*

Suddenly, she felt a hand on her shoulder, her body calming down as the presence of the others made her remember she was not alone.

"You are not that being anymore, Reye," Ca-to assured her. "We *Know* you have changed and are healing. If you were still the 'Hy-mun Horror,' would you feel the way you do now?"

"No," Reye replied. "If I were, I would be feeling thrilled. Instead, I feel sick and scared because I know I *would* have felt that way not too long ago."

"Then that should tell you that you are becoming a better person after completing the Ritual. Try and feel more at ease because of that. We still have a lot more to do."

Reye, however, did not feel quite at ease as she would have liked. Through the Reconciliation Ritual, she came to terms with her past, but it did not change what she had done or taken away the memory of it. She still saw the faces of the warriors and gladiators she killed, and she knew she would probably see them for the rest of her life, only now she knew she would not be stuck in that one moment but could move past it and toward a future.

"It's time to split up and get going," the Seat of Kindness announced. The group quickly broke up into its two smaller groups led by both the Seat of Kindness with Ann and Ca-to with Reye.

"We'll be okay, Reye," Ann said reassuringly. "Just get to Lust Atrophied with Ca-to, find Stella and anyone else willing to leave Nis, and get them out of the city. I'll have a drilling machine primed and ready to take us back to the surface."

"I will," Reye said as she was led by Ca-to again through the streets of Nis.

\*\*\*

"Every member of the Tribe of Shadows, no matter how insignificant they may seem, has contributed something to The Plan." Tanas's voice continued to echo through the now empty streets. With every guard, citizen, and gladiator in Wrath Eras, Ca-to and Reye's group had no trouble moving from Maestri to Gluttony Mesh-Re.

"In life, our members contribute through city work, the digging of the Great Tunnel, creating future generations, becoming the strongest gladiators that will soon retake the surface, and finally in death." Tanas's voice paused, building to make a point. "In death, the members of our Tribe become the food that will fill our stomachs and carry us on to victory."

"It sure likes to hear the sound of his own voice," Reye realized. She had only heard Tanas speak when she was in Yam-Preen, and she knew that was not much of a meeting. Also, the Tanas she encountered during the Reconciliation Ritual was only a phantom of Tanas, not the real one. This was the first time she was actually listening to him as he spoke, and she could tell he *really* liked the sound of his own voice. He sounded like a politician making a self-important speech.

"And another thing, what is that smell?" Reye asked.

"We're passing through a Preparation Room," Ca-to said. "The smell is from the bodies. Mounds of bodies are stacked throughout the room. They are covered with silver scarabs created by Tanas's original followers, the Legions of Shadows, when they first came here. From what we have learned over the generations, the scarabs clean the bodies and keep them fresh before they are dismembered and cooked. The smell is a by-product created by them."

However, it was not the smell, or the scarabs crawling over the bodies, that were now catching Reye's attention. The idea that Reye was surrounded by dead bodies made her peer out from beneath her blindfold; she needed to. She collapsed in shock, taking Ca-to with her, as she quickly pulled the blindfold back over her eyes. She had recognized each face stacked in the Preparation Room. She kept seeing them in her nightmares. They were the bodies of the warriors she had killed when she rampaged through Nis as the Hy-mun Horror. Each face was frozen in death, and twisted into a bizarre look of fear and joy. It was almost like they were scared of dying but still glad it was happening.

"You've seen these warriors," Ca-to stated, helping Reye up and *Knowing* that she recognized them from the white mental energy and fear scents rising from her.

"I killed each one of them," Reye said shakily. "I'm sorry, I needed to see if it was them. They've all just been thrown into a giant meat locker, so a bunch of bugs can crawl over them instead of being cremated properly, yet every one of them looks strangely happy about it."

"I understand your confusion, but this is the way of the Tribe of Shadows," Ca-to replied, his monotone voice told Reye he did not like it either, but accepted that it was the path the Tribe of Shadows had chosen. "When someone dies in the Remnant, their body is buried in the ground, but for the Tribe of Shadows, it's different. When any of them die, the bodies are brought here and are slowly turned into the food that they eat."

"I thought they only did that to Hy-muns," Reye responded, remembering how she was served food made from the bodies of dead Hy-muns.

"No, they do that to all their dead, but they only eat their own kind. If you spent time with other members of the Remnant, I'm a little surprised that they didn't tell you about that."

Reye could not remember the bulk of what Ice and Dan-te told her, both during their incarceration in Wrath Eras and during her rampage through Nis.

*They were right next to me the whole time,* Reye thought ashamedly, *and all I remember, all I* wanted *to remember, is that they turned Hy-muns into food and sport and that they wanted my help to steal a veil. I never tried to listen or remember anything else.*

"I see," Ca-to mused. Reye quickly realized that Ca-to must be *Knowing* the shame Reye was feeling over not being able to remember anything Dan-te and Ice told her except what she wanted to remember.

"So, every warrior I killed, they're all brought here to be turned into food for the city?" Reye asked, fearful that she already knew the answer.

"Every warrior with salvageable remains becomes the Tribe of Shadows' food," Ca-to stated bluntly, also realizing that while Reye was scared of the answer, she needed to hear it. "Your rampage, in one sense, merely supplied the Tribe of Shadows with more food than they've ever had in a very long time."

Reye felt sick, not because she had killed the warriors stacked in the piles before her—she already went through *that* nightmare multiple times since encountering Tanas. She felt sick because she realized that by continually killing the Tribe of Shadows warriors, she was only feeding them.

*All that time running and killing throughout Nis,* Reye reflected. *In the end, all I really accomplished was property damage and providing the Tribe of Shadows with more food than they'll ever be able to eat. Can I get any blinder?*

"We don't have the time for you to feel sorry about not realizing what you were doing," Ca-to said, shaking Reye out of her reflections. "We need to keep moving forward to Lust Atrophied. That's where your friend might be, correct?"

"Right," Reye answered, her resolve building back up as she continued to move through Gluttony Mesh-Re.

*Ca-to's right,* Reye realized, moving past more rooms reeking of bodies she knew she would recognize. *I can regret what I did and what I didn't do later. Right now, what I have to do is get to Lust Atrophied. If Stella really is the Hymun being held there, then I need to get her and get back to the surface. If I do one good thing in this entire city, it has to be that.*

Reye continued on through Gluttony Mesh-Re. Above her, the booming sound of Tanas's voice continued to echo throughout the city and beyond it to where the Seat of Kindness's group was making its way toward the Tribe of Shadows' digging machines.

# Chapter 13

"For generations upon generations since 'The Coming,' you labored toward the completion of The Plan, now those efforts will reap their rewards." Tanas's voice echoed. "Using the Veil of Shadows, you struck the Beings of Light, inciting the First Great Attempt that drove them from the surface world, leaving nothing but their creations—the Hy-muns—in their place. After they were gone, you continued to strike at the Hy-muns, creating the Second Great Attempt, which almost destroyed them and re-darkened the world. And while that attempt might have not succeeded, it did provide us with the tools to bring our greatest attempt to fruition that much quicker. Thanks to your hard work, and the stupidity of the Hy-muns. The land of our ancestors is finally within our reach."

"It certainly likes to go on and on," Ann stated as she stood outside of Nis's Ring of Fire-Stone alongside the Seat of Kindness. "The way It talks, you would almost think It was working alongside the Tribe of Shadows from the beginning. But if you actually listen, you hear It's just talking about the Tribe of Shadows' efforts and none of Its own. Reye said it best when she called It 'a deceiver who tells no lies.' From what you've told me, the truth is that Lord Tanas has been mostly a recluse since It first entered Nis."

"Indeed," the Seat of Kindness pointed out. "According to our history, when Tanas first arrived in Nis, It did work closely with the Tribe of Shadows, establishing the civilization that would become the basis for today's Nis. Doing so created the conditions that allowed It to live as a reclusive god-king while others handled day-to-day affairs for It."

"I'm still a little surprised no one ever tried to question Tanas before," Ann said.

"Why would they?" the Seat of Kindness replied matter-of-factly. "Tanas appeared like a savior to our ancient brethren, providing them with the tools they wanted for their vengeance. Also, you remember how your friend Reye looked after her encounter with Tanas, don't you? How do you think the members of the Tribe of Shadows would have reacted to seeing *that* kind of reaction?"

The Seat of Kindness had a point, and Ann knew it. When Reye was tossed into the cell after facing Tanas, she was a broken, crying mess, a shell of the Hy-mun she once was.

*If Tanas can do that to anyone just by getting close or touching them, then it would be easy for anyone to see It as something more than mortal that should be kept at a distance,* Ann realized.

"You do understand," the Seat of Kindness replied, seeing her white mental energy spark and process the information about Tanas. "But enough about Tanas, what can you tell us about these digging machines?"

Ann turned her attention from the image of Lord Tanas above them to the digging machines in front of them. Since breaking up with Reye and Ca-to's group, she and the Seat of Kindness had quickly made their way out of Nis—through an unguarded main gate—and into the Ring of Fire-Stone. The jagged slabs of rocks set up in a ring around the perimeter of the city, illuminated by the magma, gave them the illusion that they were on fire. It was also where the digging machines used by the Tribe of Shadows were parked. They had been left outside by the Tribe of Shadows' diggers, and Ann could tell from the first glance that they were built before the Great Rainbow War in the Violet Dominion. The bodies of the machines and the drills themselves were coated with a rare titanium alloy, making them extremely resistant to heat and pressure. The metal of each one shimmered with a particular grey color only known to be found on the Violet Dominion's plateau.

"With machines like these, it's no wonder the Tribe of Shadows could get close to a magma vein," Ann marveled. "Since the Great Rainbow War, the ability to construct any kind of digging machine of this nature has become all but a lost art. I've only seen machines similar to these twice now. The first was at a Terranaut Exposition in the Red Dominion. It was what made me want to become a terranaut in the first place. The second time was at Spectral Academy when one was put on display in the Academy's museums. After that, all I've ever done was to study them in books."

"But, can you operate them?" the Seat of Kindness asked. He could see the white mental energy radiating from Ann, it was dim and hazy. He *Knew* she recognized the machines, but was unsure of their operation.

"Let's find out!" Ann shouted, resolving to put whatever knowledge she had to good use. "I've only studied how these machines work and operate in books, but let's see what I can do."

Ann climbed up to the door of the first machine and began to look it over as the Seat of Kindness stood at her side.

"These doors were built so they could be opened from the outside by either entering a code on a keypad…"

"What's a keypad?" the Seat of Kindness asked.

"A flat surface with buttons and numbers on it," Ann explained. "But I don't think we'll be able to use it. The keypad should be under a panel near this door to protect it from damage. First, we need to find it, and then we would need to figure out the right numerical combination needed to open the door."

"How many combinations could there be?"

"Since I've read that each of these doors used a different nine-digit combination, three hundred sixty-two thousand eight hundred and eighty," Ann answered, quickly doing the math in her head.

"We could look at the keypad and *Know* which numbers were pressed by the residual energy radiating from each of them," the Seat of Kindness suggested, knocking on the side of the door where he felt lingering energy. "We'll be able to figure out the code from that."

"I don't doubt we'll be able to figure out the code," Ann said, examining the other side of the door. "But what we don't have is time, that's why I was going to suggest we use this."

Ann pushed a panel on the side of the door that quickly popped out before sliding upwards.

"Right where the schematics said it would be." Ann laughed as she looked at a circular latch behind the panel.

"Okay, help me pull this," Ann instructed, grabbing the latch along with the help of the Seat of Kindness and beginning to pull. With a popping sound, it came out, and Ann turned it counterclockwise as far as it could go.

"Release!"

The door popped open.

"Good," Ann cheered before turning to the Seat of Kindness. "All the other digging machines can be opened the same way we opened this one."

"Understood," the Seat of Kindness replied before running out the door and telling the other members of the Remnant how to open the digging machines. "What was that device?"

"The emergency manual override," Ann explained. "The doors were designed so that if the emergency release were activated, the doors would pop open. Let's get to it."

Ann and the Seat of Kindness climbed inside the digging machine.

"Now that we're in, what's next?" The Seat of Kindness asked, returning to Ann's side. "How do we use these machines?"

Ann did not answer, she knew this was where the *real* challenge started. The inside of the digging machine looked like the pictures she had seen of Terranaut ships, only smaller and more compact.

*And to think that there used to be lots more ships and machines like this before the Great Rainbow War,* Ann thought as she marveled at the technology before her.

"Ann," the Seat of Kindness asked again, snapping Ann out of her state of awe, reminding her where she was and what she had to do.

"Right," Ann said, bringing herself back to the present moment. "This is where I am going to need your help. Can you see the residual energy from the Tribe of Shadows' diggers in here, where and what they touched?"

The Seat of Kindness looked around the digging machine's cabin and soon was able to *Know* every general location that the diggers moved in, what they touched, and where they sat and ate.

"Yes, I can see and feel their energy," the Seat of Kindness replied. "What do you need?"

Ann sat down in one of the seats and looked over the operating controls, piecing together what she would have to do to operate the machine from what she learned at Spectral Academy.

"I need you to tell me the order that the controls were used in the start-up procedure."

"Wouldn't you know something like that?" The Seat of Kindness asked.

"I worked on simulators that were already started," Ann explained. "Once the machine is started, I'll be able to make it go where we need it to go, but first we have to get it started."

The Seat of Kindness nodded, seeing the white mental energy radiating from Ann and *Knowing* that she was concentrating and trying her hardest to figure out the quickest way to solve this problem.

"Okay, the diggers will have needed to use the same start-up method every time they started the machine," the Seat of Kindness said to himself as he studied the controls and the lingering energy hovering over all of them. "The energy on the start-up controls should be the stalest and the most constant, unlike the other controls, which could have been used randomly at different times."

# The Second Coming

For a regular member of the Remnant, *Knowing* which minute traces of energy were the right ones would literally have been like trying to find one specific member of the Tribe of Shadows in the entire city of Nis. Thankfully, the Seat of Kindness was not a regular member of the Remnant. He was a member of the Remnant's Council, meaning he could *Know* in a way that went far above and beyond what the rest of the Remnant had been able to achieve.

"The first step, flip that switch," the Seat of Kindness instructed, pointing to a switch on the control panel.

"Got it," Ann said, reaching over and flipping the switch, bringing the control panel to life. "Okay, what do I do next?"

"Look out!" The Seat of Kindness exclaimed, grabbing Ann before jumping away from the controls.

"What?" Ann wondered, just as the entire control board exploded behind her.

"Sorry about that," the Seat of Kindness apologized. "I hope I wasn't too rough just now, but after you flipped that first switch, I *Knew* the controls were going to explode."

"No problem," Ann coughed, slightly winded from being lifted off the seat and pulled away. She had forgotten for a moment how much stronger the members of the Remnant were compared to her. "Did I flip the wrong switch?"

"No, you hit the right switch," the Seat of Kindness confirmed, looking at the melted remains of the controls. "When those lights started flashing, I suddenly caught a flash of molten heat energy plus a smell rising quickly from under the panel. I recognized the smell from Reye when she was first thrown into Maestri, the smell of the explosives she used throughout Nis."

"Magnesium Mining Charges, or MMCs for short," Ann realized as she looked at what was left of the controls. They were beyond melted and useless now, reducing the digging machine to a giant paperweight. The way they were dissolved, and the unmistakable smell that now hovered over them, were all characteristics of MMCs.

"All together I *Knew* that the controls were going to explode," the Seat of Kindness explained. "But what I don't understand is why."

"The diggers must have rigged them," Ann reasoned, moving away from the controls.

"Rigged?"

"Yeah, the controls must have been wired with MMCs so that if anyone tried to operate them, they would explode and make the machines useless. We better warn the others."

Ann and the Seat of Kindness started making their way out of the digging machine when another member of the Remnant stopped them.

"Seat of Kindness, the controls on one of the digging machines just exploded right in front of us." Ann and the Seat of Kindness looked at each other, mutual understanding crossing both of their faces. "No one was hurt, but everyone else is staying away from the controls. We don't want to risk losing any more digging machines."

"Good choice," Ann confirmed. "How many machines are left?"

"Four," the member of the Remnant answered. "Do you think you can keep the controls from exploding?"

Ann did not know. When it came to explosives, Reye was the expert, but Ann was no dunce concerning them either. Still, she had never tried disarming one before.

"I'll have to find out," Ann said, sweat beginning to build on her brow. "Find me some tools and let me at the next machine."

Finding tools turned out to be easier than Ann thought as she made her way to the next machine, but instead of making her feel confident, it only made her feel more nervous. Thankfully, no one said anything as she climbed into the third machine and began to loosen the screws holding down the control panel.

*The members of the Remnant and the Tribe of Shadows can see emotional energy as colors,* Ann thought as she loosened the last screw and began opening the control panel. *I bet I'm radiating all kinds of energy right now. I need to calm down and focus on what I need to do.*

"Move!" The Seat of Kindness shouted, causing Ann to drop the panel and jump back, shielding her face as another explosion reduced the panel to a melted heap.

"I just barely opened the panel." Ann coughed out, completely surprised and thrown off guard by the second explosion.

"I realized that," the Seat of Kindness said, coming up to Ann and placing a hand on her shoulder to steady her. "It's not your fault; whoever rigged these ships must have wanted to make sure that no one could use them. We still have three ships left we can try to operate. We will need to be very cautious about how we proceed."

*And I think we both know who rigged these ships,* Ann thought to herself as she moved away from the melted panel and out of the machine. *Tanas. He must have anticipated someone trying to take them and use them to either alter the Great Tunnel or something else entirely, so he took precautions.*

Ann made her way out of the digging machine and looked at the remaining three, three final chances to potentially stop the Third Great Attempt.

*I wonder how many more* precautions *he took to make sure that the Third Great Attempt is executed without any interruptions.*

# Chapter 14

"Professor Heart was right." The Tribesman gasped, riding down the Great Tunnel. "It does feel like I'm moving through fire. If it wasn't for this new suit, I don't know how I could make it. I wonder how the Tribe of Shadows even made it this far in the first place?"

Since leaving Professor Heart and returning to the Great Tunnel, it had become increasingly hotter. Even with his new suit, the Tribesman felt like his skin was slowly being burned by the heat.

"If this is how bad it is with the suit, I wonder how bad it is without it?" the Tribesman wondered, tempted for a second to take the suit off until he noticed a black spot in the fearful pink energy of the tunnel. Pulling over to investigate, he found a small group of diggers from the Tribe of Shadows, their own suits open, and their bodies scorched and baked beyond recognition. On each of them was a note, "Don't leave the digging machine, or this happens."

"So, that's what happens." The Tribesman gulped at the grim example the diggers left behind, and the realization he almost made a fatal mistake.

"I can just imagine what happened. The group is in the digging machine and making their way to the magma vein; it's too crowded, a fight breaks out, or dissenters rise up wanting to return to Nis. Either way, their taskmasters toss them out of the digging machine, and they get incinerated by the sheer heat of the tunnel. The taskmasters then throw the notes out as a warning to other diggers. Those bodies look so badly burned I would almost think their deaths were caused by the Light. I doubt that even the best Preservationists in Gluttony Mesh-Re could make them into food for the Tribe of Shadows, which is probably why they were left here."

Unfortunately, the Tribesman did not have any more time to consider the bodies as a more immediate concern caught his attention. A sudden rise in the temperature and an increase in the molten heat energy beneath him made him step on the accelerator, moving the cart forward as a jet of hot gas erupted from the ground. More powerful jets of hot gas quickly followed, spewing randomly from various cracks and fissures throughout the tunnel walls, marked only by the rise in temperature and the molten heat energy in the spots where they would burst.

*I'm getting close,* the Tribesman realized, sweat running like a river down his face and into his suit. *Very close.*

All around the Tribesman, the energy of the land was becoming ecstatic as the fearful pink energy grew more vibrant. The Tribesman *Knew* the Land was afraid, and the closer he came to the Keyblast Point, the more frightened the Land was going to become.

*I better keep going,* the Tribesman thought as he moved on in the electric cart. *I can't stop now when I'm this near the end.*

The Tribesman continued down the Great Tunnel, the temperature rising the further along he went until the Great Tunnel opened up into a large cavern. Fearful pink energy and molten heat energy radiated so intensely through the cavern that it threatened to block out everything else. The temperature was unbearable, rocks glowed red and orange from the intense heat, the suit felt like hot metal and fire against his skin, and rivers of sweat ran down his face and other parts of his body. Yet despite everything, the Tribesman smiled. Even with all the sweat obscuring his vision, he could clearly see the piles of silver crates stacked up against the far wall of the cavern. Carved into the wall above them was a declaration.

"Here, the Third Great Attempt begins. Let our ancestors be avenged as we return to our ancestral home on the surface."

"This is it, the Keyblast Point." The Tribesman gasped, not caring if he wasted energy or not. He was so happy he felt like he could have run all the way back to Rem. The Tribesman drove over to the crates, hopped out of the cart, and began examining them. Each one was bolted shut except for a mechanical device that fed into it.

"These crates must be larger versions of the Magnesium Mining Charges that Reye used throughout Nis," the Tribesman theorized, trying to grab one, but quickly pulled his hand back from the heat of the container. "They've become so hot from sitting here that I can barely touch them, yet they don't explode. I wish Reye were here. She's the expert on...No! I shouldn't even think about wanting

Reye here. I don't need Reye here. I can do this myself. Relying on Reye because of her strength and desire is exactly what caused the being I was to be killed by the being I am now. I can't, especially after coming this far, let myself fall into apathy again."

The Tribesman grabbed one of the crates. Despite the protection from the suit, the heat and pain raced into his hands and through his body. Every second felt like a year of being burned alive as he pulled the crate down and began examining the device on it.

"What's a little pain?" the Tribesman winced as he started to look at the device. "Compared to the pain Reye suffered since the attack that cost her brother his life, cumulating with the assault on Lord Tanas that I led her into, this pain is nothing. Now, let's look at this thing."

The device was a small metal box with a thin cord going into a small hole right next to it, and a transparent panel on the top of it protected two metal slits.

*Keyholes,* the Tribesman wondered as he looked at the rest of the device. Next to the keyholes shined two Hy-mun made artificial lights—a red one and a white one—and on top of that, a small rod.

"Well, since I don't have any keys, assuming these are keyholes, let's try snapping this rod." The Tribesman grabbed the rod and began twisting and pulling at it, but the rod refused to move.

*Okay, I can't snap the rod, can I break the whole crate open?* The Tribesman's mind suddenly went back to the destruction of the E-gle Building and the Great Staircase. The Tribesman remembered vividly how each structure looked as it slowly melted to the ground just from the regular sized MMCs. The memory sparked a new fear into the Tribesman.

*If I force open just one of these crates, will that cause it to explode?*

The Tribesman remembered that when Reye destroyed the E-gle Building, the MMCs in the building triggered other MMCs that did not explode, increasing the size of the explosion and quickening the rate of its destruction. The one MMC that he was handling now was many times larger than the ones Reye used. If just one of them went off prematurely, it could easily set off the others and start the Third Great Attempt.

*I can't just break any of these containers open,* the Tribesman realized since the early detonation of any one of them could cause the very disaster he was trying to prevent. *What about breaking the wires?*

The Tribesman looked at the wires leading from the device into the crate. There was only a small amount of exposed wiring, nowhere near enough for him to be able to pull them out.

*Are there any small rocks lying around with a jagged edge?* the Tribesman wondered as he began sweeping the cavern floor; unfortunately, there were none. Either the Tribe of Shadows cleaned them out as part of their preparations to make sure nothing could interrupt the Third Great Attempt, or he was just unlucky.

"Now what?" the Tribesman asked himself, looking back at the electric cart he rode in on, giving him all the inspiration he needed.

"That's it!" the Tribesman exclaimed, grabbing a large rock and smashing it into the electric cart, not caring if he needed to walk back to Rem on foot now—assuming he walked back at all—until he had a piece of metal in his hands with a sharpened end on it. Taking his "knife" to one of the crates, he positioned the sharpened end over the wires and muttered a silent prayer.

*Please First Ones, don't let this crate explode on me.* The Tribesman cut the wires, and the crate did not even twitch.

"Ha!" The Tribesman exhaled, relieved that the crate did not explode. His relief was short-lived, however, as he looked at the device and noticed that the white light was still on.

"I guess breaking the wires isn't enough," the Tribesman realized, repositioning the box. "I have to get this device off it entirely."

The Tribesman inserted his knife into the space between where the device was connected to the crate. Slightly more confident that the device would not explode now, he began to pry at the container and the device until it broke off with a pop that echoed through the cavern. This time, the light on it went out after it was separated from the crate.

"That's one down," the Tribesman cheered, becoming far more serious as he looked back to the stacks of crates making up the Keyblast Point. "And many more to go. So much for Lord Tanas's precautions."

The Tribesman returned to the stack and took another crate. Ignoring the pain from the hot metal, he repeated the same procedure. The more crates he disabled, the easier it became. His body soon became numb to the burning pain coursing through his body. During his work, a thought entered his mind.

*I wonder how Professor Heart is doing?*

# Chapter 15

*Too fast, Bridget, you're working too fast,* Professor Heart thought to herself as she retracted the Arc's digging mechanism and moved through the Great Tunnel toward the next drilling site. *The Tribesman was right about using the Great Tunnel to save on the time it would take for me to get to Nis. But that doesn't mean I should speed drill the venting tubes, but what choice do I have?*

Professor Heart was currently traveling under Sand Break Border, the boundary between the Yellow and Green Dominions. Usually, a quiet place, getting its name from how the sands of the Yellow Dominion broke abruptly against the grass and soil of the Green Dominion. The border was quickly becoming the subject of study as a series of minor earthquakes and sinkholes began appearing across it, all the results of Professor Heart's digging. Deep beneath the surface, she wrestled with her own decisions and why she was making them.

*This tunnel is the same size as the Arc,* Professor Heart mused, relieved to have that much in her favor. *The problem is the vents to the surface. According to Father's calculations, I needed an entire week to dig vents under Sand Break Border that can safely withstand the force of the magma. That estimate was based on how long it would take to drill the bare minimum number of vents. Dig them slowly enough so that there wouldn't be any significant disturbance to the surface. Place MMC charges to force the magma up through them. And finally, continue onward slowly enough so that the Arc can't be tracked underground by either Hy-mun technology or anyone in Nis. Yet here I am, chewing through the ground like an earthworm and dumping crates of explosives behind me like it was nothing.*

*Drilling this fast will not go unnoticed on the surface,* Professor Heart worried as she quickly approached the next drill site. *The faster I dig the vents, the higher the odds are that they could collapse in on themselves prematurely, seal themselves up, or open to the surface. I've already picked up reports from the surface about quakes along the border and sinkholes opening up under some of the vents. But what choice do I have!*

Professor Heart's worry only increased when she shifted her gaze down to both her father's journal and the timetable that the Tribesman gave her.

*When I first looked through that journal, I found notes, equations, diagrams, an exact plan laid out on how to defuse the supervolcano and stop the Third Great Attempt.* Despite everything, Professor Heart was still flabbergasted at the sheer scope and depth of her father's work. *My colleagues have often called me a genius, but I'm nothing compared to him. He managed to figure out Tanas was going to create a supervolcano to darken the skies, where he would ignite it, and what would have to be done to defuse it, saving as many lives as possible both above and beneath the surface. The problem is time.*

Faced with the immediate threat presented by the Third Great Attempt, Professor Heart decided on a high-risk option. Following her father's designs and disregarding the time it would have taken her to drill the vents to the surface along Sand Break Border as inconspicuously as possible, she had been digging as fast as her equipment would let her despite the risks. But as a former terranaut, she knew exactly what that would mean for the surface, and it was eating her up inside. Yet what was worse was she knew what would happen if she *didn't* proceed this way, and that was even more maddening.

*You told me to save as many lives as I can, Father,* Professor Heart fretted, thinking about the consequences of her actions. *But how many lives will I really be able to save, or am I only going to put* more *lives in danger by attracting Hy-muns to the vent sites and by potentially creating faulty vents. But what choice do I have! We don't have the time. Do I not make the vents and just save the Remnant of the Tribe, Hy-muns, and any defectors from Nis that are here in the underworld and let Tanas's supervolcano wipe out life on the surface? Or do I make the vents carefully, protect the surface world, and sacrifice everyone in the underworld. They have as much a right to live as we do—despite what some of them might have done? What do I do?*

Professor Heart kept looking at the situation again and again from as many different angles as she could imagine. But each time she kept coming back to the same conclusion: no matter what happened, she had to proceed with her current plan.

# The Second Coming

*I might be endangering more lives with this course of action, but it's what I have to do,* Professor Heart willed herself again as the Arc's drill finished drilling its next vent. *By* not *drilling these vents, I'm endangering far more lives than I am by digging them. Then there are the cities of Nis and Rem. I have no doubt that the members of the Remnant of the Tribe who live in Rem will come with me, especially after I tell them who I am and mention Cacci-guida like the Tribesman said. But Nis, on the other hand, is a different story. The Tribe of Shadows have been brought up seeing Hy-muns as an enemy to be conquered and the Third Great Attempt as a good thing. Not only that, they think the supervolcano will erupt in the Red Dominion. When I show up and start telling everyone that the magma is coming toward the city and that I'm trying to save them, how do I know that they'll even believe me and not think I am trying to trick or destroy them? Wait, what did I just think?*

Professor Heart suddenly remembered another part of her father's last testament. He warned her about Kai Aphas and the Hammers of the Orange Light, who had approached him trying to take the Arc but instead left with a copy of the Arc's plans.

*I already understand that both Kai Aphas and the Hammers are dangerous,* Professor Heart reasoned. She knew that anyone like Kai Aphas, who could go from being a condemned criminal to an advisor for several Virt Princes and the head of a secret organization, was beyond dangerous.

*But what would he want with the Arc or its plans? Is he also planning to invade Nis? No, he couldn't do it without the Arc. But he did take the designs. No, I'm overthinking this. My father spent years just to build this one ship. There's no way Kai Aphas could have recreated it for his own plans with the short amount of time he had since he took them, could he?*

Professor Heart did not have an answer to her own question. All she could do was keep working. The idea that someone else was working on getting to Nis, someone just as dangerous as Tanas, made her forget her own fears and get back to her work.

PJ Fenton

# Part 4: The Final Moments before the War

# Chapter 16

"It will be worth it, brother, you'll see."

Kai Aphas was in his private compartment aboard the Antaeus. He watched as the final members of the Hammers of the Orange Light boarded the ship so it could begin its descent toward the city of Nis. At the same time, similar reports from the Antaeus's sister ships, the Og, Nimrod, Typhon, Alops, and Tityos, were also coming in. All six ships were modeled after the plans for Dr. Noah Heart's Arc, with his own personal modifications, and built secretly in record time with the full support of four of the Seven Dominions. In the meantime, Kai Aphas was having a private conversation with a photograph of his stepbrother Able, taken soon after he shot him.

"You see, brother, I really had no choice. I mean you, Hope, and Noah were buying into the demon's story that they were descended from a race of beings native to Prism that were driven underground by the Nag-el. I mean, we both know that couldn't be true. The Nag-el and Ash Addiel are divine, they are good and infallible, and they don't do things like conquer and devastate."

Kai Aphas had this same conversation with his stepbrother's photograph at least three times a day since he first saw the picture, and every time he started it, he could hear his brother contradicting him.

*But Tanas was a Nag-el, and he conquered,* Able's voice would say. *He devastated the Ancient Tribes homeland in "The Coming," almost destroying them, then turned on Ash Addiel himself.*

# The Second Coming

"No!" Kai Aphas rejected harshly. "Tanas stopped being a Nag-el so he could become a traitor to Ash Addiel and later become the shadow to his light."

*You're lying to yourself. You know Tanas was always a Nag-el when he betrayed Ash Addiel. After his failed rebellion he was altered, but he was still a Nag-el.*

"No, Able, you're trying to deceive me again, just like you did in Nis when you tried to make me sympathize with the creatures there. The Nag-el create civilizations, we Hy-muns create civilizations, those demons are not capable of creating one—even with Tanas present."

*But then what would you call the City of Nis?*

"That is not a civilization, Able!" Kai Aphas screamed. "That so-called city is a mockery. Just demons created by Tanas playing at civilization. The only true civilization can come from the Nag-el."

*But Tanas is a Nag-el.*

Kai Aphas kicked a table over and started pacing the room. Every time Kai Aphas had this conversation, it always made him extremely angry, it was why he only held it in private away from the ears of any of his brother Hammers. He did not want any of them to think he was cracking in his old age, especially now that the Hammers were so close to their final victory.

"You're still mad that I left all of you in Nis, aren't you, brother? Well, I had to do it. I needed to get to the surface. Warn the Virt Princes about Tanas, his demons, and that the rest of you had been compromised."

*I never said that Tanas wasn't a threat that had to be dealt with.*

"But you wanted to make peace with the demons," Kai Aphas threatened accusingly. "How could you want to make peace with demons?"

*You know the Tribe of Shadows and its sister group, the Remnant of the Tribe, are not demons. They were the first natives of Prism and have just as much of a right to it, if not more of a right to it, than we do.*

"They die in sunlight. What else, but a demon dies in sunlight?"

*We can die from sunlight,* Able's voice said punishingly. *Or have you forgotten about how you got seriously sick once from a bad sunburn?*

Kai Aphas punched the side of his compartment. He hated talking to Able since he always opposed him and knew just what to say to contradict him. However, he could not stop talking to him. Talking to him, getting angry at him, helped keep him focused on the goal he could finally see ahead of him now, a world without Tanas, without any Tempters from the Tribe of Shadows sneaking into Hy-muns' shadows to tempt and provoke them into misdeeds. No more cave snatchers would kidnap explorers to turn them into food or their own personal amusement; a world the Great Master Ash Addiel and the Nag-el can finally return to.

*You won't reach the end your seeking,* Able's voice said again in warning.

"Yes, I will, brother," Kai Aphas said confidently. "And when I reach the end; when the world is finally free from Tanas and at peace, the Great Master Ash Addiel and the Nag-el will return. Then you'll see, every action the Hammers and I have taken, they will all be justified. It will be worth it, brother, you'll see."

# Chapter 17

*No matter what* precautions *Tanas might have in place, I doubt he is ready for my Hammers of the Orange Light,* Kai Aphas mused to himself excitedly as someone knocked on his chamber door.

"Sir, the Virt Princes, they are here to see you," a voice called from outside.

"Send them in, brother," Kai Aphas replied, returning the last piece of overturned furniture to its proper place, as the door opened and a Hammer led in four individuals. Each one was in their mid-forties and wearing a different color robe—red, orange, yellow, and violet.

"Welcome, Virt Prince Noah Virt Red-Scipian of the Red Dominion, Lucan Virt Orange-Licht of the Orange Dominion, Moses Virt Yellow-Lien of the Yellow Dominion, and Ovid Virt Violet-Esprit from the Violet Dominion. We've waited for this day for a long time." Kai Aphas shook each of the Virt Princes' hands and embraced them as he welcomed them into his chamber. The anger and madness in his voice and actions were instantly hidden and replaced by sentiments of friendship, brotherhood, and comraderies.

"We have been waiting a long time for this as well, Kai Aphas," Ovid said, stepping to the front of the group. "Our dominions have sacrificed decades worth of resources in the form of building material, food, armaments, technical expertise, and lives to keep this project a secret."

"But for the destruction of Tanas and his evil, we all agreed any sacrifice would be worth it," Moses interjected, stepping up alongside Ovid—almost challenging him as a sneer crossed his lips.

"Actually, it was our fathers who first agreed to that," Lucan said, speaking up from behind Ovid and Moses. "It was their illuminated minds that saw the brilliance in Master Kai Aphas's plans and actions all those years ago. It was back when he first appeared from the underworld like the sun rising in the sky, freeing his stepbrother from Tanas's influence, and alerting our fathers of Tanas's existence, who would then share that information with us."

Kai Aphas could not help but smile whenever he listened to Lucan talk. Out of all the Virt Princes that supported him, Lucan was his most stalwart supporter.

"And just like you suggested, we kept the information secret from our immediate families. As far as any of them know, we are at a private meeting about Dominion finances, and not one of them knows about Tanas or Nis. Isn't that right, Noah?"

"Yeah, I did whatever you said," Noah answered, looking more scared to be there than anything else.

*I can always count on Lucan to follow my instructions,* Kai Aphas thought with a smile. *Ovid and Moses would tear each other apart if they both didn't want to see Tanas destroyed even more, and as for Noah, he's the coward of the four. From the moment he took over his father's position ten years ago, he's done nothing but follow the group's direction so that there wouldn't be any problems in it. And since the group is mainly led by me, with Lucan, my most stalwart supporter, and Ovid and Moses following to see Tanas destroyed, I don't have anything to worry about. Once Tanas is gone, I won't need any of them or the Hammers anymore. Their children can clean up after them.*

"It's just a shame the other Virt Princes can't be here," Noah muttered, thinking no one would hear him but quickly receiving harsh looks from the other Virt Princes.

"We don't need those cowards!" the other Virt Princes said in unison.

"Archimedes Virt Green-Gander can stay in his flower bed in the Green Dominion. It's all he cares about. And Aeneas Virt Blue-Canoe is even worse. He might as well be a bum instead of a Virt Prince with the way he acts." Lucan spit out, thinking about the Virt Princes of the Green and Blue Dominions.

"Then there is Hesiod Virt Indigo-Castitas, who hides like a coward in the Indigo Dominion behind *your* plateau Ovid," Moses added with a sneer. "Neither he nor his father had the guts for our plans and made it his prerogative to have as little to do with the other Dominions as possible."

# The Second Coming

"I can't speak for the Indigo Dominion," Ovid said, maintaining his composure. "They just keep to themselves and do whatever they want."

"Gentleman," Kai Aphas announced, ready to get the focus back onto the matter at hand. "Now isn't the time to worry about men who are not wise or illuminated enough to share in our vision. We can only thank the Great Master that none of them ever let the knowledge of our plans slip to the outside. We could not afford to let Tanas become aware of them."

*Or anyone else for that matter,* Kai Aphas mentally added as the four Virt Princes nodded in agreement with Kai Aphas's words. *If the general public knew of the sacrifices we had to make toward defeating Tanas, I doubt many would be as willing as my brother Hammers or these four Virt Princes. When Tanas thinks of "sacrifices," he thinks of something that needs to be given up for the greater good. But in our case, the "sacrifices" that we have made are in Hy-mun lives, taken in secret to keep our activities hidden and Hy-mun culture on its "proper" course, both technologically and ideologically.*

*I've kept my eyes on the Virt Princes of the Green and Blue Dominions, and thankfully they've kept their mouths shut for the last few decades, worrying more about their own Dominions than anything else,* Kai Aphas thought, thinking about the actions of the other dominions. *As for the Indigo Dominion, all my spies could do is get into the Dominion and tell me they are mostly isolationists. As for the Virt Prince and his family, except for their eldest son Homer who is out among the people regularly, not even my best spies could find anything else out about the rest of them. Only that they seem very tightlipped, and are also not making any apparent moves against me or my plans. We shouldn't have any problems with them.*

"Is something wrong, Master Kai Aphas?" Lucan asked, a worried expression crossing his face. "You are looking tense."

"I'm just thinking about our plans, Lucan," Kai Aphas happily replied, his smile erasing the worry from Lucan's face. "We should be leaving for Nis in ten minutes." Kai Aphas looked over to the countdown clock to double-check that time and saw that it was ten minutes and counting before the ships departed for Nis. "If the four of you want to watch the launch, you better leave now."

"Watch the launch? We are coming!" the four Virt Princes said in unison, both surprising and slightly irritating Kai Aphas.

"Our fathers, the previous Virt Princes, started this with you following the end of the Great Rainbow War and we want to see it through with you to the end," Lucan announced, bursting with pride at each word—a feeling that the other three Virt Princes equally shared.

*Just what I need,* Kai Aphas thought irritably, realizing he would now have four uninvited guests on this mission, but did not dare show it outwardly.

"In that case, my brother Hammer outside will then get you outfitted quickly and to a staging area." Kai Aphas knocked on his door, and another Hammer walked inside to escort the Virt Princes out. "Once we have departed, it should take twenty minutes to reach Tanas's city, ten minutes to drill through the plateau and another ten to reach Tanas himself. I suggest you prepare yourselves."

The Hammer led the four Virt Princes out of Kai Aphas's chamber, leaving him to complete his own launch preparations. Taking another glance at the photo of his brother, he whispered to him again. "Soon, brother, it will all end soon."

# Chapter 18

"Soon, brother, it will all end soon," Dan-te whispered to herself as she watched the countdown clock tick closer to zero. At her side, she could feel Virgil's hand squeezing her own, trying to offer whatever comfort he could. She understood why Virgil was not speaking openly, and she did not blame him. They were in a confined pod with eight other members of the Hammers of the Orange Light, Hy-muns who would kill them both if they realized who they were. Watching the last few minutes tick down, Dan-te could not help feeling a sense of dread over what was about to happen.

*Ice first came up with the idea of using the Veil of Shadows to go to the surface and alert the Hy-muns living there about Lord Tanas and the Third Great Attempt. We figured one of us would slip into someone's shadow, encourage them to talk to a Hy-mun leader for us, and get that leader to send an army underground to take care of Lord Tanas. Now that I think about it, that idea was so naïve and half made I should have laughed out loud when I first heard it.*

Dan-te would have laughed over how ridiculous a plan she and Ice originally conceived if she could. Yet despite the craziness of their idea, she succeeded in stealing the Veil, thanks to Reye's actions in the Grand Coliseum, and made it to the surface. Only to be cut off from the shadow, she appeared in to get stuck *outside* the "Reversed State."

*When I reached the surface, I was alone, stuck in a room filled with books, and outside of the "Reversed State" because of the damage to the Veil. One yank on it, and I would have been burned alive in the sunlight. But the room*

*I was in turned out to be your room, Virgil.* Dan-te cast a grateful glance at her traveling companion, considering all he was doing and giving up to help her. *You were a Hy-mun I could talk to directly* because *of the damage done to the Veil. Not only that, but you even turned out to be the son of a Virt Prince, precisely the type of person I originally was hoping to meet. You understood what the Third Great Attempt really meant for us all, and the inherent problems with my original plan because of the forces active in Hy-mun society.* Knowing *that, you gave up your old life to help me.*

*Without you, I would have been lost and probably dead on the surface for a while now.* Dan-te remembered how hungry and tired she was when she first came to the surface. The number of times she passed out *Knowing* aspects of Hy-mun culture, she needed Virgil to carry her, and she remembered the times she was almost exposed by technology crafted by the Beings of Light. She *Knew* she needed Virgil just to make it this far.

*When I was hungry, you fed me, tired, and you gave me a place to rest, faint of heart, and you carried me, in danger, and you shielded me. Now, you're returning with me to the city of Nis, along with the "army" that I initially wanted to "do something" about Lord Tanas.*

Dan-te felt sick with herself, *Knowing* the army she was returning to Nis with wasn't made up of soldiers ready to fight Lord Tanas and stop the Third Great Attempt, but the absolute worst the Hy-mun race could produce in the Hammers of the Orange Light.

*When you first told me about the Hammers of the Orange Light,* Dan-te remembered. *That they were the extremists that destroyed technology during the Tribe of Shadows' Second Great Attempt—the Hy-muns' Great Rainbow War. Later butchering your friends in the Alien Astronaut Movement, I initially thought they were a bunch of intolerant thugs and killers. But after encountering them, I* Knew *they were far worse. They're no different than the Beings of Light from "The Coming." Their only real desire is to kill anything that moves underground that they perceived as being associated with Lord Tanas; in other words, everyone.*

Dan-te shivered, gazing at the other Hammers in the pod alongside Virgil and herself. Each one of them, despite their orange suits, radiated the same crimson energy that she witnessed coming from the gladiators and members of the Tribe of Shadows, tainted with an intense rosy lustful energy. She *Knew* these Hy-muns wanted nothing more than to start killing as soon as possible. They were filled with anger and rage toward Lord Tanas, the Tribe of Shadows, and anyone who lived underground, blaming them for all the misfortunes that the Hy-mun race had known since its creation.

# The Second Coming

"Attention all Hammers of the Orange Light!" Kai Aphas's voice echoed in the pod through its speakers.

"The final minutes have come. Soon we will descend on Tanas and his Tribe of Shadows like the Nag-el from the stars and obliterate their shadows from our world. You are my brothers as we embark on this mission, ridding our world of shadows once and for all, for the glory of the Great Master and his light!"

The pod erupted with noise as the other Hammers began cheering for Kai Aphas and the coming fight. Virgil also started cheering. But as Dan-te listened, and saw the energy coming off him, she *Knew* Virgil's cheering was only meant to disguise his identity so that no one in the pod would suspect he was not a member of the Hammers of the Orange Light. The Hammers' voices were filled with excitement, pride, and the lust for conflict. The short speech from Kai Aphas caused each one of them to emit the teal-colored energy of pride. Virgil's voice, however, only sounded excited on the surface, but unlike the Hammers, there was no passion or emotion within it. And while Virgil tried to feel nothing toward Kai Aphas, Dan-te could see the sparks of the same horrible red energy she had seen on Reye along with umber colored contentment and flaxen yellow negativity bubbling out of him after listening to Kai Aphas, the Hammers, and their cheering.

*Virgil doesn't like having anything to do with these Hy-muns,* Dan-te thought to herself. *Not that I blame him. They are the ones who massacred his friends in the AAM and used his friends from Spectral Academy as bait to learn the Tribe of Shadows and Nis's exact location. Even without the ability to* Know, *I can tell Virgil is struggling just to keep himself in check. I don't want anything to do with them either. But like it or not, they are going to Nis, and we need the ride.*

Dan-te quietly watched the count-down clock in the pod quickly approach zero.

*We went through all of this to stop the Third Great Attempt,* Dan-te remembered, thinking about the task still ahead of her and Virgil. *But was it all worth it? Hy-muns already knew about the Tribe of Shadows and were planning to go underground and fight them anyway.*

Dan-te did not wonder too long about her own question, she only had to feel Virgil's hand in her own for the answer.

*Yes, it is worth it. The Hammers of the Orange Light might want to attack Nis, but they don't know anything about the Third Great Attempt, nor do they seem to be the kind who would listen to a warning from either a member of the Remnant or the son of a Virt Prince. Getting to the digging machines and using them to try and defuse the supervolcano, that's our job, and once it's completed, we'll need to warn Rem and get it protected as soon as possible.*

"One minute to go!" a Hammer exclaimed who was watching the count-down clock intensely. "Count-down time, fifty…forty-nine…forty-eight…"

*Well, this is it.* Dan-te prepared herself for what she expected was going to be an extremely bumpy ride back to Nis, nothing like traveling via the Veil of Shadows, which was quick and easy.

"Three…two…one…zero!"

As soon as the Hammer shouted zero, the whole ship began to vibrate and shake as its digging mechanisms came to life and started burrowing into the ground. Dan-te slowly felt herself, and the entire ship, sink into the ground as it began to tunnel its way through the plateau.

*I saw how big this plateau was when we arrived in Tri-Dominion City,* Dan-te mused. *This ship has to dig straight through it, and then through however much ground separates the surface from Nis before it arrives. I wonder how long it will take?*

Dan-te soon realized it might not take as much time as she thought. She could feel the ship quickly building up speed the faster it descended into the ground. She *Knew* it would not be long now before the Tribe of Shadows received a very unwelcomed and unexpected surprise.

# Chapter 19

*What is Lord Tanas going to say next?* Met-on wondered, hanging on every word of Tanas's speech in the Grand Coliseum.

"Each part of the Tribe of Shadows' society is worthy of praise," Lord Tanas's image continued. "First, we must remember the martyrs who gave their lives and bodies to the services and survival of Nis. Next, the current Seven who live in Circle Emporium and make up my private counsel, all members of the Tribe of Shadows who have served Nis for so long that they have perfected their tempting and earned the privilege of living in Circle Emporium. Next, we remember the Branders who presented each member of the Tribe of Shadows with their brandings, placed upon them after completing a mission from the Wardens of the Circles.

"We must also honor our civil servants. From the teachers and instructors of Envy Opal-Lo to the planners, runners, office workers, telecommunication operators, and more in the three ruling circles of Greed U-Sez, Pride Aster, and Circle Emporium. Even more so to the breeders of Lust Atrophied, who even now are still holding true to their ancient promise to me to remain in their circle to protect it and provide future generations for the Tribe of Shadows *no matter what*. But no one in Nis can survive without food, and for that, we need to thank the chefs and preservationists in Gluttony Mesh-Re.

"The members of the Tribe of Shadows stationed in Gluttony Mesh-Re have long been responsible for the care of the dead and feeding of our living. I want to make a special note to thank them all for their generations of tireless work. It is by their skilled hands that every member of the Tribe of Shadows recovered after death is cleaned, preserved, processed—removing all waste products—and turned into the food which has fed this city and every member of the Tribe of Shadows in it since its beginning."

Lord Tanas's speech paused as the inhabitants of Gluttony Mesh-Re stood up—like the other members of the Tribe of Shadows' society present before them—to receive echoing applause for all of the work they had done over the generations. Met-on also noticed they were carrying bags and that they were seated extremely close to where he, and the other members of the Tribe of Shadows with Rodent-blood, were standing.

*I wonder what's in those bags,* Met-on mused. *And more importantly, is Lord Tanas going to say something about us too?*

"And of course," Lord Tanas's image continued, "no congratulations could be complete without mentioning the Tribe of Shadows' finest, our proud gladiators."

From the coliseum's various entrances, rows of gladiators emerged to the cheering of the crowds. Met-on had seen a few gladiatorial fights in some of the other circles, but he *Knew* the gladiators of Wrath Eras were in a league of their own compared to the others he had encountered.

*They're so focused.* Met-on was in awe as the gladiators approached him and the rest of his group. *I can feel their crimson energy focused directly on us, sharp as a blade, unlike the blunt club-like energy I've felt in other circles. Their bodies are fully developed and bear the scars of all the battles they have lived through just to make it to this point. These gladiators really are the* best *that the Tribe of Shadows has to offer, especially after the Hy-mun Horror's rampage through Nis.*

"These gladiators have prepared for the eventual attack on the Hy-muns," Lord Tanas's image continued. "Now, before we begin the Third Great Attempt and leave this city to attack the surface, they have only one final duty to perform. Purging our city and our Tribe of Shadows of the *filth* you see before you on the coliseum floor. These Rodent-spawn, who dare to think of themselves as members of the Tribe of Shadows, believe they would be allowed citizenship into its ranks no matter what they tried. Their pathetic attempts, flattery, and whatever brandings they earn, have always been and will always mean—just like their lives—absolutely *nothing.*"

"What!" Met-on screamed, a sentiment equally shared by the others around him who were yelling their shock and surprise at Lord Tanas's declaration.

# The Second Coming

"You can't mean this," Met-on pleaded, his eyes raised to the image. "Our lives, everything we've done, everything we've gone through for you, it can't have been for nothing."

Yet Met-on was silenced, closing his eyes as something wet and smelly hit him in the face. Wiping the substance from his eyes, he saw what it was. *Excrement*, he thought curiously. *Relieving oneself is easy in Nis, everyone does it in private over holes leading to the magma streams so that the magma incinerates it. How could I be hit by it?*

Met-on did not have time to wonder since he was soon hit by another wad of excrement, and he was not the only one. Every member of Met-on's group was being pelted with them. They were being thrown from the stands above them. Looking up, Met-on noticed the throwers were the preservationists from Gluttony Mesh-Re. They were taking the excrement out of the bags that they were carrying and throwing it at them.

*At least that explains the excrement,* Met-on's mind thought frantically. *The preservationists clean and remove all by-products from a body, including excrement, before it can be served as food. After the Hy-mun Horror affair, who knows how many corpses they received, and how much excrement they were able to collect from the martyrs' bodies.*

However, having that question answered did not erase the more significant burden on his head. Lord Tanas had just proclaimed that he and every one of them present with Rodent-blood in their veins was useless to the Tribe of Shadows. Everything in his life was meaningless. He did not know what to do.

"Gladiators of Nis," the image of Tanas ordered. "Rid the Tribe of Shadows of this filth once and for all."

Met-on watched in horror as the gladiators slowly marched toward them, each one of them radiating the red and rosy energies of anger and lust. Around him, total panic was breaking out. Some threw themselves on to their knees, pleading to Lord Tanas's image, asking what they had done to deserve this. Others manically asked each other questions about what they could do. And a few, realizing they had nothing left to lose, decided to charge at the gladiators with nothing but their fists, only to be grabbed and slowly killed before everyone's eyes. Looking around, Met-on noticed his teacher collapsed on his knees, a look of complete defeat across his face. He was muttering under his breath, scratching in vain at his branding until his skin started to bleed, and pulsing with hazy white energy. He remembered something.

"Teacher," Met-on said, taking his hand before he could hurt himself more.

"You were right, you were right all the time, and I didn't listen," Met-on's teacher rambled, intense sadness dripping from every word.

"Who was right, Teacher? And about what," Met-on asked. Met-on's teacher looked into his eyes, and he could see tears forming in them. He *Knew* he was reliving a painful memory.

"I can't even remember her name," Met-on's teacher sobbed. "She was a Rodent, no, she was a member of the Remnant kept in Lust Atrophied. The first female I ever Joined with, and at the time, the only person I ever thought about. I made every attempt to be with her, not just to Join with her, but to talk with her. I couldn't get enough of her."

*I can relate,* Met-on thought to himself. *From the first time I Joined with Stella, she's been the only "person" I could think about too. And not just because of my mission. It was because I could talk to her, and she listened to me, no one has ever done that before. I felt safe around her.*

"Then, one day, she asked me to take her out of Nis and back to Rem," Met-on's teacher continued. "She told me that I would be welcomed there, that no member of the Remnant would blame me for any actions I made in Nis under Lord Tanas's direction. Naturally, I refused, praising all the good that Lord Tanas had done for us over the generations and what he still promised to do for us in the future through the execution of the Second and Third Great Attempts.

"Yet she told me not to listen, that 'Lord Tanas is deceiving all of you. What It wants isn't to give the surface back to the Tribe of Shadows, but something else. That once It gets what It wants, I'm sure It will get rid of us all. You told me how members of the Tribe of Shadows whose mothers came from the Remnant are treated. When It has what It's after, I'm sure It will get rid of all of you first. You won't even get the chance to earn a single branding.'"

"You must have known this female before you received your first branding," Met-on replied. "The fact that you have two only proves she was wrong."

"I still denied her, leaving her that day feeling crushed and confused. It was then that the Warden of Lust Atrophied approached me with a mission to earn my first branding."

"What was your mission?" Met-on asked.

"To kill the Rodent I had been Joining with, and I had to do it bare-handed," Met-on's teacher replied, tan sandy shame radiating from his face. Met-on *Knew* that his teacher carried out his mission and killed the female Rodent immediately. He would have done the same. But secretly, Met-on *Knew* he regretted the decision.

"I still remember how she looked at me as the last bits of breath, and silver life energy left her body. I kept telling her, 'She was wrong, I would get a branding, Lord Tanas wouldn't forsake us,' but she was right all the time."

# The Second Coming

Met-on looked away from his teacher and back to the gladiators. They had encircled Met-on's group and were now slowly approaching them. He *Knew* that the gladiators wanted to enjoy watching Met-on's group squirm for as long as they could before killing them, just as much as they wanted to take their time killing each one of them if they attempted to fight back. They were pausing every few minutes just to clean their weapons of the excrement that was getting on them, and to display the dead bodies to the increasing roar of the crowd and the scared mass that made up Met-on's group. Looking at the gladiators, he felt their rosy lust and horrible red energies pulsing off of them. He *Knew* they wanted to kill them and that his turn was fast approaching.

"I lived my life devoting myself to Lord Tanas," Met-on's teacher continued. "I wanted to prove to her that I was right, burying her memory deep into my mind. But while I could forget her name, I couldn't forget the time we had together, nor what I had done, my branding wouldn't let me. All I could do was hide it, but it doesn't seem like there is any more use for doing that. The time for hiding things is over."

And then the cavern's roof exploded.

# Part 5: War Comes to the City of Nis

# Chapter 20

"We've breached Nis's cavern! Launching Sun Spheres! All Hammers prepare for freefall, stabilization burn, and then launch. Good hunting to all of you, for the glory of the Great Master."

No sooner had the words been spoken than Virgil and Dan-te felt lifted out of their seats from the Antaeus's sudden drop into the open air of the cavern. Only their harnesses kept them from flying out and crashing into each other. But it did not stop them from screaming their lungs out in fright.

*How long is this going to last!* Dan-te screamed in her head, trying to will the Antaeus to stop falling so she could get herself out of the pod, get the disguise off, and scream out the rest of the energy she had been holding up inside of her since she and Virgil first walked into the Hammer's camp.

Dan-te did not have to wait long for a reply, the Antaeus's engines soon roared to life. With a jolt, she was back in her seat as the ship slowly made its way down to the signal it was receiving from Nis. The ship landed with a thud. But before she could be grateful for being back on the ground, another message began echoing through the pod.

"Pod 33-ES, launch malfunction, commence manual egress."

Immediately, the harnesses unfastened, and the door popped open, letting the other Hammers race out of the pod, leaving Dan-te and Virgil alone.

"Here we go," Virgil whispered, preparing himself for what was coming next.

# The Second Coming

*One way or another, everything ends now,* Dan-te thought, preparing herself too as she walked out of the pod with Virgil while the other Hammers streamed through the Antaeus. Each one headed out to various locations in Nis to the panic and surprise of every soul watching—including Tanas.

\*\*\*

"Curse those hybrid mutants! Between all their infighting, when did they manage to create something like that?" Tanas shouted from his ship deep at the bottom of the Great Lagoon.

"Since the Second Great Attempt ended forty years ago, no one Dominion should have been left with enough resources to construct machines like that. With Tempters and their own natural suspicions keeping them divided, they shouldn't have been able to unite like this. They *can't* unite like this. Good thing I was ready for this contingency."

Ever since encountering the Hy-mun named Able during the Second Great Attempt, another Hy-mun born without the genetic submission programming, Tanas knew that a Hy-mun invasion could be possible. Inputting a few commands into the ship's computer, he activated the first part of his "Hybrid Mutant Invasion Contingency Plan."

\*\*\*

"What just happened?" Kai Aphas bellowed.

From Decca-Ju Tower, a pulse of blue-white light suddenly flashed through Nis, turning the inside of the Antaeus dark as the Hammers rushed to their assault.

"Electromagnetic pulse," a Hammer replied, "similar to what was used during the Great Rainbow War. We'll have the Antaeus's systems back up in a moment, but the Sun Spheres are out. They're dropping onto the city like stones and will have to be restored on-site."

Kai Aphas sneered out of a window to the top of Decca-Ju Tower as the power was restored. The tower was only a short walk away from where the Antaeus landed, and he was certain Tanas was waiting for him there.

"Have Hammers rerouted to the Sun Spheres to get them working so these creatures can burn. In the meantime, activate the Lightning Lamps on the hull so none of them can hide using their Veils. First, these demons tempt and corrupt us, now they steal and copy our technology—pretending to be us. It's time to expose these monsters for what they are and watch them burn to death!"

"Burn to death!" the other Hammers repeated as Kai Aphas left them and returned to his chambers, intent on picking up the weapons he wanted to use to end Tanas personally. Meanwhile, outside the Antaeus and the other ships arriving in Nis, the orange-yellow light of the Lightning Lamps blazed to life while Tanas watched in complete safety from his ship.

"Playing Hybrid Mutant Announcement," Tanas chuckled, throwing a switch on his control board.

\*\*\*

"Tribe of Shadows, hear me!"

All eyes in the Grand Coliseum turned to the image of Lord Tanas the moment the cavern ceiling exploded. The Third Great Attempt, the purging of the Rodent-blood, everything was forgotten as the giant tubes began descending toward the city, shooting out smaller pods as they soared above the city, and caused other parts of the cavern to rain rocks down upon it. A collective fear had gripped everyone present, a terror that could be expressed in three words, "the Second Coming," one that only increased when Lord Tanas's image vanished briefly following a flash of blue-white energy from where the ships were landing.

"Tribe of Shadows, what you have feared since the days of the Beings of Light has come to pass: the Second Coming is here."

A deathly silence gripped the entire Grand Coliseum. There was not a being alive in Nis who did not know the story of "The Coming," the genocidal slaughter brought down by the Beings of Light and did not fear that they, or the Hy-mun after them, would return to finish the job.

"But do not be afraid," the image of Tanas continued. "I am with you now, and as long as I am here above you, the Hy-muns will not be able to move against you. You have long prepared for this conflict if it ever came to Nis. You will not be driven from your home again, you will not be exterminated again. I call on all the pure-blooded men of the Tribe of Shadows, abandon your current duties, gather your weapons, and destroy the invaders who would seek to do to you what the Beings of Light did to your ancestors. Go!"

The image of Lord Tanas stopped speaking, remaining expressionless above the Grand Coliseum, but it had done its job. The noise echoed through the Grand Coliseum as seats quickly emptied. Every member of the Tribe of Shadows raced from the Grand Coliseum to grab a weapon and fight. On the arena floor, the gladiators turned from the stunned Rodent-blooded members of the Tribe of Shadows and hurried out of the Grand Coliseum to meet the Hy-muns in battle. Soon, the only ones left in the Grand Coliseum were the Rodent-blooded members of the Tribe of Shadows. Met-on, standing next to his teacher, looked up silently at both the image of Lord Tanas, the falling pods, and the rocks raining down upon the city.

"I'm going to fight!" an older member shouted. Met-on did not recognize him, but he had one branding and had tried to fight the gladiators. "I'm not about to let myself be burned like our ancestors, and I'm definitely not going to run and hide like the Rodents, or just wait to be killed. I'm going to fight the Hy-muns, and if I can prove myself, maybe Lord Tanas will change his mind about us. He is still watching. Anyone willing to come with me?"

The older member's enthusiasm was contagious. Soon almost every member of Met-on's group was cheering and ready to go and aid the rest of the Tribe of Shadows, racing out of the Grand Coliseum to fight the Hy-muns. Met-on and his teacher were soon left as the only two members still standing where they were.

"Why didn't you join the others?" Met-on asked his teacher and himself, unable to figure out why he did not join the others to go and fight the Second Coming.

"I have lived a long life, Young One. Lord Tanas, no, Tanas never changes his mind. You heard what he said just as much as I did, 'no matter what they tried.' Even if Rodent-blooded members like us manage to stop the Second Coming, Tanas would undoubtedly kill us afterward. You also heard what else he said, 'I call on all the *pure-blooded* members of the Tribe of Shadows,' he doesn't even want or consider us worthy of mention."

"So, what are you going to do?" Met-on asked.

"Stay here," Met-on's teacher answered, sitting on the ground, and looking up to the cavern ceiling. "As I said, I've lived a long life, far longer than anyone might think. I'm too old to keep doing this, I don't mind ending my life here, but you are different."

"Me?" Met-on replied.

"You are the youngest member of the Tribe of Shadows here with Rodent-blood, the blood of the Remnant of the Tribe, in you. You also *Know* the reason why you didn't go with the others. You don't believe in Tanas anymore, and you have something else you want to live for, don't you?"

Met-on realized his teacher was right. He *didn't* believe in Tanas anymore. From the moment Tanas betrayed them, claiming that all their efforts were worthless, ending his dream of being accepted as citizens of the Tribe of Shadows, and setting the gladiators upon them to kill them all, he had lost all faith in Tanas. His teacher's question also brought Stella's face to his mind, he again remembered their last meeting, how he had joyfully told her the news that he would be going to the Grand Coliseum, and how she had responded.

"Think about what just happened to us, Young One," Met-on's teacher mused. "And what is still to come. You really don't need me to tell you what it is you need to do, right?"

Met-on did not need to ask, realizing how simple the answer was all along, especially after hearing his teacher's earlier story. Bowing respectfully to his teacher for the last time, Met-on left his teacher's side and started running.

PJ Fenton

*These are Hy-muns that are invading Nis,* Met-on thought frantically. *Stella's a Hy-mun, she belongs with them. If I can get her to them, they can take her back to the surface.*

A large piece of rock collapsed into the Grand Coliseum's seats, destroying them and sending them spilling into the arena close to where Met-on was running, causing him to dive for cover. In another part of the Grand Coliseum, a pod shot from one of the ships crashed into it, popping out giant bags that cushioned it as it hit the ground and rolled into the wall where the Veil of Shadows once stood.

*It would be better if I found her first and took her to the Hy-muns instead of trying to lead them to her myself,* Met-on figured, not wanting to try and explain himself to the other Hy-muns as he picked himself up and continued running out of the Grand Coliseum. Behind him, his teacher watched him go and looked at the Hy-muns emerging from the pod. Each one was dressed in orange robes with dark masks over their faces and radiating the same horrible red energy as the gladiators. However, once they left the pod, they suddenly dropped to their knees, the red energy dissipating as they gazed up at the image of Tanas

*I hope young Met-on has a better future then we did Mar,* Met-on's teacher silently prayed. He laughed out loud as he realized it was the first time he ever said "hope" in his life and that he never did forget the name of the woman he knew from the Remnant. Rising to his feet, he opened his arms to the Hy-muns leaving the pod, paralyzed by the sight of Lord Tanas.

"Welcome to the city of Nis," he proclaimed.

The Second Coming

# Chapter 21

*No, not again, you won't make me submit to you again!*

Kai Aphas had returned to his private cabin for weapons when Tanas's image reappeared over Nis. Upon seeing it, he and almost every Hammer of the Orange Light became paralyzed. The word "submit" echoed through their heads while a feeling of powerlessness swept through their bodies, making them think that they could not fight against Tanas. The genetic programming found in almost all Hy-muns was doing its job.

*This isn't the same as the Grand Coliseum, I'm not some scared child you can intimidate with a glance. I've grown stronger since then, I've built an army since then, all to kill you.*

*Yes, you did build an army,* Able's voice whispered in his mind. *You created an army hoping its members would be "charmed" like I was.*

*It is not the same!* Kai Aphas wanted to scream but was still paralyzed by the image of Tanas. *Tanas himself charmed you, or do you not remember him making that claim. Why else were you the only one able to move when he looked at us in the Grand Coliseum while the rest of us remained frozen?*

*Like I said, I didn't know, but it wasn't some charm from Tanas, and you were a fool to believe him. The fact that I wasn't paralyzed meant that I was able to earn Cacci-guida's respect and later friendship, and aren't you hoping some of your Hammers will be "charmed" too?*

*My Hammers and I will move by the blessings of the Nag-el!* Kai Aphas claimed. *Not because they are charmed by Tanas.*

*But Tanas is a Nag-el,* Able's voice reminded him.

*Not this again!*

Elsewhere, a Hy-mun was moving despite seeing Tanas's image.

\*\*\*

"That's Lord Tanas?"

"Honestly, I don't know, Virgil. It's my first time seeing It too. But more importantly, why aren't you like them?"

"I don't know, Dan-te. Let's just be thankful I am and that we landed where we did. We might find a way to stop the Third Great Attempt from right here."

Dan-te and Virgil had left the ship with the rest of the Hammers of the Orange Light just before Tanas's image reappeared over the city. But unlike the Hammers, Virgil found he was not paralyzed by Tanas's image. The two of them were now forcing their way into Decca-Ju Tower and heading for its highest level.

"This tower has been Tanas's home since It first arrived in Nis generations ago," Dan-te explained as they ran up the stairs. "It's the one thing in all of Yam-Preen that hasn't aged or decayed since it was built. Lord Tanas must have something here that can control the Third Great Attempt."

"I hope so, Dan-te," Virgil agreed, opening a door at the top of the steps and entering Lord Tanas's private chambers, finding them empty inside.

"No, this can't be it. This can't be all there is!" Dan-te panicked. Lord Tanas's room was deserted except for a few pieces of furniture. "There has to be more, a plan, controls, *something*!"

"Try and calm down, Dan-te," Virgil begged. "You're right, there *has* to be more. We just have to find it. Tanas couldn't have been gone for long."

"Yes, It has," Dan-te countered. "Dust is already settling on the furniture that is in this room. The air tastes stale, it hasn't been breathed in a while. There's also the ambient energy from the Antaeus. It's flooding through the window and filling the room. If Tanas were still here, the energy would be drawn to it."

"Then follow the energy," Virgil quickly encouraged. "If Tanas creates an energy vacuum, then like you said, the energy from the Antaeus will be drawn to him. We just have to follow it."

Virgil and Dan-te raced back down the stairs, following the energy until it took them to the lowest level of Decca-Ju Tower.

"What is this?" Dan-te gasped, staring at a strange device enclosed in a glass box.

"Some kind of relay terminal," Virgil answered. "I've seen them before back in the Indigo Dominion and on the Platinum Throne. They send signals out to devices so they can be operated remotely."

"So, if Tanas isn't here, then does that mean It needs *this terminal* to trigger the Third Great Attempt."

"Exactly," Virgil smiled. "Wait here, I'll be right back."

Virgil left Dan-te in the bottom of Decca-Ju Tower, soon returning with a war hammer taken from a paralyzed Hammer of the Orange Light.

"I might despise the Hammers, but this time I'm going to take a page from their book and smash that glass and terminal to bits."

"Do it, Virgil!"

\*\*\*

"What!"

Tanas stared in shock and surprise at the image in the ship's monitor. One of his alarms warned him of something attacking the security glass around the main relay terminal in the base of Decca-Ju Tower. Checking the monitor, he not only found two Hy-muns in orange suits unaffected by his image, but one of them was also hitting the glass and trying to get to the terminal.

"This is bad," Tanas fretted. "If the relay station in the base of Decca-Ju Tower is destroyed, I might lose all ability to work anything in Nis remotely. If those two also find the tunnel from Decca-Ju Tower to here, I'll be cornered by two mutants with the same genetic anomaly as *that* hybrid mutant. Good thing I planned for this too."

Tanas's mind worked fast, his hands faster, imputing a set of commands into his control panel.

"This will cause me to lose the projection of myself above the city. But if those two think that there's nothing else down there for them to find, then there's a high probability they'll stop searching the area. Meaning they won't find the tunnel."

Tanas pressed a button.

\*\*\*

"Look out!"

Dan-te tackled Virgil to the ground and away from the terminal as it suddenly began emitting molten energy before exploding in front of them.

"Did you do that?" Dan-te asked, looking back at the now scrapped terminal.

"No." Virgil coughed, winded from being tackled by Dan-te. "It must have been rigged to self-destruct if it was tampered with."

"Did we just stop the Third Great Attempt?" Dan-te asked incredulously.

"I doubt it would have been that easy," Virgil replied.

"Agreed. Let's get back to making our way out of the city to find a digging machine."

Dan-te helped Virgil up, and the two of them ran out of the room and back to the entrance of Decca-Ju Tower.

\*\*\*

"Well, that takes care of those two," Tanas happily hummed, watching Dan-te and Virgil leave Decca-Ju Tower while he brought the backup relay terminal online. "They didn't even think I had a secondary terminal buried under the stairs that I could shift my Third Great Attempt Commands too. Plus, another one after that hidden elsewhere in the tower. But to use it, I had to sacrifice the image of myself above the city. That means the mutants will be able to move again. No matter, the spectacle provided will be the perfect entertainment while I finish my preparations; now, to add a bit more fuel to the fire."

Tanas reached over and activated another of his recordings.

\*\*\*

"Tribe of Shadows!" Tanas's voice echoed through Nis. The sudden disappearance of his image had caused the Tribe of Shadows to stop hunting the Hammers, allowing the Hammers to recover and mount their own offensive.

"The Hy-muns have invaded our sacred site of Yam-Preen. My image can no longer be with you while they are here, I must fight them myself now. But my voice is still with you, and I am always with you in spirit. Fight on! Purge Nis of these Hy-muns! Stop the Second Coming once and for all!"

\*\*\*

"Hey, you two!"

Dan-te and Virgil nervously approached a group of Hammers at the base of the Antaeus. As soon as they left Decca-Ju Tower, they noticed three things. Tanas's image was gone, his voice was echoing through Nis to encourage the Tribe of Shadows to fight, and the Hammers were quickly recovering from their paralysis—one of whom had just called them to him.

"Did you find Tanas or anything important in that tower?"

"No," Virgil lied, trying not to tip his identity. "Tanas must be in the main city."

"Well, climb back onboard. We fixed a few of the damaged pod launchers, and we're launching now. We have to get to the Sun Spheres to reignite them for the glory of our Lord and Master."

"Right away," Virgil replied. Dan-te nodded and followed close behind, taking his hand as soon as they were in the crowd again. Both of them thought the same thing as they climbed back into one of the pods, strapping themselves into the harness.

## The Second Coming

*This is the quickest way we can get to the edge of the city and to the drilling machines parked there.*

"Sun Sphere repair pod, launching in 5, 4, 3..."

*This is it,* Virgil and Dan-te thought to themselves.

"2, 1, launch!"

Dan-te, Virgil, and the Hammers in the pod suddenly felt the air pushed out of them, cannoned from the ship, and into the escalating war being fought throughout the city of Nis.

# Chapter 22

Tanas watched as the members of the Tribe of Shadows clashed with the now unfrozen Hy-muns across Nis. He smiled at the entertainment they were providing him while his ship's systems booted up before his departure.

"I'm glad I decided *not* to have a backup in case my projection failed." Tanas laughed as the carnage unfolded. "This spectacle is far more enjoyable when both sides can fight. I wonder if there will be a winner before I wipe them all out with the Third Great Attempt."

Tanas watched as the Hammers, now active, began spreading throughout Nis. He watched as several groups started making their way toward the spheres that crashed throughout the city, while another group worked toward Envy Opal-Lo and its vaults, while others moved toward the outskirts of Nis—all looking for fights wherever they could find them. Yet the last group of Hammers also worried Tanas.

"I've already found two with the anomaly in Decca-Ju Tower. No reason to wait and see if any more are like that and attempt to use the digging machines against me."

Tanas turned back to his controls and pushed another button on his control board.

"Program two, go."

\*\*\*

"Now what?" Ann shouted, running back into the digging machine. After Ann's attempt to start a digging machine resulted in triggering a charge that destroyed the controls, she tried opening the panel to disarm the bomb from the inside. Unfortunately, that also triggered an explosion that destroyed the controls and left Ann with only three more ships to try to operate. She was starting on the next one when an explosion brought her and the other members of the Remnant out to look at the spectacle descending upon Nis.

Ann was speechless. Multiple terraships, bigger then she had ever seen, were punching through the cavern ceiling and descending down to Nis. Each one ejected pods and giant spheres that came crashing down. Looking at the other members of the Remnant, they had dropped to their knees, pure terror streaking across their faces. Even the Seat of Kindness looked like he had seen a ghost as the ships began descending upon the city. The image was made ghostlier by a sudden blue-white flash that pulsed from the center of Nis to where Ann was standing.

"Tribe of Shadows," the image of Lord Tanas bellowed from above Nis. "What you have feared since the days of the Beings of Light has come to pass; the Second Coming is here."

*That explains why everyone is scared all of a sudden,* Ann realized. *I remember the stories the Seat of Kindness told me about "The Coming," the Beings of Light, and the destruction they brought down upon the Remnant's ancestors. For the members of the Remnant, this must look like something out of a nightmare.*

"But do not be afraid," the image of Tanas continued. "I am with you now, and as long as I am here above you, the Hy-muns will not be able to move against you. You have long prepared for this conflict if it ever came to Nis. You will not be driven from your home again, you will not be exterminated again. I call on all the pure-blooded men of the Tribe of Shadows, abandon your current duties, gather your weapons, and destroy the invaders who would seek to do to you what the Beings of Light did to your ancestors, go!"

*That proclamation is going to make every soul in Nis fight whoever is on those ships with no mercy,* Ann considered, thinking about the situation. *What's worse, if Tanas's image paralyzes the invading Hy-muns the same way it did Reye, then they won't stand a chance. However, this could be useful. Those ships have to be more advanced than these and must be equipped with modules for independent drilling. If we can get one...*

But before Ann could complete her thought, Tanas's image vanished from above Nis.

"What?" Ann and the Seat of Kindness snapped.

"Why did he shut off the image?" Ann wondered, fear starting to grip her. "We're not too late, are we?"

"No," the Seat of Kindness replied. "The land is still emitting its fearful pink energy, it's not dying. The Third Great Attempt hasn't started yet. But I understand your confusion. If that projection is so effective against Hy-muns, and Nis is stuck in the middle of a Second Coming instigated by Hy-muns, Lord Tanas wouldn't stop it for no reason. Something must have happened."

"Tribe of Shadows!" Tanas's voice suddenly returned. Only now it was booming throughout the city instead of coming from the image over them. "The Hy-muns have invaded our sacred site of Yam-Preen. My image can no longer be with you while they are here, I must fight them myself now. But my voice is still with you, and I am always with you in spirit. Fight on! Purge Nis of these Hy-muns! Stop the Second Coming once and for all!"

"I seriously doubt that Tanas removed his projection simply because Hy-muns were now in Yam-Preen, or that he has any intention to fight," Ann puffed.

"As do I," the Seat of Kindness agreed. "There must have been Hy-muns in Yam-Preen who were unaffected by Tanas's image like yourself and managed to disable it. Lord Tanas simply decided to change tactics after that. But with Its image gone, every Hy-mun on those ships will now be free to act as they please. So, what do we do now?"

Three more explosions from the remaining digging machines answered the Seat of Kindness's question. Ann ran into the nearest one to find the controls a melted pile of wires and metal.

"Now what?" Ann asked. "Did someone else try and disable the bomb?"

"No," the Seat of Kindness replied, joining her. "Everyone was outside watching the Hy-mun ships and listening to Tanas's proclamation. But we have bigger problems, the controls in the other machine have also exploded, we have nothing we can use now."

Now, Ann was worried. If all the digging machines were out of commission, then there was no way to alter the Great Tunnel. Ann did not know why the controls exploded, but she had a pretty good idea.

*The machines' controls were rigged to explode the moment someone tried to tamper with them,* Ann hypothesized. *If someone could do that, then why can't they also rig the bombs to be detonated remotely if the bomber felt the machines were going to be used against the Third Great Attempt? The real problem is what we do now.*

Ann took some paper and a pen from an undamaged part of the digging machine and walked back out with the Seat of Kindness to the rest of their group, all looking extremely scared.

"Seat of Kindness," one of the members said, approaching him, "with the digging machines destroyed and the Second Coming upon us, it's only a matter of time before they go to Rem. A few of us want to head back and warn the city, get it moving deeper into the underworld before anyone can reach it."

"That might be a prudent action," the Seat of Kindness replied. "However, it is also a futile action. The Third Great Attempt is still a threat to us. If it is started, then it doesn't matter where we move Rem. No place will be safe anymore."

"So, we stay?"

"We'll stay until the last possible moments, but that doesn't mean we won't be idle. Ann, you're the expert on volcanoes and these machines, what can we do now?"

Ann, who had been brainstorming ideas and working on diagrams and equations since the Seat of Kindness's exchange began, looked up from her work. The stress on her face clearly showed as white mental energy poured from her head.

"What *can* we do?" Ann stated, to herself more than anyone. "These drilling machines might have been our best shot. However, those ships busting in on us might actually help us stop the Third Great Attempt. The passages they made coming from the surface are going to give the supervolcano more places to vent its magma and pressure. But I just don't know if it's enough. Maybe, if I have a couple more of those ships digging holes, a few smaller terranaut ships, or digging machines like these to form stable pathways in the Great Tunnel, then I could do something. But I just don't know."

"If we need more ships, can't we try calling one and asking for help," the Seat of Kindness suggested. "Those invading ships, even these digging machines, must have a way to talk with each other."

"Of course!" Ann exclaimed, slapping herself in the head in frustration and running back into one of the digging machines. "All of these machines have emergency radios used to contact other ships should they become disabled. They are also kept away from the main controls in case something happens to them. Now with any luck."

Ann hammered the far side of the machine, eventually popping open a compartment and revealing a box-like device that she carried back out of the ship, joyful jam radiance pulsing from her with every step.

"We have a radio!" Ann shouted. "It's old, but it should be able to reach terranaut ships that are active near Nis. And if we can get more help, we might just pull this off yet."

Ann turned on the radio and prepared to make her broadcast. She felt more confident now as she stared back toward Nis, thinking of both Reye and the other ships, hoping she could call more to help to alter the Great Tunnel.

*I hope Reye has found Stella by now,* Ann thought as she began broadcasting a distress message over the radio.

***

"Stella?"

"Hy-mun!"

Reye had barely enough time to close the door again and bar it before its occupant, a lithe female member of the Tribe of Shadows, attacked her. Reye and Ca-to's party arrived in Lust Atrophied just as the Hy-mun ships broke through the cavern's ceiling. They had heard Tanas's broadcast call every male member of the Tribe of Shadows to fight the invading Hy-muns, but the female members were still in Lust Atrophied and ready to fight anyone who approached them. After Tanas's second announcement, stating that his image was gone, Reye removed her blindfold and saw the ships for the first time. She not only felt stunned by their size and presence, but she was also relieved and excited.

*More Hy-muns, a rescue at last,* Reye initially thought as the ships descended. *Now I just have to find you, Stella. Then we can get to one of those ships and go home. As for the Tribe of Shadows, the Hy-muns who came down here can take care of these.*

Reye mentally checked herself when she realized she was about to refer to the Tribe of Shadows as *creatures* again. Not thinking of the Tribe of Shadows as sentient beings was one of the first mistakes she made when dealing with the Tribe of Shadows and the members of the Remnant. She did not want to make that same mistake again.

*Just find Stella,* Reye thought to herself as she and the rest of Ca-to's group began to split up and search Lust Atrophied after Tanas's image vanished, and Reye removed her blindfold.

"This entire circle is like one giant underground hotel. How does anyone know where anyone is down here?" Reye guessed the answer to her own question as soon as she said it. "They *Know* where everyone is, don't they?"

Reye still did not understand the Remnant's or the Tribe of Shadows' ability to *Know*, but she had seen it used for finding things. Back when she was bulldozing through Nis, Ice had used it to find the right path for them to follow; and since entering Lust Atrophied, she had seen Ca-to and other members of his group open only select doors. Behind those doors was an extremely grateful female member of the Remnant who came out and joined their group.

"The women from the Remnant are kept far apart from each other," Ca-to explained, joining her for a moment. "The Tribe of Shadows don't want to run the risk of them coming together and making any joint plans. Your friend is most likely kept surrounded by the Tribe of Shadows' women as well."

"But why haven't you been trying to save any of the women from the Tribe of Shadows?" Reye asked as she opened another door next to them.

"Wait!" Ca-to shouted, but Reye had opened the door and was looking at a female member of the Tribe of Shadows.

Reye remembered what Dan-te looked like when they were imprisoned in Wrath Eras, and this woman could have been Dan-te's twin from the Tribe of Shadows, except she did not have the starved and ragged look Dan-te had when they first met. This woman's body was lithe and well taken care of; she had the same blue skin, pointed ears, and red eyes that were common to all the members of the Tribe of Shadows, and a bewildered expression on her face. She looked like she was waiting for someone else to come into the room, but as soon as she saw Reye and Ca-to, her expression quickly changed.

"A Rodent and a Hy-mun!" the woman screamed before reaching under her bed and pulling out a whip, quickly lashing at both Reye and Ca-to, giving them both a few cuts each before they could shut the door and bolt it.

"Over the generations, we've learned that the Tribe of Shadows teach their women to be completely subservient to any male member that enters their rooms," Ca-to explained. "They're taught to be that way because it's the women who provide future generations for the Tribe of Shadows. That said, they *also* teach them to defend themselves vigorously from anyone who *isn't* a member of the Tribe of Shadows."

"Do you mean that every female member of the Tribe of Shadows is…" Reye let her question hang in the air as she processed what Ca-to told her.

"A trained warrior," Ca-to answered. "And like us, they heard Tanas's message. They know that Hy-muns have invaded the city and that Tanas had called every man to fight them. That's put them all on edge and is making them emit a scarlet hunting energy while they wait for someone to come. Yet it's too ingrained into them to leave their rooms without orders, only to fight anyone who enters their rooms and isn't expected."

"But if all the Tribe of Shadows' women are dangerous, why not just lock the doors?" Reye asked. "I'm guessing you are using your ability to *Know* to tell which rooms have your women in them, so why not just lock the ones with the Tribe of Shadows' women?"

"Because if Hy-muns come here looking for a fight, then they'll unlock the doors themselves. Also, if the doors are unlocked, then at least the women of Nis can have the choice to follow their teaching or do something else. That is still far better than being locked up in a room, don't you think?"

Reye nodded her head in agreement and looked on to the next unexamined area of Lust Atrophied. "I'm going to continue on by myself. It will help us cover more of the circle. If I open any doors, I'll be careful."

Ca-to nodded, realizing that Reye wanted to find her friend as soon as possible and that she was also right, it would help them search the circle quicker.

"Just be careful," Ca-to replied as Reye took off.

Since then, Reye had tried over a dozen doors, and most contained women from the Tribe of Shadows who almost attacked her before she closed the door again, but a few contained women from the Remnant who thanked her before heading back toward Ca-to's group.

"I know you're in here, Stella," Reye shouted, hoping Stella might hear her somewhere in Lust Atrophied. "I'm going to find you!"

# Chapter 23

"Ha, ha, ha, ha!" Tanas laughed maniacally as he watched the chaos unfold before him from the safety of his ship. "The savages and the hybrid mutants slaughtering each other is better entertainment then I thought. And with every drilling machine disabled in Nis, I know they can't alter the tunnel. Thousands of years of waiting and planning, thinking about every single thing that could go wrong, factoring out who was a threat and who wasn't, all leading up to this final moment.

"Program three, go!" Tanas shouted, pressing another button on his control panel.

***

*I'm going to die here,* the Tribesman thought to himself as he put his wedge of metal between another device and crate and proceeded to hammer it off as he had done to dozens more before it. *And that's okay, I'm glad to die here, disabling each of these explosives so that the Third Great Attempt can't be activated. I should have done this when I was still Ice. Now, where is the next one?*

The Tribesman had been working diligently, working through so much pain that his body had become numb to it. Looking around, he saw that there was only one crate left that had the same device on it that he had been smashing off of every other container he could get his hands on. Crawling on all fours, the Tribesman struggled to get to it.

*The last one, there's just one more crate left, and then Tanas's plans are finished for good.* Joy filled the Tribesman's heart; he *Knew* this was the right course of action, what he should have done from the beginning instead of using Reye to kill Tanas. He was putting himself into harm's way to stop the Third Great Attempt and ensure Tanas's plans failed. Around the Tribesman, the heat from the Keyblast Point slowly ate away at his suit, and he *Knew* it would not be much longer now until the suit ultimately failed him. But before he died, he was going to make sure that every one of these devices was disabled for good.

*Just…one…more,* the Tribesman struggled as he crawled over to the last crate, using the metal wedge for support to make sure he did not collapse. The container was not even half his height, but from the ground, it could have been a mountain. His arms trembled, just reaching up to it.

*One more device, one last time.* The Tribesman's legs felt weaker than his arms, his whole body shook as he fitted the metal wedge between the crate and the device that would activate it.

"Break!" The Tribesman screamed, the first time he spoke in a while, throwing his entire weight onto the rock and wedge, and finally snapping the device off the crate, the Tribesman's own body collapsing with the strike and falling motionless at the side of it and the device. Lying on the ground, the heat unbearable, the Tribesman weakly opened his eye and managed to see a reflection of himself in the last crate.

"You've…come…back…to life," the Tribesman said as he immediately recognized the image reflected in the crate, a reflection that was *not* the one he saw in Maestri. The being before him was energetic, diligent, ready to act quickly. The pale umber contentment in his eyes was gone. It was replaced with pearl-colored dedication, the energy of someone dedicated to doing whatever needed to be done to help others—even if it cost him his own life. The gluttonous dark-green energy in his eyes was gone, too, and the look he had when he was dazzled by power. Instead, his eyes shined with blue resolve, the resolve to trust in himself and in his own abilities, and not to use anyone else to do his work for him.

"Welcome…back…Ice," he whispered as he closed his eyes.

Ice was happy. He had disabled each of the bombs at the Keyblast Point, the Third Great Attempt would not happen, and he had managed to bring his old self, Ice, back to life. It was extremely rare, but he knew that members of the Remnant who died the Death of the Self did have a chance—albeit a small one—to bring their old selves back to life after performing both the Reconciliation Ritual and a lifetime of penitential work. But for him to *Know* he brought his old self back to life again before he died was the greatest gift he could have received, and the fact that he did not hear or see what happened *after* he died was perhaps the greatest mercy anyone could have given him.

\*\*\*

"Signal Failure!" Tanas screeched. "Unable to detonate. Did something happen at the Keyblast Point?"

Tanas knew the Keyblast Point should be deserted. That way, no one could tamper with the explosives. Even if there was someone there, he knew that the conditions at the Keyblast Point were so severe that it would be suicide to remain there long enough to disable each device physically. That is why he chose the spot.

"No matter," Tanas calmly replied, regaining his composure. "Activating program 3-a."

\*\*\*

"Signal received through secondary internal detonator," all the disabled crates replied in unison throughout the Keyblast Point. "Initiating internal detonation in two, one, zero."

Ice never heard the crates announce that they were going to explode. The heat had killed him by that point. Each one exploded together in a flash of white light and magma, consuming Ice's body instantly and flooding the Keyblast Point with magma that started rushing down the Great Tunnel toward Nis. The Third Great Attempt had begun.

\*\*\*

"Signal received and accepted." Tanas cheered. "Just one last detail, Program four, go."

Outside the ship, Tanas heard the bombs detonate as the tunnel linking his ship with Nis was destroyed, severing his contact with Nis, and leaving him isolated inside of his ship.

"Now that the Third Great Attempt has started, it should only take a couple of hours until the supervolcano erupts and darkens the sky."

Tanas turned on one of the ship's monitors. On it, a countdown was displayed.

"Three hours," Tanas read aloud from his computer screen. "Three more hours until I can finally leave this planet once and for all. I better get the ship ready."

Tanas left his computer to complete the preparations for takeoff, not even giving another thought to the Hy-muns, the Tribe of Shadows, or the city of Nis. He let the events there play out as they may.

# Part 6: Paths Converge Within an Ocean of Chaos

# Chapter 24

"Calling all terraships, calling all terraships!"

"I know that voice!" Professor Heart shuffled to the radio. The voice belonged to her student, Ann Branley. Professor Heart could barely contain her excitement. Ann was alive.

"Ann, this is Professor Heart, can you hear me?"

"Calling all terraships, my name is Ann Branley, and I am a survivor of the Demp Cavern Mining Project disaster. This is not a drill or joke. I am reporting a Class S emergency."

"She can't hear me," Professor Heart whispered. "She must be using an old or damaged radio."

"I am currently imprisoned deep beneath Tri-Dominion City in need of immediate evacuation alongside others. There is a powerful land-based volcano that will erupt here in the immediate future. We need ships to divert the magma now before the eruption. Once more, this is not a joke or drill."

Ann's message was suddenly drowned out by an alarm that screamed through the Arc's command deck.

"Now what," Professor Heart asked herself, turning off an alarm, and looking at the Arc's sensors to find out what had set them off.

"Great Master, help us." Professor Heart gasped. Heat sensors she had been dropping since entering the Great Tunnel were spiking exponentially before their signals were cut off. She knew it meant only one thing.

# The Second Coming

"The Tribesman wasn't able to prevent the detonation at the Keyblast Point. The magma is on its way to Nis." Professor Heart frantically worked the Arc's keyboard, calculating how long it would take the magma to reach Nis. "I just finished drilling the last vent for the magma when Ann's message arrived. I also planted charges throughout the Great Tunnel designed to periodically block the magma and force it up through them. But considering how fast I was working, there's no guarantee that they'll even work. How long will it take?"

The Arc's screen displayed the result.

"Two hours and forty-five minutes, at least, assuming nothing can stop the magma," Professor Heart said to herself. "From where I am now, it will take me another two and a half hours just to reach Nis. No time to think about it. I have to move."

Professor Heart returned to the controls and attempted to push the Arc even further down the Great Tunnel. The magma was on its way. That meant Nis and Rem were doomed, and potentially so was the surface of Prism and everyone living on it. Regardless, if she wanted to save as many lives as she could, she needed to get to Nis and Rem, fast.

***

"Tanas!" Kai Aphas screamed, a squad of Hammers and the Virt Princes behind him. "Face me demon, betrayer, corrupter, it has been forty years, but I have finally returned to end you and your monstrous Tribe of Shadows once and for all!"

Kai Aphas, after being freed from the paralysis, had gathered an elite squad of Hammers and the Virt Princes and was leading them into Decca-Ju Tower to assault Tanas. He had forced open the door to the chamber at the top of Decca-Ju Tower, the place he remembered hearing was the personal home of Tanas back when he was a prisoner in Nis expecting to find him waiting. Yet no one was there.

"Where is he?" Lucan asked, coming up alongside Kai Aphas.

"He's here somewhere," Kai Aphas shouted. "We all saw him above the city after the Antaeus landed addressing the Tribe of Shadows. My Hammers, search every inch of this tower. Find him!"

The Hammers scattered, searching every inch of Decca-Ju Tower while Kai Aphas and the Virt Princes remained in Tanas's chamber. Yet there was no sign of Tanas, or anyone else, anywhere in the tower.

"Keep looking!" Kai Aphas screamed, standing at Tanas's window and looking out to the Antaeus and Nis just as another Hammer from the Antaeus quickly joined them.

"Have you found him?" Kai Aphas asked greedily.

"No, sir," the Hammer answered. "Although we have been receiving a strange message over the radio. Someone is claiming to be a survivor of the Demp Cavern Mining Project and that a powerful land-based volcano is going to erupt here."

"Lies!" Kai Aphas screamed. "A trick by the Tribe of Shadows to get us to leave Nis. Exterminate them and find Tanas. Send a message to the other ships to ignore that broadcast too. It's just a lie created by a Tempter."

"Yes, sir," the Hammer replied before returning to the Antaeus and leaving Kai Aphas alone with the Virt Princes.

"Perhaps we should have more Hammers search around the Tower," Lucan suggested, looking at the base of the Tower and the landscape around them. "There might be a clue there to Tanas's current whereabouts, and we'll need the perimeter once the Tribe of Shadows arrives."

"Do that," Kai Aphas barked. "Destroy whatever you have to. Tanas might be hiding in one of those rotting buildings. Demolish this entire wasteland."

*This is a mistake, brother, and you know it*, Able's voice began whispering again in Kai Aphas's head. *You remember what Cacci-guida said about Yam-Preen, the center of Nis. The Tribe of Shadows sees it as sacred land. They are going to come at you with everything they have.*

"Let the Tribe of Shadows come," Kai Aphas murmured, not realizing he was talking aloud. "We will destroy every one of those demons."

"Bravery even in the face of a race of demons," Lucan gasped in awe. "You are truly the one who will end the shadows that are hiding within Prism."

"Thank you, Lucan," Kai Aphas replied, quickly covering himself. "Take the Hammers and prepare for battle."

"Yes sir," Lucan readily agreed before returning to the ship to muster more Hammers at the tower's base.

"You see," Kai Aphas whispered again to the voice of Able in his head. "This isn't a mistake, this is the right course of action."

"It had better be Kai Aphas," Ovid responded. He had come up from behind him to join him at the window. "Every one of us has committed far too much now for this whole enterprise to have been a mistake."

"It is not a mistake!" Kai Aphas screamed, hating having to hear someone else doubt what he was trying to do.

*Just being back in this city is having a corrupting influence*, Kai Aphas decided, eying Ovid carefully. *Lucan can still see the light, but is Ovid becoming corrupted by Tanas's influence? Who knows if Noah and Moses won't become corrupted as well? I might have to remove them before we return to the surface.*

# The Second Coming

*Like I had to be "removed" because I had been "corrupted,"* Able's voice whispered again. Kai Aphas noticeably twitched at his stepbrother's constant reminders of his actions, a twitch that caused Ovid to take a step away from Kai Aphas.

While Ovid always supported Kai Aphas's goals of ridding Prism of Tanas and the Tribe of Shadows, Kai Aphas himself always made him a little nervous. Yet at the sound of a massive gate opening, and the roar of a mob echoing through the cavern, Ovid knew his own thoughts about Kai Aphas's eccentricities would have to wait. Joining Kai Aphas and the other two Virt Princes, he could see the source of the noise from the window in the tower. The massive gate in the wall surrounding Yam-Preen was opening. Scores of warriors from the Tribe of Shadows poured into Yam-Preen roaring battle cries as they charged the Antaeus and Decca-Ju Tower. All of them could hear the chants from the Tribe of Shadows echoing in the air.

"Death to the Hy-muns! Halt the Second Coming! Avenge Yam-Preen!"

"Get that perimeter established!" Kai Aphas ordered. "Send word to the Sun Sphere repair crews to get them operational again right now and for the Antaeus to focus its Lightning Lamps around us and on the Tribe of Shadows. We don't want any of Tanas's demons trying to slip by invisibly."

The three Virt Princes' eyes opened wide when they saw the approaching force, hesitating for a moment before scrambling into action.

*This is what separates a Hy-mun like me from Hy-muns like them,* Kai Aphas mused. He noticed the shock and fear in the Virt Princes' eyes and was glad to be rid of it.

*These Virt Princes, unlike their parents, haven't done anything but sit on their Ziggurats since the end of the Great Rainbow War, handling the day-to-day affairs of state. Not one of them has faced any* real *fear or danger in their entire lives. Well, that's about to change. Now it's time for the Tribe of Shadows to be afraid.*

Kai Aphas watched as dozens of Lightning Lamps blazed to life on the hull of the Antaeus, shining bright orange-yellow light down across Yam-Preen and the approaching hoards from the Tribe of Shadows. The oncoming mob hesitated for a moment, expecting the light from the Lighting Lamps was going to affect them in some way before being rushed by an opposing force of Hammers led by Lucan at the front.

"For the glory of our Great Lord and Master and the Hammers of the Orange Light!" Lucan screamed, charging into battle with the Hammers of the Orange Light against the Tribe of Shadows.

From his vantage point atop Decca-Ju Tower, Kai Aphas watched as Lucan and his forces, armed with guns and martial weapons, weaved through the warriors from the Tribe of Shadows. If Lucan and the other Hammers did not think they looked monstrous before, then they did now. All around them, warriors and Hammers clashed, fueled by vengeance, willpower, and pure adrenaline, only to get bullets put into their faces or swords run through their chests.

"Now that Lucan and the other Virt Princes are fighting the Tribe of Shadows, my Hammers can work in Nis to restore the Sun Spheres, and I can get back to finding Tanas." Kai Aphas began ransacking Decca-Ju Tower again, looking for anything he could have missed. "This battle won't truly be won until Tanas is dead."

# Chapter 25

"Wake up, wake up!"

Dan-te struggled to open her eyes. Her head felt like it was a gladiator's personal punching bag. After their pod was fired from the Antaeus, some of the internal cushioning had failed to deploy. It caused everyone in the pod to get more shaken up than they would have liked when they finally hit the city. Dan-te could not remember much of the initial impact and the time after it, but she thought she heard Virgil telling someone to "go on."

*I'll get up, I'll get up,* Dan-te thought to herself. *Just stop the pounding in my head.*

Dan-te actually got her request. Her next sensation was that of a cold hand rubbing her head and hair, which actually made the pain go away.

"Ah, yes, that's it," Dan-te mumbled. "Right there, top of the head, behind the horn, wait…what!"

Dan-te's moment of bliss ended abruptly when she realized that if someone was rubbing her head and horn, then both her helmet and head covering were off, and anyone would be able to tell that she was not a tall Hy-mun, but a member of the Remnant of the Tribe. Sitting up abruptly, she found herself in the pod, her head coverings off just like she thought, but with only Virgil at her side.

"Good, you're finally awake," Virgil said, his voice filled with relief and his face glowing with the blue and violet energies of care and protection. "I was almost afraid I was going to have to try giving you mouth-to-mouth to get air into your body."

"What happened? Where is everyone?" Dan-te asked, immediately self-conscious about being exposed and back in Nis.

"You got knocked out when we landed. It took some fast talking, but I was able to convince the others in the pod to go on and join up with the Sun Sphere repair crew while I made sure you were okay, telling them we would meet up later. After that, they left me this."

Virgil showed Dan-te a small beeping device. "It's a tracking device that shows me where each Hammer, pod, and Sun Sphere is located so I can find them. I've been watching the device while trying to get you up. Most of the Hammers are making their way to the Sun Spheres. But they haven't been moving quickly. I'm guessing the Tribe of Shadows is not making it easy for them."

"And you would be right," Dan-te said, standing up and getting ready to move again. "We had better get going. I can find my way through Nis by feeling the latent energy flowing between each circle from where others have gone before. There's just one problem, with the Hammers now in Nis—"

"The pathways between circles are going to be more crowded than ever with soldiers from both sides looking for a fight," Vigil said, finishing Dan-te's sentence and realizing the obvious problem that they were going to face. "Not only that, we can't really get rid of our disguises yet. If we do, then we'll have two sides trying to kill us instead of just one."

"You're right," Dan-te sighed. Picking her helmet off the ground, she placed it back on her head. Dan-te did not like the Hammer's uniform and would have been glad to tear it off and toss it into a magma river, but she knew Virgil was right. If the suits helped them avoid trouble from the Hammers, then wearing them was a small price to pay.

*And as much as I hate these uniforms, I* Know *Virgil hates wearing them even more than I do,* Dan-te mused as she climbed out of the pod. However, as she walked out, the sight before her made her stop in her tracks, and her blood run cold.

"Dan-te," Virgil asked, as soon as he saw her stop, "what's wrong?"

Virgil might not have been able to *Know* the way that Dan-te could, but he had been with her long enough to realize when something was bothering her, and something was *really* bothering her.

"We're too late," Dan-te sobbed, dropping back to her knees as tears began rolling down her eyes. "Ancient Tribe save us. We're too late. The Third Great Attempt has begun."

"What!"

Virgil was on his knees with Dan-te, pulling off both of their helmets and embracing her the second she said the words, "The Third Great Attempt has begun." Virgil knew what the Third Great Attempt's execution meant. It meant that the magma vein in the Red Dominion was tapped, and magma was flowing, nonstop, straight for the city, and nothing could stop it.

"Talk to me, Dan-te," Virgil pleaded, both encouragingly and as gently as he could. He realized the important thing now was to get her talking and moving so she would not shut down in fright and despair like he almost did after the AAM was wiped out by the Hammers. "I do not doubt you. But tell me, how do you *Know* the Third Great Attempt has started, and how much time do you think we have?"

"It's the cavern," Dan-te sputtered out, also realizing Virgil's intentions. "Its energy is dying. Do you remember how I told you that for a long time now, this cavern and other parts of the tunnels were emitting a bright pink fearful energy because the Land itself was afraid of the Third Great Attempt?"

"Yes, I do," Virgil said, remembering their first meeting back in his room at Spectral Academy.

"Well, now it's changing for the worse," Dan-te wept. "The fearful pink energy is rapidly leaving the cavern, leaving it null, black, and dead. It's already black in the direction of the Great Tunnel. That means only one thing. The Third Great Attempt has begun. We're too late."

Dan-te continued crying while across Nis, the change in the cavern's energy was not only going unnoticed, but it was also causing its own effects across the various factions struggling throughout the city.

***

"The fearful pink energy is leaving the cavern!" Ju-Nian screamed as he and the other chefs from Gluttony Mesh-Re fearlessly fought against the Hy-muns that landed in an out-of-the-way section of Gluttony Mesh-Re. The Hy-muns were trying to reach a giant sphere that Ju-Nian's group was trying to destroy.

"It is a sign from our ancestors! Lose your fear and fight. We will not be exterminated again!" Ju-Nian was on an adrenaline high. He had just cut off his own right arm at the elbow after it was shot by a Hy-mun weapon, cauterized the wound, and was now eating that same arm raw for energy. The sight of him eating his own arm, combined with his declaration about a sign from their ancestors, was rallying the warriors from Nis and destabilizing the Hammers.

"What are these things?" a Young Hammer stuttered. "They eat their own bodies and preach about signs. Are they really—"

The young Hammer's words were silenced as another Hammer whipped his gun onto the first Hammer's shoulder, aimed at Ju-Nian, and shot him clean through both his face and the arm he was eating, earning cheers from both the Hammers and warriors from Nis.

"These things are just monsters," the new Hammer exclaimed to his allies. "But do not fear my brothers. We have Light, Right, and the Nag-el's tools on our side. Push through for peace, His glory, and the glory of the Hammers of the Orange Light."

The Hammers, revitalized by the new Hammer's speech, continued fighting and were soon breaking through the Tribe of Shadows' warriors, reaching the Sun Sphere. After the fight, the leader of the Hammer's group approached the Hammer who had invigorated the others to give him both praise and new instructions.

"You are doing your grandfather proud, Sol," the old Hammer said, looking at the Hammer who had invigorated his brothers-in-arms. "You have your grandfather's passion, the gift for encouragement, and you are an excellent shot and fighter, too. I want you to make your way to Beta Point, see if you can help them secure the Sun Sphere in that location as well."

"Yes sir," Sol replied readily, making his way to the Hammer's Beta Point. Elsewhere in the city, different fights were being fought.

\*\*\*

"What do you mean?"

"I mean *ma'am* that all terranaut ships have been ordered to return to the surface for yearly inspection and repairs. There are no Terranaut Crews available to pilot them. Orders direct from 'the powers that be.' Now, this joke of yours has gone far enough. Have a good day, ma'am."

The radio clicked silent, and Ann could hear her own nerves clicking and breaking right along with them. Ann had finally managed to contact a Terranaut Base with the radio in the digging machine. Unfortunately, the one on the other end was unwilling to listen or even believe a word she said. Even worse was that all of that base's ships had been called back for service.

"If Worm were here, he would probably say that this can't be a coincidence," Ann fumed. "Now, what do we do?" Ann turned from the radio to the Seat of Kindness, who for the last few minutes had been staring intensely at the cavern roof.

"Keep trying," the Seat of Kindness answered, his voice half panicking and half pleading. "Just keep trying, someone, anyone, needs to listen."

"Is something wrong?" Ann asked. She might not have been able to *Know* things about other people like the Seat of Kindness could, but anyone listening to him right now would know that he was scared. Something was changing, and it was changing for the worst.

"The Third Great Attempt has begun," the Seat of Kindness whispered, causing Ann to stop what she was doing and let the full weight of the Seat of

Kindness's words sink in. When she found her voice again, all she could do was ask one question.

"How much time do we have left?"

"I honestly don't know," the Seat of Kindness responded. "I know that the Third Great Attempt has started. The energy dying in the cavern, starting in the direction of the Great Tunnel, is proof of that. But there is something else about the way the cavern is losing energy. It's too slow, something has altered the Great Tunnel."

Hope began to spark in Ann at the thought of the Great Tunnel being altered.

"If the Great Tunnel has been altered, maybe the magma won't even reach here," Ann suggested hopefully.

But the Seat of Kindness shook his head as sadness streaked across his face.

"The magma will reach here, and from here it will go to Rem, that much I *Know* for sure. Hoping that it won't happen when the proof is before our eyes is pointless. As for whether or not the supervolcano will be defused, I just don't know."

Ann could see the pained expression on the Seat of Kindness's face.

*It's not just that he doesn't know if the supervolcano will be defused,* Ann realized. *He honestly doesn't know what to do. The magma is coming, and anyone caught in its path is going to be killed. The only thing I can think of doing is keep calling for help and hope someone listens to me and brings a ship down here.*

Ann returned to the radio, her mind running through every open and private terranaut frequency she had ever learned.

"Someone will hear me and listen," Ann reassured the Seat of Kindness as she continued her broadcast. "This is an emergency, please respond!"

*** 

"We're too late."

Dan-te looked utterly defeated, and Virgil could understand why.

*Dan-te's forced herself to do plenty of disagreeable things since coming to Nis,* Virgil realized. *Enduring starvation, fighting, killing, all just to get a chance to find help on the surface and bring it back here. Only to return and discover she's too late, that it was all for nothing. Soon she and everyone else she knows will be consumed in volcanic magma. That's enough to crush anyone's spirit.*

Virgil, however, was not about to let Dan-te give up now after they had both come this far together. Lifting Dan-te back to her feet, steadying her on him like he had done many times before, he started her walking.

"The magma isn't here yet," Virgil said, trying to sound confident, but realizing they now had only a short time to do anything of use. "'Dum vita est, spes est,' 'where there is life, there's hope.' We just have to move on and work faster. We're still alive, so we have to hope we can do something to change this for the better. Now, where are we and where do we go from here?"

Dan-te started walking, taking in what encouragement she could from Virgil's words.

"You're right," Dan-te replied. "We have to keep going. It's the only thing we can do now." Dan-te looked around and soon was able to get her bearings, recognizing the distinctive architecture of the area belonging to only one circle.

"We're in Envy Opal-Lo, it's the fourth circle in Nis out from Maestri where the Tribe of Shadows teaches their young. If we head this way, we'll be able to get to Lust Atrophied. From there, we go to Gluttony Mesh-Re, Maestri, and then out of the city where the digging machines should be located."

"Then let's get moving." Virgil cheered as he and Dan-te made their way through the streets of Nis.

# Chapter 26

"There's one of them, after it!" The voice cried out from behind Met-on as a piece of the building he was hiding under exploded, and a group of orange-suited Hy-mun started running toward him.

Met-on had made it out of both the Grand Coliseum and Wrath Eras. He was now back in Envy Opal-Lo and making his way to Stella in Lust Atrophied. But since Lord Tanas's image had vanished from above Nis, the entire city had fallen into complete chaos. Fighting between the warriors and the Hy-mun invaders had broken out in every circle of Nis. To make matters worse, debris from the cavern ceiling had started to rain down on the city from where the Hy-muns' ships had broken through. Looking up, Met-on also noticed the cavern losing the fearful pink energy that it had been radiating lately.

"That can't be good," Met-on mumbled, watching the radiant pink energy of the cavern slowly change to black from the direction of the Great Tunnel onward. In the distance, he could hear different groups of warriors from Nis cheering about it, calling it a sign from their ancestors. But after what happened in the Grand Coliseum, he had been questioning everything he had ever learned in Nis.

*Is the Third Great Attempt* really *going to allow us to return to the surface?* Met-on wondered again. *Or has the Remnant been right the whole time, that the Third Great Attempt is going to kill us all? The way the energy is leaving the cavern now is just like how energy leaves a body. Then there are the Hy-muns, have they really been our enemies? Or have we been theirs?*

Met-on did not have an answer to his questions. His experience with Hy-muns was limited to Stella and the ones invading Nis. One thing he did *Know* was that the invaders were *not* friendly.

*If I had met Stella outside the city, is this what she would have been like?* Met-on wondered, ducking down an alley into a nook, pulling a rotting body over himself to mask the stench of excrement still lingering on him, and watching as the other Hy-muns ran past him.

*Could Stella really be like these Hy-muns? And if not, would she really be safe with them?*

After Tanas's orders to execute all the members of the Tribe of Shadows with Rodent-blood was interrupted by the arrival of the Hy-muns, Met-on decided to return to Lust Atrophied and free Stella. Earlier, she challenged him to take her out of the city instead of going to the Grand Coliseum; he failed. Now, he planned to free her. Initially, he was going to bring her to the invading Hy-muns so they could take her back to the surface, but the more he saw of them, the less he trusted them. Climbing out of the nook and making his way out of the alley, Met-on paused as a new sound reached his ears.

"Kill every Hy-mun, Rodent, or half-Rodent, you see my fellows-in-arms. All hail Lord Tanas!"

*And I thought the hunt for the Hy-mun Horror was intense,* Met-on thought, ducking back down into his hiding place to avoid an oncoming troop of warriors from the Tribe of Shadows heading off to fight the Hy-muns that had just gone by. *Back then, the warriors of Nis were only hunting* one *Hy-mun. Now, they're hunting* everything.

Met-on waited again until he could not hear the warriors any more before leaving and continuing on his way.

*One of the advantages of being a half-Rodent in Nis is that one quickly learns where all of the best hiding places are, as well as finding all the best and untraveled shortcuts leading between circles.*

*The Jac-ob Way—not that I could use it—is currently filling up with dead Hy-muns who are trying to take it. I learned* that *already,* Met-on considered, thinking about the fastest ways to get to Lust Atrophied and some of the news he gleamed hiding from both forces. *The next quickest way is through the back alleys and passageways Teacher taught me about. I just need to pass a few more back streets, go through the air duct on a bunker, and I'll be at the entrance to Lust Atrophied.*

Met-on rechecked his mental map as he got to the next junction, the entrance to the air duct that went through the bunker. However, once he reached it, he discovered the path was no longer what he expected. The bunker had been blown clean open, a pod sitting inside of it.

# The Second Coming

*That pod must have gone through the ceiling and blown the bunker wide open,* Met-on figured, creeping slowly toward the opened bunker to see if he could slip through it. The bunker was part of the wall between the Circles, and Met-on used the air duct as a means of going through the wall instead of using the Circle's main entrance. But if the bunker was open, maybe he could slip through it and continue on normally. As he approached the bunker, keeping himself low, Met-on could hear voices coming from inside it.

"This place is a treasure trove."

"Agreed, I've never seen so much pre-Rainbow War technology in one place before. We have to tell the other Hammers about these vaults. The material here is worth a fortune."

Met-on crept closer to the bunker, keeping to the sheltered alcoves created by debris and falling rubble to avoid being seen. He found it crawling with Hy-muns slithering from the pod, into and through the bunker, and taking whatever technology they wanted from it.

"Snake Unit, take as much as you can carry and then get to Beta Point," another of the Hy-muns shouted. "The Sun Sphere isn't going to reactivate itself. Be certain you alert other Hammers about these vaults as well. Once the Sun Spheres are active, and these demons are wiped out, all this technology will be vital to the new, proper, and Tanas-free world."

*Those Sun Spheres they are talking about sound like trouble,* Met-on realized until he was suddenly grappled from behind.

"What?" Met-on muttered, his mind racing as he tried to fight back the panic that was quickly building up inside him. But before Met-on could respond, his assailant pinned him to the ground.

*So, this is it,* Met-on figured, closing his eyes and preparing for the end. However, the killing move Met-on expected never happened; instead, he heard a voice whisper into his ear.

"Don't move or make a sound."

*A woman,* Met-on wondered, opening his eyes and finding he could turn his head and look at the person who pinned him.

*A Rodent woman,* Met-on realized in shock. The woman was dressed in the same suit as the Hy-muns, but she had taken off her helmet, revealing she was *definitely* a Rodent, a member of the Remnant of the Tribe. She had the same pure white hair and skin complexion, silver eyes, and silver and gold horns around her head that culminated in a single horn on her forehead—unlike Met-on's black horn.

"We're not going to hurt you. There are more Hammers, the invading Hy-muns in the suits like these, nearby. You were too focused on the ones in the vault to notice them. Close your eyes, listen, and you'll *Know* I'm right."

Met-on closed his eyes, not willing to argue with anyone who had him pinned to the ground, and listened. He already made out the sounds of the Hy-muns in the bunker, but soon he heard more, a lot more. The Rodent was right, he was too focused on the bunker, and because of that, he missed hearing the other Hy-muns—and the Rodent—approaching him.

*But what is a Rodent doing here?* Met-on wondered, looking back at his assailant. *And why is she wearing the Hy-mun's robes? Also, why does she look familiar?*

Met-on, however, did not have time to wonder because the approaching Hy-muns soon started swarming over and around the alcove where Met-on was hiding and began racing into the bunker. As more Hy-muns snaked into and out of it, they began emitting a gluttonous dark-green energy to go with the red energy that all the Hy-muns and the warriors of Nis were equally generating. Glancing back at the Rodent, Met-on noticed that she radiated different kinds of energy. She pulsed fearful pink energy—she was afraid of something—and he saw a mix of blue and violet energy that he had only seen in a few places throughout his life—mostly from Stella.

"What do you see, Virgil?" The Rodent looked back, and it was then that Met-on noticed her companion, another Hy-mun dressed in the same robes as all the others; but Met-on *Knew* that *this* one was completely different from the other Hy-muns invading Nis. This Hy-mun, Virgil, was generating the same energies as the Rodent.

"It looks like those Hammers are just concerning themselves with stealing whatever they can from the bunker before making their way to the Sun Sphere," Virgil surmised.

"And Kai Aphas was spouting all that nonsense about this bringing peace to the surface," the Rodent said in disgust. "It looks like they're just a bunch of thieves as well as butchers."

"Dan-te, that's a sad and unfortunate truth of every conflict," Virgil said, his voice tainted with shame for his own people. "In every conflict throughout history, there have always been people who just want to kill and then slither in and grab whatever loot they can afterward."

*Dan-te, that's it!* Met-on's mind snapped in recognition as he suddenly recognized the Rodent woman pinning him. *About a week before the Hy-mun Horror Hunt began, two Rodents—Dan-te and Ice—were part of a large group of Rodents that surrendered themselves to Nis, preaching against the start of the Third Great Attempt. They entered the gladiatorial arena, fought up to the Grand Coliseum in Wrath Eras, and tried to steal the Veil of Shadows with the Hy-mun Horror. During the attempt, the Veil of Shadows was destroyed with Dan-te right alongside it. Ice and the Hy-mun Horror escaped afterward, beginning the Hy-mun Horror Hunt. But how is she here now?*

Met-on's mind was racing with questions. He never witnessed Dan-te, Ice, and Reye's fight in the Grand Coliseum, but he had heard about it. Not only that, but he had also seen Dan-te and Ice fight once in Envy Opal-Lo before they were sent to Wrath Eras. It was clear how much she changed.

*When I first saw her, she was on the point of starvation,* Met-on thought, realizing that the reason why he did not recognize her sooner was that Dan-te was now full and fit instead of the starved gladiator he had seen before.

"We had better keep moving to Lust Atrophied," Virgil concluded. "Can you find a way around them?"

Dan-te closed her eyes, took a deep breath, opened them, and started looking around. Met-on realized that Dan-te was trying to feel the latent energy running throughout the city, but guessed she must be having problems doing it because of the constant fighting and the debris everywhere. Otherwise, what reason would they have for coming this way, unless they were trying to find these Hy-muns?

"I got it," Dan-te replied, before turning her attention toward Met-on.

"Now, please listen to me," Dan-te said, amazing Met-on by the amount of sympathy in her voice. It immediately made him think of his last meeting with Stella. "I *Know* you think I'm nothing more than a Rodent, but you have to get out of Nis. Go wherever you want, just get out of the city and as far away from it as you can. It doesn't matter who wins this fight anymore, everyone in this city *will* be killed. So, get out of here now!"

Dan-te released him after that, stood up, and began walking away with the Hy-mun named Virgil.

"Wait," Met-on called to them, surprising himself that he would even talk to a Rodent. "What makes you think I won't try and attack you, and why do you think everyone in this city is going to die?"

"The energy," Dan-te responded. "Since I've made it back to Nis, almost everyone has been generating horrible red energy: Hy-muns, the warriors of Nis, even the few like you who carry the blood of the Remnant. Everyone is generating the same red hateful energy and seems bound to kill one another. You must have noticed."

Met-on did notice, as the energies and scents became more intermixed throughout Nis, it was increasingly harder to *Know* who was Hy-mun and who was a warrior of Nis anymore.

"But then while Virgil and I were making our way through this circle, we spotted you, a single radiant beacon of the violet energy of protection among all this energy of hate. After seeing it, I had to talk to you. Because unlike the rest of the Tribe of Shadows, you have someone in this city that you want to protect, and you want to protect that someone more than you want to hate the Hy-muns. You want it so badly that you are emitting the energy of protection instead of the energy of hate. I'm was hoping that you would listen to me."

Met-on did listen, but he did not know what to think.

*This Rodent, Dan-te, and the Hy-mun, Virgil, they purposely looked for me because of what she* Knew *in my* energy. Met-on was amazed that they would even put themselves at risk just to find him.

"But what about Nis?" Met-on asked. "Why is everyone in the city going to die?"

"Because its energy is dying," Dan-te said, her voice turning grave and sympathetic. "The Third Great Attempt has started, it was never meant to trigger a volcanic eruption in the Red Dominion, it was meant to start one *here*. The city is soon going to be flooded by volcanic magma before being blown to the surface. That's why the cavern's energy is dying, and that's why everyone in it will die no matter what side they are on. Believe me or not, but it's the truth. So, if there's anyone you want to protect, get them out of Nis as soon as you can. Maybe then you'll have a chance." Dan-te rejoined Virgil, and the two of them continued down a path Met-on quickly recognized, the one leading around the bunker to Lust Atrophied.

*She only half believes that any of us has a chance,* Met-on thought, considering what Dan-te told him. *If she had told me this before the purging order, I wouldn't have believed her. I would have defended Tanas, the Third Great Attempt, and the Tribe of Shadows to the death. But now, I'm not so sure anymore.*

Met-on *Knew* Dan-te was completely sincere with him. He had also seen the fading energy in the cavern and recognized it as a sign of death. Then there was what Dan-te said about someone he wanted to protect.

*Stella...* The image of Stella in her room flashed into Met-on's mind again. *I do* want *to protect her, or at least I want to get her somewhere safe, but if the city is going to be swallowed in magma, what place is safe? It's not like Dan-te said...*

Met-on paused mid-thought, realization striking him like a piece of falling debris.

*If the city* is *doomed, why did Dan-te come back to it, and with a Hy-mun no less? Do they know a way to save Nis, or maybe someplace protected from the magma that they are planning to retreat to? They* are *going toward Lust Atrophied.*

Met-on looked back toward the bunker, the Hy-muns were finishing taking whatever they wanted out of it and leaving for their Sun Sphere. Met-on focused all of his efforts into sticking to the shadows to make himself invisible, giving a silent thanks to whoever could be listening for letting the Hy-muns be so wrapped up in their own work. Creeping around the edges, he made his way to the entrance of the air duct he once used as a shortcut. He soon popped out on the other side of the bunker in Dan-te and Virgil's path—surprising them both.

"Can you two save the Nis?" Met-on asked.

"I don't know," Dan-te responded, sadness tinting her voice. "We had an idea, but it needed us to get back here before the Third Great Attempt was triggered. I don't know if we can do anything."

"Then, can you get back to the surface, or at least somewhere safe from the magma, if you wanted to?"

Dan-te looked to Virgil for that answer, and Met-on could see the sparks of white mental energy flashing around his head.

*The Hy-mun wasn't expecting to return to the surface,* Met-on realized, guessing that Virgil did not make any plans to return to the surface when this was all over.

"If I can get one of the digging machines outside the city, or get back to one of the terraships—the big ships that landed in the city—we should be safe from the magma, and from there get back to the surface. Why?"

Met-on could tell by the tone in Virgil's voice that he was making the plan up as he went, but he was still acting differently than the rest of the Hy-muns in Nis. Met-on *Knew* if he were going to entrust Stella to anyone, Virgil would be the best choice.

"I want to protect a Hy-mun girl in Lust Atrophied named Stella," Met-on said, not missing the instant recognition that appeared across Virgil's face.

*Virgil's familiar with her,* Met-on realized. *That will help.*

"I want to get her out of the city and back to the surface. I can show you shortcuts leading to Lust Atrophied and through the rest of the Circles, but you have to get her out of here. Can you do that?"

Virgil looked back to Dan-te, a questioning look crossing his face.

*He's wondering whether or not I'm telling him the truth,* Met-on figured. *Virgil can't* Know *like I can, so he's trying to find out if I said anything that was a lie.*

Dan-te also looked at Met-on before turning back to Virgil, smiling and nodding in affirmation.

"I can't promise anything," Virgil began. "But I'll do whatever I can to protect her and keep her safe. Is that good enough?"

"It is," Met-on agreed. He could tell that Virgil was nervous, the familiar smell of fear that everyone in Nis *Knew* hovered around him.

*He's worried he won't be able to do anything at all.* Met-on realized. *But not once has his, has either of their energies, wavered. If they can, they will protect Stella. And bringing her to someone who can do that is the least I can do for her.*

"So, where are these shortcuts?" Virgil asked, extending his hand to Met-on, which Met-on curiously took. "And what's your name?"

"My name is Met-on. We start by going this way."

# Chapter 27

"The technology being found in this city is worth an untold fortune!" Ovid gasped, reading the newest report to arrive at Decca-Ju Tower from the Hammers in the city. "Prototype water purifiers, land re-claimers, every one of them marked 'Do not use until after the Third Great Attempt,' whatever that means, but do any of you see the possibilities of what this technology could do?"

"Of course, I do. That technology was originally developed in the Yellow Dominion," Moses said smugly. "It was developed to turn the Yellow Dominion's uninhabitable regions into fertile grasslands and to make even the foulest water drinkable again, and I imagine you are thinking of similar uses for it on the Violet Plateau."

"I am," Ovid said greedily. "The Violet Dominion will be able to produce more food, recycle, and use more groundwater than ever before, and this is literally just the start of what this technology can do. Once Tanas and his Tribe of Shadows have been eradicated, we could be looking at the start of a new golden age."

"Yes, Ovid," Moses agreed cautiously. "A new age."

Kai Aphas watched and listened to the exchange, creating his own plans for when they were finished in Nis. He stood at Tanas's window, feeling extremely satisfied with the work his Hammers were accomplishing. Below him in Yam-Preen, cremation fires burned as thousands of warriors from Nis lay dead and dying alongside the dead Hammers of the Orange Light; and Kai Aphas knew it was still only the beginning. From across the city, reports continued to come in about similar successes as well as the discovery of lost technology hidden in vaults throughout Nis's Fourth Circle, Envy Opal-Lo. The news of the find sent Virt Prince Ovid and Moses of the Violet and Yellow Dominions back to Kai Aphas in a state of ecstasy to make their report. Kai Aphas, on the other hand, was hearing something very different in their words.

*Tanas's influence is corrupting both Moses and Ovid,* Kai Aphas thought, listening to the two Virt Princes banter. *If left alone, they will start a second Great Rainbow War over control of the technology we are recovering. They will have to be removed. I have met both of their heirs. They're innocent and naive enough, and they know nothing about Nis, the Tribe of Shadows, or where the technology will have really come from. I can easily talk them into the correct choice of actions to firmly establish a "Golden Age" worthy of the Great Master's return.*

*Then you are no different than Tanas,* Able's voice echoed again in his head.

*I am not the same!* Kai Aphas twitched at his stepbrother's remark, fighting hard to keep himself from vocalizing it. *I am nothing like Tanas!*

*Then what do you call the scene playing right outside this window? What do you call what you are planning to do to two of the Virt Princes?*

Kai Aphas looked out the window again and over the city and display before him, if only just to silence Able's voice.

*I see a glorious work in progress, Able. I see thousands of demons, who, for years, have been a constant threat to the peace of Hy-muns everywhere, being destroyed along with the nest that spawned them. I see my Hammers of the Orange Light recovering the lost heritage of the Hy-mun people. And I see myself taking whatever steps I need to, to ensure lasting peace for all Hy-muns, an order that will surely bring the Great Master's return.*

Able's voice was silent, allowing Kai Aphas a moment to relax and exhale a breath he had been holding since this latest bout with his stepbrother's ghost began.

"He's gone, at last," Kai Aphas mumbled.

"Who's gone?" a voice asked, grabbing his shoulder and surprising him from behind.

Kai Aphas turned quicker than he had ever turned in years—his old combat instincts as sharp as ever, drawing the same knife he had brought from Nis clean across the throat of Noah, the Virt Prince from the Red Dominion. Noah's blood gushed over both of them, and with a gasp and spasm, he dropped to the floor dead to the shocked expressions of the other two Virt Princes.

# The Second Coming

*Well, might as well remove Moses and Ovid now,* Kai Aphas realized, deploying a silenced gun in his suit and killing both Moses and Ovid with a quick shot to their heads, leaving him alone at the top of Decca-Ju Tower.

*That was unfortunate,* Kai Aphas thought, looking back to Noah. *You should have known better than to creep up on me like that. At least now, I've managed to remove Tanas's influence from Moses and Ovid. As for Noah and the Red Dominion, his own heir is just as weak-willed as he was, he'll go along with whatever I say, too. Now, I don't have to worry about witnesses. If anyone asks, I can blame their deaths on a Tribe of Shadows assassin who managed to sneak into the tower. Best of all, Able's voice is finally gone.*

*I'm not gone,* Able's voice rang in Kai Aphas's head, louder than ever. *I just decided to be quiet for a second to see what you would do. Now, let me tell you what I see. I look out, and I see the Tribe of Shadows' worst nightmare come to life. I see intolerant invading monsters who don't even want to try and see the ones they are invading as "people," but are comfortable with calling them "demons." I see the invaders destroying lives, homes, and looting the city with all the greed and gumption that every invading army has done throughout Hymun history, doing it* without *the influence from the Tribe of Shadows. I see you, a regicidal killer, murdering three Virt Princes with plans to tempt their heirs into following your way of thinking. I see our people becoming* exactly *like the Nag-el who all but exterminated the Tribe of Shadows' ancestors and* you *becoming a new Tanas.*

"I am not Tanas!" Kai Aphas screamed, no longer worried about being overheard.

*You are Tanas,* Able's voice repeated. *You destroy civilizations. You call beings that are different from you "demons" for no other reason than their outward differences. You kill family and comrades to hide your secrets. You tempt and lie to further your own ambitions. You are* Tanas!

"I am not! I am not!" Kai Aphas raved like a maddened baby. What little furniture left in Tanas's room was smashed as Kai Aphas picked up almost anything he could find, including the bodies of the three Virt Princes, and started throwing them against the walls of the chamber. Soon, it was covered in the blood of the Virt Princes as each one of their bodies became a broken mess of dead flesh, skin, blood, and bones, eventually resting in a heap with the rest of the destroyed furniture. All the while, Able's voice continued to echo the same phase.

*You are Tanas, you are Tanas...*

Kai Aphas finally returned to the chamber window and began to look out to the Antaeus and beyond it to Nis.

*I am not Tanas,* Kai Aphas replied to his stepbrother's voice—as many times as he could—but Able's voice would not be silent, and neither would he. Reaching for his radio, one of the few things not destroyed in his rampage, he called his forces acting throughout the city.

"Lucan, status update," Aphas inquired.

"This is Lucan. Our forces are moving splendidly throughout the city. Two Sun Spheres are fixed and awaiting activation. Repairs are continuing on the other three. One, however, is encountering heavy resistance. I am heading there right now with forces to eradicate the demons so the last one can be activated, and we can bring our light into this city."

"Excellent, Lucan," Kai Aphas responded, inwardly questioning Able. *How can I be Tanas? Did Tanas ever have followers who would know how to act without me needing to tell them, did he ever have followers as loyal to him as Lucan is to me? No, all he has are his demons.*

But Able's voice never stopped.

*You are Tanas,* it repeated yet again.

"Lucan, how is my grandson Sol doing?" Kai Aphas asked, ignoring his stepbrother's voice to ask about his grandson.

*That is a way I am not like Tanas,* Kai Aphas mentally sneered. *I have my grandson. What family does Tanas have?*

"We've lost contact with Sol," Lucan reported, making Kai Aphas's blood freeze. "My reports tell me he was moving toward Beta Point when his squad lost contact with him after he entered the next circle in from where his pod landed."

Kai Aphas mentally pictured Nis in his mind. He knew where his grandson's pod landed and mentally calculated where he should be.

*Sol should be somewhere in the circle these demons call Lust Atrophied.*

"But I wouldn't worry about Sol," Lucan's voice called over the radio. "He is every bit the Hammer that you are with all the strength that his youth can provide. I am sure he will show up at Beta Point soon and will personally report in before we activate its Sun Sphere."

"Of course," Kai Aphas replied confidently. "He is my grandson and a far better Hy-mun than any of these demons could ever hope to be."

Kai Aphas clicked off the radio. Unfortunately, the one in his head would not turn off. Able's voice continued repeating the same message that he was Tanas, a message he would not and could not accept.

*I am not Tanas,* Kai Aphas mentally screamed again. *I am the one who will destroy Tanas, his demons, and bring the Hy-muns into a new age, one worthy of the Grand Master. How can any Hy-mun capable of doing that be Tanas?*

But Able's voice would not stop. Turning on his radio again, Kai Aphas called another group of Hammers.

"Beta Point, this is Kai Aphas, come in."

"Sir," a nervous voice answered, "we didn't know you would be calling us. The Sun Sphere is almost operational."

"Good," Kai Aphas interrupted, cutting off anything else the Hammer would have said. "But I want you to do something special for me."

"Anything, sir," the voice responded enthusiastically.

"My grandson, Sol, is heading for your position. Radio me when he arrives."

"Affirmative, sir," the voice replied before clicking off.

Kai Aphas stood in Tanas's chamber, a chamber that started to smell of the dead bodies of the Virt Princes and looked back to the city, Tanas city, soon to be purified and left free of every last demon and shadow that could ever haunt or tempt Prism again. The voice of Able would not stop now, but at least he could find something else to focus his mind on instead of Able's words.

*I'm going to end this city soon, brother,* Kai Aphas repeated in his head. *And I will do it with my grandson by my side; he just has to call in.*

Kai Aphas repeated those phrases, again and again, each time his stepbrother called him Tanas, partially to convince Able's voice that he was not Tanas and to give himself hope that his grandson was still fighting somewhere in the city and would soon join the other Hammers in the destruction of the Tribe of Shadows. Sol, however, was facing his own difficulties.

# Chapter 28

*Curse these demons!* Sol fumed as he made his way through Lust Atrophied. Soon after entering the circle, he decided to try one of the many chamber doors hoping to find something that he could use in the Hammer's fight with the Tribe of Shadows. Instead, he encountered his first female demon.

"Hy-mun," she screamed, before reaching to the side of her bed and picking up a spiked club that she began swinging wildly at Sol.

Sol barely had enough time to notice that he was in a fight before dodging the club's first swing and countering with his sword, his preferred weapon in close combat fights.

*This female demon fights madly*, Sol thought. *Swinging that club around with no form whatsoever.*

Sol, however, was a disciplined fighter and more than aptly trained in how to challenge someone who fought like a berserker. Keeping to his sword form, Sol soon parried himself around the female's attacks and ran his sword clean through her heart—dropping her dead at his feet. As the body lay there, Sol used the opportunity to get his first real look at a female member of the Tribe of Shadows.

*The creature, she seems designed to stimulate lust,* Sol thought to himself as he examined her body. *The female is slightly shorter than I am. She also has the same distinctive hair, eye, and skin coloring that the males do, and is also very well-endowed. I remember my grandfather telling about a place where the Tribe of Shadows keep their women so they can spawn more demons and teach their men about seduction and corruption. This must be it. This creature must have been one of those seductresses, vicious, but made to look physically attractive to Hy-mun eyes, and having about as much decency as the women in the Blue Dominion, dressed in nothing but a slip.*

Sol looked around to each door surrounding him in the circle, guessing that they must all contain female demons as fierce as this one.

*I had better call this in,* Sol thought to himself, reaching for his radio. *If we're going to eliminate every demon in this city, I'm going to need help to clean this nest out.*

But once Sol reached for his radio, he noticed it was only half there. Sol's radio and the tracker he used to navigate the city with were both destroyed.

"How did?" Sol gawked before realizing what had happened. "When that female took her first swing at me with her club, she came close to hitting me but only barely missed. It must have been then, the club missed me but hit my radio and tracker. Curse these demons!"

Sol knew that without his radio, he could not tell the other Hammers about the demon nest he stumbled into, and without his tracker, he had no way to find any of his brother Hammers, or find his way to Beta Point. He was going to have to try and navigate the circle by himself.

"I have to get to Beta Point." Sol realized, considering his options. "But I can't leave this nest alone, and that's assuming I'm the only Hammer who is here now. But once the Sun Spheres are activated, each one of these rooms will become a cell, trapping their occupants inside. My brothers can then take their time weeding these demons from their nests and exterminating them. But can I really leave them alone. What would grandfather do?"

Sol did not have to think about his grandfather for long before deciding what to do. He had grown up listening to his grandfather's stories about Nis, the Tribe of Shadows, and what they had cost him long before he officially joined the Hammers. He had heard the stories about how his grandfather's first love was lost to him because of these demons, listened to the pain in his voice when he described how she was lost to him, and—unknown to his grandfather—witnessed parts of his mad raves. Raves, Sol later decided must have been the Tribe of Shadows attempting to tempt him when he learned about the Tribe of Shadows' Tempters and fought one on the surface for the first time.

"I can't leave these demons where they are," Sol realized, looking through the pouches inside his suit to see what other supplies he still possessed. "I have chalk for marking my path, a pistol with a silencer, spare ammunition, and emergency food. If I'm going to exterminate as many of these demons as possible, I'll use the pistol first until I run out of ammunition. I'll also only destroy a demon every so often unless one confronts me. That way, I can keep moving through the circle, marking my path with the chalk until I meet up with more Hammers. Then I can continue on to Beta Point and make my report about this circle. Who knows how many Hy-mun have been tempted into acts of depravity because of these monsters? Well, there tempting ends now."

Sol began searching the circle, marking his path with chalk, kicking open doors, and firing upon the surprised occupants inside as they reached for clubs, whips, or attacked him outright. Sol, however, soon realized he was not alone with the demons in the circle. Every so often he spotted what looked like a pure white demon running through the Circle with him. Other times though, he saw two of the white demons together, and there were also a few times he spotted a white and grey one running down a different street.

"Where are you monsters?" Sol screamed, grinding his teeth at the game these white and grey monsters seemed to be playing with him. "I am Sol Aphas, the grandson of Kai Aphas, the Hy-mun who once escaped from this city swearing to return one day and destroy it, and I will fight and destroy you. Come out!"

***

From behind a closed door, Ca-to listened to Sol's ravings while hushing the room's occupant, a middle-aged woman from the Remnant of the Tribe who had almost burst into tears when Ca-to entered.

*This Sol is no different than a newly made gladiator,* Ca-to thought, listening for Sol's footsteps to lead away from the door before he could exit and lead its occupant out. Ca-to had spotted Sol a few times while searching Lust Atrophied for women from the Remnant, as well as women who were of mixed heritage who did not answer Tanas's summons to the Grand Coliseum. He only saw Sol a few times, but those few glimpses let him *Know* everything he needed to find out.

*He radiates the same red energy as the invading Hy-muns and the warriors from Nis,* Ca-to realized. *Considering what I can see in Sol and hear in his voice, he also pulses with a streak of teal pride and dark-green gluttony. He hungers to prove himself worthy of being a descendant of his grandfather. Then there's his voice. It grinds with an inherited hatred that refuses to listen or even attempt to see another point of view. Lastly, there is a cold white mental energy behind all of it.*

Sol's footsteps began leading away from the door. When Ca-to was sure he had gone, he led the room's occupant back out into the circle and started taking her back toward Maestri, but not before turning around and gazing in the direction Sol was heading.

*When Reye became the Hy-mun Horror, it was because unexpected grief and madness joined with other parts of her personality. Reye never entirely chose that path for herself. But this Sol, he* has *chosen this path and has utterly devoted himself to it, and that makes him even more dangerous than Reye was when she was still the Hy-mun Horror.*

Not letting his thoughts linger too much on Sol, Ca-to took the woman he rescued and started leading her back toward Maestri.

*Reye, I hope you've found your friend,* Ca-to prayed, looking back to the cavern ceiling again, *Knowing* that the Third Great Attempt had begun. *We don't have much time.*

***

"Another chalk mark, there is definitely another Hy-mun around here."

Reye struggled through Lust Atrophied, looking for Stella. Every door she opened so far turned out to belong to a woman from the Tribe of Shadows, a woman who nearly attacked her before she closed the door and left the room. To avoid more attacks, Reye started a new method of checking the doors. She knocked in the rhythm of a song Stella regularly listened to back at Spectral Academy, hoping that if Stella were behind one of the doors, she would be the first to recognize the song and try to answer, but so far, each knock was met with silence. Thankfully, none of the rooms' occupants emerged to attack her. Still, Reye knew the task of finding Stella in this circle was a challenge in itself, one with an ever-shrinking amount of time. Yet the discovery of the chalk marks gave Reye new hope.

"A member of the Remnant of the Tribe of Shadows would be able to find their way through this circle without any problems," Reye realized. "These marks could only mean one thing, that the marker needs them to figure out where they are going, and the only ones that would need to figure that out would be Hy-muns like me. Maybe Stella escaped and is around here right now."

Reye wanted to call out Stella's name, hoping she might reply, but when she turned a corner indicated by another chalk mark, she was hit by an extremely familiar odor.

*That smell,* Reye thought as she noticed a room with a chalk "X" on the door. *The odor could almost be called metallic, and a rotting stench that could only be cadaverine.* Reye recognized the smell at once. She had caused it plenty of times. It was the stench of blood and death.

"I have to know," Reye said as she opened the door, preparing herself in case the dead body that she knew was behind it turned out to be Stella's body.

"By the Great Master," Reye gasped, seeing the corpse laid out before her. Reye knew she was responsible for more death and destruction in Nis than anyone. After encountering Tanas, she re-witnessed all of it. And after that experience, she thought she could take seeing another dead body. She was wrong. The body before her was like nothing she had ever seen before—or expected to see.

"This woman, she's been shot."

Lying on the floor, a woman from the Tribe of Shadows was dead with a bullet wound going clean through her head. Until then, every death caused by either her or by the Tribe of Shadows had been with hand-to-hand martial weapons, such as swords, spears, or war hammers. But seeing a dead body sprawled across the floor as the result of a gun shook Reye in a way she did not think could happen.

"I should have stayed with Ca-to," Reye stuttered, as she slowly closed the door, feeling that Nis had suddenly become much more dangerous, and tried her knocking method on another door.

"No answer," Reye mumbled, as she continued down the path indicated by the chalk marks. Yet inwardly, Reye was still shaking, the sight of the woman killed by gunshot had brought a new reality into Nis that did not exist before, one Reye had no choice but to accept.

*It's not like I didn't expect the Hy-mun rescue party would be armed,* Reye thought, knowing full well that the marks she had been following now were not left by Stella, but by one of the Hy-muns who came aboard the terraships.

*Of course, they would bring weapons. They must have heard from Sol, about the kind of beings the Tribe of Shadows are so they would be armed and ready for a fight, a fight that would leave members of the Tribe of Shadows— male and female—dead as the result of Hy-mun weaponry. Besides, after all the death I caused, am I really going to be shaken by seeing another one created by our weapons?*

But Reye already knew the answer. She was shaken, a shaking that only increased as she passed another door with an "X" on it, looking inside to find a similar scene as the one she had just discovered and was shaking because of the realities the gunshot deaths introduced into the city. First, the two deaths she saw by gunshots were women, and second, she realized the Hy-muns she believed were here to rescue them, would waste no time and effort in pointless killings.

"Another 'X,'" Reye murmured as she found a third marked door and dead body behind it. But this time, as Reye opened the door, she heard it hit something metallic. At Reye's feet was a small gun with a silencer attached.

*Well, at least this means there should not be any more gunshot deaths,* Reye thought to herself as she picked the gun up and examined it. *I wonder how many times this gun was used before I stumbled onto the chalk markings.*

The gun was still a little warm, so Reye knew its owner must have tossed it recently. It could hold up to six bullets, but that did not mean it could not have been reloaded at some point before Reye found the trail.

# The Second Coming

*I really wish I stayed with Ca-to,* Reye thought again, leaving the gun in the room, closing the door behind her, and walking back into the circle. Ignoring the chalk marks this time, Reye set off again on her own path, knocking on doors and hoping for a response from Stella. Soon she found herself in a narrow alley divided by a tall gate.

*I can climb this,* Reye thought confidently, gripping the gate and using the walls to climb to the top of it. Catching her breath at the top, Reye was about to jump down when a figure appeared.

*What?* Reye wondered in shock and surprise. At the end of the alley was a Hy-mun in an orange containment suit. Reye knew it had to be a Hy-mun since she had seen plenty of warriors from Nis, and none of them ever went around in the orange containment suits Hy-muns wore when they entered dangerous territories. The Hy-mun looked as lost as Reye felt and was about to call out to him when he took off again. Reye quickly made her way back down the gate and to the end of the ally, turning in the direction the Hy-mun went when she noticed another chalk mark on the ground.

*Well, at least I know for sure now that there's one Hy-mun around here,* Reye thought to herself as she followed the mark in the direction the orange-suited Hy-mun was traveling.

*That Hy-mun is following the same marks I'm am, maybe even the one making them. If that Hy-mun is responsible for the chalk marks, could that also mean he's responsible for...*

Reye let the thought hang in her head uncompleted. The idea that the Hy-mun in the orange suit was responsible for the chalk marks brought an unexpected chill to Reye's back as she followed the next one. She knew that after all the death and destruction she caused in Nis, based on nothing more than her need for vengeance, she had no right to criticize anyone who wanted to attack the members of the Tribe of Shadows with lethal force. But despite what this Hy-mun might have done since arriving in Nis, he was still another Hy-mun. Reye had to find him.

*He might know something about Stella,* Reye thought, chasing her through Lust Atrophied. *And how to get all three of us—me, Ann, and Stella— back to the surface, I have to talk to him.*

# Chapter 29

"What was she like?" Met-on asked, turning back to check on Virgil and Dan-te.

"What was who like? Stella?" Virgil inquired, a bolt of white mental energy flashing around his head, signaling he was instantly curious about Met-on's question.

"Yes, Stella. I met her in Lust Atrophied. She was given to me since my mother was a R...was like Dan-te so that I could experience my first Joining with a woman. The experience was so intense I found myself asking for her to be reserved for me, a request that was granted since no one wanted to have anything to do with a Hy-mun, and because the Warden of Lust Atrophied gave me a mission regarding her. If I could make her admit that she loved me or get her pregnant, I would receive my first branding. So, I kept going back to her, more times than I could count and Joined with her, especially during the Hy-mun Horror incident when no one noticed someone like me disappearing to go back to Lust Atrophied to see her again," Met-on stuttered mid-sentence. He noticed an abrupt change in Virgil.

Virgil was getting angry, right at the point where Met-on was explaining his mission. The same red energy Met-on witnessed throughout Nis, flaring uncontrollably on warriors and Hy-muns alike, was beginning to boil up through Virgil's blue and violet energies.

# The Second Coming

"Virgil, are you alright?" Dan-te asked, her concern ringing loud and clear in her voice as her own blue energy seemed to grow around her almost enwrapping Virgil like giant arms.

"I'm fine, Dan-te," Virgil said, his voice projecting a monotone and controlled pitch. "It's not like I didn't expect something like this could happen. Met-on, please tell me more about your *experiences* with Stella."

"Of course," Met-on mumbled, realizing something about what had happened between him and Stella must not have been acceptable for a Hy-mun from the tone of Virgil's voice and the red energy rising at the mention of their encounters. Yet Met-on could also hear the desire in Virgil's voice when he asked for more information about their time together, and if Met-on wanted his own question answered and doubts settled, he knew he had to tell Virgil everything.

"I kept going to see Stella," Met-on continued. "I never used any of the physical methods I was taught to make the Joining better, Stella seemed too frail for them. I just used the gas everyone uses, Joined with her, and then left. Eventually, she started talking to me, asking me questions about the Tribe of Shadows, Nis, and our history. No one ever talked to me like she did before. No one ever seemed to pay attention and notice me like she did before. I *really* started enjoying her company, just talking with her. I actually thought she was starting to develop feelings for me. Then I told her I was going to the Grand Coliseum along with all the other members of the Tribe of Shadows who were like me, and suddenly she became scared for me. At the time I was confused. I thought she might have been testing me, trying to make me choose her over the Tribe of Shadows. But now, I think there was more to it, and I know why she didn't tell me what was really scaring her. She knew I wouldn't have believed her."

Met-on turned his eyes down at the memory. Virgil couldn't *Know* like Dan-te could, but he realized that whatever Stella said to him must still be haunting him. That much was clearly visible on his face.

"After the Hy-muns arrived and I saw their own energy, identical to the warriors of Nis, and the way they were rampaging through Nis, I started wondering if Stella was like that before she came to Nis; or if she was someone different. Can you tell me if she was like these other Hy-muns, or was she someone different?"

Met-on looked into Virgil's eyes, his stare pleading for an answer. Virgil, however, did not answer Met-on immediately, and that made him even more nervous. Met-on could still see angry red energy bubbling up out of Virgil. Thankfully, there was not as much of it as there was before. But now Virgil was also generating white mental energy around his head. He *Knew* from the energy and the expression twisting across his face that Virgil was thinking. He wanted to choose the right words to answer Met-on's question.

"The Stella I knew wasn't anything like the Hammers of the Orange Light; the Hy-muns fighting Nis's warriors," Virgil began. "She was a kind person who valued her friends, wasn't above getting into a little trouble, and loved just being one with her surroundings, remembering every detail in case she might never see it again."

*So, she wasn't like the other Hy-muns,* Met-on realized, his mind and step becoming lighter with the relief that Stella was a different kind of Hy-mun than the suited ones Virgil called the Hammers of the Orange Light.

"However," Virgil continued, almost making Met-on miss a step, "I don't think she's that same person now."

"Why?" Met-on asked. "I'm the only one she had ever seen since she was brought to the city, and I never did anything wrong to her."

"Not by *your* standards." Met-on could not help but feel threatened by Virgil's voice. He almost sounded accusing when he talked about standards. "But by Hy-mun standards, your constant Joining with her, without her consent, while she was gassed, would be considered a horrific and criminal act."

"You mean what I was doing could have had me sent to a Hy-mun Maestri?" Met-on gasped, thinking about the first circle prison where lawbreakers were sent to, and the punishments handed to them.

"It could have you killed on sight," Virgil shouted. Anger, the hunting smells that extruded from the gladiators, and his red energy bubbled up out of him again. "And you would *not* be remembered as some kind of martyr for it. In fact, you wouldn't be remembered at all. As for Stella, I'm familiar with the practices of her home dominion. Everything you've done is more than enough for her family to banish her, and for her to live in shame until she died!"

"Then, did I *Know* her completely wrong?" Met-on wondered, his voice quivering. "Does she really hate me enough now that she wants to kill me? Did I turn her into a Hy-mun just like these Hammers? I thought she liked me."

"Honestly, Met-on, I don't know what she is thinking right now," Virgil answered. "I do think she wants to kill you because of everything that you've done to her. But I also don't think she could afford to hate you enough to do it. That's why I don't know what she could be thinking right now."

Met-on thought about what Virgil said as they turned down the last passage leading them through a crack in the border and taking them into Lust Atrophied.

*Virgil is being completely honest,* Met-on realized. *There isn't a single lie in his words, but plenty of anger. But it's not just anger directed at me because of what I did to Stella. It's anger toward Nis itself. Yet Virgil's anger seems to be tempered with understanding. He gets that this is the way Nis works, and while he's angry about it, he isn't chastising it. He's merely accepting it as reality and moving on so he can learn more. Would I have done that?*

*No, I wouldn't have,* Met-on realized as they made their way into Lust Atrophied. *Despite Stella's pleas against it, I willingly walked into the Grand Coliseum, blindly trusting and praising Tanas, the Tribe of Shadows, and their ways my entire life. I did whatever they asked of me, hoping for a branding that in the end, was always going to be meaningless and believing that Nis was the most perfect city ever. I was always taught that Hy-muns were the enemy, a plague mocking civilization that spawned uncontrollably. I was wrong.*

*How much more could Stella have told me about the surface, Hy-mun culture and customs, and herself, if she wasn't accommodating my own cavern-sized ego?* Met-on wondered, thinking now of all the opportunities that he missed. *How much more could I have learned if I didn't look down on Hy-muns in general and accepted them and their civilization and tried to learn as much about them as I could? For that matter, how much more could I have learned about the Remnant if I honestly tried listening to them instead of seeing them as rodents and treating them that way?*

Met-on watched as both Virgil and Dan-te walked through Lust Atrophied. Met-on's horn itched with the fact that half the blood in his veins came from a female member of the Remnant, a female who could still be alive here.

*That's the Tribe of Shadows' way,* Met-on remembered from his lessons. *"The Tribe of Shadows itself is our parent. Everyone has to ensure another generation follows the previous one. No one is different in that respect." But that was never true, was it?*

Even before meeting Stella, Met-on knew his black horn and grey skin marked him as a lesser member of the Tribe of Shadows. Yet when it came to providing future generations, Met-on thought he was still equal to any member of the Tribe of Shadows, a belief that was only further encouraged by both the fantastic first Joining he experienced with Stella and the mission he later received from Warden Cha-les.

"I thought I was the same as the other member of the Tribe of Shadows," Met-on mumbled, a sick feeling growing in the pit of his being, "the equal of every other one of my peers here in Lust Atrophied. Then after I got my mission from Warden Cha-les, I thought I was even better since I would be the first to earn a branding. But in the Tribe of Shadows' eyes, I was always just 'the spawn of Rodents' meant to be exterminated when they saw fit. Now it turns out I'm worse. I should have died in the Grand Coliseum. I deserved to be killed."

"No one *deserves* to be killed!" Virgil barked, shocking Met-on with the passion behind his words and how quickly his blue and violet energy suddenly flared up. "What you did to Stella may be punishable on the surface, but it is the way things are done here. You had no way of knowing anything about Hy-muns until after meeting her. Whatever hatred she has for you, I'm sure there must be at least some understanding by now."

"But if I've violated her so much, what could I possibly do now?"

"What you're doing right now," Virgil encouraged, putting his hand on Met-on's shoulder. "You're getting us to Stella so we can get her out of here. If you want to do more, than live and make sure nothing like this happens to her or anyone else ever again."

Met-on looked into Virgil's eyes. They sparkled with an old white mental energy. He was reliving a similar memory from long ago, his voice holding a faint echo in it. The blue and violet energies around him had softened from their earlier flare-up and become gentler, more comforting, a sensation Met-on could feel transmitted through Virgil's touch.

*I'm guessing Virgil must have felt the same way as I have once,* Met-on thought, looking across to Dan-te and noticing her nodding her head in acknowledgment. *Dan-te* Knows *it even better than I do. In fact, those words he told me just now, to "live and make sure nothing like this happens to her or anyone else ever again," I'm sure someone told him those very same words.*

Met-on was about to ask Virgil more when he suddenly noticed Dan-te's expression change as radiant pink fearful energy and scents began pouring from her.

"Quake!" she screamed, just as the entire city began shaking.

# Chapter 30

"Met-on, are you alright?"

Met-on coughed and picked himself up off the ground. The quake hit hard and fast. The surrounding building and walls were cracked open, but the real damage was above them. More pieces of the cavern's ceiling broke free and plummeted down onto the city, raining down like the Hy-muns' pods and doing as much damage. Turning around, he found that a good piece of the surrounding wall and ceiling now separated him from both Virgil and Dan-te.

*So that's why Virgil suddenly grabbed me and tossed me away,* Met-on realized, wondering why—during the quake—Virgil suddenly picked him up and threw him as far as he could from the rest of them. *You saw the wall falling and was trying to get me away.*

"I'm okay, Virgil. How about you and Dan-te?"

"We're both all right," Dan-te responded from behind Virgil. "But the two of us are now cut off from you by the debris."

"So, what do we do now?" Met-on asked.

Virgil tore off a piece of his suit before opening it up and digging into a pocket and pulling something out.

"Take these," Virgil instructed, reaching his hand through the debris and handing Met-on two pins. "That first pin, the one that looks like an orb over a cave, is a tracker that allows the other Hammers to find each other. I have one of their tracking devices, so I will be able to follow you. Keep going to Stella and get her out of here. Just make certain you also show her the other pin."

"What's so important about the other pin?"

"That pin is branded with my family's coat of arms. They are extremely rare, and only a few people have ever seen them. The first time I met Stella, she noticed me wearing it and a pendant with the same insignia, paying very close attention to the details on them. Show it to her. Tell Stella I'm coming right behind you, and to *not* trust the orange suited Hy-muns."

"I understand," Met-on replied, *Knowing* full well how dangerous the Hy-muns in the orange suits were.

"Let me just give the two of you one quick warning. The women of the Tribe of Shadows are trained to fight anyone who enters their rooms they don't recognize, so don't open any of the doors."

"Got it. Now, get going."

Met-on nodded to Virgil before running down a passage. Virgil, removing his sword from the suit, expecting to use it soon, began down another passage with Dan-te.

"Do you think Met-on will be okay?" Virgil asked, turning to Dan-te.

"He genuinely wants to help Stella and has realized his past mistakes. If I didn't *Know* we could trust him, I wouldn't have suggested we save him in the first place."

"I'm not worried about whether we can trust him. I'm worried if he'll be okay. He still has to face Stella again."

"Why don't we just get moving? That way we can meet up with him sooner rather than later and then make sure he'll be okay."

"Good idea," Virgil replied, racing down the passage and following the Hammer's tracker with Dan-te at his side, and also following Met-on's energies.

\*\*\*

"That was a magmatic quake," Ann exclaimed, fear rising throughout her body.

"Just try and stay calm, Ann," the Seat of Kindness encouraged, but he knew it was hard because he could feel the fear rising in him just as quickly.

*I don't understand what a "magmatic quake" is*, the Seat of Kindness fretted. *But I* Know *what it must mean.*

From the moment the quake swept through the city, the Seat of Kindness *Knew* that the magma would be here soon and that the opportunity to escape back to Rem was gone.

*Even if we could reach Rem, it would only be a temporary escape. As soon as the magma incinerates Nis, Rem will be next. The only chance any of us have for survival rests with contacting more terraships.*

# The Second Coming

"How can I stay calm?" Ann blurted out. "None of us are going to make it out of here alive. This is a volcano, my specialty, and I know we're all dead. It's just a matter of time now until everyone else realizes it as well."

Ann was panicking, and the Seat of Kindness did not blame her. It was taking all of his own self-control to keep from panicking, too. The Seat of Kindness *Knew*, especially after being a member of the Council, that even if one wanted to panic, it was never a good idea to do it in front of others. The rouge energy of panic, an energy that Ann was pulsating, was as infectious as any disease. If he started to panic, that *would* mean the end for them.

"Just try the radio again, Ann," the Seat of Kindness said, edging Ann back toward the radio. "It's not like it's going to hurt anyone now, is it?"

Ann shook her head and returned to the radio, broadcasting again on the open frequency.

"Please, is anyone out there? This is Ann Branley, formerly from Spectral Academy. Is anyone out there?"

Again, the silence was Ann's only response.

"You see, we're all going to—"

"Ann, Ann, are you there?"

Ann was cut off mid-sentence as the broadcast suddenly began blaring over the radio. Ann's expression and energy quickly changed, from panicked to joyous when she heard the familiar voice coming over the radio.

"Professor Heart! Yes, it is me," Ann cried, tears of joy rolling down her eyes. "The last time I saw you, we talked about my supervolcano theory before I left for the mining project. Are you down here? What are you doing?"

"Finally, the radio is working," Professor Heart yipped. "I'm glad to hear you're still alive, Ann. While down here, I met a member of the Remnant of the Tribe called the Tribesman. He told me he was trying and stop the Third Great Attempt's igniting. Since then, I've been trying to divert magma out of the Great Tunnel and get to Nis using my father's instructions and his ship, the Arc. So far, it seems to be working. But I was rushing it. I honestly don't know if all the vents I made will hold. I'm making my way to Nis now. Let's rendezvous at the entrance to the Great Tunnel. After meeting up, we'll head for Rem and try and save as many members of the Remnant of the Tribe as we can before the magma gets here. So, if anyone in Nis is looking to survive, have them meet up with me now."

"Understood, Professor, we'll be there."

Ann clicked off the radio, grabbed the Seat of Kindness's arm, and pulled him into a big hug.

"That was my teacher, Professor Heart. She's coming to the city right now in the Arc, a terraship her father built. We have a way home and a way to live!"

Ann's last comment brought a round of cheers from everyone in the group. Not one of them cared about the fact that they were just outside of Nis and could possibly be surrounded by either the warriors from Nis or Hammers of the Orange Light at any moment. All any of them cared about was that now there was hope, real physical hope that they could jump into and ride to safety.

"The Professor said she would meet us at the entrance of the Great Tunnel."

"Then we better make sure everyone is accounted for," a new voice called out from behind the crowd.

Everyone looked to see Ca-to returning with a group of women from the Remnant, the youngest possibly in her 30s and the eldest in her 50s. Looking around the group, Ann noticed that there was still no sign of Stella or Reye.

"Is that everyone, Ca-to?" The Seat of Kindness asked.

"Everyone except Reye and her friend," Ca-to replied. "Reye went searching on her own, I was about to go back for her now that I've brought this group back."

*Especially after I noticed that one Hy-mun wandering around Lust Atrophied in the orange suit,* Ca-to privately added to himself. He was sure the Seat of Kindness also knew he had a secondary reason for wanting to go back for Reye from the look in his eye and the white mental energy sparking around his head.

"Do that, Ca-to, find them both and bring them to the Great Tunnel's entrance where we will meet Ann's teacher, Professor Heart. We'll wait for you as long as we can."

"I'm on my way, Seat of Kindness," Ca-to responded, heading back into the city while the rest of them made their way toward the Great Tunnel, during which the Seat of Kindness noticed Ann examining the notes she took while talking on the radio, white mental energy surging from her brain as she stared intensely at them.

"What are those notes?" The Seat of Kindness asked.

"Volcanic calculations," Ann explained. "You heard Professor Heart. Before making her way down the Great Tunnel, she met the Tribesman. He told Professor Heart that he was on his way to the Keyblast Point to try and stop the Third Great Attempt from starting."

"Unfortunately, he didn't succeed," the Seat of Kindness mourned. He cast his eyes down for what he realized must have been the fate of the Tribesman once the explosion went off at the Keyblast Point.

"Agreed, but Professor Heart has also been working. On her way here, she dug multiple volcanic vents to attempt to diffuse the supervolcano and slow the magma. These are equations based on what she produced. I'm trying and find out if what she did was enough. Supervolcano theory is my specialty."

"And what do you think, did it slow the magma, will it diffuse the supervolcano?"

"It won't slow the magma enough so that it won't reach the city and cause the eruption here," Ann replied regrettably. "But as to whether or not it was enough to defuse the supervolcano, I just don't know. If I assume each vent worked, then the best chance I can give for its success is only 50 percent, and that's still a big 'if.' The only ones who could possibly tell if it's working now are the people on the surface."

***

"Antaeus Command Deck, this is Mr. Pot in communications, we've detected more strange seismic activity moving toward our location, can we get confirmation of that from the other ships? Please respond?"

Mr. Pot, the head of communications aboard the Antaeus, was in the radio room since the ship reached Nis. His job was to coordinate among the teams of Hammers throughout the city to ensure their operations ran smoothly. Yet as things stood, it did not seem like there were going to be any problems. The campaign was running smoothly, until now. The brief quake had made him review all the recent seismic data. Something was wrong, he could feel it.

"Communications, this is Antaeus Command Deck. Just continue with the operation and keep the channels clear for our brothers in the city. Don't concern yourselves with a quake, leave that to the people in command."

"Yes, sir," Mr. Pot replied, doubting whether Command was taking the quake as seriously as they should.

"Mr. Pot!"

Another member of the Antaeus's communications staff ran into the radio shack. He looked exhausted and frightened, like he had not only run from one end of the ship to the other, but he had also seen something terrifying in the process.

"The report from the seismologist department you asked for just came in. You won't believe it, but several *land-based* volcanoes have just erupted across Sand Break Border."

"What!" Mr. Pot screamed. He, like everyone else, knew that volcanoes only formed out in the Great Lagoon and the Seraph Sea. The only land-based volcanoes in the world were the ones found in the Red Dominion.

"It's true, we're getting reports about it over every open wavelength on the surface. Listen for yourself."

Mr. Pot clicked the radio to an open surface frequency, and sure enough, everyone was talking about the land-based volcanoes. Volcanologists everywhere were in an uproar about them and were pushing to get as close as they could to study them. The fire departments in the Green Dominion were also on high alert to make sure nothing threatened any of the food production abilities of the dominion. The Oasis Forces in the Yellow Dominion were also trying to keep people out of the volcanoes' way, making sure lava did not touch any of them.

"There's something else, sir."

"What else?" Mr. Pot asked the nervous crewman who handed him a report.

"The seismic activity we're tracking is heading toward Nis, and each volcano has erupted in its wake. The people in the seismologist department don't think it's a coincidence."

Neither did Mr. Pot.

"Contact all the ships and Hammers in the city," Mr. Pot instructed his staff. "Regardless of what Command says, I'm putting everyone on standby for evacuation. We either have to finish this job now or return to the surface."

*Before it's too late for any of us,* Mr. Pot privately added to himself.

# Chapter 31

"Antaeus Command Deck, this is Kai Aphas. What is the status of the campaign following the quake?"

Kai Aphas stood back up. The sudden quake had knocked him off his feet, but he was quick to recover once the shaking had stopped. Nis, however, did not look as fortunate. The quake had caused massive quantities of rock, stalactites, and debris to rain on it like incoming missiles, with the highest amount of damage near where each of the terraships drilled into the cavern. Clutching his radio, Kai Aphas awaited information.

"Communications with the surface is unclear," the radio officer replied. "We are getting reports of volcanoes appearing on land."

"No need to worry about that," Kai Aphas responded. "It's just a trick of the Tribe of Shadows. They are tempting Hy-muns on the surface to give false reports to try and trick us into leaving the city. What about the campaign? How is my grandson fighting? How soon until the sun spheres are activated?"

"No news on your grandson. I'm afraid, he is still missing in action."

"Not to worry," Kai Aphas said, more to himself than the radio officer. "He's my grandson, he can survive this city just like I did. What other news do you have?"

"Not good news, I'm afraid," the radio officer said, causing Kai Aphas's features to worsen. "Two of the Sun Spheres were destroyed by debris, it will be impossible to repair them."

"Not once we access the technology the Tribe of Shadows has been hoarding in Nis," Kai Aphas lied, knowing he had no way to repair the Sun Spheres if they were destroyed. "We'll be able to repair them with that. Until then, we just have to make do with the ones we have and fight harder to make sure every last demon is exterminated. Anything else?"

"During the quake, Virt Prince Lucan fell in combat."

Now Kai Aphas's blood ran cold.

*Lucan, he was my most loyal follower,* Kai Aphas thought, thinking of how he watched Lucan grow up admiring him like a second father and following every order he was ever given with a smile on his face.

*He was my son Alpha's best friend before he died and the best Hammer suited to watch over the rest of them if something happened to me before Sol could take my place.*

"Command Officer, connect me to every Hammer in Nis," Kai Aphas ordered.

"Yes, sir." A moment later, the radio officer came back over Kai Aphas's radio. "You're on, go ahead."

"My brother Hammers, hear me! I know you are all suffering from the effects of the quake just now. It has cost us two Sun Spheres and worse, our noble Virt Prince Lucan, a braver man than any I've ever known. He sacrificed his life fighting to make sure Tanas and his demons would be purged from Prism forever. You must not let his loss be in vain. Remember the sacrifice he has made for us. Carry on to ensure that no more noble souls like his are ever tempted and lost to Tanas and his demons again. Fight with everything you have, my brothers. The other Virt Princes and I will be joining you in combat soon. We will not let you fight alone. Complete the remaining Sun Spheres and activate them. If you hear a call to retreat, ignore it. It is just another of Tanas's temptations. Fight on for Virt Prince Lucan, for a Tanas-free future. Fight for the glory of the Great Master Ash Addiel!"

Kai Aphas clicked off his radio's transmitter. But he could clearly hear the cheers from hundreds of Hammers coming over the receiver. Each one of them was becoming inspired by Kai Aphas's words and resuming their fight, fighting harder than ever before. Standing at Tanas's window, Kai Aphas thought he would feel proud of himself, but instead, all he could feel and hear was his stepbrother Able's presence and voice.

*You have really become Tanas,* Able whispered, his voice filled with both pity and regret for everything his stepbrother once was and has done since they first entered Nis over forty years ago.

"Never," Kai Aphas screamed. "I am Kai Aphas, the leader of the Hammers of Orange Light. I have brought the light of the Nag-el into this dark world, and I am the one who will exterminate these monsters that plague it. I am the one who will ensure that it will be ready for when the Great Master finally returns to us, and he will be pleased!"

*You are the one who willingly brought a foreign and lethal substance into a world with no real defense against it to begin a campaign of extermination,* Able's voice responded. *You are the one who has degraded another sentient race into monsters merely because they look and act differently than you do. You are the only one who believes he is making the world fit for the Great Master Ash Addiel. You are the one who has killed and lied to conceal the truth and mask your own crimes and problems, creating every kind of contingency for whatever new issues emerge. You are the one who glorifies the death of your comrades and turns them into a rallying point to continue fighting. Everything you have done is precisely the same things that Tanas has done, only over a much shorter period. And you and your grandson will both die a death similar to his.*

"You are wrong Able," Kai Aphas raged, staring out over the city and wondering where Tanas was hiding. "Tanas is going to die at the hands of a Hymun. Maybe even my grandson's hands. Then we will both return to the surface along with the rest of the Hammers as heroes. And when we do die, it will be surrounded by our brothers and family before our spirits join the Nag-el in the heavens. That is not the way Tanas is going to die, you will see Able."

*Yes, we will see,* Able replied before finally going silent in Kai Aphas's head.

"He's finally quiet." Kai Aphas gratefully exhaled, returning to Tanas's window to look out over Nis. "Now, back to the business of destroying Tanas and these demons. My grandson is still out there, I know it, and I am certain he is hunting as many of these demons as he can."

***

*These females seem to only serve two purposes,* Sol thought as he hobbled his way through the circle. *Procreation and mutilation.*

Sol shuddered at the thought of needing to be mutilated just to procreate, but on the other hand, it made his task that much easier. Sol was in combat when the quake hit, and it could not have caught him at a worse time.

Sol stormed into a room. Out of bullets for his gun, he sprinted in to make a quick kill with his bare hands before the female member of the Tribe of Shadows could grab her weapon when the whole room started shaking. The quake knocked Sol to his feet, twisting a foot in the process, and popping the latches on his helmet. The female, however, was not as severely affected by the quake. With Sol at her feet, she quickly grabbed a club from her bedside and brought it down on his head in an attempt to kill him. Luckily, he pulled his head out of the helmet before it was crushed by the female's strike, giving him the opening to make a quick and lethal counterstrike. But after both the quake and fight, Sol realized he would not be able to fight again anytime soon.

*Curse these demons again,* Sol thought, testing his foot as he made his way back into the circle. *I can walk and jog easily enough, but that's it until this foot heals. Now, what do I do?*

Sol's thoughts paused momentarily by the sight of something ash-grey and smelly moving past him through the circle's halls.

*What was that?* Sol wondered, attempting to follow the strange creature. Keeping far enough away from it so he would not be noticed, but close enough so he could still follow it and mark his way, he managed to get a better view of the creature. He was slightly puzzled by what he saw.

*It's not a regular demon, that's for sure; this one has grey skin where the others I fought had blue. This one also has a black horn coronet around its head, and it stinks of rot and excrement. Could this be some kind of demon Virt Prince?*

The idea that this demon could be some kind of Tribe of Shadows royalty excited him.

*There is only one reason why a royal demon would be in a place like this. He's going to Tanas!*

Sol, as well as every other Hammer of the Orange Light, knew what Tanas looked like. Even without seeing the projection of him over the city after they landed, Sol's grandfather had created plenty of pictures from memory of what Tanas looked like. So, Sol knew the grey demon was not Tanas. But since it was not fighting like the other blue demons, and seemed to be wearing a coronet, he figured it could at least be a form of royalty. And in this city, there was no one more royal than Tanas.

# Chapter 32

*Take the third left and then the fifth right after that...*

Met-on did not need to mentally say the directions to Stella's room in his mind. Between the numerous times he had gone there, and the fact that Stella's own energy radiated differently than any of the other occupants in Lust Atrophied, Met-on *Knew* he could find his way there anytime he wanted. But the running commentary helped him to take his mind off of what he would say once he reached her.

"All right," Met-on proclaimed, prepping himself for when he would face Stella again. "There's the entrance to the Jac-ob Way."

The entrance to the Jac-ob Way, a small guard station built into one of the circle's buildings, led to a staircase going down to the Way. From it, Met-on could smell a familiar odor rising up from beneath the city, the smell of death.

"With all the fighting going on throughout the Circles, who knows how many bodies have filled the Jac-ob Way. I'll bet the guards abandoned their posts immediately after Tanas called everyone to the Grand Coliseum—probably leaving every booby trap turned on before they left. Now, from here, I take three more lefts. After the third left is the long alleyway leading down to where I have to go."

Met-on opened his hand. Inside were the two pins that Virgil gave him. Both Virgil's and his Teacher's voices now rang in his ears.

*"If she is alive, what do you think you should do?"* Met-on's teacher had asked him, fully aware that Met-on already knew the answer. It was the same thing that Virgil told him.

*"What you're doing right now,"* Virgil said. *"You're getting us to Stella so we can get her out of here. If you want to do more, then live and make sure nothing like this happens to her or anyone else ever again."*

"Here I come, Stella," Met-on announced. Taking the first left, he made his final sprint toward Stella's room, while behind him, a solitary Hy-mun followed a safe distance away.

***

"What is going on out there?" Stella wondered, slamming at the door with her cord and body, trying to force it open and finally escape from Lust Atrophied.

Stella was frantic since Tanas's first announcement. At first, she was sure one of the guards was going to open the door and kill her. Thankfully, no one did. Instead, the proclamation that Nis was invaded by Hy-muns stirred up numerous thoughts and emotions within her.

*Hy-muns are here, I'm saved!* Stella thought exuberantly, but quickly changed her mind when she remembered other vital facts. *Wait, do the Hy-muns even know that I'm here? As far as the surface of Prism is concerned, I must have died in the mining attack. And if they do know I'm alive, what will they do to me once they find me? I'm carrying a child fathered by one of this city's inhabitants.*

Her child brought even more thoughts colliding together into a chaotic mess in her head.

*Met-on told me how the Tribe of Shadows always feared there would be a Second Coming. Something to finish what Tanas and the Nag-els began. If he died in the Grand Coliseum...*

Stella let that point hang in her head for a moment. She knew she would have killed Met-on herself if she had the chance because of everything he had done to her. Still, he was the father of her child and the closest thing she had to an ally in Nis. To say that their relationship was weird would have been an understatement.

*I'll wager dying in the Grand Coliseum would have been the highest point in Met-on's life*, Stella figured. *But even if I reach the Hy-muns and get out of this city, how free am I? I still can't safely return to the surface as long as I'm carrying this child. Will any of us even survive there? And if I could go to the surface, who would take me in?*

Stella's mood did not improve after the quake. Instinctively, once it started, Stella tried to brace herself in the door despite the guard's possible presence. The heat from the magma vents also intensified as a few sputters of it popped up to the vent, melting it away.

"Forget guards," Stella barked, not caring anymore if someone heard her or not. "Forget other Hy-muns or the surface. This city is going to explode, isn't it? Someone, anyone, get me out of here!"

Since then, Stella had been wrapping and rewrapping her cord up and down her arms and slamming it at the door, trying to force it open. When that did not work, she tried pacing the room, making sure to keep clear of the magma vents in case more magma sputtered out, to try and take her mind off her situation. The longer nothing happened, the more scared and crazier she became, and the closer it seemed that a time bomb under her feet was going to explode.

"Something needs to happen, something just needs to happen," Stella rambled until she was distracted by a foul odor coming from the door.

"What is that?" she wondered as the smell came closer. "Whatever it is, it means something is coming toward the room, and that means it's my chance to get out of here."

Stella retook her position behind the door, waiting, ready to leap out and attack whoever might walk through the door. "One way or the other, something is finally going to happen."

***

*Stella's scared,* Met-on realized as he approached her door. *In fact, she's terrified.*

Despite the stench of excrement coming from him, the smell of fear coming from Stella was even greater, quickly filling up her room and seeping into the hallway. But much worse than the aroma was the energy radiating from the edges of the door, an energy that only grew brighter as Met-on opened the deadbolt holding the door in place.

*Stella's been radiating pink fear, flaxen yellow negativity, and so much horrible red energies that it's flooding the room. With all the fighting between the warriors and the Hy-muns going on throughout the city, the quakes, and no means of finding out what's going on around her, not to mention the other feelings Virgil said she must be feeling, she's ready to snap. I have to get her out of here.*

"Stella," Met-on called as he pushed opened the door and entered the room, suddenly finding himself choking as a knotted cord looped around his neck.

***

Stella's eyes lit up as she found her cord wrapped around a very familiar figure.

"Met-on," Stella gasped, surprised that he was here. "Perfect!"

All the rage, shame, and sadness she had been burying since she first woke up in Nis flooded to the surface in one burst of vengeful fury. And she was enjoying every second of it.

"What you did to me!" Stella muttered as her rage boiled over. "What you did to me!"

"Stella," Met-on struggled to say, twisting his head just enough to meet her eyes, feeling the depths of her emotions in that one connection.

*Virgil was right,* Met-on thought, his body becoming weaker as Stella continued to choke him. Met-on realized he could have broken Stella's grip with ease, but after looking into her eyes, he did not want to. Even Virgil's advice to "keep living" faded from his mind. He *Knew* and understood the full measure of hurt and shame he had caused Stella.

*You* do *hate me enough to kill me, and I deserve it,* Met-on despaired. He saw the full measure of Stella's various energies—her horrible red, flaxen yellow negativity, pink fear, and tan sandy shame—glowing vibrantly in her eyes.

*What I did to you had nothing to do with anything you, the Hy-muns, or the Beings of Light, did to me, or the Tribe of Shadows,* Met-on lamented. *All I ever did was blindly follow my people's rules and customs regardless of how someone else might see them, and you were hurt because of that. If my life can give you back even a piece of what I've taken from you, then kill me, my life is yours.*

Stella loosened her rope a little, not out of mercy, sympathy, or pity, but because she was surprised. Met-on was crying, genuinely crying as his face twisted into a scene of regret and acceptance.

*Is he actually* sorry? Stella thought in shock. *Well, it's far too late for that.*

Stella did not know if Met-on could tell what she was thinking or not, but he raised his arm toward the open door next to them, uttering one sentence through the loosened cord.

"Escape, help, coming."

Met-on opened his hand and let the two pins he was carrying fell to the ground. The sight of both of them quickly made Stella forget where she was and what she was doing—releasing Met-on, who collapsed to the ground panting for breath. Dropping to her knees, she picked up the pins and examined them. One was a pin just like the one Sol had given her and every other member of the mining project before they made their descent into the Demp Caverns. The other was a platinum pin with an indigo serpent forming an ouroboros around an indigo ziggurat, with the serpent's head and tail resting where the top of the ziggurat would be. Stella gently turned the pin over, almost afraid that it might disappear in her hand, and looked at its flip side, seeing the same emblem on the other side of it.

"Where did you get these?" Stella whispered, not able to believe her eyes as a vivid encounter from her past suddenly flashed into her mind.

*** 

"Trust me, Stella," Reye said, walking Stella into the restaurant. "This guy is as big into religion as you are, and a great listener, I'm sure you'll like him. There he is over there, flipping that coin in his hand. Hey, Worm!"

The man Reye identified as Worm turned around, a pin Stella had seen once before attached to his shirt glowing in the restaurant's light. The sight of it and the man quickly shocked her. Pulling her hair around her, she shrank as she became self-conscious of her surroundings.

*What's* he *doing here?* Stella wondered, not understanding why the son of a Virt Prince would be on the Platinum Throne. Why had Reye called him Worm, and why was he acting natural about it?

"Hi, how are you doing?" Worm asked.

"Great," Stella squeaked. She had hoped she would never see this Hymun again for the rest of her life. Now, she realized she was going to see him across Spectral Academy for as long as they were students together. It was quickly scaring her.

*** 

*That was one date I'll never forget,* Stella whiffed. *It was how I was re-introduced to Virgil Virt Indigo-Castitas, now going by the nickname Worm. The same person who kept me from getting in trouble in the Indigo Dominion. The same person I continue to be nervous around every time I saw him because I expected he would use that secret against me in some way. Now, deep underground, I'm holding Virgil's pin, given to me by the last person I would expect to have it.*

"Met-on?" Stella asked again, the tone in her voice taking on a commanding note. "Where did you get these?"

Met-on stared at Stella, still gasping for breath after she tried to kill him. Met-on *Knew* he now *Knew* the *real* Stella. The Stella he had *Known* before had always kept parts of herself hidden from him, which made it hard for him to completely *Know* her. But now, she was not hiding anything. Her explosion of rage brought all of her buried pains, hurts, sorrows, and fears to the surface, allowing Met-on to *Know* them all.

"Stella…" Met-on began, *Knowing* full well the kind of pain she had endured because of him, but stopping mid-sentence as he felt something else approaching, fast.

"Move!"

# Chapter 33

"That quake was even worse than the last one," Virgil said to himself as he looked around to survey the damage after the quake suddenly hit them. Streets were cracking open as the magma beneath them bubbled even closer to the surface. Walls throughout the city were also beginning to collapse in on themselves, crushing rooms, and altering the entire labyrinthine structure of the circle.

"I hope Met-on and Stella made it through in one piece."

"Me too," Dan-te agreed, her head now visible. After the quake, she chose to throw away her helmet, deciding that whatever happened next, she did not want to be hiding behind it anymore. "I've already lost my brother here, I don't want to lose anyone else."

"Agreed, but first, we have to *find* Met-on and Stella. Then we can see about getting out of here alive."

Virgil looked at the tracking device to check Met-on's position, but Dan-te quickly placed her hand on it and made him lower it.

"Don't even bother with that anymore," Dan-te explained. "The quake opened up a new path for us. I can get us there faster now. But we need to hurry, something's happened to Met-on; he's hurt—badly. There's also something else."

"What else?"

"I can feel two sharp energies nearing Met-on. One of them has dulled, but the other is still sharp and approaching Met-on quickly. I've also felt the sharper energy before, lingering in front of rooms with dead bodies in them. Whoever is generating that sharp energy is dangerous."

"Then lead the way," Virgil encouraged. He trusted Dan-te's abilities without question. If she said something was wrong, that someone dangerous was approaching Met-on, that was good enough for him.

*** 

Met-on screamed just as the quake started.

Stella, however, was not in the mood to move anywhere. She had just tried and failed to kill Met-on, the half-blood member of the Tribe of Shadows who had spent every chance he could get trying to impregnate her as part of a mission he received for a branding. She failed when she discovered he was carrying one of Sol's pins, and the pin Virgil was wearing where she met him again at Spectral Academy. Seeing Virgil's pin awakened every nervous feeling she used to have whenever she was around him. All Stella could do was release Met-on and ask him how he got his hands on the pin, and she was not going to do anything until she had an answer.

*All the hateful red energy she was emitting has given way to white mental energy,* Met-on thought to himself. He *Knew* she wasn't going to be moved until she was given an answer. *I've seen this before on my teacher whenever he began reminiscing. He would generate white mental energy and then sink into the memories of his past. But this episode is far worse than anything my teacher ever produced.*

*Stella will wait for an answer until the whole city collapses down on her head,* Met-on realized as cracks developed in the walls surrounding her and in the floor around the magma vents as the entire room began to shake.

"Stella, you have to move now!"

"No!" Stella screamed. "I don't have to do anything for you. Do you understand, anything!"

What occurred next seemed to happen in slow motion. Met-on ran to Stella as the walls around her began to cave in on themselves. Picking her up, Met-on threw her clear of the rubble as the wall and ceiling collapsed on him. In that instant, their eyes met one last time, and Stella could see the regret and need to apologize for what he had done to her etched into his eyes. They seemed open for the first time. He not only understood that what he did to her was wrong by Hy-mun standards, but he also desperately desired to make up for it.

"Met-on," Stella coughed as she looked through the clearing dust and rubble, but there was no sign of him. The corner wall and ceiling had collapsed in on itself, giving Stella her first view of Nis since she arrived in Lust Atrophied.

"Where are you?" Stella coughed again, standing up and making her way to the pile of debris. She didn't know how much was there, but she knew Met-on was buried under it.

*Wait, why am I even worried?* Stella asked herself, stopping mid-step. *I know he's stronger than me, he should be fine under that mess, and after everything he did to me, why am I even concerned about him? Just because he saved me, because he realized he was wrong, because he wanted to make up for it. There is no making up for it; serves him right.*

Stella started walking away from where Met-on was buried toward the newly made exit when a new figure began making its way through the dust and debris and into Stella's room.

"Met-on," Stella whispered, fearful he was not buried after all, but soon realized she was wrong as the figure came through the dust and into view. The person wore an orange Hy-mun containment suit, the kind that Hy-muns used when operating in dangerous, diseased, or contaminated areas and did not want to expose themselves to the danger. But the wearer of this suit was not wearing a helmet, giving her a clear view of the wearer's face. He was the first Hy-mun Stella had seen since the mining project, and more importantly, he was a very familiar one.

"Sol," Stella squeaked, hardly believing that he was standing right in front of her. In what seemed like a heartbeat, all of Stella's feelings for Sol—feelings that seemed like part of a past life—rekindled themselves. Stella looked at the same cool demeanor, stoic expression, and calm eyes that were able to take anything thrown at them and not even blink, remembering what she felt about him.

"You're here, you're really here," Stella cried as she staggered toward Sol and reached out to grasp him.

*It's time to finally end the sun and star dance, Reye,* Stella thought to herself. She was ready to embrace Sol, thank him for coming to get her, and finally tell him everything she had ever held back from him, regardless of his response. But just as Stella was about to embrace him, Sol backhanded her to the ground.

# Chapter 34

"If that quake is any indication, we don't have much time left," Reye fretted to herself as she moved through the dust. "Where are you?"

Reye had been following the trail left by the mysterious Hy-mun until the second quake hit. The new one had cracked open pathways and collapsed several of the buildings around her, forcing Reye off the chalk trail. But once the dust started to clear, she found herself walking through a vacant building, spotting Stella on the other side.

"Stella, you are alive," Reye coughed through the dust, far happier than she sounded.

Ever since the Remnant's Reconciliation Ritual, Reye knew she never once tried to find out if Stella—her best friend—was still alive after escaping from the Grand Coliseum. Instead, she had focused only on her revenge. It was a choice that had been haunting her ever since she accepted that she made it. Now, Reye knew Stella was alive, she had a second chance to save her and bring her home. And as she slowly walked through the building to reach Stella, she found she would not be the only one to get to her as another familiar face joined them.

*Sol! You came back.* Reye's happiness was doubling. The last time Reye had seen Sol was when he used a strange device during the attack on the mining camp to paralyze and burn the warriors from the Tribe of Shadows. Afterward, he escaped to the surface using the one man return rocket. Seeing Sol again, Reye's mind quickly came to life—in a way that it had not since leaving Spectral

Academy. She was trying to figure out what he must have been doing since the attack.

*Sol went back to the surface for help,* Reye thought, trying to figure out his actions. *He went back to alert other Hy-muns about the Tribe of Shadows. The Hy-muns attacking the city right now must be here because of him. Sol came back to rescue us.*

Reye watched Stella slowly rise up to meet him. She was dressed in a slip of clothing similar to what the other females in Lust Atrophied wore. Her hair was ragged and disheveled, and her body thinned and moving slowly. But there was also a determination Reye had never seen on Stella's face before. The expression on Stella's face was one of mixed wonder and excitement. Reye knew Stella did not know why Sol was there, nor did she care. She was just glad that he was here, and by the way she was approaching him, arms outstretched, Reye guessed what Stella was finally going to do.

*Do it, Stella,* Reye mentally encouraged her as she slowly moved through the dust to join them. *Tell Sol how you've always felt about him, we're all alone, stuck in an underground city with the possibility of death all around us. Now couldn't be a better time. After that, I'll join you, and the three of us will have the happiest reunion imaginable. I can tell Sol about the Remnant and how they mean us and the surface no harm. He can pass that information on to his comrades, and then we can get Ann and get ourselves back to the surface.*

But all Reye's fantasies suddenly froze as stiff as she did as understanding left her as the situation changed once Sol backhanded Stella to the ground, and he started shouting insults immediately afterward.

\*\*\*

"Don't touch me, filth!" Sol screamed, his voice dripping with venom. "I honestly didn't think any of you arrogant fools were still alive after the Tribe of Shadows' attack."

"Wait, you already *knew* about the Tribe of Shadows?" Stella gasped, picking herself back off the ground, instinctively shielding her belly, and recovering her wits as quickly.

If there was one thing Stella's experiences in Nis had taught her, it was adaptability, finding herself in Lust Atrophied, learning that it was not a dream, and doing whatever was needed to survive and gain information. They had all proven to be excellent lessons in adapting to changing situations. She was not going to let Sol's revelation get to her *that* much. She had already been through worse.

"Of course I knew," Sol shouted, his eyes focusing on Stella like he was painting a target. "Why did you think I had a prototype Sun Sphere launcher with me? I was hoping Tanas's demons, the Tribe of Shadows, would show up. You, the mining crew in the Demp Caverns, all of those other idiots from Spectral Academy, and especially that silly and warped girl Reye and her brother from the Orange Dominion. All of you were chosen by us, the Hammers of the Orange Light, to be in the Demp Caverns for one reason. You were to have the noble honor of being bait for the Tribe of Shadows so we could conduct our prototype Sun Sphere test, to see if it was going to be as effective as we thought. We expected the Tribe of Shadows would take your corpses, and the tracking pins I gave you right back to this city so we could find it. Then we could attack it and wipe Tanas, his Tribe of Shadows, and everything else beneath the surface of Prism out of existence. I honestly didn't think they would keep any of you *alive*."

Now, Stella was rattled.

"The Demp Cavern Mining Project," Stella gasped. "The project Reye—a silly and warped girl—Raymond, myself, close to a thousand other students, and all the miners. We were all chosen just so we could be bait for the Tribe of Shadows and sacrificed in a *weapon test*. You hoped our bodies, or more precisely your pins, could then be used to find this city. And you call it a 'noble honor'?"

Sol did not show a single sign of remorse for the lives lost in the attack. He called their deaths a "noble honor," yet Stella could not remember Sol *doing* anything "noble" during the attack. Now, hearing him preach how he and his allies were going to wipe "everything else beneath the surface of Prism out of existence" gave her a horrible feeling about what was next.

Reye's feelings were even worse. *Sol had always been stoic and tight-lipped*, Reye remembered. *He kept his own feelings hidden and focused on his schoolwork—despite the constant heckling—like a model student, hearing him talk as much as he was now is a rare thing in itself. But listening to him, his true feelings, the mining project's secret.* The revelation was shocking her to her core.

*I don't understand*, Reye whiffed, transfixed by Sol's declaration. *This isn't the way it's supposed to happen, I don't understand. The project was a weapon test, we had the* "noble honor" *of being the bait for the Tribe of Shadows. The workers at the site, the other students from Spectral Academy, my twin brother, all chosen so you could sacrifice them in a* test!

Reye remembered the Reconciliation Ritual. The Phantom Raymond had told Reye, "At this point, maybe you should think I was merely killed by another Hy-mun." Those words were now taking on a new meaning for her.

*I always thought that it was just bad luck that the Tribe of Shadows attacked the mining project. But you knew, "the powers that be" knew that they were going to be there the whole time. We were chosen, and then sacrificed, just so you could lure the Tribe of Shadows out to test your weapon, smile at its success before running away, and you call it a* "noble honor!"

Reye still remembered sitting in Zirconium Auditorium when Professor Heart read her name, confirming that she was chosen to take part in the Demp Cavern Mining Project. She remembered how overjoyed she felt. Later hearing from Raymond she was so enraptured, she could barely hear or acknowledge anything else. She believed that despite all the odds, she was one of the chosen students for the project. But now, learning that she, Raymond, Stella, and everyone else was selected just so they could be used as bait for the Tribe of Shadows was breaking her all over again.

*I can still hear the squeals from the other students as each one of them was killed in the darkness,* Reye remembered. *The fear of knowing that any moment I was going to die. The hope I felt when the cavern was suddenly illuminated by the orb of light that not only revealed the Tribe of Shadows but also burned them as well. Watching as you smiled joyfully over the effect the light seemed to be having on them before leaving on the one-man return rocket. And then sinking into despair and madness when Raymond was killed when a warrior from the Tribe of Shadows took out his leg and crushed his head like an egg. And yet you, and your superiors, wanted that to happen!*

Reye reached to her chest, attempting to grab something she could throw, and remembering she dropped it during her failed attack on Tanas.

*Those pins, you gave them to us expecting the Tribe of Shadows would take them alongside our bodies back to Nis so they could lead you here. Myself becoming a gladiator, Stella being stuck here, my rampage through Nis, all the death and destruction from the mining project onward to the failed attack on Tanas, all of it, part of a Hy-mun plot just to lead your forces to Nis. What have I been doing?*

Reye dropped to her knees in shock. The Remnant's Reconciliation Ritual had allowed her to come to terms with both herself and her mad and revenge-driven actions throughout Nis. But one thing she never expected was to learn that, from the beginning, it was all part of a Hy-mun scheme to find and destroy the city of Nis. Even worse, as someone who carried one of Sol's tracking pins right to Tanas's front door, she realized she was doing precisely what Sol's superiors wanted since long before the project even started.

"A *noble honor*!" Stella's scream brought Reye back to her senses. Stella, standing back up to face Sol again, shook not only from Sol's revelation but from pure anger and rage.

"All the workers in the Demp Caverns, the other students who knew nothing about what was happening to them. You used us all as bait, watched as they were killed before you could run back to the surface, and you call it a *noble honor*! Do you have any idea what they must have felt during the attack, not knowing who it was that was attacking them? Do you have any idea what *my life*

162

has been like since the attack, and you dare to call me filth? *You're* the one who's filth, you, and every one of your comrades."

Sol slapped Stella again, harder than the first time, causing her to roll past him toward the collapsed wall and ceiling where Met-on was buried. Stella, however, never broke Sol's eye contact. Using one hand, she protected herself from the fall, and the other to protect the child that she was carrying. Yet she never stopped glaring at him. Her eyes burned with rage and betrayal. In that short instant, all the feelings she ever held for Sol vanished, replaced by the anger she had been bottling up since her first encounter with Met-on, turning it toward Sol and his allies. The ones who *chose* her for the project, turned her into bait for the Tribe of Shadows, the *real reason* for everything that had happened to her since the mining project was attacked.

"Don't you dare call me and my brothers filth!" Sol screamed, drawing a sword from behind his back and taking his first steps toward where Stella sat in the rubble. "The Hammers of the Orange Light are the ones who have worked to smash everything acting against the Great Master Ash Addiel since before the Great Rainbow War. It is because of us that heresies have never taken hold in the Seven Dominions. It is because of us that silly fools on the surface like you and those crazy Orange Dominion siblings could live lives ignorant of the demons beneath their feet. And it is because of us that we will wipe this filth out of existence once and for all."

*The Hammers of the Orange Light,* Reye thought, a memory stirring within her. *That was one of the extremist groups Worm was researching the day I was chosen for the mining project. And if my own actions have taught me anything, it's that extremism is never a good thing.*

"Filth is anyone who acts against what is right by the Great Master Ash Addiel," Sol continued. "Anyone who touches it will be just as defiled. Don't think I haven't seen other demonic women in this city dressed in the same manner as you are right now, nor have I missed the way you're protecting your stomach. You've been taken by them, you are no better than one of them; you're carrying one of these demons within you!"

*What?* Reye whiffed, wondering if Sol was telling the truth. *It can't be, Stella can't be* pregnant. *Even if she was taken, we can't interbreed with the members of the Tribe of Shadows, can we?*

Yet Stella never broke her gaze.

"Yes, I have been taken, and I am pregnant, and why did that happen?" Stella asked, challenging Sol through her eyes. "Was it because of anything I did? No, it was because my own people decided to turn me into bait for their own purposes."

Stella felt far less ashamed about it than she thought she would as she continued to slam Sol.

"The father of this child isn't even a full member of the Tribe of Shadows. But he's no demon. In fact, right now, I think he's a saint compared to you. Whatever he did to me, and no matter how angry I am about it, I can at least understand a little bit about why he did it. It was part of how their civilization redeveloped after it was all but destroyed ages ago by the Nag-el and then rebuilt under Tanas's influence."

"The Nag-el create civilizations! None of them are capable of destroying one." Sol yelled, almost imitating one of his grandfather's speeches.

"And yet Tanas himself is a Nag-el," Stella countered.

"Heresy! You are worse than filth, you have become a demon yourself," Sol said shakily, hearing Stella proclaim that she was pregnant by one of the creatures in Nis, calling one of them better than him—a Hy-mun, a member of the race created by Ash Addiel, listening to her call the Nag-el destroyers, and that Tanas was also a Nag-el. It was precisely the kind of heretical nonsense Sol had been warned about by his grandfather since he was a child.

"Demon, you will not tempt me into following your example. You cannot fool me into thinking I can trust you over my fellow Hy-muns. What peace can exist between your kind and mine, between those who walk in Ash Addiel's brilliance and those who can't? None!"

Sol gripped his sword with both hands and raised it over his head like an executioner ready to cut off a criminal's head. Stella, however, refused to move, at peace, for speaking her mind and refusing to act the way she knew Sol wanted her to.

*I'm sorry,* she internally spoke to her child. *I not giving him the satisfaction of running, turning my back on him, giving him the pleasure of hunting us down, just because he decided we needed to be killed for the good of the Hy-mun race, regardless if we're Hy-mun or not. It's precisely what he wants. If he's going to kill us, I want him to look me in the eyes as he does it. We will not be bait, or a pawn, for "the powers that be," that was why I tried leaving home in the first place. Nor will we be just a couple of nameless "demons," we will be a mother and child that* will *be remembered by him every day for the rest of his life.*

Stella felt a twitch inside her, the first feeling she ever received from her child and was suddenly filled with both courage and hope. In that one twitch, she could feel her child acknowledging her decision, and telling her, "I'm proud of you, and it's not over yet." Elsewhere, Reye was still masked in the opposite building and frozen in place, seemingly incapable of moving closer to Stella and Sol.

# The Second Coming

*Move,* Reye pleaded with herself. *Move! Why can't I move? Stella is right there, and about to be killed by the person she used to have a crush on. Why can't I move?*

"Die demon, for the glory of the Great Master Ash Addiel, and the Hammers of the Orange Light!" Sol cheered as he brought his sword down in a final killing strike. Only the blade never reached Stella. Another sword stopped Sol's mid-stride in an earsplitting crash of metal against metal as another Hymun suddenly appeared between them.

"You talk too much," Virgil exclaimed, his own eyes—even fiercer than Stella's—focused directly on Sol.

# Chapter 35

"Worm!" Sol and Stella barked, neither one expecting Worm's sudden appearance.

The whole scene looked so cliché it could have come right out of a movie Reye and Stella were watching back on the Platinum Throne, complete with the shocked and mind-numbing expressions on Sol, Stella, and Reye's faces.

"Worm," Reye squeaked, still watching the events unfold before her. "What are you doing here? You're not also one of these Hammers, are you?"

Reye remembered how Virgil—known to her as Worm—was researching extremist groups before she left for the Demp Caverns. She also knew that Worm was a very secretive individual when it came to his past, a past she never bothered asking about. But now, after seeing him rush past her with another figure by his side, dressed in the same suits as the Hammers, and suddenly saving Stella's life, she realized she should have.

*Worm can't be one of these Hammers,* Reye wondered as she stared at him. *He just saved Stella, that has to mean something.*

Yet Reye had already realized that she did not know the people around her—including herself—quite as well as she thought she did.

"Worm," Stella whispered in shock, opening the hand that still carried the pin Met-on had brought to her. "You did come."

"Are you okay, Stella?" Virgil asked, never taking his burning eyes off Sol.

"Yes, I'm alright," Stella replied, feeling infinitely better and more alive than she thought possible.

Stella knew from the moment she saw the ouroboros pin, it could only mean a few things. One of the invading Hy-muns had one that looked just like Virgil's and dropped it, allowing Met-on to pick up. Or Virgil himself came to Nis and either lost it or gave it to Met-on; the latter option turning out to be correct.

"Worm, what are you doing here? You're not a…" Sol stopped talking as his gaze shifted toward Virgil's sword. "That sword, a cured single edge made from semi-transparent metal, capped with a unicorn's head on the pommel, *you*!"

Virgil's reaction was instantaneous. The moment Sol recognized Virgil's sword, Virgil threw all his weight onto the blade, forcing Sol away from Stella and back to the corner of the room where they started to fight.

"You have no idea how much and how long I waited to do *this*," Virgil hissed, sounding angrier than Stella or Reye had ever thought he could possibly become as he clashed with Sol.

"Not only is this infernal city a nest of demons," Sol spit between sword swings. "It's also a magnet for heretics as well. Who knew you, the lone survivor of the AAM, would be found here? If I had known you were the masked heretic Uni sooner, I would have killed you myself back at Spectral Academy. Filth like you deserves to die."

"*No one* deserves to die," Virgil shouted in reply as he parried and responded to Sol's sword attacks. "Not Stella, the citizens of the Underworld, or my friends in the AAM. None of them were heretics. All they wanted to do was travel into space and learn. But I'm guessing a hypocritical bigot like you, who defines people as either filth or Hy-mun, can't understand that."

"Space is the realm of Ash Addiel and the Nag-el, heretic," Sol replied. "You and the rest of your heretical brethren, building that ship in the Violet Dominion's Dawn Palace two years ago, deserved death. My father and I were personally there to make sure it succeeded. He died, ensuring that your kind was wiped out and that the world thought it was an industrial accident. Knowing he failed, and left one survivor, is a blight on his efforts, one I plan to erase."

Sol and Virgil continued fighting, neither one gaining a clear advantage over the other as Sol tried to force his way back into the room, and Virgil tried to keep him out of it. Stella continued to watch, transfixed by their fight until a hand touched her shoulder, causing her to turn around and see that another newcomer had joined them.

"You must be Stella," the newcomer said. "My name is Dan-te. Met-on told us about you. He said he wanted to get you out of Nis and back to the surface."

Stella looked at the newcomer who called herself Dan-te. She could have been Met-on's elder sister or cousin on his mother's side.

*She must be a member of the Remnant*, Stella realized. *She has a horn like Met-on's, but it's silver and gold instead of black. She also has chalk-white skin and hair, and eyes that looked like they're made out of pure silver. Wait, did she say they're here because of Met-on?*

"Met-on told you about me?" Stella asked, not even sure she heard Dan-te correctly. "You're saying he wanted to get me out of the city and back to the surface. Don't make me laugh, you don't know what Met-on has done to me. All with a smile on his face, no less. There's no way I can possibly return to the surface. I'm actually relieved he was crushed under that debris, it saved me the trouble of doing it myself."

The look in Dan-te's eyes changed from concern to pity. Stella found herself quickly shutting up as she turned her head to avoid Dan-te's pitying and somewhat prying gaze.

"You're wrong," Dan-te replied, her voice softer than Stella expected. "I *Know* exactly what he did to you and what he gave you. Virgil and I heard you and Sol as we were running over here."

"You did?" Stella asked.

"Yes," Dan-te replied with a nod. "Met-on also told us exactly what he did to you, and I would be lying if I said Virgil wasn't fighting against himself to keep from lashing out at Met-on when he heard it."

"Yet, I wouldn't judge Met-on too harshly," Dan-te continued, bringing Stella's focus back onto her. "You can't judge someone that easily. Everything that Met-on did to you—regardless of how disagreeable it was—has long been a part of the Tribe of Shadows' way of life. It would have been as natural for Met-on to behave the way he did as it would have been for you to act as naturally with someone close to you by your own laws and standards. But I can tell you this. When we met Met-on, after being betrayed and disillusioned by Tanas, and learning some of the differences between his culture and yours, he was genuinely sorry and filled with regret."

"I can't see how he could regret anything," Stella spit. But inside, she knew Dan-te was not lying. Dan-te's words reawakened the last few moments she had with Met-on before the rubble collapsed on him. She was sure that there was regret and apology in his eyes when she had him by the throat, almost like he was telling her he was sorry and that he deserved to be killed for his actions. Stella had brushed it off at the time to her imagination, but hearing Dan-te talk about Met-on's feelings of regret brought the image back.

"And if you do still have doubts, why don't you ask Met-on yourself?"

# The Second Coming

"Met-on is alive?" Stella asked, surprised that anyone could have survived being crushed by the collapsing wall.

"Barely," Dan-te answered, turning her head to the pile of debris. "I can still see his silver life energy under the rubble, but it's weak."

"Don't tell me you are going to dig him out?" Stella asked.

"I wanted to let you decide that," Dan-te replied, causing Stella to blink in shock. "I *Know* how angry Virgil was at Met-on for the things he did to you. I also *Know* how angry you are right now. I can see the same horrible red energy of anger boiling off you that I can see simmering off Virgil right now. You are also producing the same harsh smells of anger. So, if you want to save him, it has to be your choice. I'll help you dig him out, but if you want to leave him, we'll leave him, it's your choice."

Stella looked at the rubble. Underneath was a member of the Tribe of Shadows—little more than a teenager by Hy-mun standards—who had frequently drugged, Joined with her, and eventually impregnated her. And he did it all with an innocent smile on his face, utterly unaware of the wrong that he was doing.

*There probably isn't a Hy-mun alive that would blame me for leaving him,* Stella thought to herself as she looked at the rubble. *Most would say I am in the right to abandon him, so why am I hesitating!*

Stella knew she could walk away, that she *wanted* to walk away, but every time she tried, Met-on's last seconds replayed in her mind. She could see the look in his eyes as she strangled him, begging for an apology, and the fear for her life when he pulled her away from the collapsing rubble.

*Just walk away, Stella, forget about him and just walk away.* Instead, Stella walked to the pile of debris and began digging through it. Dan-te quickly joined her, digging next to her as a gentle smile appeared on her face.

"Don't get the wrong idea," Stella yapped. "Just because I'm digging him out doesn't mean I've forgiven him or that I have any feelings for him. It's just that leaving him here to die this way is too good for him. You said that he was genuinely sorry for what he had done and filled with regret. Well, I'm going to make him show me just how sorry he is, either for the rest of his life or until I'm satisfied—whichever comes last."

"Whatever you say," Dan-te replied, smiling. *But you've made the right choice,* she thought as Dan-te noticed Stella's red energy dimming as she worked to clear the rock pile. *No one should be left to die buried where they can't move or do anything about it. Yet with the way the cavern is losing its pink fear energy, who knows if we'll even get the chance to do anything before the magma arrives?*

Of course, the magma was not the only thing Dan-te was worried about. Glancing back to look at Virgil and Sol's fight, she suppressed a tremor. Both of them were producing the same horrible red energy that Reye did back in the

Grand Coliseum and the same scents of anger, rage, and adrenaline. They also were bursting with a hazy white mental energy, their minds drifting.

*The two of them aren't* here, Dan-te realized as she watched them fight. *They're back in the Alien Astronaut Movement's camp, continuing the fight that they started. The only difference between them is that Virgil is also producing a violet energy of protection. He wants to protect himself, and us, as well as fight Sol.*

Still, Dan-te could not keep her nerves entirely in check. This was her first time seeing Virgil enraged. She was not going to lie, it was scary.

# Chapter 36

"Tell me, *Uni*, do you remember how many of those AAM heretics died just to make sure you escaped," Sol taunted. His sword connected with Virgil's again, each strike now threatening to push him back into Stella's room.

"Damnant quod non intelligunt," Virgil replied, countering Sol's attack as he attempted to push him back into the hallway and away from Stella and Dan-te while they worked to dig Met-on out of the rubble.

"So, I condemn what I don't understand." Sol laughed. "I don't need to understand; I know that you should be dead. The only reason you're not is that you must be an extremely important, or an extremely cowardly, heretic. Otherwise, why would those fools go to such lengths to keep you alive?"

"Don't you *dare* call me a coward," Virgil accused. "You and the Hammers slaughtered my friends at night in a surprise attack all because we wanted to learn and explore. You sacrificed hundreds of innocent lives in a plot to find this city instead of looking for it yourselves. Now, you almost butcher a woman because of circumstances far beyond her control, circumstances that you and the Hammers are responsible for. It's you and the Hammers who are the cowards!" Virgil increased the ferocity of his attacks, forcing Sol further backward.

"I'm the coward," Sol laughed, amused at seeing the normally mousy Worm becoming mad and unhinged. "At least my brothers and I finish our job, datum perficiemus munus—we shall accomplish the mission assigned—just like how I'll finish you!" Sol dodged one of Virgil's strikes and attempted a piercing lunge for his head. Vigil, seeing the incoming attack, dropped to the ground and rolled backward, avoiding the strike and parrying Sol's next one.

"Why am I not surprised you know Platin?" Virgil mumbled. "After the Great Rainbow War, almost all of the Dominions suddenly agreed to do away with the language to create a standard form of communication. I imagine your grandfather had something to do with it."

"Ancient Platin versions of the Tome of the Ouroboros revealed Light Bringer and Tanas to be the same person," Sol confessed. "My grandfather witnessed firsthand how that kind of knowledge could be corrupting. He agreed, along with most of the other Virt Princes at the time, that the knowledge would be better lost to give the public a *clearer* view of the Tome; for their own piece of mind."

"Humph, omnis traductor traditor, every translator is a traitor," Virgil mumbled before continuing the assault.

Back in the cell, Dan-te silently kept an eye on Virgil as she and Stella dug Met-on out from under the collapsed wall. She was worried about Virgil and what this fight was doing to him.

*Virgil's been radiating the same horrible red energy as Reye from the moment the fight started,* Dan-te fretted. *It's not as bad as Reye, but it's getting there. Virgil's struggling just to keep himself under control. He's not just fighting a member of the Hammers of the Orange Light, he's fighting against one of the very Hammers who killed his friends in the AAM. Worse, he was near him every day at Spectral Academy, and he never even knew it. Virgil's mind is pulsing with white mental energy every time Sol mentions the AAM. Virgil remembers the attack as if it's happening right now.*

Dan-te stole a quick glance at Sol. The energy and scents he was producing were even more worrisome than Virgil's.

*Sol, however, has utterly drowned himself in the horrible red energy, especially after recognizing Virgil's sword and realizing that he was the last surviving member of the AAM. I already Knew that the Hammers were no better than the Nag-el. But Sol is in a league by himself in terms of horrible red energy he is producing and how much he has given himself over to his cause. Even if Virgil wins, it may cost him more than he realizes.*

"I found him," Stella shouted, turning Dan-te's attention back to the rubble and away from the fight. Stella had uncovered the beginnings of an ash-grey form, bleeding red blood from beneath the collapsed wall.

"Good," Dan-te confirmed as they continued to dig, glad to see that even though Met-on was unconscious, and his silver life energy was weak, it was stable.

# The Second Coming

*Virgil, be careful,* Dan-te begged, her thoughts returning to Virgil for a second. *Remember who you are, don't do something that you will regret.*

Meanwhile, in the building across from Stella's room, Reye watched the proceeding before her stoically. Reye heard every word that Sol said.

*Me, Raymond, all of the members of the Demp Cavern Mining Project, were chosen so they could be used as bait to draw out the Tribe of Shadows to conduct a weapon test. Those pins were trackers meant to find Nis. Stella was used by her own people and now pregnant because of the Tribe of Shadows. Yet she considered the father of her child a saint next to Sol. Plus Sol can just knock her to the ground, call her filth, and prepare to kill her,* Reye mentally whimpered. *All while I remain frozen in place.*

*Move,* Reye told her body. *Move, I have to get to Stella. Why can't I move?*

But Reye remained fixed, watching as Sol brought his sword down to execute Stella, only to be stopped by Worm's sudden appearance.

*Worm!* Reye's mind was shocked even further as another of her friends from Spectral Academy suddenly appeared from behind her with a second figure to defend Stella. Soon afterward, Worm and Sol began fighting with a seriousness she recognized from her rampaging through Nis. Still, she remained rooted to the spot, her mind filling with too many questions.

*Why is Worm here? Why is he fighting Sol? How is it that he even* knows *how to fight like that? He's just a harmless bookworm, isn't he?* Gazing at the second figure who arrived with Worm, Reye suddenly recognized the person and understood a little of what must have happened.

*Dan-te, she's alive!* Reye gasped, recognizing the member of the Remnant of the Tribe who fought with her and Ice in the Grand Coliseum, only to disappear when the Veil of Shadows exploded.

*She must have made it to the surface, after all,* Reye figured, trying to piece together what must have happened to her. *Once there, she found Worm and convinced him to come back here with her. I have to help them, I have to help Worm, Stella, and Dan-te, I have to* move.

Yet for all her struggling, Reye was stuck, unable to move or speak.

*Why can't I move!* Reye screamed in her head. *What's stopping me!*

"It's because Sol is a Hy-mun," a voice said as Ca-to emerged from behind Reye.

"He's a Hy-mun," Reye whispered, surprised that she could speak again once she could not see the scene before her, and confused over the meaning of Ca-to's words.

"Yes, he's a Hy-mun," Ca-to replied, examining Reye as if he were a doctor before turning his head to look at the scene involving Dan-te, Stella,

Virgil, and Sol. "Your energy is shifting between being completely calm to frazzled. I've only seen that happen when close friends or family members turn on one another. I followed you here by following your residual energy and heard what those other Hy-muns were talking about as I got closer. You know all of them, don't you?"

"Yes," Reye admitted. "We were all friends at Spectral Academy. But I heard what Sol said, too. So, why haven't I been able to do anything?"

"Do you remember why you were able to easily tear through Nis, killing warriors from the Tribe of Shadows as if they meant nothing to you?"

Reye slumped down in shame, casting her eyes away as she felt her hands shake. She could still see her brother, Raymond, being killed during the mining camp attack by a warrior from Nis along with the faces of all the other warriors she killed afterward in vengeance. The words of the phantom-Raymond later chastising her about her actions during the Reconciliation Ritual echoed in her head.

*"You don't think they felt hurt, angry, or thought that they were also due vengeance. Before you encountered Lord Tanas, have you ever once thought that either the Tribe of Shadows or the Remnant of the Tribe feel the same emotions we do?"* The phantom-Raymond had accused her of not thinking of the Tribe of Shadows as similar to the Hy-muns, an accusation Reye knew she was guilty of. Reye knew she had never once thought the two species as being the same until the ritual and the phantom-Raymond made her see otherwise.

"I was able to kill them without thought because I didn't think of them as 'people' the same way I think of Hy-muns," Reye whispered, radiating shame as she spoke each word. "They were just 'creatures' to me, creatures responsible for killing my brother and turning Hy-muns into food and sport, hardly anything next to Hy-muns."

"That's right," Ca-to replied. "You saw a group of beings so different from yourself that could be blamed for the death of your brother that you mentally labeled them as 'other.' And set yourself to the destruction of the other."

"Making me no different than the Tribe of Shadows," Reye said sickly, remembering another part of the phantom-Raymond's chastising.

"At one time," Ca-to said with a shrug. "But you are improving. Yet now that Hy-mun, the one who calls himself Sol, has caused you to start re-examining the cause of your brother's death and your own actions afterward, hasn't he."

Reye did not answer, and Ca-to *Knew* she did not need to. From the moment Ca-to laid his eyes on Reye, he could see her white mental energy pulsing, twisting, and sparking all around her head. Her body might have been stunned, but her mind was working overtime.

174

# The Second Coming

"I blamed the Tribe of Shadows for everything that had happened to me, Raymond, and even Stella since the attack," Reye finally said.

"And now?" Ca-to asked.

"Now I find out that the only reason we were even in that attack in the first place was because of a plot devised by Hy-muns like me. The very beings I believed to be so much more advanced and better than either the Tribe of Shadows or the Remnant of the Tribe were the ones who sacrificed us in the first place. Every life I took, every piece of destruction I caused in Nis and against the Tribe of Shadows as a whole in Raymond's name was pointless since the Tribe of Shadows was never the real reason why he was killed in the first place. It was because of Hy-muns like me."

"So, why are you are not running to fight Sol like you did the Tribe of Shadows?"

Reye did not reply to Ca-to's remark at first. She only dropped to her knees and cried.

"It's because he's still a Hy-mun, and I just can't bring myself to fight him," Reye cried. "I look at Sol, and I see the person I knew at Spectral Academy, I see the person Stella crushed on, I see a Hy-mun just like me, and I know it is wrong and criminal to kill him. However, a part of me still considers the Tribe of Shadows and the Remnant of the Tribe to be something else, making what I did to them exempt from Hy-mun ethics, rules, and laws. But when confronted with actually having to commit a serious Hy-mun crime against another Hy-mun, I freeze up. The biggest rule-breaker and troublemaker in the Orange Dominion is stopped by the rules. It's both funny and sad."

"It just means your maturing," Ca-to replied, but his expression soon changed as the entire cavern began shaking again.

"Another quake?" Reye screamed over the rumbling.

"Worse."

# Chapter 37

Kai Aphas laughed like a mad child, and he did not care if someone overheard him or not.

"I've done it! It's over now for Tanas. With this many Hammers scouring the city, he and his Tribe of Shadows will be destroyed in no time."

This was the moment Kai Aphas had lived for since he escaped Nis, resurrected, and reorganized the Hammers of the Orange Light into the organization it had become today. The Nimrod, Og, Typhon, Alops, and Tityos sat at different points around the city, and three of the Sun Spheres were now rising to the cavern's ceiling and glowing brighter by the second. Kai Aphas was confident nothing would be able to stop the Hammers. They would find Tanas, destroy him, and every last demon crawling beneath the surface.

*You certainly have done it,* the voice of Able echoed again in Kai Aphas's head.

"So, you've finally come to agree with me, Able?" Kai Aphas asked, sensing a final victory not only against Tanas but against the phantom of his stepbrother. "This final assault will end Tanas and his Tribe of Shadows."

*No,* Able's voice responded mournfully, causing Kai Aphas to twitch in annoyance over being challenged by his stepbrother's voice yet again. *All you've done is create the very disaster the Tribe of Shadows has feared since long before Tanas, and his Legions ever joined them. You've done to the Tribe of Shadows exactly what the Nag-el did to the Ancient Tribe generations ago when they destroyed their homes, family, and culture, back when they deemed them as monsters and needed to be wiped out, all to satisfy their own twisted beliefs.*

"The Nag-el are not destroyers!" Kai Aphas screamed in reply, again refusing to accept the Nag-el as anything but the creators he was brought up to believe them to be. "And these monsters have no culture, all they have ever done is try to copy ours. They have been a plague on our race since its beginning. And every secret activity by the Dominions aligned with me, drop of blood spilled since the Great Rainbow War, it's all been to erase this plague forever."

*The only plague here is the plague of hatred that Tanas and his Nag-el legions sowed on Prism generations ago, one you continued to spread on the surface, a disease that is being further spread throughout the city even now, a plague that will only end in the manner it was started, in an ocean of light.*

"Then it's a good thing I am bringing that 'ocean of light' to Nis," Kai Aphas responded with a sneer. "The Sun Spheres are activated, and my brother Hammers are sweeping the city. My ocean of orange light will end this plague, you'll see."

*You never change,* Able sobbed. *All you ever see is what you want to, instead of what is real. No matter, you* will *see it soon enough.*

Able's voice went silent again, yet it left Kai Aphas with a puzzling thought.

"What did he mean by, 'I *will* see it soon enough,' I know what I see, my Hammers spreading their light throughout the city and ending Tanas's influence. What more do I need to see?"

***

Back in Lust Atrophied, Sol was laughing just as manically as his grandfather over the appearance of the Sun Spheres rising in the distance over the city while he fought with Virgil.

"Ha! It's over now, heretic!" Sol cheered triumphantly, sensing victory for both himself and the Hammers of the Orange Light as he pushed Virgil back into Stella's room. Stella and Dan-te had finished clearing the rubble from Met-on's bloody, bruised, and unconscious body and had dragged him to a shaded corner of the room away from the light and fighting.

"With the Sun Spheres activated, nothing can stop us from bringing our light into this dark world. All that's left are the final two spheres, and then we'll finally eradicate these monsters you've stooped to align yourself with along with every other heretic, rodent, and piece of filth we find. Once that is over, we..."

Sol did not finish his sentence. Excited and overconfident by the activation of the Sun Spheres, Sol swung his sword wildly, allowing Virgil to not only dodge it but to also counter with a rising strike that connected and cut clean across his chest. The force of the attack cut clean into his suit, drawing a mark across his chest mirroring the older one.

"Now they match," Virgil laughed, seeing both of the scars he gave him on display as he was knocked down toward the magma grates. With Sol on the ground, Virgil moved in closer to see how much his injury had crippled him, never taking his hand off his sword in case Sol was not as down as he looked.

"You think you've won, heretic," Sol spit. Virgil might not have had Dan-te's ability to *Know*, but it was clear after looking Sol over that he was not going anywhere. Sol had landed poorly on his leg and twisted it; he was out of the fight. "My brothers are going to finish everything that they find here, and that includes these demons and an AAM heretic like you."

At the mention of the AAM, Virgil brought his own sword up, making Dan-te extremely worried about what he would do next.

"Don't do it, Virgil," Dan-te shouted out, unsure whether or not Virgil would hear her.

From the moment Sol had mentioned the AAM to Virgil, he had been producing the same bittersweet scent of anger and slowly generating more and more of the same horrible red energy as Reye. Virgil's mind also pulsed with white mental energy every time Sol mentioned anything about the AAM. Dan-te had no doubt that at least some part of Virgil wanted to claim vengeance for the friends that were killed by Sol and the Hammers of the Orange Light.

"You want to kill me, heretic?" Sol continued, taunting Virgil. "Go ahead and take your revenge and finish me off. You won't be able to kill all of us. This will still be our victory no matter what you do."

"No," Dan-te shouted again, leaving Stella and going to Virgil's side. "Virgil, I know he hurt you and your friends. You're angry, and you have a right to be angry, but this isn't you. I *Know* you and the Virgil I *Know* won't kill someone for vengeance in cold blood like this. You're the one who sheltered and protected me when I arrived on the surface, carried me every time I passed out over witnessing aspects of Hy-mun culture I couldn't bear, promised he would help me—a complete stranger from beneath the surface—stop the Third Great Attempt. You *Know* what's heading for this city right now. Is killing him really worth it?"

Virgil raised his sword further over his head.

*No,* Dan-te thought. *Not again. Please don't let me have driven another Hy-mun down the same path as Reye.*

Dan-te had never forgotten or forgiven herself for causing Reye to drown herself in horrible red energy after their initial conversation in Wrath Eras. Later, when Dan-te first met Virgil, she was initially afraid that she might send him down that same path. Thankfully, he did not and had shown himself to be a caring, protective, and understanding Hy-mun. Now, Dan-te's fears were returning to her, even more so considering how much she had come to depend on Virgil. She did not want to lose him.

In a flash that made Dan-te hold her breath, Virgil whipped his sword down. But instead of injuring Sol further, he left a trail of blood across Sol's face as Virgil returned his sword to its sheath. Sol was left surprised, and Dan-te relieved, as the red energy around Virgil dissolved, leaving his original blue and violet energies.

"Surprised, Sol, I guess you don't know me as well as other people do." Virgil flashed a sly wink to Dan-te, who smiled in response to the unspoken message he sent her. "'Nemo me impune lacessit,' no one provokes me with impunity. Kill an injured, cowardly, bigot like you just because you begged me to is not going to happen. My friends whom you killed would cry if they knew I'd fallen that far. Seeing you bested and beaten by me, one of the heretics you loath is more than enough vengeance for me. Killing you is just not worth it."

Virgil and Dan-te turned away from Sol and walked toward Stella and Met-on.

*Not worth it,* Sol fumed as Virgil turned his back to him. *I'm not worth it, I'm worth* INFINITELY *more than a heretic like you. Never turn your back on a Hammer of the Orange Light.*

With a scream, Sol staggered back to his feet to start fighting again, but his cry was blocked out as the magma grates beneath him cracked wide open. Virgil, Dan-te, Stella, and Reye in the distance had just enough time to see him fall into the open vent. Looking down it, Virgil and Dan-te saw nothing left of Sol, but a pair of flaming legs and feet sink slowly into the magma. Turning away from Sol's fiery tomb, Virgil and Dan-te returned to Stella's side, where she was cradling the bleeding and unconscious Met-on.

"Let's get out of here," Virgil said, taking Met-on away from Stella and loading him across his back to carry him out of the room. Leaving the cell, and sticking to the long shadows cast by the low-hanging Sun Spheres, the small party soon found itself confronted by another figure who emerged from a cracked building in front of them.

"Ca-to," Dan-te shouted as she recognized the figure walking out of the building, "I'm surprised I didn't notice you there sooner."

"Don't be," Ca-to replied, shaking his head in a gesture of understanding. "I had seen the Hy-mun your friend referred to as Sol earlier. From what I could *Know* about him, he made me want to keep my distance from you until the fight between him and your friend—Virgil, correct? —was settled."

Dan-te agreed with him. She also witnessed how the energies and smells from both Virgil and Sol interacted with each other. She *Knew* that the fight was meant for them.

"Besides, I've had my own charge to take care of who needed me far more than you." Ca-to stepped aside, causing Stella, Virgil, and Dan-te's mouths to drop open in shock. Standing before them was Reye. Her face was stained with salt and tears, clothes were dirty and torn, cuts and scratches were all over her body, and a lingering smell hung close to her body. She smelled like blood. She looked like she had fought a war, and the expression on her face made it look like she had seen one. For a moment, nobody did anything, until Stella—shocked at seeing her friend alive—took the first step toward her.

"Reye, is that really you?" Stella asked.

"I'm sorry," Reye sobbed in reply. "I thought you were dead, I'm sorry."

Reye could not talk after that, all she did was cry as Stella hugged her in a comforting embrace.

*Reye thought Stella was dead because of me and Ice,* Dan-te thought to herself, seeing waves of syrup-colored regret spill from Reye like water bursting out of a bucket. *I can't even imagine what she put herself through after believing she was dead when we parted ways back in the Grand Coliseum. If Reye had known Stella was alive from the start, if Ice and I had only told her she could have been alive from the start, I wonder if we could have spared her some pain.*

Dan-te was generating her own syrup-colored regret about her actions since she first met Reye. Dan-te remembered it was the conversation she and her brother Ice had with Reye that first set her on an extremely destructive path.

*I* Know *the horrible red energy is gone from Reye, and I'm glad about that,* Dan-te realized. *But she has a lingering smell of blood on her, and she also has traces of the dust and herbs used in the Reconciliation Ritual. If Reye had gone through that, she must have done something horrible, to herself more than anyone else, and it was all our fault.*

"I'm sorry to spoil the reunion," Ca-to said, breaking the mode between them. "But unfortunately, we don't have the time."

"He's right," Virgil agreed. "The higher the Sun Spheres get, the more shadow we lose to hide in. More importantly, remember what's heading for the city, we need to get out of here, *right now*. The Hammers might actually have done us a favor. With the Sun Spheres active across parts of the city, warriors from Nis are going to go into hiding until they are veiled. We'll be able to escape the city because of that."

"And we already have a terraship coming for us," Ca-to added. "We just need to meet up with everyone."

"What?" Virgil, Stella, and Dan-te asked at the same time.

# The Second Coming

"I'll explain as we run. We need to get to the Great Tunnel's entrance, now!"

# Chapter 38

*Unbelievable,* Professor Heart thought to herself as she looked out of the Arc's window. She did not know what shocked her more, the city of Nis her father described, sprawled out before her; the six terraships sticking up out of it like metal towers on a stone block; the three glowing spheres slowing rising over it—casting long shadows toward the Arc; or the strange image it all made together.

*Father, you were right to be worried about Kai Aphas. If one man could unite enough people across Prism just to* build *those ships, keep them a secret, and then use them, then he's more dangerous than either one of us could have imagined. Just getting the resources together to build* one *of those ships privately would have been a monumental effort, and he has* six *of them. I better pick up Ann and the other escapees and get out of here as soon as possible. Now, where is Ann?*

Looking at a screen on the Arc's controls, Professor Heart found Ann and a group of beings similar to the Tribesman, members of the Remnant of the Tribe, running toward the ship's hatch in the shadows formed by the rising spheres. Another screen, projecting an image from the city's main gate, showed two more members of the Remnant and another three Hy-muns—one carrying someone Professor Heart could not identify—running as fast as they could toward the ship in another shadow.

*Not much time left until the magma reaches Nis,* Professor Heart fretted, looking at the clock she set for when the magma would enter the city. *And considering both the time and force that it's moving, it won't take long for it to fill this cavern and trigger the supervolcano. We need to leave now!*

Professor Heart activated the remote control on the outer door and watched as Ann and her group entered the ship. Typing a message to Ann on a keyboard, a robotic voice started speaking throughout the Arc.

"Ann, please follow the signs and come to the control bridge immediately. I need your help operating the Arc."

Professor Heart would have breathed a sigh of relief over having someone who could move without a suit on the bridge helping her. But after sending that message, a warning light began flashing. A transmission was being sent to the Arc.

"Attention Unidentified Ship, this is Martin Pot, Chief Communication Officer onboard the terraship Antaeus. This is a classified operation of the highest degree. All other terraships should be docked for mandatory service. We are preparing to terminate you unless given orders or reason not to. Identify yourself."

*Martin Pot.* Professor Heart's memory flashed to her last years of activity as a terranaut, recognizing the voice of one of her crewmates, and surprised that he was a Hammer involved in this mess. Reaching for the keyboard, Professor Heart began issuing a reply.

"Martin Pot, this is your old shipmate Bridget Heart aboard the terraship Arc."

*Bridget and the Arc,* Martin Pot thought. *That's the terraship built by Dr. Noah Heart, the one our ships are based on. Dr. Heart, like Kai Aphas, was imprisoned in Nis but became a recluse after escaping. After Kai Aphas reformed the Hammers, he became a longtime watch target but never did anything that merited his termination. I was assigned to keep an eye on his daughter during her last mission before she retired. Could that actually be her?*

"And if you think I'm lying, then how many other people remember finding you in a rather *compromising* position with that woman from the Green Dominion?"

*Yep,* definitely, *her,* Martin Pot fumed, blushing at the affair Professor Heart promised to keep secret.

"Now, listen to me because I am only going to say this once. And I am asking you, terranaut to terranaut, and more importantly, shipmate to shipmate to believe me. A cataclysmically large and fast-moving current of magma is heading for us right now. I've tried to divert some of it, and if it worked, there should be a series of new land-based volcanoes on the surface of the continent along Sand Break Border, but the magma is still flowing. It will reach this city soon, and when it hits, it will flood this entire cavern and trigger another eruption—bigger than anything we have ever seen before—right here. If you care for your life, and the lives of your shipmates, get them out of here, now!"

Professor Heart cut off her transmission just as Ann appeared on the Arc's bridge alongside one of the Remnant's members.

If Professor Heart could have cried or screamed out how glad she was to see Ann alive again through her suit, she would have, and by the expression on Ann's face, Professor Heart knew Ann felt the same way. In fact, she was certain Ann wanted to hug her right now but was holding herself back because they were not safe yet.

"I'm glad to see you, too, Professor," Ann whimpered, tears forming in her eyes. "But you have to look at this." Ann unrolled a map she was carrying. It showed Nis, a series of tunnels, and a path marked to a point called Rem. "This is Rem, the Remnant's home. Once the rest of us get on the ship, we need to get to Rem and evacuate its people onto the Arc. Otherwise, they'll be killed once the magma starts flooding all of the tunnels around Nis. How long will it take to reach Rem?"

Professor Heart looked at the map and began to mentally calculate the travel time, using the distances provided on it, what she knew of the Arc's capabilities, and her own experience piloting terraships for a reference.

"If I dig through some of the outer cavern walls around Nis to get to the tunnels sooner, it will take almost all of the remaining time before the magma reaches here. But since Rem is in a tunnel and not in a cavern, it might actually be destroyed before Nis. How long will it take Rem to evacuate?"

"No time at all, Professor," a member of the Remnant replied. "Believe it or not, my people are *excellent* at packing up and moving quickly. All I'll need is a way to let them know this ship doesn't mean them any harm."

"You have that right here, Seat of Kindness," Ann cheered from where she was familiarizing herself with the Arc's controls. "This is the ship's external speaker. Use this, and you'll be able to let every member of the Remnant know we are getting close."

"Very good," the Seat of Kindness replied. "But I am a little surprised with you right now. You are radiating more white mental energy now than when you were working on the drilling machines, but your breathing and demeanor seem much calmer. You've been here before, haven't you?"

"This ship was once on display near my home in the Red Dominion," Ann explained with a bright smile. "I've visited it every chance I could get, and studied how it worked since long before I ever walked into Spectral Academy. I can operate it with no problem."

"She's right," Professor Heart mused, remembering their discussions about the Arc while they worked on Ann's supervolcano theories. "The only two people I've ever known who probably know the Arc better are my father and me. Now we just have to get out of here without getting shot first."

# Chapter 39

Martin Pot reread the message again, and alongside it listened to more reports from the surface about the newly formed land-based volcanoes.

*"A cataclysmically large and fast-moving current of magma is heading for us right now. I've tried to divert some of it, and if it worked, there should be a series of new land-based volcanoes on the surface of the continent along Sand Break Border."*

"Well, you succeeded there, Bridget," Martin Pot feared reading the rest of the message.

*"But the magma is still flowing. It will reach this city soon, and when it hits, it will flood this entire cavern and trigger another eruption—bigger than anything we have ever seen before—right here. If you care for your life, or the lives of your shipmates, get them out of here, now!"*

*I know you have a wicked sense of humor*, Martin Pot mused. *But this doesn't sound like one of your jokes. In fact, your message, along with what I've heard on the surface, only makes me think you're right. Something very wrong is happening beneath us.*

About to walk out of communications and go to the Command Deck, he quickly stopped one of his subordinates.

"Tell me, we have drone probes, correct?"

"Yes, sir, they're standard issue on all terraships, they dig ahead of the ship and send images of what they find back to the ship that launched them. It's how terraships find magma tubes and reservoirs."

# The Second Coming

"Launch one directly below us; I want to know what's under this city."

"But what about the Arc, sir?"

"Ignore it for now," Martin Pot replied, "And send a message to the other ships to ignore it as well until operations in Nis are completed. If anyone asks, tell them it's Command's choice."

"Yes, sir," Martin Pot's subordinate replied before going to one of the phones and ordering a drone probe launched directed beneath the Antaeus. Soon, an image of dirt and rock sent from the probe appeared on a screen in the communications room.

*Nothing so far, Bridget,* Martin Pot thought to himself as he watched the probe's transmission. But his look soon changed from consideration to terror as the image changed to a pool of magma. It was more vast than anything he had ever seen before; and from the looks of his shipmates, more vast than anything they had seen either.

"Open a channel to all Hammers active throughout Nis," Martin Pot shouted.

"Yes, sir," his shipmates answered. Each one was shocked, awed, and, most important, scared by the gargantuan pool of magma sitting beneath them.

"Attention all Hammers of the Orange Light! Abort all activity and make for the terraship nearest to you. New and dangerous volcanic information has come to our attention. Nis will soon explode. We are leaving before it happens." But once the retreat order was given, the Communication Room found itself stormed by guards shooting everyone present, Kai Aphas's voice echoing over the loudspeakers.

"This is Kai Aphas sending a message to all my brother Hammers of the Orange Light. The Communications Crew of the Antaeus has tragically been corrupted by Tanas and his influence. Double your efforts, make sure Tanas and his Tribe of Shadows are rooted out and exterminated forever. But now, I must do what must be done. I order the Communications Crew of the Antaeus to be terminated at once."

*Is that what you told yourself when you shot your stepbrother?* Martin Pot steamed when pandemonium broke out throughout the Communications Room. The guards picking off each member of Martin Pot's staff, most already shot and dying, and finishing each one with a shot to the head.

*Looks like I'm not coming back from* this *trip,* Martin Pot lamented as he prepared himself for the end. *I just hope that when this whole city does blow, at least it takes both you and Tanas with it.*

\*\*\*

Kai Aphas listened to the executions aboard the Antaeus silently, while internally, his mind screamed in argument and regret.

187

*Why did you have to let yourself be corrupted by Tanas? What is it about this place that causes people to create these stories? Why couldn't you just follow my orders? Why?*

The last time Kai Aphas's mind was this tortured was just after he shot his stepbrother. No matter what happened, he could not allow anything to happen that challenged what he believed was the right course of action and was willing to take any measure to ensure that his actions would still be justified, regardless of what he had to do.

"Calling Commander Del of the Og," Kai Aphas said over his personal radio.

"This is Commander Del," a voice replied.

"This is Kai Aphas. You are closest to the new terraship contact. Do you have a shot at it?"

"Not a perfect shot, sir. If I start firing on it now, I'll probably miss it more than I'll hit it."

"Fire!"

\*\*\*

"Don't look back!" Virgil screamed over the deafening sound of the Og's guns. Reye, running at Virgil's left between Stella and Ca-to, almost did turn around, partially out of curiosity, but mostly because Virgil said not to until Ca-to put his own hand up against Reye's head to keep her looking straight toward the Arc.

"You'll only be stunned if you look back," Ca-to screamed, feeling the heat from the explosions at his back hit him like a paralyzing wave. "Just keep running to the ship. It's our only chance."

Reye nodded and kept running, focusing all her attention onto the Arc, a decision she later felt glad about as an artillery shell blew up alongside her.

"Will the Arc be okay with the Hammers firing on it?" Dan-te screamed.

"Yes," Virgil answered, taking Dan-te's hand to help her along. "That ship was built by recycling some of the strongest and toughest terraships ever built. Even by today's standards, the Arc stands as one of the most durable terraships ever constructed."

"Worm's right," Reye added, far more at ease with talking to Dan-te than she was with Stella. "Even if all six of the Hammer's ships rained shots onto the Arc, it would still take a lot of punishment before any real damage is done to it."

Reye glanced over to Stella instinctively, looking for agreement but quickly turned her head away from her as soon as their eyes met. Since their escape from Lust Atrophied, the two of them had hardly said a word to each other. While everyone was primarily concerned with escaping the city before the magma could reach it, Reye knew that if they did flee from Nis, she and Stella would have to talk, and it would not be a pleasant conversation.

*All this time she was alive,* Reye regrettably thought to herself as they made their way through and out of the city and toward the Arc. *I could have saved her, maybe even kept her from becoming pregnant by that unconscious kid Worm has loaded over his back, I could have...*

An explosion behind them silenced Reye's thoughts as a shell knocked them all to their feet. Looking up, Reye noticed Virgil was already recovering, his silent load still on his back as he helped Dan-te up from where she was on the ground. Next to her, Ca-to was also getting himself back on his feet, yet there was no sign of Stella.

*What happened to Stella?* Reye wondered. *She was just here.*

Reye glanced ahead of her and was instantly relieved to see Stella had only been blown a little further ahead of them. Reye's relief was short-lived, though, when she noticed that Stella was not moving.

*No,* Reye worried with mounting alarm. *This can't happen, not now, not after we're finally out of Nis.*

Reye staggered over to Stella and breathed a sigh of relief when she saw she was still breathing, but unconscious.

"I'm not leaving you behind, Stella," Reye muttered as she struggled to load Stella onto her back the same way Virgil had Met-on on his. Reye soon began running again toward the Arc, each step a fight in itself, as Stella's unstable form constantly shifted on Reye's back.

*How is it that Worm can keep Met-on stable on his back?* Reye thought, glancing at Virgil as they neared the Arc. *Then again, how is Worm doing any of this? Appearing suddenly in Lust Atrophied with Dan-te, sword fighting like a master, carrying an unconscious person through a crumbling city, he's nothing like the bookworm I took him to be.*

A wave of shame washed over Reye as she realized that not only Virgil but also none of the people she knew—including herself—were who she took them to be.

"You were right, Raymond," Reye said to herself, remembering the Reconciliation Ritual and the phantom of her dead brother. "I only listened to what I wanted to listen to, knowing and understanding only what I wanted to, instead of what was actually true. Well, now at least I can do what you really wanted me to do when you told me to 'run, fight, and live.' You wanted me to take Stella, run, and fight my way out of the mess we were in and live through it. Well, now, I am. I just hope it's alright if it's better late than never."

Despite the bombardment, the Arc's body held up against it, only showing black marks from where the shells hit. Soon Virgil, Reye, Dan-te, Ca-to,

Met-on, and Stella were onboard the Arc alongside the Remnant members who were waiting for them at the door before closing it behind them. From inside the Arc, the attack from the Hammer's terraships continued to beat down on the hull, a loud echo following each hit, but as Ann's voice sounded over the intercom, everyone let out a collective sigh of relief.

"Welcome aboard everybody, you're the last group. Now let's get out of here and make for Rem to rescue the other members of the Remnant."

From deep inside the Arc, everyone could hear and feel its engines and drilling devices come to life as the Arc slowly started to move, snaking out of the Great Tunnel like a train before re-digging into another cavern wall amidst the shaking caused by the Hammer's bombardment.

"Assuming all goes well, we will reach Rem soon," Ann continued over the intercom. "But, it will go quicker if I had another pair of hands up here to assist me."

*I should head up there, but if I do...* Reye knew that before coming to Nis, she would have jumped to pilot any terraship and would already be making her way to the bridge. But now, all that mattered to her was being there when Stella woke up.

"I'll head up there," Virgil replied, a look of understanding appearing on his face as he watched the way Reye gazed at Stella with the same honest eyes and expression he had when he was back in Spectral Academy.

"Thanks, Worm," Reye replied as Virgil walked to the bridge.

"Reye..."

Reye looked and now saw the familiar figure of Dan-te standing over her. Compared to the first time they met, Dan-te now looked fed and refreshed compared to the haggard appearance she had then. Reye could guess what Dan-te wanted to talk with her about; after all, they both had brothers.

"Please tell me what happened to Ice after the Grand Coliseum."

"Ice stayed by my side after you disappeared in the Grand Coliseum. Once we escaped, he led me through Nis on my mad and bloody rampage all the way to Decca-Ju Tower. I ended up facing Tanas himself, but once that happened..."

Reye broke off and started shivering at the memory of her encounter. Her voice was tinged with fear and shame. Dan-te did not need Reye to explain what happened to her when she faced Tanas. She had seen it on the Hammers when they first arrived in Nis. She was also familiar with the Stories of Rill, just like all the other members of the Remnant. Dan-te did not know what happened to Reye when she encountered Tanas directly. But looking at her, seeing how the energy around her became pale and icy just from trying to remember it, she *Knew* all she needed to about her reaction to Tanas's presence.

# The Second Coming

"After Tanas, I just don't know. I felt like I was trapped in a nightmare. When I finally woke up, I was a blubbering mess and crying in Ann's arms in Maestri. I don't know what happened to Ice after that."

"Ice died," Ca-to answered mournfully. "He suffered the Death of the Self. The tribesman that was brought into Maestri with Reye claimed to be Ice, but he wasn't Ice, it was a different tribesman altogether. That tribesman was later taken to the Great Tunnel, I would assume by now—especially with the magma coming—that he has died the Death of the Body as well."

"I see," Dan-te replied. She had already guessed her brother must have died at some point during their mission into Nis. They had considered it a suicide mission from the start. But still, to hear how it happened, that he suffered the Death of the Self, stung.

*Ice, you idiot,* Dan-te thought to herself, remembering the last time she saw her brother. *You were supposed to help Reye get back to her old self, not make her worse. Then you go and suffer the Death of the Self. What were you thinking?*

"You should go to the bridge and help Worm," Reye said, breaking Dan-te out of her reminiscence. "You came back here with him to help your people; you should be there with him to finish this."

"With Worm?" Dan-te asked, taking a second to register Virgil's nickname.

"Right, with Worm," she agreed before walking off in the direction Virgil had taken.

"You should be on the bridge, too," a voice squeaked from beneath Reye, causing her eyes to bulge and look down.

"They're going to need everyone they can get to help run this ship," Stella whispered, smiling as she looked up at her friend. "I know how much you must want to pilot this ship. So, get going."

"No," Reye replied, shaking her head. "I have something more important I need to take care of right here. I called you my best friend, but all it took was a little doubt to make me write you off as dead and charge off on my own revenge-driven mission instead of trying to find you. Then, when I finally did find you, I was so shocked by Sol's revelation that I could not even move to protect you. If Worm did not show up when he did, you would be dead, and I might still be frozen like a statue in Lust Atrophied. I'm not leaving you behind again."

Stella chuckled. Of all the responses Stella could have given her, Reye was expecting shouts or a stern talking; she certainly was not expecting laughter.

"So, I should blame you for getting distracted and lost in your own little world," Stella asked Reye comically. "I've stopped counting a while ago the number of times you've done that. I'm just happy you've finally come to realize that fault about yourself."

"I just wish it could have come at a lower price," Reye sobbed, turning her head away from Stella. "I mean, with what happened to you…"

"Why don't I tell you what happened to me?" Stella said, cutting Reye off and turning her face so that their eyes locked. "I was being attacked by Hymuns like myself. They blasted me with cannon fire, and it almost killed me. Then I saw you appear next to me, pick me up on your shoulders, and carry me to safety. I heard you say, 'I'm not leaving you behind,' and you didn't. You got me to the safety of the Arc, and you can keep us all safe by being on its bridge. So, go catch up with everyone. Better late than never, right."

Reye smiled and realized Stella was not as unconscious as she believed after they were nearly hit from the Hammer's attack. Clasping Stella's hand one more time, Reye stood up to find Ca-to by her side.

"I'll personally take care of your friend, get going."

"Thank you, Ca-to," Reye replied and began making her way to the bridge.

***

"What took you so long?" Reye heard a strange voice ask as she walked onto the bridge.

Reye looked to a part of the bridge where Professor Heart—encased in a giant, fluid-filled suit—was standing with Virgil and Ann at the two pilot seats of the Arc.

"The same as you, Professor Heart, and let me just say I am glad to see you here." Reye laughed happily, surprised at how many unexpected people kept showing up in the last place she would have expected to find them. Even through the fluid in the suit's helmet, Reye could tell from the look on Professor Heart's face that she was also overjoyed to see her alive again after believing her to be dead.

"I'm afraid we'll have to save the reunions for later," Ann called from where she was seated. "Reye, if you're not too busy being stunned, get over here and help me pilot this ship."

Reye did not need to be told twice. Forgetting, for a moment, the pain and guilt she felt over her past actions, Reye let herself enjoy the same childlike joy and excitement she always felt when she thought she was getting near her dream—only this time it was actually happening.

*I'm finally doing it*, Reye thought to herself as she sat next to Ann. *I'm piloting a* terraship.

Reye knew that terraships needed multiple pilots to accurately maneuver through dirt and magma flows. While one pilot could do it alone, it put far more stress on the pilot and reduced accuracy. As Reye took the seat next to Ann and grasped the steering wheel, she could feel her fingers tingle with an excitement she had not felt since she was rampaging through Nis, which also frightened her.

*Why am I feeling this way again?* Reye wondered, taking a deep breath to try and calm her nerves. *Why do I feel like I'm about to go killing throughout Nis? I should be glad. Isn't this what I've always wanted to do?*

Reye instantly knew the answer. *It is what I wanted to do,* Reye realized somberly. *I wanted to kill the Tribe of Shadows, just like I wanted to pilot a terraship. Joy is joy, right Raymond.*

Reye remembered the phantom-Raymond's words about how joy was joy regardless whether or not the actions were good or evil. Reye found joy killing the members of the Tribe of Shadows, and now she was finding it at the wheel of a terraship.

*If I feel scared or sick now, it's all my fault. I needed to find out what else brings me joy.*

A quick punch to her arm brought Reye out of her thoughts, and into Ann's eyes, who was staring at her angrily.

"Now isn't the time to put me off again and go into your own little world. I need you here with me at these controls. Worm!" Ann turned to Virgil and Dan-te. "Take the navigation desk with your friend there. The two of you should have no trouble getting us to Rem. Once we're there, the Seat of Kindness will announce who we are from the communications desk." Reye looked to her right and saw the Seat of Kindness was already seated at the communications desk, waiting for action. "Let's go, this is one time I don't want anything going wrong."

Reye gripped the steering wheel tighter and felt the bulk of the Arc as it tunneled through the rock, moving at the turn of the wheel. Glancing to her left, she saw Virgil and Dan-te were both seated at the navigation desk studying a map and scope in front of them.

"No offense, Ann," Reye whispered briefly, "but shouldn't Professor Heart be giving the orders, and does Worm know enough about terraship navigation to even navigate us properly?"

"Don't worry," Ann replied reassuringly. "I examined all of these controls before your group arrived and got Professor Heart's permission to act as her proxy while she works the systems from her station. You certainly can't expect her to quickly give orders from inside that suit."

"True," Reye agreed, having already seen how difficult it was for Professor Heart to move and talk in the suit. It would make sense that she would have someone else act as her stand-in so orders could be relayed clearly and quickly.

"As for Worm being at Navigation, don't worry. Professor Heart's father, Dr. Noah Heart, was an even bigger genius than any of us ever realized. After completing the Arc, he not only predicted Tanas's plan, and a way to counter it, but also invented equipment that can be operated with only the bare minimum of knowledge, something that Worm already has."

"Adjust course by four degrees starboard," Virgil shouted from his position. "It will put us into a softer patch of rock and increase our speed."

Reye and Ann made the adjustments and soon felt the Arc's speed go up as it dug through the looser ground.

"Wow," Reye gasped, surprised at how quickly Virgil was adapting to the ship's navigation.

"Dr. Heart wanted to make this ship easy enough to operate in case he never lived long enough to use it himself and needed to entrust it to someone who may have not even been a terranaut and had to learn how to use it fast. Now, less talking and more operating, you can bet the Hammers are making plans to come after us right now. And if they don't come after us, the magma is. A lot can still go wrong."

*Ann's right*, Reye mentally agreed. *We might be finally out of the city, but that doesn't mean we're safe yet, and that's assuming anywhere is safe. The Arc will protect us from the magma, but not from Sol's companions, and they're probably making plans to come after us right now.*

# Chapter 40

"I want the Og to lower itself so that it can chase after that ship. I'm positive more of Tanas's demons are onboard, maybe even Tanas himself. If he escapes this will all be for nothing. I want that ship hunted down and destroyed!"

Kai Aphas was not taking the news about the Arc's departure gracefully.

"We can't just lower the Og down and chase after the escaping ship," a bridge officer tried to explain to Kai Aphas for the third time. "The fighting has started to intensify again throughout the city, the demons are now robed to protect themselves from the Sun Sphere's effects, they are returning to battle. Plus, the manpower needed to defend the remaining two Sun Spheres while the other three rise to their optimal height is too taxing. We just don't have the manpower. It will take ninety minutes for us to get the required men together and get the ship on the ground, at least."

"You have thirty minutes," Kai Aphas responded coldly. "The longer it takes, the more time you give for Tanas's demons to escape." Kai Aphas clicked off the radio, furious that creatures were escaping him and even more determined than ever to hunt them down.

*You know Noah's ship isn't harboring demons,* Able's voice whispered again into Kai Aphas's head.

"Of course it's harboring demons," Kai Aphas spit. "I should have killed Noah Heart and just appropriated his ship for the Hammers when I first confronted him. It was a mistake leaving him alive like I did. I honestly never thought he would try to return to Nis."

*The only one who should have never returned to this city is you. You know you are not going to accomplish any of your goals.* Able's voice echoed

"You're wrong Able," Kai Aphas screamed. "The three active Sun Spheres will soon rise to a point where they won't need the remaining two, and then and my loyal Hammers will crush the remaining demons in the city before chasing after the escaping ones."

*The same loyal Hammers you killed aboard the Antaeus,* Able challenged. *And what about the Virt Princes? You really think that after killing them that the Hammers won't start questioning your judgment?*

"No one questions my decisions, Able! My Hammers' loyalty to me and to the cause is paramount. No one dares question a decision I make if it will bring about the destruction of Tanas."

*Just like the loyalty between Tanas and the Tribe of Shadows,* Able regrettably moaned.

"No!" Kai Aphas threw his radio across Tanas's chambers, smashing it against the wall as he began punching the other walls and turning over the remaining bits of furniture in a fit of rage. "My Hammers and I are nothing like Tanas and his demons. We are Hy-muns, a race created by the Great Master Ash Addiel, with real bonds, feeling, and a sense of purpose. Tanas is a creature who dies in the sunlight, and his demons are monsters he created with the same weakness. The only feelings and bonds they have are the ones Hy-muns foolishly imagine they have, and their only purpose is to tempt, destroy, and corrupt us; they are monsters."

*I wonder, Kai Aphas, I wonder,* Able's voice fell silent again, leaving Kai Aphas alone in Tanas's chamber with his hands bloodied from punching the walls, his radio destroyed, and the remaining furniture overturned.

*I need a new radio,* Kai Aphas said to himself as he examined the broken radio before looking at his watch. *Humph, it can wait. I've waited forty years for this day, I don't want to miss one bit of it.*

Kai Aphas returned to Tanas's window and looked out over the city of Nis.

"My Hammers are exterminating the rest of Tanas's demons, hunting for Tanas in whatever hole he is hiding himself in, and soon the Og will chase after the Arc and hunt down the demons that escaped on it. The plague of Tanas and the Tribe of Shadows will soon be exterminated by our cause's light."

Kai Aphas laughed maniacally over his own speech, proclaiming the destruction of Tanas at the hands of the Hammers, patiently waiting for the moment when the Sun Spheres finished rising over the city and their light penetrated every corner of Nis.

"Soon, it will all be over."

# Part 7: The Death of the City of Nis and Resurrection of the Ancient Past

# Chapter 41

"Praise the Sun Spheres! Praise the Divine Tools of the Nag-el!"

The Hammers watched as the Sun Spheres rose to their zenith above Nis, flaring with illumination as bright as the sun. The three Sun Sphere's effect over Nis, once they had reached this point, had radically changed the course of the battle between the Tribe of Shadows and the Hammers of the Orange Light.

"Light!" One warrior screamed before turning black and bursting into flames as his veil was torn off in the fight with Hammers. Other warriors suffered the same reaction as the remaining forces from the Tribe of Shadows, now robed in Veils of Shadows, attempted to continue the fight against the Hammers of the Orange Light, only to have their veils ripped from their bodies and, like their ancestors before them, burn to death in the Sun Sphere's light.

Across Nis, cheers were rising from the Hammers of the Orange Light. The Sun Spheres had turned the battle decisively in their favor. Hammers now took their time breaking open doors and dragging warriors and women, who from the shade would fight tooth and claw, into the light where they would burn black and die. At the center of Nis, Kai Aphas deeply breathed in the smell of burning skin on the air in the newly lit cavern. He knew his task was almost complete.

"With the Sun Spheres at their max height, maybe now my Hammers will be able to get the Og on the ground and go after the Arc," Kai Aphas laughed manically.

# The Second Coming

Since the Arc's departure, Hammers were working to lower the Og so it could go after the Arc while still fighting the Tribe of Shadows. Kai Aphas's decision to move men back to the Og to prepare it for a chase had given the Tribe of Shadows a brief opening to push back against the Hammers of the Orange Light. But it passed the moment the Sun Spheres reached their max altitude and all but removed the long shadows from the city. Now, with the Sun Spheres working, and the destruction of the Tribe of Shadows seemingly imminent, there were only three things left to accomplish in Kai Aphas's mind.

"First, my Hammers will exterminate the rest of Tanas's demons that are still fighting in the few pockets of shadow left throughout the city," Kai Aphas raved, feeling success within his grasp. "Next, we will chase down the Arc and the demons in it and destroy them to ensure that a new race of demons isn't created. Finally, I will watch Tanas himself burn to death in our beautiful light. Once that is done, it will finally be over. No more Tempters pulling Hy-muns into acts of depravity, no more whispers from the shadows, the world will finally be ready for the Great Master Ash Addiel's return."

Kai Aphas had not felt this excited and pleased with himself since the day he escaped from Nis and swore, whatever the cost, that he would return to Nis with the means to erase it from Prism completely. All of the sacrifices, the bloodshed, were finally proving that his actions were justified.

"Now, where's my radio?" Kai Aphas asked himself, looking around the chamber, and finding it smashed in the corner of the room.

"That's right," Kai Aphas grumbled, "I need a new radio." But just as Kai Aphas was about to leave Decca-Ju Tower and return to the Antaeus, another quake hit, the most violent one anyone had felt yet.

\*\*\*

"What's going on?" Reye screamed, sirens suddenly roaring across the bridge as the Arc—now traveling in the tunnel leading to Rem—began shaking so badly that it felt like it was going to break open. Professor Heart only said one word from within her suit.

"Magma!"

\*\*\*

Magma began gushing into the cavern from the Great Tunnel faster than anyone could have ever imagined. The area around the Great Tunnel's entrance was quickly turning into an ever-expanding magma lagoon that reached Nis's main gate in minutes. Hammers and the few remaining warriors from the Tribe of Shadows in the area were incinerated instantly in the oncoming rush that was quickly filling up the cavern. On the bridges of the terraships, panic and pandemonium were breaking out while the captains shouted several orders to try to save themselves.

"Re-seal all open ports!" An officer on board the Antaeus shouted to his panicking subordinates. "Close off access to Nis! Get the men to magma rafts!"

But it was no use. Each terraship in Nis had its pod and exit ports open when the magma hit, and at the rate the magma flowed, it quickly entered each ship, disabling their drilling mechanisms, and quickly turning each ship into molten metal. The worst was the Og since it was in the process of being lowered when the magma hit. The force of the magma caused the ship to topple over, crack open, and melt from the inside out. From atop Decca-Ju Tower, Kai Aphas watched the magma flood quickly overtake the city and terraships with a mix of shock, awe, and fear as a crewman from the Antaeus called to him from the door.

"Kai Aphas, the city is lost! Wait, what happened here!" The crewman could not believe it. Kai Aphas stood alone in a room splattered with blood, smashed furniture, and the broken bodies of the three remaining Virt Princes. He was oblivious to the carnage around him and the danger fast approaching them. "Anyway, we have to get you back to the Antaeus and to a magma raft. It's the only chance you, or any of us, have!"

But Kai Aphas was not listening to the crewman, he was not listening to the rumblings that had started since the magma first poured into Nis. All he could hear was laughter, mocking laughter he was sure belonged to Tanas, and the words of his stepbrother moaning in his ears.

*In an ocean of light…*

Kai Aphas turned away from the crewman and stayed in Tanas's room, sitting silently in the throne, the one piece of furniture still intact. The crewman, realizing that Kai Aphas would not be moved, and far more concerned about his own life, attempted to return to the Antaeus, which was leaning in the rising tide of magma and launching its own magma rafts alongside the other terraships. Each magma raft was a miniature terraship meant to carry crewmembers through the magma streams if the main terraship was critically damaged until it could be recovered by another ship or reach an outlet to the ocean. Unfortunately, with the number of Hammers scattered through Nis when the magma hit, and the general state of panic on the ships, the number of rafts being launched was low. Kai Aphas, however, did not care about that anymore, he did not care about the Hammers or Nis anymore. Seated on Tanas's throne, only one thought was on his mind.

*Laugh all you want, Tanas, I erased your city, your demons, I even took your throne, and no one will take it away from me. I win!*

With that thought in mind, Kai Aphas began laughing maniacally, and he did not stop until the magma eventually rose to the top of Decca-Ju Tower and melted him away, along with everything else he believed he had won.

\*\*\*

# The Second Coming

Far from Nis, at the bottom of the Great Lagoon, Tanas was laughing. The final program he activated might have cut him off from Nis, but he could still calculate what was going on in the city.

"By now, the city is filling with magma," Tanas gleefully chuckled, imagining the looks on both the faces of the Hammers and the Tribe of Shadows as it washed over them. "The Third Great Attempt is almost complete. Soon the supervolcano will erupt, and after the sky is darkened, I'll finally be able to escape this prison and say good-bye to both the Hybrid Mutants, the Savages, and my past for good and all."

Tanas rechecked his computer, resetting his clock based on the magma's arrival.

"Fifteen more minutes," Tanas happily chirped. "Then I'll be free of this prison once and for all."

# Chapter 42

"Stop the Arc!" Dan-te screamed, the fear, fierceness, and surprising note of joy in her voice, gaining the attention of everyone on the bridge, especially Reye and Ann, who quickly applied the brakes.

"You better have a good reason for stopping us, Dan-te," Reye replied from her seat. "The magma is right behind us and will catch up to us shortly, and we still haven't reached Rem yet."

"We don't have to," Dan-te exclaimed with a big smile. "Rem came to us!"

Everyone looked at the external monitors and was shocked to see the tunnel ahead of them filling with members of the Remnant of the Tribe running toward the Arc carrying children, the old, the infirm, and bundles of belongings.

"They *Knew* we were coming," Ann whispered, further amazed by the ability to *Know* that Dan-te, and the Seat of Kindness's people, possessed.

"Open the front hatch by the drill, Professor Heart," the Seat of Kindness instructed excitedly, flipping on the external speakers. "We are going to have company."

Professor Heart nodded, opening the hatch on the front of the Arc. Outside, as hundreds stared at the Arc in wonder, the Seat of Kindness's voice began blaring from the Arc's external speakers. "My friends and family, as you *Know*, time is short. Proceed to your left, and at the point where the drill meets the ship's base, you will find an open hatch. Hurry!"

# The Second Coming

The Remnant of the Tribe did not need to be told twice. Like the magma in Nis, they streamed into the Arc, picking up anyone who stumbled to ensure that they would not be trampled with an efficiency born out of generations of evacuating and moving Rem to escape the Tribe of Shadows' continuous expansions. The Remnant of the Tribe was soon safely onboard the Arc. As the last members boarded the ship, the tunnel began to vibrate from the force of the magma.

"Seal everything!" Ann screamed as Professor Heart frantically worked the controls. "This is it!"

The force of the magma hit the Arc hard causing blackouts and disabling systems across the ship. Back in the flooded cavern that once contained the city of Nis, the few surviving magma rafts belonging to the Hammers of the Orange Light were smashed into the cavern ceiling and walls. The mixing Magnesium Mining Charges and building seismic pressure finally reaching their critical point. Pushing itself through the holes formed by the Hammer's terraships, the supervolcano finally erupted.

On the surface, the explosion was seen as far as the Platinum Throne. A pillar of ash shot into the sky. Hy-muns all across the continent, especially the ones examining the new volcanoes forming along Sand Break Border, stared openmouthed and scared as the summit of the Violet Plateau burst into flames around Tri Dominion City. They watched as the ground pulsed upward, exploding with the force of the magma pooled beneath Nis that began raining down the sides of the plateau. The only one who wasn't scared was Tanas.

\*\*\*

"It's done! I've done it at last. The Third Great Attempt is a success!"

Tanas had not been this happy since he first came to Prism and began the genocidal slaughter that the Ancient Tribe would remember as "The Coming." After thousands upon thousands of years being locked underground, unable to return to the surface because of the effects of the Methuselah Drug and the Ziggurat Security System, with no company except for the descendants of those very savages his legions all but exterminated, he was free.

"The supervolcano has been erupting for a day now," Tanas cheered, checking his clock. "More than enough time for it to darken the skies above the continent with enough ash and soot to neutralize the Ziggurats. Time for me to finally leave this planet and rendezvous with Ash Addiel's ship in orbit. Once there, all I have to do is extract the blood I need to neutralize the negative aspects of the Methuselah Drug, set him and the rest of the sleeping Nag-el on a course leading into the sun, and then no one will ever get in my way again."

Tanas gripped the controls of his ship with joy and pulled up, feeling the craft, after being sunk for millennia, slowly rise from the bottom of the Great

Lagoon. With each foot Tanas ascended, his own joy equally mounted. He knew he was returning to where he belonged and that the thousands of years he spent imprisoned within this planet would soon be nothing more than a horrible dream.

"Freedom!" Tanas screamed as his ship broke the surface of the water.

Tanas's ship froze in midair.

The instant the ship broke the water, all seven Ziggurats and the Platinum Throne flared to life as eight beams of light, one from each structure, captured Tanas's ship mid-flight, destroying it, and suspending him in the air.

*Impossible!* Tanas fumed, unable to speak as the beams of light held him over the water's surface. *The supervolcano erupted, the skies should be dark, so why aren't they, why is the Ziggurat system still active?*

As Tanas gazed toward the Cherubi Continent, he received his answer.

*Why are there volcanic spouts up and down the continent? There should only be one volcano over Nis's location. Why are there more? What happened to my plan, my Third Great Attempt? What happened?*

The questions only mounted as Tanas felt his body begin to stiffen as the lights from the Ziggurats activated the nanotech programming in the Methuselah Drug.

*A fate worse than death,* Tanas panicked as he realized what was happening to him. *Carbonized Crystallization!*

The light from the Ziggurats triggered a program in the nanotech part of the Methuselah Drug set to activate if Tanas ever crossed the boundary of the surface again. Slowly and steadily, the nanotech machines started to react with the carbon in his body, stiffening and hardening his body until it became an immobile piece of crystal. Tanas, however, remained conscious throughout and after the whole process, and while it only took a minute, it felt longer and more frightening than all the years he spent underground.

*I can't smell or taste the air, I can't smell or taste anything,* Tanas reeled as his first senses, scent and taste, were stripped from him. What made Carbonized Crystallization so terrifying was that it left the victim alive but immobile and stripped of almost every sense he had, leaving him nothing but a conscious statue at the mercy of chance and circumstance.

*My hearing's gone, I can't hear the water beneath me. Please, not this!* Tanas knew he was pleading to no one, but faced with Carbonized Crystallization, even he succumbed to fear as his senses continued to be stripped from him, pleading helplessly for it to stop.

As Tanas's sense of touch was taken from him, the last to go before he was left as a conscious crystal statue with just his sense of sight remaining, the beams of light from the Ziggurats released Tanas and he fell back into the Great Lagoon. Tanas could not move against the water, feel it, hear it, taste it, or struggle for breath. All he could do was sink helplessly into the Great Lagoon and watch as the world slowly became dark, darker than the caverns beneath Prism could ever be, and think.

*Why didn't it work?* Tanas repeatedly asked himself. *I prepared for everything, sabotage at the Keyblast Point, attack from the caves, disabling and neutralizing the hybrid mutants' technology, everything. I planned for every imaginable circumstance, and ran every calculation hundreds upon hundreds of times over. Why didn't it work? Tell me, why didn't it work?*

Tanas kept asking himself those questions as he sank further into the Great Lagoon, down to where no light reached him until he came to rest face down on the sea bed half-buried in the silt, a constant thought eternally screaming in his mind.

*Why!*

# Chapter 43

"What!"

It had been a few days since the supervolcano erupted. Since then, Ann and Reye had piloted the Arc blindly, drilling into the magma pool that fed the supervolcano, and into the various magma streams that ran beneath the continent as they made repairs. The force of the magma had knocked out power to most of the ship, including critical systems like navigation. Thankfully, life support remained intact. During that time, Reye, Stella, Ann, and Virgil, caught up on what had happened to each of them since their last encounter at AB's. Virgil's own revelation regarding his past and family received its own *unique* set of responses.

"You're the son of a *Virt Prince*!" Reye screamed, staggering backward and falling onto her backside, unsure how much more Virgil could shock her. "And you already *knew*?"

"Well, I did say he was *odd*," Stella countered. Stella knew that when she said Virgil was odd, Reye assumed she meant that he was just weird, not that he was Hy-mun nobility who usually would not even leave his Dominion, much less attend Spectral Academy and mingle with them.

"A Virt Prince's son, really," Ann said, shocked so severely she had a big freaked out look on her face that was entirely out of character for her. "Well, time to work on the navigation systems. Can anyone help me?"

"Let me help you," Virgil offered, walking away with Ann—who could barely stay on her feet from the surprise—to the navigation council. "You look like you need it."

Over the next few days, everybody on the Arc worked to restore its systems. The navigation system was the last to be fixed. Without it, the Arc just tunneled blindly through the magma currents without any real way of knowing where it was under the planet. But it was unanimously decided that immediately going to the surface would be a bad idea. Every member of the Remnant would die if exposed to sunlight. So, until a safe place could be found for them, the Arc had to stay underground until a spot was discovered where the Remnant could be left in peace.

"Okay, Virgil," Ann asked from beneath the navigation council, still feeling weird about calling "Worm" by his real name. "Try it now."

Virgil flipped a switch on the navigation council, and the panel came to life as instruments and sonic cameras across the Arc turned themselves on.

"That did it, Ann. We have navigation."

"Great," Reye added. "So, where are we?"

"Unknown," Professor Heart answered through her suit's systems. "We're in an unexplored region deep beneath the Violet Plateau, and Great Lagoon, deeper than any ship has traveled before. No known cave systems…"

Professor Heart's words were cut off as a loud ping echoed from the navigation controls, quickly gaining the attention of everyone on the Arc's bridge, including Dan-te, who was returning for her next communications shift.

"What was that?" Dan-te asked, joining the others at the navigation council.

"Impossible," Reye gasped, unable to believe what the sonic radars were telling her. "This says we're near the entrance to a cavern, a *big* cavern, but there shouldn't even *be* any caverns this deep."

"Can we enter it?" Dan-te asked.

Reye did not know what to say. She knew what Dan-te was thinking.

*A cavern large enough could mean a new home for her people,* Reye realized. *But entering a new cavern, especially from a magma stream, is no easy task. First, the ground around the cavern needs to be checked so that if it's disturbed, it won't cause the cavern to collapse and fill with magma. Then it has to be approached from the floor, not from the walls or ceiling. Otherwise, we could puncture it and let the magma in. Lastly, there's the cavern's air, assuming there's any air even in the cavern. If it's poisonous, then nothing can live there.*

Reye looked to Professor Heart. She was already back at her desk, working the calculations based on the readings from the sonic radar. It was going to be her decision whether or not they attempted to enter the cavern. Professor

Heart looked up from her desk, smiling through her helmet, and made a thumbs-up gesture.

"Let's go for it," Dan-te cheered excitedly.

Reye snickered as a sly look was thrown at Dan-te from two members of the Remnant—the Seats of Diligence and Patience—stationed in the driver's seats and was sure Professor Heart was giving her one, too.

*They think* she's *acting like the ship's captain,* Reye giggled. Not that Reye could blame her. With the prospect of a new home right in front of them, it was easy to forget protocols.

"Sorry, Professor Heart," Dan-te quickly apologized, realizing her outburst was slightly out of line. Professor Heart merely responded by sending a stream of information to the navigation council and a short message.

"Don't worry about it. Instead use that excitement to help us get to the new cavern."

"Yes, ma'am," Dan-te replied, taking her shift at communications while Virgil resumed navigation duties assisted by both Reye and Ann.

For the next hour, the Arc plunged further into the magma flows beneath both the surface and the Great Lagoon. Finally, it reached the estimated floor of the new cavern. Once the Arc was under the cavern, it departed the magma stream. Drilling into the hard rock and stone that made up the crust of the Prism, the Arc collapsed the passageway behind it to ensure that magma could not follow it until it was safely anchored within breaching distance of the cavern.

"Launching probing drill," Virgil announced, pressing a button to activate a small drill on the top of the Arc that began burrowing through the rock until it penetrated the cavern.

"Air is present in the cavern. Checking air composition now. The air is a breathable nitrogen-oxygen mix, no lethal gases detected, temperatures are habitable, the air pressure is normal, it seems safe to enter and examine further."

Reye could not help noticing the rising smiles on Dan-te and the other members of the Remnant Council who had joined them on the bridge to hear all they could about the newly discovered cavern.

*This could be a new home for them,* Reye thought, a wave of longing for her own home back in the Orange Dominion coming over her. *I dreamt for years about getting away from the family farm, becoming a terranaut, and traveling the magma streams beneath Prism. But now that I've achieved my dream, all I want to do is go back to that farm. I wonder what that says about me?*

"Reye!"

Reye snapped out of her trance to see Ann looking at her from the opposite driver's seat.

"Everyone wants us to come and see the new cavern. Are you coming or not?"

Reye turned around and saw Professor Heart, Virgil, Dan-te, and the members of the Remnant Council staring at her, waiting for a reply.

"Let's go," Reye said, standing up and making her way to the excavation drill staircase leading out of the Arc and into the new cavern.

# Chapter 44

"Activating Excavation Drill," Ann announced, throwing a switch in a chamber near the top of the Arc, and starting the drill to burst into the new cavern.

The Excavation Drill was connected to a hollow shaft with stairs in it. After breaking into the cavern, they would walk through the passage and into it. News of the new cavern had spread to every member of the Remnant on the Arc. As the sound of the drill rattled through it, everyone eagerly waited for it to break into the cavern and for it to determine whether or not the Remnant would call this cavern its new home.

"We're in," Ann cried, feeling the drill move easier once it broke the shell of the cavern and soon cleared enough distance so that the entry hatch would be clear of the estimated internal cavern floor. "Let's see what we've found."

Reye, Stella, Ann, Virgil, Dan-te, Professor Heart, Ca-to, and the Remnant Council climbed up the stairs in the entry passage leading to the door. Reye realized she could not *Know* like Dan-te or the other members of the Remnant, but she did not need to; each one of them was clearly wearing the same feelings across their faces.

*They're all hoping that this will be their new home, and fighting down whatever fear they feel that it won't be.*

# The Second Coming

"Well, this is it," Ann said, about to open the doors until she turned to the Remnant Council. "Would one of you like to do the honors?"

The Council quickly grouped together, muttering to themselves, until an old female member of the Council, who looked like she could have been Met-on's much older aunt, stepped forward.

"I will open the door."

*The Seat of Hope,* Reye thought, recognizing the daughter of the Tribe of Shadows' gladiator Cacci-guida, as she stepped up and pressed a button that caused the doors to swing open and take everyone's breath away.

To say the cavern was big would have been a gross understatement, it was gargantuan. As the party stepped, almost reverently, into the cavern, they noticed that the penetration drill broke through at only a small corner of it where a finger of rock was protruding out. But the fact that they could *see* in the cavern was not even the most mesmerizing thing of all.

The cavern glowed and sparkled with light, all kinds of light, blues, indigo, violets, greens, and so many more that no one could possibly count them all. But the light was natural, it did not feel warm like sunlight—or even artificial light—it felt cool. Watching the dazzling display before them, Reye and Stella compared it to a sight they were more than familiar with.

"It's like the kaleidoscope of light on the Platinum Throne," Stella gasped, shocked at the sheer majesty of what they were looking at. "Look, it even seems like there are stars on the ceiling."

Reye did and realized that Stella was right.

*The lights don't just cover the cavern floor*, Reye marveled, *but are also scattered across the ceiling in an ever-shifting pattern resembling the stars in the night sky.*

Looking at Dan-te, Ca-to, and the members of the Remnant Council, Reye noticed that they were having a more extreme reaction to the cavern's display. All of them staggered before silently dropping onto their knees, a look of pure bliss etched onto each of their faces as waves of tears began running from their eyes.

"Dan-te," Virgil whispered, kneeling down next to Dan-te and cradling her in his arms. "What is it? How do you *Know* this place?"

Dan-te turned her head slightly so she could just meet Virgil's gaze; she did not want to stop looking at the sight before her anytime soon.

"I've never really *Known* it before Virgil," Dan-te squealed, happier than she ever sounded. "I've only *Known* it through stories and in my dreams. But it's the Glow. The Glowing Land from our stories, the way the Land was before 'The Coming.' The bio-luminesce land you told me about back in Spectral Academy. It's here, and it's alive! It's just like the stories described it, a warm land that

211

glowed with life, not just the silver energy of life but all the expressions of life living in peaceful harmony."

*The Glow...* The words triggered a memory in Reye from the Reconciliation Ritual.

*The last sight I witness just before waking up, sharing Evening Supper back home in the Orange Dominion with members of the Remnant in peace. The land glowed in more colors than I could imagine, just like it's doing now. The phantom Raymond, who now looked like a member of the Remnant, said, "This is the Glow the members of the Remnant speak of; and the dream of the world. The world has never forgotten what it was like before the Nag-el first came to it, and the world dreams of returning to what it once was. This is the world's dream, one where it can shine with the Glow again and live in harmony with* all *its people."*

*Is this what you were talking about when you said that the Glow was a dream the world keeps buried within it?* Reye asked herself as she knelt down to feel it better, only to discover it was not the rock glowing beneath them, but the dirt and grass. Looking back to where the Penetration Drill entered into the cavern, Reye saw the drill was also covered with glowing dirt and grass from where it broke into the cavern, and in the distance, a new sound caught her ear.

"A surf, what is this place?" Reye marveled. Her own wonder about the cavern left her at a loss for any other words. She had never heard of a cavern with dirt and grass in it, never heard of a cavern that could glow with the same kaleidoscopic effect as the Platinum Throne. And she certainly never heard of one that contained a surf, meaning that there was water, a *lot* of water, in it, making it far bigger and far more mysterious than it seemed.

"What is this place?" the Seat of Kindness pronounced, rising to his feet and looking happier that Reye had ever seen him. "I'll tell you what this place is. It's our new home! I'm going to tell our people, they need to see this for themselves."

With that, the Seat of Kindness ran back into the Arc to tell everyone the news about the cavern. Standing amidst the other members of the exploration party and seeing their reactions, Reye felt a sense of longing.

"You would have loved to see this, Raymond," Reye mumbled, thinking about her brother, and about how he always wanted to become an explorer and discover something new. "Here I am, standing in a glowing cavern that shouldn't exist, surrounded by a race of beings whose history and way of life predate the Hy-mun species, and you're not here to see it. Take a look at Ann, she's changed, she's more hopeful now than she ever used to be, yet still the pessimist. Now that the Seat of Kindness has declared that this cavern is going to be their new home, I'll bet she's already looking for ways that the whole cavern could cave in on us now that we've entered it."

# The Second Coming

Reye was right. Ann did have a worried expression on her face, counting on her fingers the dangers of building a new society in an unexplored cavern.

"Then there's Stella. She looks completely enraptured by the cavern's glow. In fact, considering all that she's been through, I didn't think anything could make her look peaceful again. But looking at her now, she looks almost as peaceful as she did when she would bathe herself in the light of the Platinum Throne."

Stella did feel strangely at ease. The kaleidoscopic effect of the glowing cavern had invoked her memories of the Platinum Throne, but she was also at ease for another reason. Since discovering her pregnancy, and choosing to carry the baby to term, her mind had been filling with questions about where she could deliver the child safely and with whom. Now she had her answers.

"I've decided," Stella whispered to herself, below the range that anyone could hear.

"Then there's Worm, or should I say, Virgil," Reye mused, looking at Virgil as he cradled the enraptured Dan-te. "Son of the Virt Prince of the Indigo Dominion, member of a heretical movement, master sword-fighter, scholar, and the grandson of the hero Able the Peacemaker who ended the Great Rainbow War and was also a prisoner of Nis himself. I couldn't have pegged him more wrong if I tried. Before this started, if I went to his home in the Indigo Dominion, I would have expected to find that he lived in a library, not the Tanzanite Ziggurat. I'm not even trying to guess what he's thinking now."

A noise caught Reye's attention as she turned to the Excavation Drill to see more members of the Remnant streaming out into the cavern: male and female, young and old, each one barely able to contain their excitement, shock, awe, and wonder, at the new—but in some ways anciently familiar—cavern stretching out before them.

*I can't blame them,* Reye thought with a smile as Ann tried to keep everyone calm and warn everyone not to get their hopes up too high since they did not know if there were any dangers in the cavern yet. *This is more than just a new cavern and home; it's like someone carved a piece of their ancient past and preserved it just for them, and now they've found it. They've finally come home.*

# Chapter 45

"I just want to make sure there are no surprises later," Ann kept saying. "You don't want to wait until it's too late."

The next couple of hours were a frazzle of activity both on and off the Arc. Exploration teams scoured the land to find edible plants, trees, and water. While the members of the Remnant claimed they *Knew* the cavern was safe to live in and its plant life was safe—having moved and lived in caverns for generations—Ann insisted on checking the cavern's soil and air compositions on board the Arc. The most significant find in the cavern came from the discovery of the source of the surf noises Reye heard earlier.

"An ocean," Reye gasped, the body of water stretching out before her. She joined the exploration team because she thought it was what her brother would have done. In the process, they discovered two freshwater rivers bubbling up from underground springs and the ocean. "This cavern, no, super cavern would be a better description, must be bigger than anything ever recorded for there to be an ocean in it. The water itself is glowing, just like the land."

"That's because it's also filled with life and the Glow," Ca-to explained, also amazed by the pre-Coming world preserved in the cavern. "And look across the water, more land has survived, and who knows what else might be there waiting for us."

# The Second Coming

In the distance, Reye could see more land glowing with the same soft light as the land they were standing on. She could easily guess what Ca-to was thinking.

*Ca-to is hoping that somehow more of his people might be here,* Reye figured. *If not, then perhaps animals from before "The Coming." The possibilities are both hopeful and exciting.*

Meanwhile, on the Arc, Professor Heart, Virgil, and the Seat of Kindness were able to determine the cavern's location beneath the surface of Prism and theorize how it and the Glow managed to survive there.

"This cavern is not so much a 'cavern' as it is a giant time capsule," Professor Heart explained. "It's located under the Great Lagoon, near the fingers of land belonging to the Blue Dominion, and beneath the Indigo Dominion. Now, it's been long theorized that the Indigo Dominion was once a part of a much larger landmass. Correct, Virgil?"

"Yes, Professor Heart," Virgil agreed. "It's long been believed that the peninsula and islands that make up the Indigo Dominion were once a part of a greater landmass that sunk into the sea. If this cavern is that landmass, then we should be underneath the Indigo Dominion right now. I actually wouldn't be surprised if there are massive stalagnates in this cavern that are connected to the islands of the Indigo Dominion."

"Stalagnates?" the Seat of Kindness asked.

"Stone pillars created when a stalagmite joins with a stalactite," Virgil explained. "Now, according to your story, during 'The Coming,' that landmass *did* exist. It was part of the Indigo Dominion. But it sank into the ocean from the force of the Nag-el's, the Beings of Light's, invasion."

"That is correct, Virgil," the Seat of Kindness confirmed. "It was a forested land precious to the First Ones. They were last seen on it before it sank. This *is* that land, I *Know* it is, even if I have never seen it. But what I don't understand is how it managed to survive and get here."

"The estimated top of this cavern is located deeper than any terraship has ever traveled." Professor Heart explained. "The reason why they don't go this deep is that the deeper they go, the greater the pressure on the ship becomes, and the lower the chances are that they will find anything of value. That said, no terraship ever travels deeper than a certain point. It's too expensive, risky, and impractical to try otherwise. As for how this cavern survived, my theory is that when the land and ocean sank, it sank so fast that it created a massive air pocket around it that was held in place by the rocks surrounding it as the magma sealed it shut."

"You mean how air pockets form in landslides and avalanches?" Virgil asked.

215

"Exactly," Professor Heart continued. "The sealed cavern then sank into the magma until it came to rest here where we found it. The plants sealed inside preserved the air, keeping it clean, and turned the cavern into one giant underground ecosystem based on Prism's ancient past. The only thing that it's missing is the Remnant's people."

"And that's assuming none of my people are already here," the Seat of Kindness hoped aloud. "According to the stories, my people had always lived in harmony with the world around them before 'The Coming.' After it, the Remnant still found ways to live in harmony with its new surrounds despite having to keep running from the Tribe of Shadows. If any of my people are here, I'm sure they will be alive; and if we are the last, I *Know* we can start over here."

"Than that just leaves one question," Virgil stated, voicing a question that he knew would come up. "Once all of the members of the Remnant are off the Arc and settled, what do we Hy-mun do?"

# Part 8: Returning Home to an Unknown Tomorrow

# Chapter 46

*Something is about to happen,* Reye realized as she returned with the exploration team.

A meeting was taking place with the Remnant Council, Professor Heart, Ann, Virgil, Stella, and the members of the Remnant at the Excavation Drill. Rushing up to the back of the crowd to listen to the meeting, she heard, "So, after finishing our examination, we have determined the cavern is indeed safe to live in. I, Professor Bridget Heart, as a representative of Hy-mun society, also believe that it is in the best interest of both our races if I not only return to the surface but not reveal the existence of this sealed cavern, or the Remnant of the Tribe, to anyone."

*We're going back,* Reye realized. *We're* finally *going back to the surface!*

Reye was overjoyed. While she definitely found the cavern beautiful and knew her brother would have loved to explore it if he were still alive, she longed to be back in the open air and under the sun again. Her adventure had been one she would never forget, but also one she wished she never had had. Now, it was finally time to go home to the Orange Dominion.

"Because the Arc was spotted in Nis, I believe it is dangerous to bring it back to the surface in case more Hammers of the Orange Light, or their allies, are up there," Professor Heart continued. "The Arc's navigational black box could be exploited and used to find this cavern. That's why I intend to leave the Arc docked where it is beneath the cavern and use the Arc's magma rafts to return to the surface. The Arc, its supplies, material, and technology, I am leaving for the Remnant of the Tribe to use as you see fit in the rebuilding of your society."

A cheer of thanks rose up from the assembly at Professor Heart's declaration. Over the last week of traveling through the magma, it had been discovered that the Arc was loaded with seeds, non-perishable food, building and gardening tools, and other materials; all of the building blocks needed to begin a new society. Professor Heart, after finding the stockpile, realized her father must have not only been planning for the day when the supervolcano erupted, but also for what would be needed afterward. However, until Professor Heart's decision, none of the Remnant had considered using any of them. They still thought of the supplies as her property. Now they knew they were free to use them as they wished.

"Now, for the other Hy-mun representatives present." Professor Heart's gaze shifted to Ann and across the assembly to where Reye was looking not only at her but also at Stella and Virgil. "You've known each other far longer than I have, so I feel I am in no position to order or ask any of you to return to the surface with me. I leave the choice of returning to the surface or remaining here to you. Please choose whether you wish to return or remain here with the Remnant of the Tribe."

Ann walked alongside Professor Heart, taking a step beyond her so the assembly could see her better.

"I am Ann Branley, and I will be speaking for myself now," Ann said, taking a deep breath to prepare herself. "After much personal consideration, I have decided that I will return to the surface with Professor Heart. I thank the Remnant of the Tribe for everything it's done for me, and I promise I will keep its existence a secret, but I need to be back on the surface. The new land-based volcanoes created by Tanas's Third Great Attempt and our own attempts to stop it are going to need study so that Hy-muns can face the dangers presented by them. I can't stay safe down here when I already know what can go wrong on the surface. I have to return."

Reye noticed Ann's face was reset into her classic, pessimistic frown, but there was now a determined look in her eyes.

*She's already decided, not just about returning to the surface, but what she's going to do once she gets there,* Reye thought, looking into Ann's eyes. *What am I going to do once I get back? Ever since I found myself in Nis, besides vengeance, all I wanted to do was go back to the surface and go home to the Orange Dominion. But once I get home, what am I going to do?*

Reye knew that most of her desire to return to the surface was rooted in her quest for vengeance, bringing back an army to destroy Nis. But now that Nis was gone, what was next?

The Second Coming

*I don't want to return to Spectral Academy, I'm positive about that. After Sol said I was chosen for the mining project just so I could be used as a sacrifice, I don't want to be anywhere* near *the powers that be in case they wonder how I could still be alive. Nor do I want to be a terranaut anymore. I knew that once I was in the seat of the Arc and actually piloted it for some time. The price of becoming a terranaut was not what I thought it would be. If becoming a terranaut meant I had to sacrifice Raymond's life, subject Stella to all the pain she went through, and butcher scores of warriors in a mad rampage, then that's not the life for me. But what can I do now?*

"According to Professor Heart, we'll leave tomorrow, that will give us time to secure the Arc, say our good-byes, and for the rest of us to make our decisions to stay or leave. It has been an honor to have known you all."

Ann's final comment brought heartfelt applause from every member of the Remnant.

*None of them are going to forget us,* Reye thought as she looked around the cavern, basking in the Glow, and realizing that this cavern is what the Remnant had been searching for its entire life. Reye was so dazed she did not notice Stella approaching her until she touched her shoulder.

"Reye."

"Stella," Reye gasped in surprise. "I'm sorry, what is it."

"There's something I have to talk to you about."

\*\*\*

*Where are you, Virgil?* Dan-te thought as she moved through the familiar patterns of energy swirling about the other members of the Remnant around the Arc. Thankfully, after traveling with Virgil for so long, she could pick out his blue and indigo energy even among a crowd of similarly colored ones.

"There you are," Dan-te sighed with relief as she approached the Arc and saw near the ship scanning the crowd the familiar Hy-mun figure that she had come to *Know*. Virgil was looking for someone, too. His white mental energy was pulsing, and his blue energy of resolve was even more robust than usual. Something was on his mind, and Dan-te could guess what it was.

*He's made his decision about leaving with the magma raft,* Dan-te figured, stopping in her tracks as a cold wave of fear hit her. *Is he going to go back to the surface?*

Dan-te remembered that Virgil promised her to take her safely back to Nis, to do whatever he could to stop the Third Great Attempt, and to help her and her people. Dan-te realized Virgil succeeded in getting her to Nis. She also realized that in the end, he was not able to do anything to sabotage the Third Great Attempt. Professor Heart and the Hammers of the Orange Light's terraships did that for him. All he could do besides getting her back was save

Stella's life, carry Met-on—who was still unconscious—to the Arc, and do whatever he could onboard the Arc to help navigate and bring it to this cavern.

*If he thinks he's failed, does that mean he's going to leave and return to the Indigo Dominion?* Dan-te *Knew* she had developed feelings for Virgil, and she also *Knew* Virgil carried similar feelings for her. Yet, neither one of them dared discuss them with the Third Great Attempt, and the threat it posed to both of their people, continually hanging over their heads.

*But that threat is gone now,* Dan-te realized. *If Virgil doesn't think he's fulfilled his promise to me, or that it would be dangerous for him to stay, is he going to return? He* is *Hy-mun royalty, maybe he feels he needs to go back.* The prospect of Virgil leaving scared her more than she realized. She did not hear Virgil call her name until he was almost in front of her.

"Dan-te!" Virgil shouted, breaking her trance.

"Sorry, Virgil," Dan-te stuttered, trying to recollect herself. "I guess now that the danger is over, you're going back to the surface and returning home to the Indigo Dominion."

"Why do you think that?" Virgil asked, confused.

"You couldn't do anything to stop the Third Great Attempt, you're the son of a Virt Prince, and you can go home, that's why."

"You're right, I couldn't stop the Third Great Attempt," Virgil admitted. "But I only said I would try, not that I would, so I didn't break any promises. We both knew that it was a long shot that I was going to be able to do anything at all."

"That's true," Dan-te agreed.

"And I *did* get you back to your people. Besides, we could be under the Indigo Dominion right now. Right here in this cavern, there could be stalagnates that connect to the islands of the Indigo Dominion. A terraship might not be the only way to get here. Someone should be here in case Hy-muns find this place."

"Wait, what are you saying?"

A bright and wiry smile appeared on Virgil's face as he took Dan-te's hand and placed it over his heart. Dan-te suddenly felt new energy flow into her, an energy she recognized in herself and in other members of the Remnant as Dan-te *Knew* all she ever needed to know about Virgil's decision—wiping her fears away.

"Look around us, in this new world I feel like I'm constantly surrounded by the stars in the night sky. I can't think of anywhere else a guy like me who once dreamed of reaching the stars would want to live."

"Then, in that case," Dan-te chuckled. "I have this really crazy and bad idea I want you to support me on, and you did promise to support me the next time I came up with one."

# The Second Coming

"I just hope it's not too bad of an idea," Virgil reminded her. Dan-te moved closer to him and whispered her idea into his ear, a smile appearing on Virgil's face the moment he heard it.

"Yes," Virgil answered, "if you'll have me."

Dan-te threw her arms around Virgil, holding him like never before and making sure not to impale him with her horn or crush him.

"We need to tell the others."

\*\*\*

"You're going to stay!"

Reye had suffered enough shocks to make her think she would be used to it by now. She was wrong.

"Why do you want to stay, you have a family that must think you are dead back in the Violet Dominion. Don't you want to go home and let them know you're alive?"

"Family is the reason why I *want* to stay." Stella declared adamantly, cradling her womb and the child she carried. "There is no way I can give birth to this child on the surface. While captive, I learned from Met-on that there have been other cases of mixed-blood children between the Tribe of Shadows and Hy-muns; they were produced to see if they could stand sunlight, but none of them could. I checked out the story with the members of the Remnant, and they confirmed it. If I give birth on the surface, the child, and possibly myself, will die as soon as the sunlight touches him or her. But here, my child can not only be born safely but also be raised in peace. As for my parents in the Violet Dominion, they're probably glad I'm gone."

"What! How could you say that?" Reye asked. "Why would they want you dead and gone?"

"You have no idea how strict my parents are about traditions. My older sister had to be banished from my family just to marry someone from a different dominion."

Reye's eyes popped open. Stella had never revealed this part of her past to her. She could not conceive of any family being okay with banishing one of their own.

"My own entry into Spectral Academy was also met with skepticism after the Violet Dominion couldn't use me as a pawn to get a foothold into the Indigo Dominion, which was how I first met Virgil. Then there was something Sol said."

"What?"

"That me, 'the mining crew in the Demp Caverns, all of those idiots at Spectral Academy, and especially that silly and warped girl Reye and her brother from the Orange Dominion' were chosen by the Hammers of the Orange Light to be in the Demp Caverns. Just so we could be bait for the Tribe of Shadows. An organization that could assemble the manpower and resources to secretly create six large terraships, launch them, and invade an underground city *picked* and wanted *us* dead. If any of them made it back to the surface, or are still on the surface, and learn that we're still alive, try to imagine what could happen?"

Reye had imagined it. Anyone who started talking about what happened down here would either be declared insane or killed to keep the Hammer's existence a secret or the status quo intact.

"If you need someplace to stay, you can stay with me. I plan to go back to my family's farm in the Orange Dominion; we can find a way for you to give birth safely there. There are plenty of dark caves near my home, you can…"

"I can what," Stella challenged. "Live in a dark cave with my child, isolated, for the rest of our lives? Keep him or her there like a pet that I'm hiding? I can't do either of those things. But here, I have a new world where I can raise my child, and he or she will be safe with people who will help me until a time when perhaps I can return to the surface. This is the best choice for both of us."

"But you'll be the only Hy-mun here," Reye argued, unable to face losing her friend for a second time.

"No, she won't," a new voice said from beside them.

Reye turned to her side and saw Virgil walking up to them with Dan-te by his side.

"I'm also staying."

"You can't stay!" Reye and Stella exclaimed in unison.

"You're the son of a Virt Prince," Reye rambled. "You're needed in the Indigo Dominion. What if you need to take over, what if they're looking for you now, what if…"

"Relax," Virgil explained. "My brother Homer is the heir to the title of Virt Prince, and while we might be twins, we're fraternal twins, we look nothing alike. Also, my family already knows I might not be returning at all."

"What do you mean?" Stella asked.

"Before leaving Spectral Academy, I sent out several letters. The last was a coded letter to my mother—using a code only we know and can decipher—explaining what I was about to do, where I was going, and most importantly, why. I also explained that there was a high chance that I wouldn't be able to return and if I didn't than to tell anyone who asks that I had died in an accident."

"But you can't leave *your* family wondering whether you're alive or dead," Reye chastised.

The Second Coming

"I won't," Virgil answered, taking Reye's hand and placing a pin and letter in it, the same one he had given to Met-on, only to be later picked up by Stella, and then returned to Virgil by her while they were on the Arc.

"I want you to tell my family what happened."

"Me?" Reye gasped, scared at the thought of even approaching a Virt Prince.

"Send that pin and letter to the Tanzanite Ziggurat," Virgil instructed. "It explains what happened here. Besides, they're also holding the books you and Ann gave me before you left Spectral Academy. The letter also tells them where they can forward your stuff to."

Reye chuckled weakly, but it did not help her mood.

*Stella is staying here to start a new life, and I bet Virgil planned to do something like this from the start,* Reye realized, looking at the determined expressions on both of their faces. *He even sent our stupid books to his home so they can be sent to us later. Now he wants me to send a letter to his parents, a Virt Prince and Princess, explaining everything that happened.*

"And then what?" Reye mumbled. "I've lost my brother. My dream turned out to be not what I wanted it to be. Now, I'm losing two of my friends, and you're asking me to deliver a message to your parents once I get back to the surface, but then what? My plans for the future only extend as far as going home. What do I do after that? Please, one of you, tell me what I should do?"

Virgil, Dan-te, and Stella each looked to the other, realizing the same thing.

*Reye focused so much of herself on her dream, revenge, finding Stella, and going home that she doesn't know what she should do now,* Dan-te thought, watching Reye's energies swirl chaotically around her. *She's at an internal crossroad but doesn't know where to turn. The last time I tried talking to her, it ended badly.* "I think you should say something, Virgil."

Dan-te squeezed Virgil's hand, signaling him to talk.

*Stella's trying to come up with something,* Dan-te realized. *But her white metal energy is only simmering. Yours, however, is flashing throughout your head. You have something in mind.*

Vigil nodded to Dan-te's prodding, taking the initiative.

"What would Raymond be doing right now?" Virgil asked.

"Raymond?" Reye popped open in surprise. Reye certainly did not expect to hear him mention her brother. Virgil had learned how Raymond died and knew it was a sensitive topic.

"Raymond would be on an explorer's high right now. This place would have been a dream come true for him. If he were here right now, he would be talking to people, collecting plants, making up ideas about how they generated light, why they died in sunlight, and if there was a way we could overcome that and transplant them to—"

Reye stopped mid-sentence, a scene from her vision during the Reconciliation Ritual, vividly replaying itself in her head along with the phantom-Raymond's words.

"The world has never forgotten what it was like before the Nag-el first came to it, and the world dreams of returning to what it was once was. This is the world's dream, one where it can shine with the Glow again and live in harmony with *all* its people," Reye said aloud, a new light brightening her eyes as her mind began creating plans for a new project, a project she would give the rest of her life to finish if needed, but one she *would* finish.

"I need your help," Reye asked hysterically. "All of you."

"Of course," Stella, Dan-te, and Virgil agreed unanimously as they ran back into the Excavation Drill for supplies. Reye knew she had a lot of work to do, and not a lot of time to do it in.

# Chapter 47

The rest of the day was a fury of activity for Reye, Stella, Virgil, and Dan-te. Together they gathered as many plant and seed containers as possible, collecting samples of every glowing plant, blade of grass, piece of soil, and seed they could find until the magma raft could not hold anything else other than its passengers.

*This is the kind of thing Raymond would do,* Reye thought to herself, working with more passion and energy than she ever did as the Hy-mun Horror.

*Raymond, after finding this place, would want to bring these plants back and find a way to grow them on the farm. That's what I can and will do. I'll find a way to make these plants survive on the surface in sunlight. I'll make Raymond's dream, the world's dream, come true.*

Alongside her, Dan-te, Virgil, and Stella smiled at the change in Reye.

"Reye's mind is buzzing with white mental energy, and her natural brown energy is rippling all around her excitedly," Dan-te whispered to Vigil as they followed after Reye. "She *Knows* what she wants to do now and is willing to do it. How did you figure out that mentioning her brother would do this?"

"I didn't," Virgil replied. "But Raymond meant more to Reye than anyone else in the world, and finding a place like this was his greatest dream. I thought that if I reminded her of that, she might think of something on her own. But Reye needed to come up with the answer herself. If she couldn't, then she would either end up relying on what I told her, or she wouldn't believe me.

Thankfully, she's wised up enough that she doesn't need me, or anyone else, to give her advice anymore."

"You really *Know* her, you realize that, don't you?" Dan-te commented as she watched Reye work.

"I don't think I really *Know* her, but I do think I understand her, and *Knowing* and understanding are two very different things."

When the time of their departure finally came, Reye, Ann, and Professor Heart were seen off by Stella, Virgil, Dan-te, Ca-to, the Remnant Council, and as many members of the Remnant that could fit in the magma raft launch bay. Professor Heart carried a large device that Ann explained to the assembly.

"This is a special two-way radio. It connects the Arc with only this magma raft. If there are any problems, or if you simply want to say hello, use the Arc's radio to call us."

"We will," the Seat of Hope responded. "But I hope it won't be used for anything more than social calls."

"It shouldn't have to," Professor Heart replied. "With all the trouble I'm expecting on the surface, I doubt anyone will even want to try and explore this deep and re-find the cavern. And now that I've turned off the Arc's beacon, I doubt I'll even be able to re-find it."

"Still, I hope you have a good journey." The Seat of Hope embraced both Professor Heart and Ann as they made their way into the magma raft. Reye waited a moment to say one last good-bye to both Stella and Virgil.

"I guess this is it," Reye squeaked, realizing that now it really was the last time she would probably see them again.

"Yes, it is," Stella replied, equally uncomfortable about this being the last time they would see each other.

"Graduation came early for all of us," Virgil interjected, breaking the mood and getting both of their attention.

"Graduation?" they asked, confused.

"Yes, graduation," Virgil explained. "This is our graduation, summa cum laude—with the highest praise. We're all about to begin new lives. Look at yourself, Reye. You're leaving for the Orange Dominion with your brother's dream literally in your hands so you can continue and complete it on the surface. By the way, do you still have the letter I gave you and remember the other details I told you about?"

"I do," Reye answered, feeling the inside of her pocket where the letter was resting. "And I remember how you told me it also asks your family for all the gardening and botany books and supplies you have. That they are to be sent to me to help with my project to find a way to make the cavern's plants thrive on the surface."

"Right," Virgil agreed before turning to Stella. "Stella, you're starting your own personal journey, one you thankfully won't have to face alone. You have a whole new extended family waiting to help you."

"I can't say I'm as excited as you make it," Stella admitted. "I didn't want this, any of this. But I'm here now because of my choices. And I have to live with the consequences of those actions and to make the best of them. It's unfair blaming anyone, including Met-on, and especially this child, for decisions and circumstances beyond their control."

"Has Met-on even woken up yet?" Reye asked.

"No," Stella answered. "And I'm not looking forward to when he does."

"I'm willing to bet you'll find that he'll have changed for the better," Virgil assured her. "Like I said, we're all graduating from our old lives and entering new ones. Just like we would have if we had finished Spectral Academy. We're just doing it a lot sooner."

"So, what's next now that you've graduated?" Reye asked, a smirk appearing on her face. "What are your plans?"

"*I* don't have any plans," Virgil said, turning his head toward Dan-te.

"But *we* do," the two of them said in unison.

"Okay, now *this* is getting interesting." Reye giggled, a familiar sensation washing over her as she now looked at both Virgil and Dan-te.

"We are going to go off and fully explore this new underground world," Virgil explained.

"Just the two of you?" Reye asked.

"It was my idea. We've traveled together before, and we can do it again." Dan-te assured her. "Virgil thinks that if we search the cavern, we might even find giant stalagnates that could one day connect this cavern with the Indigo Dominion, assuming it doesn't connect with it already. If there's another way for Hy-muns to get down here, we need to know about it so we can be ready in case someone else finds their way down here."

"And if someone *does* find their way down here," Virgil continued, "it might be better if they find a Hy-mun waiting for them. Less chance for a 'Third Coming'."

"Don't even joke about that," Dan-te shot back, elbowing Virgil in the ribs.

Looking at the two of them, Reye smiled and imagined what the future was going to hold for all three of them.

*Stella is going to make a wonderful mother*, Reye mused. *I can't think of anyone kinder. As for Virgil and Dan-te, I'll bet those two are going to be like a couple of romantic explorers on an exotic adventure. Raymond, you would have loved to be in his shoes.*

"Reye, it's time to go!" Ann called from the bridge of the magma raft.

"Stella, take care of yourself and your child." Reye cried, hugging Stella for what she knew could be the last time; tears now running down both of their faces as the final moments sank in. "Again, I'm sorry I wasn't there for you sooner."

Stella looked into Reye's eyes and could see that she still blamed herself for not trying to save her during her captivity in Lust Atrophied.

"Reye, as I've already told you before, I've forgiven you for that, and for everything else. Now get back to the surface with Raymond's dream and find a way to make those plans thrive on the surface. I'm hoping that one day I'll be able to return to the surface and find your family's farm is covered in them."

Reye nodded before hugging Stella one more time before backing into the magma raft, never taking her eyes off Stella, Virgil, and Dan-te.

"I expect to hear how all of you are doing soon," Reye screamed just before the doors shut. "Good-bye."

The doors sealed shut, and Reye made her way through her samples to the bridge of the magma raft where Professor Heart and Ann were waiting for her.

"So, are we just going to head straight up and come out in the Great Lagoon?" Ann asked.

"Too dangerous," Professor Heart answered. "We don't want anyone questioning how we ended up there or risk sending any seawater back toward the cavern. It will take some time, but we're heading for the Red or Orange Dominions. We'll break through the land there, and if we're found in that region, it will look less suspicious since magma rafts are tested in the Red Dominion."

"At least we'll get home sooner," Reye said, trying to sound cheerful, but found it hard knowing her friends were staying behind.

"Yes, we will," Ann agreed. "Let's go home."

Ann started the magma raft's drilling mechanisms, moving the raft back into the magma streams, and beginning its long journey back to the surface.

# Chapter 48

"We'll be entering the cave system shortly," Ann cheered from the controls of the raft as the view on its screen changed and showed an open cavern ahead of them.

"I hope so," Reye exhaled. "After being stuck in this raft for a week, I feel like a piece of canned meat."

"Try being stuck in this suit for as long as I have," Professor Heart butted in. "*Then*, you can talk to me about feeling like a piece of canned meat."

The three of them laughed despite themselves as they waited for the moment when they would finally be out of the raft. A week had passed since Reye, Ann, and Professor Heart had left the cavern, leaving Virgil and Stella behind with the Remnant of the Tribe in their new home.

To further ensure that no one could trace them back to the Remnant, Professor Heart had disabled the raft's navigation, tracking, and distress systems. They had spent the last week traveling through the magma streams of Prism using nothing but paper maps, hand navigation tools, and pure mathematics. Professor Heart's best estimates had them somewhere between the Red and Orange Dominions; they were now trying to surface, having discovered a cave system near their current location after reactivating the raft's navigation systems.

"Breaching…now!" Ann shouted as the raft burst from the ground and emerged into a cave.

"Then let's cover our cargo, turn on the lights, and find out where we are," Reye sang, heading to inspect and cover the plants they were carrying.

Reye knew that artificial light was not harmful to the plant samples, but all it would take was one beam of sunlight, and her project would be over before it began. And since their estimates showed them to be slightly underground, it was more than likely that the roof of the cave could collapse and let the sunlight in.

"Cargo covered," Reye confirmed, putting a dark tarp over the last glowing plant. "Let's find out where we are."

Ann popped the hatch, and the three of them stepped out into the cave. Once in the cave, Professor Heart opened a valve on her suit, allowing the fluid inside it to flush out. Taking her helmet off, she looked as though she had been in a bath for a week.

"I *never* want to do that again," Professor Heart exasperated. "That's it, this was my last adventure underground. I am never using this suit again."

"But if you didn't use it, then it really would have been our *last* adventure," Ann joked.

"Which is why I know I'm never using it again," Professor Heart laughed, walking into the cave but stopping short when she heard something break underneath her foot."

"What was that?" Reye and Ann asked.

"A broken lamp," Professor Heart answered, picking it up and showing it to both Ann and Reye. "Someone's been in this cave before. That means there's a way to the surface from here."

"Let me see that lamp," Reye exclaimed, rushing over to take the lamp from Professor Heart, a look of shock and familiarity appearing on her face.

"Can we really have ended up *here*?"

"What is it, Reye?" Ann asked. "Don't tell me you actually know where we are?"

"I do," Reye whiffed before turning back to the ship and grabbing a trio of lanterns so they could see better.

"I know this cave," Reye explained. "Our estimates were off, we're in the Orange Dominion. Follow me."

Reye took off through the cave, Ann and Professor Heart close behind her. The trio soon emerged from the cave into a forest of amber-leaf trees in the late-afternoon sunlight. The sight alone; the sun, the forest, the feeling of fresh air filling their lungs, brought all three of them to tears. After being underground, fighting for their lives in Nis, for what felt like a lifetime, just being on the surface again and enjoying a peaceful moment in a forest bathed in sunlight was the best thing any of them had ever experienced.

# The Second Coming

*I'm back, Raymond,* Reye mused, basking in the sunlight. *I've finally made it back to the surface, back to the light, and now I've only got a little way further to go.*

Moving again, Reye took off through the forest, her steps happier now as the trees and worn pathways around her became more familiar, soon coming to a large hill just outside the forest. Racing to the hilltop with Professor Heart and Ann, Reye was soon looking down on a view she last witnessed through the Remnant Reconciliation Ritual, her home.

"I'm back," Reye cried softly, falling to her knees at the sight before her. "There's my family, Ann. They are preparing Evening Supper. We've popped up right on my doorstep. I've finally come home."

The sight of Reye on the hill was soon noticed by the rest of her family as looks of sheer shock, fear, and happiness suddenly began racing through the farm as her family started running up the hill to meet them. Soon, Reye was surrounded by her parents, extended family, and the farmhands who worked there. Everyone was asking where she had been and what had happened to her, Raymond, and the rest of the mining project. Reye knew she would eventually have to answer those questions, but for now, only one thought filled her mind.

*I'm home, after so long. I've finally found my light. I've come home.*

# Chapter 49

"Another failed try," Reye muttered. "What is it that I'm missing?"

Reye walked through the cave carrying a lantern in one hand, her mail, and the burned up remains of her latest attempt at breeding a plant from the Remnant's cavern that could withstand sunlight in the other. Even after a year of trying different methods, she still had not found a way to make the glowing plants from the Remnant's Cavern thrive on the surface. But failure had only made her determination grow as she made her way to her sealed garden in the cave near her family's farm where the magma raft was now docked.

*I can't let myself get discouraged*, Reye mused, approaching the metal wall that now sealed the rest of the cave. *No one said that figuring this out was going to be easy, but if I'm going to make this work, I've got to keep trying. There has to be a way to make these plants survive in sunlight.*

Putting down her lantern, Reye took a key out of her pocket and unlocked the door. A sign on it read "Keep Out – Project: Raymond's Dream." Stepping through the door, she walked into her garden containing the glowing plants and specimens she brought back with her from the Remnant's glowing cavern. The magma raft she, Ann, and Professor Heart used to reach the cave from the Remnant's cavern was now anchored on the far side of it. So far, she had only managed to cultivate the plants in both the cavern's own soil and soil taken from the cave. The plants still could not grow if they were planted on the surface, or even with the dirt taken from the surface, but she had not given up.

# The Second Coming

Taking a seat at her desk, Reye opened her mail: a new book from Virgil's family in the Indigo Dominion, and a letter from Ann.

"It's been quite a year," Reye mused, thinking about everything that happened after finally reuniting with her family. "Everyone wanted to tell the whole Dominion that I had come home safe and sound. But after hearing what happened to Raymond, Nis, the Hammers of the Orange Light, and how we were originally chosen by 'the powers that be' to be used as bait for the Tribe of Shadows, everyone could understand why I wanted to keep my return a secret. Not that the other Dominions could probably spare me a thought, especially with everything else going on. The world has changed."

Thanks to the volcanic tubes dug by Professor Heart and the entry passages dug by the Hammers' terraships, Tanas's supervolcano did not erupt like he had planned. Instead, it defused through a series of eruptions that ran across the area formally known as Sand Break Border, now known as the Volcanic Spine, to Tri-Dominion City, where a new ring of volcanoes surrounded it. Miraculously, Tri-Dominion City survived. But it was now caught between the magma falls running around and down each side of it. Unfortunately, after the eruption, the Dominions were quick to demand answers from the leadership of Tri-Dominion City and the Virt Princes of the Red, Orange, Yellow, and Violet Dominions about how this happened since all four of them were in Tri Dominion City at the time of the eruption. The leaders of Tri-Dominion City were quick to give a statement; that the Virt Princes died and to send all questions to the new rulers of each Dominion. The new rulers, none of whom were even aware of their father's activities with Kai Aphas or the Hammers, soon retreated into the Ziggurats and were using committees and bureaucracies to keep the people at bay while they tried to understand their new world.

"None of the new Virt Princes are going to be able to give the people what they need any time soon," Reye realized. "The real improvements are being made by private organizations. Most of the Dominions were led by Kai Aphas and his agenda for so long they don't know how to think and act for themselves. If not for Virgil's father and the Virt Princes of the Green and Blue Dominions, we might have already descended into worse chaos then the Great Rainbow War."

After the eruption, Virgil's father, Hesiod Virt Indigo-Castitas, in a rare display of openness, reached out to the Virt Princes of the Blue and Green Dominions and started a united front to aid and support reconstruction organizations. The entire Virt Indigo-Castitas family even traveled to each of the Dominions to visit the new Virt Princes and offer their support to the new rulers.

"They've been nothing but helpful from the moment I told them Virgil's story," Reye mused. "Thinking back, I wouldn't be surprised if the only reason that they came to the Orange Dominion was just to see me."

While in the Orange Dominion, Virgil's family surprised Reye and her family with a secret visit to their farm. The letter Virgil sent them was in hand the moment they arrived, along with all the books he said they would give her. Reye still remembered the day everyone met them.

"When everyone realized they were serving a Virt Prince and Princess, they nearly freaked out," Reye remembered, still able to see the shocked expressions on everyone's faces. "Yet Virgil's mother was the last person I would have figured to be a Virt Princess; she dressed, spoke, and acted as if she were raised on a farm herself. I can see where Virgil got his personality from. It completely shattered everyone's preconceptions of what a Virt Princess would be like."

But Virgil's family did not simply show up to work on the farm and deliver books, they also wanted to hear the details of what happened to him, and everything else that went on in Nis; including why Virgil wished to stay, from someone who lived through it. Virgil was also right when he said that his brother Homer did not look anything like him.

"I still can't believe *that* was Virgil's twin brother." Reye puffed. Virgil's pin, and a picture of herself with Homer, now sat on her desk, reminding her of their encounter and the sharp contrast between them. "The only things Virgil and Homer shared were their complexion, hair, and eye color; after that, they were built entirely different. Where Virgil was lean and looked skeletal at times; Homer was a solid mass of muscle. He looked like he spent his whole life training to be a bodybuilder; he actually laughed about that.

"All of Virgil's family have been nothing but supportive of this project. Especially Virgil's mother, I still remember the look on her face when she first saw the samples we brought back from the cavern."

***

"I never thought they would look this beautiful," Virgil's mother gasped. "And these are just *samples*?"

"Small samples," Reye explained, leading Virgil's mother through the magma raft. She insisted on seeing for herself what Reye was trying to accomplish and get an idea as to where Vigil had chosen to live. "The cavern was infinitely better."

"I can understand why Virgil would choose to live there," Virgil's mother said with a knowing sigh. "You said he found an inner peace living there with the Remnant that he couldn't find on the surface. If these plants are just a small sample, I can't even imagine the beauty of the cavern. It brings a sense of peace to both the mind and heart that no one could say no to."

\*\*\*

"I still didn't tell her about you and Dan-te," Reye reflected, gazing at the pin. "But I bet she suspected it. This adventure changed us all. The farmhands see it in me every day. I used to be the wild child, always the first to get into the newest activity or mischief with Raymond right on my heels. Now, I'm the calmest one around, staying as far away from attention as possible so I can work on making these plants grow on the surface. If Raymond were here, he probably would say I've finally reached the point where I don't need him anymore. And if you were here, I'd bet you would say something in Platin to describe the situation; that I'd found a calling, one that means everything to me. I wonder if we'll ever see each other again."

Turning back to her mail, Reye opened the final piece, a letter from Ann.

"It's about time, Ann," Reye yipped, tearing into the letter. "I've been wondering if there's been any news."

Ann was working with Professor Heart, and the two of them had taken the radio connecting them to the Remnant. So, Reye was eagerly awaiting this letter and wanted to read it in the privacy of her garden in case there was anything about Stella, Virgil, or the Remnant's cavern in it. Ann and Reye always wrote their letters using Virgil's nickname, they didn't want to take any chances.

"Dear Reye," Reye read aloud. "How have you been? Is your garden project showing any new results? I heard that last year, you had a visit from Worm's mother to see the garden in its preliminary stages and that she was completely stunned by it."

*You don't know the half of it,* Reye mused as she continued reading Ann's letter.

"I've been working hard as Professor Heart's assistant up and down the Volcanic Spine. Since the initial eruption, the new volcanoes have remained semi-active, burping up ash every so often but not making any major eruption— except for the ones around Tri-Dominion City. Professor Heart thinks that the magma feeding the volcanoes from the magma pool beneath the city's location is keeping them active. Meanwhile, I've been seeing how the new volcanoes have affected the soil in the Green Dominion—making it more plentiful. Professor Heart has been working like a woman possessed to create channels from each volcano to the Seraph Sea and the Great Lagoon, so if there are any more eruptions, they won't be as damaging."

"Professor Heart feels guilty over what's she's done," Reye realized, reading the letter and its hidden messages. "She created the volcanoes now making up the Spine. Granted, the alternative was a world-ending supervolcanic eruption, but that still doesn't make the decision any easier, not that I'm one to talk about having guilt on my conscious."

Even though Reye had made it back to the surface and mourned the death of her brother with her family, she was still pained by the lives she took in Nis as the Hy-mun Horror. It was a pain she knew she would feel for the rest of her life, and one she should not forget either. Remembering the kind of person she was, and the mistakes she made, was one of the galvanizing forces that kept her motivated toward the completion of her project.

"Now, for the information, I know you want to hear," Reye read as she continued the letter. "We received a call from our old friends."

*They're heard from Stella and Worm,* Reye thought excitedly as she continued the letter.

"Star's pregnancy went longer than expected, a result of who the child's father was, but she's given birth to a boy named Raymond after your brother. That strange kid who used to hang around Star and had been in a coma finally woke up; only his long-term memory is gone. The only thing he can remember is Star and a desire to serve her, which Star is taking full advantage of. Worm and his girlfriend look to be getting married soon too; as soon as they get back from their cruise to the surrounding islands. I plan on being in the Orange Dominion next month, if I get the chance, I'll stop by and say hello. Your friend, Ann."

*So, Virgil and Dan-te are getting married,* Reye mused. *I'm not surprised. And it seems that Met-on has finally woken up, with amnesia, and Stella is really working him because of all he did to her.*

Reye heard about Met-on, the half-blood Tribe of Shadows/Remnant member responsible for both Stella's pregnancy and leading Virgil and Dan-te to Stella in time to save her from Sol after he had been dug out from under a wall and carried to safety on Virgil's back.

*When I first heard about him, I thought that Stella would have left him buried under that wall. He deserved it. But it seems he's woken up now and can only remember Stella and the desire to serve her. Virgil said that after learning about the differences between the Tribe of Shadows' and Hy-mun's cultures, Met-on not only felt sorry for what he had done but also wanted to make it up to Stella, something that Stella said she was going to see that he did.*

*I doubt Stella will get too out of hand with Met-on,* Reye mused, thinking about what Stella might do to him. *But if she does, I'm sure the other members of the Remnant will be there to keep her in check.*

*But the best news is that Stella's given birth!* Reye jumped out of her seat to look for some water so she could have an impromptu toast. *Maybe now she'll consider coming back to the surface, even if just for a visit. And she's named her son Raymond. Brother, if you were here now, I bet...*

At the mention of both her brother and Stella's son, Reye's mind flashed back to the Reconciliation Ritual's final scene. She remembered her home at night covered in the same glowing plants and light as the cavern, and the phantom-Raymond who now looked like he was a member of the Remnant. He showed her the Evening Supper with all the members of her family and the Remnant and told her that it was the world's dream.

*Could that have been more than just a vision needed to help me come to terms with my past?* Reye wondered, looking at the growing plants surrounding her, and suddenly feeling more inspired.

"In the last part of that vision, I saw the land, plants, and buildings all glowing like the Remnant's new home in the cavern," Reye whispered to herself, her mind turning at the possibility. "My family, the members of the Remnant, including the one who looked just like Raymond, were seated together enjoying the Evening Supper. I said to the Remnant Raymond that the vision told me that my family can eat and live in peace with members of the Remnant. He also said that it was the world's dream, 'one where it can shine with the Glow again and live in harmony with *all* its people.' The vision was *supposed* to just help me reconcile myself with my past, with what I had done as the Hy-mun Horror, but what if it was more?"

Reye looked to the plant samples growing throughout her garden and began to picture them growing across her farm. She would watch the sunset behind the hill, and the whole farm come to life with the Glow as it illuminated the farm around them. Reye pictured a future where Stella, her son now Raymond's age, would leave the cavern at night to enjoy the Evening Supper with the rest of the Remnant, each one of them enjoying the other's company. But it all depended on one thing, making Project Raymond's Dream a success.

"I'll just have to make it a success," Reye whispered, sitting back down and burying herself into her work, determined to one day see all her friends again when she made that vision a reality. She knew she had a mountain of work ahead of her. Gardening and botany were never her fields of expertise, but she had the determination, drive, and now the vision from the Reconciliation Ritual urging her on. The ritual helped her come to terms with her past. Now, it had given her something else, a goal for the future.

"I survived the city of Nis, seen Tanas face-to-face, lived through both the Third Great Attempt and the Hammers of the Orange Light's invasion—the Second Coming. I was then able to return home again after witnessing a sight more beautiful and long thought lost from the planet since before our creation."

Reye mused, remembering everything that she had seen since leaving Spectral Academy for the Demp Cavern Mining Project.

"If I'm still alive after all of that, then I can and *will* make that vision a reality."

And in time, she would.

The End.